TWO
IF BY
SEA

S. TAYLOR SAFLIN

Printed in the United States of America

This is a work of fiction. Names, characters, places, and incidents either are the product of the author's imagination or are used fictitiously. Any resemblance to actual events or locales or persons, living or dead, is entirely coincidental.

Dedicated to all of the men and women that serve in the military as well
as the intelligence services of the free governments of the world
and
especially to the only part of our lives that really matters,
our families and our children.

They are the reason we are here.
They are the reason we must fight for peace.

Prelude

We are all targets. It is very likely that terrorists have the materials to produce nuclear weapons.

The rationale for choosing their targets is impossible for any peace-loving human to understand. Sometimes there simply is no rationale. They are driven by the most primitive thoughts. The only thing that matters to the terrorist is that they create fear, chaos and panic. Their insatiable desire to drive terror is veiled by some twisted ideal that they are trying to achieve peace. But think about the recent terrorist acts. Are these the acts of a people that are striving for peace at every turn? They are more synonymous with the acts of a person that is truly evil.

For us however, their existence is no surprise. They seem to counter every rule that promotes harmony and peace in a civilized world. The willfully take positions that contradict the very definition of peace and they try to offer the world a reason for their despicable acts when none really exists. And these evil sociopaths have been responsible for every chaotic and negative event in the history of mankind.

For two thousand years they have fought and they have preyed on the peace-loving people of the world. We have tried to take a position of moral ascendancy and to rise above them by helping them to understand true peace. And we have prayed for divine intercession in the past.

But now we are determined to take the matters into our own hands and fight them at any place and any time. We must take the battle to them and in order for peace to triumph and good to survive, we must fight them constantly, fight them hard, and we must win. They must know that their continued acts of terror only strengthen our resolve to defeat them.

They are losing this battle and with each passing day, they become more desperate. They are simply running out of time. They must continually increase the boldness and the audaciousness of their act.

The headlines below are factual examples of how military weapons grade nuclear material is stolen and sold to those that would use these devices indiscriminately, for the next terror attack.

The headlines should frighten you. Nuclear material is moved around in corrupt and underworld channels like a commodity.

"Two If By Sea" although a fiction, describes a scenario that is based on fact.

Read the stories behind the headlines, "Kyrgyz Security Service Agents Arrested an Uzbeki National Trying to Smuggle Plutonium via a Flight to the United Arab Emirates" or "3.8 Kilograms of Stolen Uranium Seized in Caucasus."

It isn't a matter of if; it is a matter of when. If the headlines don't frighten you, reading "Two If By Sea" will.

"Holy Michael, the Archangel, defend us in battle. Be our safeguard against the wickedness and snares of evil. May God rebuke evil, we humbly pray and do you, Prince of the heavens, by the power of God, cast into hell Satan and all evil that wander through the world seeking the ruin of souls."

Is that all we can do, pray?

Table of Contents

1

Voices Heard

Mainz, Germany - February 14 - 1847 hours – Saint Valentines Day

Darkness was all around him. He seemed to be living in that momentary plane of surreal existence where everything is just a little off of where it should be.

Even the snow made a distinctly different crunching sound under the weight of his footsteps as he walked in the still silence of the late winter's evening.

'Dry snow?' It seemed a very basic contradiction to him. But it was dry. It seemed drier than the sand on a beach.

At this temperature, the snow had the same texture under his feet as loose, dry sand. Snow was just frozen water. Water, the same life sustaining liquid that covers more than two thirds of the earth but the major difference here was that it was out of bounds. It was out of the temperature boundaries that allowed it to sustain life. Below one given temperature it was a cold solid that had the ability to suck heat from one's body quickly. Above another, it was as caustic and scalding to human life as arsenic.

Either way, outside of its boundaries, water wouldn't support life. It would in fact, take life quickly and painfully away.

It wasn't altogether as different as anything else.

Life and death, just crossing a boundary, by even such a very small degree, often made the difference between the two.

He slowed his pace as he approached the fence wires. Something perceptible was happening. He felt it all around him. The weather was changing rapidly, but that wasn't it. The temperature was rising. He felt a foreboding that left a slight sickening feeling in the pit of his stomach. He couldn't remember ever feeling something as tangible as this feeling even though it wasn't real.

He continued walking between the two concentric barbed wire fences that were five meters apart and surrounded the Secure Intelligence Facility or SCIF as they called it. Nothing was meant to live in this area between the wire boundaries. It was a kill zone.

It was in between these boundaries where the rules changed just like the boundary where water changed from its life giving properties. This was an area designed to slow intruders down a little so the military police guards could have an easier target to engage. It was well lit and had no cover or concealment. It was just an open path between two tall wire fences.

The only safe passage was through two gates that allowed people to enter the facility. Each guarded by heavily armed soldiers.

Other guards continuously roamed around inside the 25,000-foot perimeter. The soldiers carried the M9, 9mm issued Beretta pistols along with the M8, caliber .223 new automatic rifles. Security was not an issue to be taken lightly. Individual GPS units that showed the guards exact positions were monitored from inside of the highly secured facility.

One of the guards patrolling the perimeter paused. Something was moving in the shadows of the winters evening. The movement caught the guard's eye as he saw something come from out of nowhere and walked toward him in the snow. His heart rate quickened. A surge of adrenaline shot through him as he raised his rifle at the target and clicked off the safety with his thumb, the center of mass of the target caught squarely in his sights.

"Halt! Who is there?" Challenged the guard, weapon leveled at the approaching figure as it loomed out of the wood line. The features of the man grew more distinct as he continued to approach the guard. The challenger now came into view and stopped his advance.

The guard felt a sudden comfort and relief as he recognized the target.

"Whew..." an audible sigh was exhausted as the guard relaxed the aim of his rifle.

"Major Nellis, I didn't recognize you -- sorry sir."

Major Frank Nellis was the senior operations officer of the downlink and forward analysis site of a high-tech aerial intelligence collection system facility. His job was to keep the well-oiled machine running, inside and out. He'd often pull a surprise inspection on the guard force. It was a dangerous game, but his guards knew the rules of engagement and he had to check. Henry Ford once said that, people would do their best on those things the boss checks. Nellis checked and rechecked. Ford was right; checking sure made him feel like everything worked better, except for the weather. It was changing and changing fast.

"Sorry?" Nellis barked at the soldier. "What are you sorry for soldier? You're doing your job. I don't care if it is Saint Valentine himself, you keep stopping and challenging any intruder until you verify their authorization. If anyone gets through here on your watch, then you'll know the meaning of sorry!" Nellis said as he produced his ID and security authorization.

The guard examined the documents more out of conforming to a procedure than really checking the identity of his boss' boss. With a cursory check, the guard returned the documents and waved the Major through, saluting by bringing his rifle to the FM 22-5, Present Arms, prescribed position.

He paused and looked around before returning the salute. The outside temperature had noticeably increased in just the past few minutes.

"It looks like we are in for some of that wet sloppy snow now! What a difference a few degrees can make." Nellis said to the guard while looking skyward.

The thickening clouds and rapid temperature increase ominously signaled the rapidly approaching warm front.

"Probably some-freezing rain in store for us too. Make sure you drive carefully back home after your shift is over." He said to the guards. Nellis turned on his heels after returning the salute to return to the secured facility.

He couldn't help but think of the crews in the aircraft that were orbiting high overhead on the mission tonight. One of them was his boss, Colonel Seth Stephens.

Back inside the warmth of his facility, he pulled the olive drab scarf from around his neck and rubbed at the chaffing the stiff wool caused. He slide out of his Gore-Tex parka and slung it over a chair as he shook off the cold. Nellis noticed that his senior non-commissioned officer was in the same position at his console that he was when he went out to check the guards.

Jeff Pulls was working intently at his supervisor's terminal. The terminal's phosphorescence in the dark console room cast a neon-like blue hue over his intense and confused expressions. His lack of motion combined with the blue pale cast by the terminal made him look more dead than alive.

Chief Warrant Officer, Grade Four Jeff Pulls finally shifted in his seat as he watched the collected data digitally stream into his computer. The static crackled intermittently through his headset as he pulled in punctuated deep breaths. Although the environmental systems circulated newly conditioned air every minute, it still felt stale. The monitor in front of him presented a visual characterization of the data being collected and processed. To him it was as easily discernable as a criminal investigator would see differing fingerprints.

Jeff Pulls was widely known as The Signals Expert. He had the most experience in signal intercept than anyone in the business. He knew "his" system; as he liked to call it, better than the engineers that designed it did. During the testing and validation prior to moving it to field testing, the system had a few flaws. The engineers that designed it were completely baffled. They poured over the designs and drawings for days trying to find a solution. Jeff Pulls walks in and looks at a few diagnostic summaries and fixes the system within 6 hours. Now the engineers call him for help on the problems with their systems. So far, the system was working better than even he thought it would. He was more than pleased with the work that went into developing this complete intelligence system. It could detect just about anything anywhere and process the information in real time. It would soon be certified as the premier intelligence collection system in the United States inventory and not a moment to soon.

Pulls glanced at his watch. In a few more minutes, he'd suggest to Nellis that they had completed this evening's collection effort for the validation trials and recall the three aircraft orbiting high overhead. The aircraft were the antennae, the aerial vacuum cleaners that sucked up any emission data available in the electronic environment. They had been on station for nearly six hours and they were nearing bingo plus 30 minutes on their fuel levels. Bingo fuel was a short version of saying that they have enough fuel to recover to their airfield and not much more.

Pulls was about to take off his headset and reach for his coffee mug when he heard an electronic bell subtly ring in the headset.

He instinctively looked back at the monitor. The bell sounded to alert him of a new signal characteristic of the same frequency that he had been tracking. More out of curiosity than anything else, Pulls sat back down into the comfortable high-backed seats that were mounted behind each intercept analyst station and re-positioned the headset.

'What next?' The thought was passing through his mind.

Pulls moved his hands over the keyboard to catalogue and attempt to characterize the new signal. As the seconds passed, Pulls confirmed that this was again the same non-characteristic signal that he had been listening to, one that wasn't in the vast database. Hopefully it wasn't a software glitch that kept categorizing similar frequency characteristics over and over again. They were almost finished with the validation. A glitch would add time to the verification effort and delay the handoff of the system to an operational unit.

Pulls stared at the screen, 'Not now, not a glitch. Why does this happen as soon as the validation is wrapping up?' Pulls asked himself.

He switched to the expanded non-test actual validation database. Maybe that would help. Still no characteristics were available in the database that could help identify the new signal.

Pulls called to Nellis. "Major Nellis, you may want to take a look at this signal sir."

Pulls scratched his head as he was listening to the radio transmission. He pushed the headset closer to his ears as if it would generate more clarity.

"What do ya got Jeff?" Nellis grabbed an extra headset and held it to one ear.

"Hmmm... Jeff, is this on the target frequency list? Whadda you think?" Is it some kind of practical joke? Weren't you the one that told me about some neo-Nazi group that broadcasts old Hitler speeches on Adolph's birthday? Maybe they're starting earlier this year." Nellis said.

"Come on boss, I would have ruled that out if I thought we had some clown out there broadcasting old recordings. It keeps coming up. I've catalogued it three times. It has been coming across on differing frequencies with different characteristics. This transmission is definitely on a tactical frequency though, maybe even a crude frequency hopper. If someone wanted to spew some propaganda, they sure wouldn't waste the time and money to put together the equipment they'd need just to broadcast on a frequency where no one and I mean no one would hear it." Pulls said as he stared into nothing, trying to hear every word and characteristic of the transmission.

"This is bizarre." Pulls continued. "I have been listening to it since you went out to check the guards. Whoever is sending it; they definitely want this message to get to the military. Here's another twist for you Sir, the technical information of this signal just doesn't match any of the data stored in our current NSA technical data files. What are the odds of that?" Pulls didn't like surprises and this was rapidly becoming an irritant.

He continued. "No, this isn't like anything I have seen before. Look at this frequency here. It looks as if it is being generated by old vacuum tube technology from seventy years ago." Pulls was stumped and that hadn't happened since as far back as anyone could remember.

Nellis rubbed his hand over the stubble on his chin. It had been a long day that didn't seem to want to end. The validation testing of the new intelligence collection system had been their project for the past three months and it was nearly over. He was just wrapping it in a nice package before turning it over to the soldiers and aviators that would use it to collect intelligence for the CIA and NSA. No one wanted to spend any more time and resources than necessary. It was time to go home.

"Jeff, it's late. What do you think? Do we have enough data to call it a night? The aircraft have less than 30 minutes of flight time remaining until they are into their reserve fuel and the weather is moving in fast." Nellis said as he reviewed the information on the screen.

"I know that this is the validation exercise, but our general collection order still applies here. If we find signal parameters that aren't in the database, we need to follow protocol and collect as much as we can, get it in the database, and get the information back to the CIA." Pulls said as he continued to prepare the secret message to send the data collected on the signal off to the National Security Agency.

"Jeff, you sure that it isn't a few smart kids putting together a Science Lab radio kit and broadcasting old war radio transmissions... remember that analyst in Korea that called wolf a few years ago? He practically started a war on the peninsula because some electronics genius started sending North Korean attack orders over a tactical network as a prank. The Air Force is still PO'd about that one. They scrambled everyone in the Pacific." Nellis didn't get to finish before Pulls interjected.

"Sir, I have been chasing radio transmissions all of my life and one thing for sure, this isn't a Science Lab radio we are dealing with. The closest I can get to a match is with a vacuum tube, old World War II radio transmitter. Look at this power-drop here... and here it spikes. At that point something that used transistors and printed circuits would have melted. You can't put this much energy through your everyday homebuilt radio set." Pulls said as he pointed to a spot on the graph with wide varying ranges on the oscilloscope.

All Nellis could do was nod. Even though everyone was tired, Pulls was right. "All right Jeff, what's another 20-hour day any way?

Let's get the message off to NSA." Nellis said as he turned to leave the console.

"Specialist, get this data off to the National Security Agency ASAP." Pulls commanded to one of his soldiers as he transferred the electronically packaged data by merely clicking an icon. The soldier encoded the message with the latest security key encryption and sent the message off to NSA.

Pulls continued his analytic dissertation to no one in particular, although everyone listened "Look at this. Some of it is encrypted, some in the clear, some of it data, some of it voice. We've intercepted something more sophisticated here. Someone has gone through a lot of effort to make this seem authentic. We had better get it off to NSA." Pulls continued to look under his glasses and study the monitor while the computer tried to break the encrypted portions of the intercepted transmission.

Nellis knew that Pulls was right as usual. All new data warranted a review before it was cataloged and NSA needed to assign file designators to it. No one would have disputed Pulls' recommendation. He lived, ate, breathed and slept signals collection. Nellis couldn't wait to hear NSA's response.

Within seconds the information was packaged and transmitted to NSA via secure satellite. The analysts at Fort Meade would probably laugh so hard when they received the data that they could hear them here in Germany.

In a mere instant, the message was received across the Atlantic by the satellite dishes outside of the huge steel and glass NSA building at Fort George Meade, Maryland. An analyst by the name of Abner Harper received the message that Pulls had just transmitted.

Under the circumstances, it couldn't have been planned any better. Abner was in the right place at the right time.

Abner Harper had manned the analyst console at NSA's Headquarters at Fort Meade like he had for the past sixty-five years. He had begun his career during World War II as an analyst after he was classified 4F for a muscular deformity that was caused by polio when he was a young boy. He always walked with a noticeable limp so it was no surprise when the military classified him as unfit for combat. Most of Abner's friends were killed in the violent combat that occurred in the European Theater. His contribution to the war effort was working for the then Army Security Agency in a cushy office environment. He always felt somewhat ashamed of that. Even now, retiring didn't seem honorable, since his friends gave their lives for his freedoms. After he had seen most of his friends come home in a box, he vowed to never

7

retire. He had been on the job, manning his analyst position and never missed a day's work since 1943.

A lot of people thought that Abner should have retired long ago, but with the law being what it is, there wasn't much anyone could do. If this was Abner's idea of how to spend his golden years, who could argue? The edge had rounded off a little for Abner. But he was still sharp by any standard and was by far the most experienced analyst at Fort Meade.

Before he opened the message from Pulls, Abner finished pouring his tea from the same 1940's era antique, brown painted metal thermos with the red strip, just like he always did. It was just past four in the morning in Maryland, designated teatime for Abner.

'Probably just another routine message, not much happening in Europe now days. Most of the action was in those damned terrorist countries anyway where those youngsters man the consoles,' thought Abner.

He looked at the light amber colored liquid in his cup. Tea, after all, just seemed to bring a little civility to an uncivilized world. Abner raised the cup to his lips as he double-clicked the icon to open the message.

Abner paused with the cup pressed to his lips before sipping the hot brew as he read the top-secret message. He read it again and once more after that. There was something strangely familiar about the contents of this message. The characteristics of the signal seemed too familiar. Back then he'd sworn to never forget them. His recall was a little slower, but it would come. He searched his memories as he stared at the monitor. His face inched unconsciously closer. His mind slowly homed in on the memory of a project from the distant past. One that President Truman said would alter the course of the world forever.

'Oh my God,' he thought…what the hell…it can't be…this can't be.' Abner thought as he read the message again.

There was no doubt in his mind. He remembered. It was the biggest project that he had worked on during the World War II. He turned away nearly too excited to talk. His mind reviewed the signals parameters. The frequency, the hopper characteristics, the codeword, the signal strength, everything came back to him. He had to get this data to the shift supervisor. It seemed like 1943 all over again to Abner in an instant.

Without thinking, Abner forced his 86-year old body up and over his console chair and part ran, part hobbled to the Analysis Supervisor station down the hallway. His mind raced, his words couldn't form as fast as his mind wanted them to. He was spitting and sputtering like a man in the midst of a heart attack. At his age, many thought that was exactly what was happening. He managed to get just enough information out before the excitement and over-exertion took its toll on his aged body.

"*Project Victory, Project Victory*." That was all Abner could stutter clearly in his excitement before he collapsed.

Abner's Analysis Supervisor, Gil Shorant, a graying man nearing 60, had the where-with-all to scribble down what Abner muttered before he collapsed. *Project Victory.*

It took about fifteen minutes to get the commotion cleared after the medical staff was called in and for everyone to get back to the business at hand.

Gil Shorant sat back at his desk only after he was assured that Abner would be fine. No heart attack, thank God. He knew Abner and knew that only a few things would get him this excited. He turned to his computer. What had gotten old Abner so excited? The letters were pecked into the search window on his computer, the same words muttered by Abner.

'*Project Victory*, what is that?' Shorant thought as he typed. 'We'll soon find out.'

The nearly immediate results surprised Gil Shorant. He was prompted to use a special password to access the data files of *Project Victory*, the same password that would have authorized opening only the most sensitive and classified information.

He clicked enter and the screen came alive with the background and special instructions. In his nearly 35 years at NSA, he had never seen anything like this.

He had never seen a long since closed operation about to be reopened. *Project Victory* was an operation that had been dormant since the end of World War II and now he was about to reopen it.

'This is crazy.' He thought. But the instructions on the computer screen in front of him clearly stated what he was to do if a message like this happened to be received. Gil sat back to realize the full impact of his next action. The one before he put the gears in motion to declare a Priority One mission. Gil hesitated as he reached to pick up the handset for the phone.

Historians often refer to the shot heard at Concord that started the American Revolution as the shot heard around the world. When that shot was heard, it traveled at the speed of sound. This news would reach every US national intelligence facility at the speed of light. He wouldn't know at the time, but Shorant's actions and message would have the same impact on the world in these recent times as the creation of the new United States in those days.

Both had the effect of potentially changing the course of history when they were sent. Gil Shorant had no idea at the time, but the world would never be the same after this.

Within seconds of Gil transmitting, the National Security Agency was in full swing. Every US national intelligence asset was redirected and the priority of intelligence collection was reordered.

Frank Nellis was so surprised when he received the return message in his facility that started with Pulls' analysis of the intercepted transmission that he could have been knocked down with a feather.

NSA had declared the now reopened Project Victory a Priority One as a result of Jeff Pulls thinking. This meant that any and all of the information on this new radio transmission intercepted in Germany would be collected at all costs. The urgency of the mission reached Frank Nellis and Jeff Pulls in less than 15 minutes after it was sent.

"Holy shit Jeff; I don't know how you know these things." Nellis said mouth agape as he read and reread the message. "I don't believe it…all right, here we go."

Nellis paused, took a deep breath to transition in his mind from what he thought was a routine validation exercise to a live collection effort. He rubbed his forehead with his forefinger and thumb deep as his mind sorted through the fourth and fifth level thoughts firing in his brain. His orders followed with rapid precision. His aircraft were now into their reserve fuel and they hadn't even started the flight to recover.

"All right folks, let's contact the aircraft and have them maintain their collection positions until relieved. Flight Ops, contact the standby flight crews and get the relief on station aircraft up and flying and do it like 20 minutes ago. Mission Ops, develop our refined target list and frequencies. Bring in the standby facility teams and bring the guard force up to full strength. Flight Ops, those aircraft have little fuel remaining, the boss happens to be flying one. He's going to have plenty of questions. Contact Headquarters and arrange for a Situation Briefing at Wiesbaden as soon as he lands. Let's get this going… now! I don't see enough hustle in this facility! Move it folks, MOVE IT! We don't have much more information other than NSA wants more data on this signal and the Army Chief of Staff has already endorsed this as a Priority One Order." Nellis said as he was bowling over people as he moved at a dangerous pace through the confines of the facility.

"Roger Sir." Pulls added before he began barking his own set of orders.

"All right, let's get serious and settle in, we have a Priority One mission initiated here. Here is the target signal, tactical frequency of 49.55 MHz. Don't loose it. Stay on it. Your career and someone's life may depend on it. We're making history now; we've gone from a validation mission to operational. I can't say that I have had that happen to me before, but there is a first time for everything. Don't miss a thing. I want every bit of this data over analyzed." Said Pulls. It was apparent that he was in his element. He and his soldiers were on this tighter than a drum. They all loved the challenge. Sometimes you need to raise the stakes to make people sharper. Nothing would slip by these experienced men and women tonight.

Frank Nellis made it over to the communications console and broke the bad news to the flight crews on station. Argus niner-niner, flown by the unit's commander Colonel Seth Stephens, was the lead aircraft of this three-ship mission. Frank Nellis has just asked him to expend his recovery fuel because of a Priority One mission until three new fresh aircraft could relieve them.

"Okay Frank. We'll be up here until the relief flight crews get on station with the other three jets. It's gonna be tight though, weather's come down fast, freezing rain and sleet moving into Wiesbaden. Stephens out." Stephens instinctively thought of his men flying low on fuel and down at the weather that was approaching fast from the south. They were above it at 35,000 feet. But they had no other option but to descend into it to land. 'Low fuel, low visibility, not many options left.' Stephens thought.

Nellis put down the handset. He looked at the weather report for Wiesbaden. Talk about being caught having your pants down. This couldn't have come at a more vulnerable time.

The next few minutes would be an eternity for the flight crews as they flew their surveillance tracks, watched the fuel remaining in pounds click off more rapidly than anyone wanted and waited for the relief aircraft to takeoff and get on station. Minutes seemed like hours as the flight crews watched what little fuel they had remaining be consumed by the jet engines of their aircraft at 35,000 feet over Germany. They tried everything to conserve fuel, but they already operated at the maximum endurance profile, not much more left to squeeze.

The next orders issued from Frank Nellis in the Intelligence Processing Collection Facility nearly 24 minutes after the Priority One was declared brought a collective sigh of relief from the flight crews as they recalculated their remaining fuel. This was going to be close.

"Argus niner-niner and flight, cleared for immediate recovery. I say again, you are cleared for immediate recovery. The relief aircraft are in position. Argus niner-niner and flight switch data links to standby and return to base."

No one needed to tell any of them twice. The orders were authenticated and acknowledged. The flight crews were throttling back, switching their systems to standby as the relief aircraft initiated the relief on station maneuver. Descending and turning for Wiesbaden Air Base, the flight crews began their recovery maneuvers. They'd all been monitoring the weather at Wiesbaden. Things weren't going to get much better as they approached the runway. It was a race against time, weather and fuel.

2

Low Visibility and Low Fuel

Wiesbaden Army Airfield, Germany - February 14 - 2122 hours

"Aircraft ARGUS niner-niner, continue inbound, runway two-six in use, wind two-one-zero at twenty-two knots, gusting to thirty-five, report six mile final." The U.S. military air traffic controller said shaking his head as he looked out of the tower in disbelief at the weather that was pummeling the air base. The weather had changed faster than he had ever seen in the past thirty minutes.

The cacophony of the ice pellets and nearly frozen raindrops that slammed into the towers thick-glass windows made hearing the radio transmissions over his headset difficult. The low ceiling combined with the precipitation produced near zero visibility conditions, at times the wind speed and direction readout on his panel swung erratically as if he were in the center of a mid-west tornado.

The visibility was so low that if it weren't for the radarscope mounted in the tower, he wouldn't have had any visual cues that he had several aircraft inbound on the instrument approach. He could barely see the airfield service vehicle's flashing amber lights on the ramp 75 feet below. The rain falling from the sky froze on contact with anything and produced a slick and heavy glaze of ice when it struck the super cooled ground and objects near the surface.

He glanced over at his German colleagues in the tower and thought, 'They couldn't pay me enough to be out there, let alone trying to land a plane in this stuff. Man, tonight I am actually glad that I bombed out and left flight school,' he shivered at the thought in spite of the warm coffee.

'Any place on the ground would be better right now. Who in their right mind would want to try and land a 15-ton hunk of steel out there? It's wet, icy and you can't see a thing.' He thought to himself. He looked through the binoculars and tried to see the approaching aircraft. He nearly jumped as the radio came alive when the aircraft reported their positions.

"Wiesbaden Tower, ARGUS niner-niner is currently inbound, thirteen miles, ILS runway 26 approach, we'll report when we are at the final approach fix." The voice said over the radio.

"Roger ARGUS niner-niner, continue. You are number two for runway two-six." The controller said shakily. He strained his eyes to look for any sign of the aircraft on the approach. It was like looking into a void, there was simply nothing to see. If it weren't for the radar, he'd never believe they were actually there.

Colonel Seth Stephens piloted the newest version of America's manned reconnaissance airplane and was almost completed with the validation trials conducted in Germany. It was scheduled to be the new backbone of the United State's strategic and tactical aerial intelligence collection effort.

The Army's RC-680, high altitude, electronic surveillance, and reconnaissance jet aircraft was a vision that Seth Stephens turned into reality. Stephens was an Army Intelligence Officer and Test Pilot that was assigned to deliver the new system for the United States Army. As the commander, it was Seth Stephens' responsibility to complete the testing and validation for the new system in conditions similar to those experienced by operational field units. He and his men would work with the Army's Aerial Exploitation Battalion that was in charge of maintaining a rapid deployment capability that they would eventually take over and fly it to support the intelligence collection missions throughout the world.

Seth was a different kind of leader. He didn't really care for officers who would write a fifteen-page Operations Order (OPORD) and listed a step-by-step play on how to get to the top of the hill. Leadership was accomplished through the heart and not the pen.

He'd give his soldiers the objective and let them workout the details. Then he would let his soldiers tell him how they could do it. It was through their effort, their determination, and sometimes their blood that made the mission a success. If they designed it, they'd own it and they'd fight tooth and nail down to the last to guarantee success.

He'd rarely been wrong in his philosophy. All he had to do was make sure his soldiers had the resources and they'd get the job done, guaranteed. Seth always summed it up by saying, 'don't tell them how to do it, just give them the objective and the resources, they are the true experts, they'll get it done.' After all, he had never seen any mission go exactly as planned. The fog of war had too much variation. He trained his men to think on their feet, stay flexible, understand the intent and always have an option open.

The new RC-680 jet surveillance aircraft was material proof of Seth's vision. As aircraft, they were magnificent. As intelligence collecting tools, they were unequaled. The capabilities skipped the evolutionary design process and defined a break-though. The RC-680s capability was an exponential improvement over the older models.

Seth was involved in their design from the start. He ignored high-powered lobbying that wooed the Pentagon staff. He knew what the Army needed and he accepted the challenge from his mentor, General Maxwell Woodsen, the then Chief of Staff for the Army. Woodsen wanted an Army that could strike hard and fast. He realized after Desert Storm, Somalia, the Balkans, the heinous, unprovoked attack on America in September 2001 and operations in Afghanistan and Iraq that intelligence was vital in saving lives and identifying the threats to peace. The capability of these new aircraft greatly improved the strategic and tactical intelligence collection for the United States and her allies. With the integrated collection systems on board, the RC-680 could collect any type of intelligence from emitted energy to high-resolution imagery, on any target. It could collect and gather high-resolution digital imagery on the target area from nearly 500 kilometers away, flying at altitudes of up to 51,000 feet, in addition to infinite radio signals collection from anything that transmitted RF energy.

Flying his design on the validation trials allowed him to see his vision become reality. Even though right now he was low on fuel and in the worst weather that he had seen in a long time.

"I can't wait until I see Frank Nellis, I think I'll drag him out of his comfortable Operations Manager's chair and kick his ass." Said Major Mike Thomas, Seth's Executive Officer (XO) and good friend as he proceeded through the before landing checklist. Mike was as tough as an anvil. Although he was of British heritage, he grew up near Boston, in an Irish neighborhood. Confrontation was a way of life for him. He understood the importance of loyalty better than anyone that Seth ever knew. Mike was an excellent pilot and Seth couldn't have hand picked a better pilot to be with right now as they approached Wiesbaden in the weather.

Mike continued his out-loud attempt at rationalizing their situation, "I can't understand. Why do you think that Frank, the best mission manager I've ever seen, wanted us to remain on track past the planned mission time and declared this mission a Priority One, boss? Do you think it was part of the evaluation?" Mike paused and flipped the anti-icing systems switch on. Before Seth could say anything, Mike continued his soapbox ranting.

"Maybe the tests are going too well and the General may have decided to push the outside of the envelope, throw in a curve." Mike added as he tried to answer his own question over the intercom as he looked at the fuel gauge on the Electronic Flight Instrument System or EFIS as they called it.

"Mike, it doesn't sound like Frank's idea. He's too safety conscious. Whatever the reason, Frank felt it was the only remaining option. With the weather back in Wiesbaden this bad, some additional fuel would be nice though. We don't even have enough to rendezvous with the tanker." Seth said as he studied the gauges and estimated time remaining before the fuel was gone.

"Maybe Mr. Putin decided that Gorby's Perestroika wasn't such a good idea after nearly twenty years, especially after the Beslan terrorist attack and Frank wanted to hear about it before the newspapers printed it." Mike said sarcastically.

Seth smiled at the thought provoking comment. Gorbachev's idea of Russia's reform was the breakthrough years ago that President Reagan needed to drive the stake into the heart of Communism. It was as if Gorbachev himself was a member of the Republican Party of the U.S. political system, after all he did spend quite a few years near Warrenton, Virginia. Perhaps the CIA's "endorsement" didn't hurt in his election. Putin however was facing steep and sharp criticism over the handling of Chechnya and he was slipping back into the old communist ways.

"Wiesbaden Tower, ARGUS niner-niner is six miles." Mike called as he looked at the distance information click off 6.0 nautical miles and watched the blue symbol flash on the flight instrument indicating that they were near the outer marker of the instrument approach.

"ARGUS niner-niner, cleared to land runway two-six. Be advised that you are following a C-120 just inside the outer marker, 3 miles ahead. Spacing looks good." The Tower Controller said checking the positioning of the targets on the approach with his radar.

"Roger, niner-niner has three down and locked." Mike called as Seth selected the landing gear handle down and the three green lights illuminated, confirming that the landing gear was down.

Mike and Seth kept their scan over the instruments methodical and precise as the aircraft instruments followed the approaches navigation signals.

Suddenly, Mike's eyes locked on the fuel gauges as they approached critical levels and heard the hair-raising call from Wiesbaden canceling their landing clearance.

"Attention all aircraft inbound for Wiesbaden, emergency in progress, all aircraft on the ground hold position, aircraft in the air make immediate go-arounds, ARGUS niner-niner, turn right to 010 degrees, contact Frankfurt Departure on frequency 120.15." The tower controller called over the radio frequency in a voice teeming with stress. They all recognized that this was not a good situation.

Seth Stephens looked at the fuel gauges as the Controller was announcing that there was an emergency happening at Wiesbaden. Aircraft wouldn't be able to land on its single runway and would be sent to their alternate landing field.

"You have got to be kidding me. 700 pounds of total fuel remaining, less than 10 minutes at this altitude. If they don't get things cleared up in a hurry we'll be emergency number two." Mike said to Seth as he heard the Controller's announcement.

"Mike, get Frankfurt's airport information programmed. That's our designated alternate and that's where we'll need to go to land. We don't have enough fuel to wait for them to clear this up." Seth said as Mike scrolled through the aircraft Flight Management System.

"Frankfurt, this is ARGUS niner-niner, four thousand feet, heading 010 degrees, minimum fuel, vectored due to the emergency at Wiesbaden, requesting landing at Frankfurt, I say again, minimum fuel." Mike said over the radio calmly, but urgently. He had already had the approach at Frankfurt set in the Flight Management System before the emergency was called. Always better to have a contingency plan at your fingertips rather than digging into your pockets. There just isn't time. Seth told him many times.

"Guten Tag, ARGOOS niner-niner." The pronunciation of the ARGUS call sign sounded a little different with German controllers.

"Radar Contact. I acknowledge you are declaring minimum fuel. Turn right to 080 degrees and maintain 4000 feet on altimeter setting 30.10. This will be a vector for the ILS 25 Left at Frankfurt. State your fuel remaining in minutes." The German air traffic controller stated in a very confident tone over the radio.

The controllers here in Frankfurt were on par, capability wise, with the approach and departure controllers around Chicago, Dulles, JFK, O'Hare, Los Angeles, and Miami.

The familiarity of the voice confirmed that he had talked to this controller before during the validation flight tests. She was one of the controllers that could handle the peak times at Frankfurt. She would probably talk to at least fifty aircraft this hour, maybe six or seven at one time. She could handle it. As long as another aircraft in the long line of traffic heading into Frankfurt didn't also declare an emergency.

"Frankfurt, ARGUS niner-niner has ten, I say again one zero minutes of fuel remaining, just enough for the approach." Mike said as he saw Seth nod his approval on the fuel estimate given by the Flight Management System and confirmed by their calculations.

"Roger, ARGOOS niner-niner, I can help you land before your fuel is exhausted." The Controller stated as matter of fact.

"Vielen dank Frankfurt." Seth said over the radio. The controller recognized the voice too. Through the many weeks of validation testing, they had talked to one another over the radio quite a few times and were confident in the other's ability even though they had never met.

The fuel gauges seemed to move even more quickly toward empty now that he watched them every few minutes. Over seven hours of flight time so far, this will be a record. Flying the south track near the Austrian border always had its drawbacks. It was a little further away that the other two tracks that the flight of three aircraft used to collect data for the tests. That was the secret to the super accuracy for the RC-680s. Three aircraft would see the target at the same time and the computers would calculate the targets location based on these three estimates. The more information, the tighter the elliptical error, and the easier it is to locate the target area. The other two RC-680s made it back into Wiesbaden before the emergency at the Air Base. He was the last off the surveillance track and consequently the last to return to base.

"ARGOOS niner-niner, contact the director, one-eighteen point nine five, Guten Nacht, ARGOOS niner-niner." The Controller said in a very calm voice.

"Roger, the director 118.95, wieder heren, Frankfurt, thanks for the help." Mike said as they continued to press on flying in the low dense clouds and near freezing rain toward the runway at Frankfurt.

"Frankfurt director, ARGUS niner-niner, four thousand feet." Mike called in after pressing the button to change to the new frequency.

"Guten abend, ARGOOS niner-niner, turn right 120 degrees, descend to two thousand, five hundred feet, altimeter 30.09, vectors for ILS 25 right at Frankfurt, state fuel remaining in minutes." The director and final approach controller said as Mike made contact.

"ARGUS niner-niner is out of four thousand for two point five, right turn to 120 degrees, I have nine minutes of fuel remaining." Mike said as calmly as if he were driving the autobahn in an S-Class Mercedes instead of flying in thick weather low on fuel.

"ARGOOS niner-niner, roger, standby for base turn, perform landing checks. Do you require any emergency assistance from the ground crews?" The director asked.

"Negative Frankfurt, just a place to land." Mike said as he tuned in the approach on the standby flight display.

"Roger, ARGOOS niner-niner, we can do that." The director replied.

The German controller was a former military controller and he was amazed at how calm this American pilot was. All the American pilots were that way. He had always respected and admired the coolness of the pilots he controlled, but the Americans stood out from all the others. They were calm as their minds raced through procedures in their checklists and the jet raced toward Frankfurt

"ARGOOS niner-niner, the weather at Frankfurt is wind two-seven-five degrees at twenty-eight knots, gusting to thirty-eight, ceiling eight octaves (which was a European aviation code for saying that the clouds were very dense), sky obscured, visibility is 100 meters with freezing rain and fog." The director said in a rapid manner, trying to sound very optimistic, but the facts painted a more dismal picture to the flight crew.

"Roger Frankfurt, ARGUS niner-niner." Mike acknowledged over the radio. "I liked the weather in Wiesbaden better," Mike said out of one side of his mouth to Seth over the intercom.

"Navigation radios tuned to the localizer frequency, decision height 200 feet is on the radar altimeter. I've got good identifiers on all beacons." Mike confirmed the flight displays configuration of the approach.

"Confirm arrival check." Seth said going through the cockpit procedures for landing.

"Arrival check confirmed." Mike replied as he toggled through the checklist on the display in the center of the cockpit.

The navigation signals that would guide the aircraft down the final approach into Frankfurt were tuned on the radios designed to receive guidance. The flight management system was programmed with a satellite guidance system to back up the ground system. Without them the approach would be impossible. With the Instrument Landing System (ILS), it would be like following an electronically created road in the sky to the runways approach end. At two hundred feet, Seth would take over visually and land.

"ARGOOS niner-niner, turn right to 230 degrees, descend and maintain 2000 feet until glide slope intercept, altimeter 30.09, you are cleared for the ILS approach 25 left into Frankfurt, report passing outer marker." The director said as Seth maneuvered the powerful jet into the approach's arrival gate.

"ARGUS niner-niner, right turn 230 degrees, descend and maintain 2,000 feet until glide slope intercept, cleared ILS into Frankfurt." Mike repeated the director's instructions back verbatim.

"Seth, I am sure that you've been counting too but the number one engine low fuel lights have been on for fourteen minutes." Mike said to Seth as he verified the fuel readings from the flight management system. Seth glanced over to check – the fuel was too low to register on the gauges.

"Well, we better land on this runway or somewhere in the German countryside will be our next and only remaining option." Seth said as Mike glanced over at him. Seth offered his characteristic off center smile, which was a combination of concentration and determination.

"Yeah, I'll report the runway in sight at two hundred feet one way or the other...I'm an optimist." Mike said.

"Mike, verify the before landing check." Seth said as he stole another look at the engine gauges. Mike was already running the checklist to make sure that the aircraft was ready for landing. Mike knew what Seth had in mind.

"Roger." Mike responded as he moved through the before landing checklist.

"Localizer azimuth indicator is alive." Mike called as he watched the needle on the guidance instrument go from one side to the centered position indicating that the aircraft was on course.

"Roger, correcting. What are the winds Mike?" Seth asked as he looked at the EFIS display.

"170 degrees at 24 knots." Mike said as he checked the updated weather report from the display on the center console.

"Seth, There's sixteen minutes on the low fuel light, I hate to say this, but, I am preparing for a flameout on the number one engine." Mike said as he looked up. Still, there was no sign of the runway ahead in the dense fog.

"I thought you just said you were an optimist." Seth said injecting a little humor.

"Most of the time, but nothing like being prepared for the inevitable. Just like my boss, a really good guy, always tells me." Mike said with a little matter of fact attitude, struggling through an attempt at humor.

"Altitude 1,850 feet, glide slope intercept at 1500 feet." Mike added as he watched the instruments.

"Roger, glide slope is captured. On course, on glide slope." Seth called as the jet started the final descent.

"Frankfurt Tower, ARGUS niner-niner, inbound ILS Two-Five left." Mike called making contact with Frankfurt Tower.

"ARGOOS niner-niner, cleared to land runway Two-Five left, wind calm, report runway insight or missed approach." Frankfurt's tower controller announced.

"ARGUS niner-niner, roger, cleared to land runway Two-Five left." Mike said repeating the controller's clearance.

"Now there's a sense of humor...report runway in sight or missed approach...where does he think we'll go after the missed approach?" Mike asked rhetorically.

Suddenly, Seth felt the jet pull to one side. He didn't need to see the instruments to know what had just happened. As if the night wasn't already exciting enough.

"Flameout number one engine! Turbine speed dropping rapidly, turbine gas temperature dropping rapidly, engine out confirmed boss." Mike said as he reached for the checklist page.

Seth was acting instinctively; his hands were already on the controls trying to salvage what was left of the approach on one engine. He pushed the power lever up on the engine still running.

"Roger Mike, I'm on it... checklist on the failed engine." Seth said to Mike in a calm but direct manner.

"Frankfurt, ARGUS niner-niner flameout number one engine, declaring an emergency, continuing inbound on ILS Two-Five left." Mike said.

"Roger ARGOOS niner-niner, rolling crash trucks now." Said the Tower Controller as he pushed the crash alarm on his communications console. In an almost immediate response to the alarm, the crash trucks headed for the runway to wait for the inbound plane. They raced in the fog-shrouded airport, through an icy mist toward runway Two-Five left barely able to pick out familiar landmarks.

Most psychologists would say that the normal reaction to danger is to remove one's self mentally from the situation. A pilot experiencing an emergency like this doesn't have time to remove anything. Anyway, where would they go? Seth knew what was happening completely. He could do nothing worse right now than remove himself from the situation. He wasn't a good spectator anyway. He'd rather be mixing it up and running the plays than coaching.

"Seth, four-hundred feet to decision height, airspeed 125 knots." Mike said calling off the altitude and airspeed.

"Roger." Seth acknowledged.

Mike was straining his eyes to see the runway lights or something that would let him make out the runway's boundaries. He was trying so hard to see it that his mind started to create a runway didn't exist. He had to consciously remove the teasing image from his eyes and look for the actual runway.

Each second was an eternity. Everything was happening in slow motion. He'd read about it, temporal distortion, where time is stretched to infinity. Mike snapped himself back to the task at hand. He wasn't going to be a statistic.

"100 feet to decision height, airspeed 125 knots." Mike continued his call-outs.

"Roger Mike." Seth sounded calm.

"Decision height boss!" Mike blurted, leaning so far forward that his forehead was pressing against the windscreen.

"Roger. Continuing. Verify landing check." Seth called.

"Auto pilot, confirmed disengaged, yaw dampener, disengaged, gear indications, rechecked, flaps full down." Mike said as he quickly verified switch positions and indications. He returned to search for the runway. It just wasn't out there. There was nothing there but an empty void. They were 200 feet above the ground at Frankfurt International Airport, but they could have been anywhere.

"Mike, I'm beginning a slow deceleration and continuing down. Get on the controls if we aren't lined up when the runway comes into sight." Seth commanded while remaining intensely cool as he concentrated on flying the machine.

Seth focused on the radar altimeter. He knew it was the only instrument giving him the height above the touchdown zone. He tried to coordinate his airspeed loss to coincide with the loss in altitude. If he did it just right, he'd touch down with the aircraft teetering on the edge of a stall. He watched as they passed 100 feet above the ground.

The momentary silence in the tense cockpit was punctuated suddenly with Mike's shout, "runway in-sight, ten feet left of centerline, maintain course!"

The powerful jet plodded through the moisture-laden air. Its nose was jutting into the air at a high angle of attack as if it didn't want to land. The high pressures developed by the underside of the jet's wings squeezed the moisture into contrails streaming off the wing's trailing edges. The extended flaps and unweighted, extended landing gear gave the aircraft an appearance of a majestic eagle swooping in on its prey, its talons sharply extended. As its descent continued, the heavy dual wheels of the landing gear met and angrily grabbed the tarmac with a protesting scream as they rapidly spun from a dead stand still to match the jet's landing velocity of over 140 miles per hour. The energy from the friction produced by the tires contacting the runway instantly vaporized the water it touched on the runway into hot steam that mixed with the smoke from the heated rubber of the tires.

Mike let out a deep sigh of relief so loud that Seth swore the controllers could hear it without the radio. Mike deployed the speed brakes as Seth held off the nose gear to jam as much flat plate drag into the slipstream as possible to slow the big machine. The jet chewed up the slick, cold, and almost ice covered runway at a rate of 2 miles a minute as the speed bled off. The nose gear finally touched down shooting a plume of smoke and steam to each side of it as a protest from instantly accelerating to 100 miles an hour from a dead stand still. Seth noted the radar altimeter when Mike called runway in sight, before he looked up, 30 feet was its indication when Mike called runway insight. This was definitely a first for both pilots.

"Frankfurt, ARGUS niner-niner, rollout on runway Two Five left." Mike called over the radio.

"ARGOOS niner-niner, Welcome to Frankfurt, take the first available turn off to the left and contact military control on frequency two thirty-five, seven-five. Gut ARGOOS niner-niner! Gut!" The tower controller said as Seth taxied the RC-680 off toward the south end of the airport, where the U.S. Air Force had maintained a small operations base.

"Thanks Frankfurt... ground on UHF two, thirty-seven, seven-five." Mike replied.

A truck with a big sign on it saying FOLLOW ME was barley coming into sight as they made the left turn. Visibility was down to 35 meters in fog. Taxiing was almost as dangerous as flying. Unseen object appeared seemingly out of nowhere as they taxied cautiously to their parking place.

"Mike, that was the lowest reported 200 feet I've ever seen." Seth said sarcastically as he glanced over at Mike knowing full well that they had to descend below the minimum altitude to see the runway and land. It was the only time he had ever descended below minimums to make a landing, but the alternative of going around and crashing in the German countryside was a certain outcome if they hadn't.

Mike was soaked with sweat and as wet as if he had just come out of a sauna. He was still sweating as they made the turn behind the follow me truck.

"Yeah, we earned our flight pay today." Was all Mike could manage as a response remaining unusually quiet.

The ground crew met the jet and was as usual very efficient. Seth and Mike had finished the other engine shutdown sequence. Seth got out of his seat first as Mike set the switches.

Seth opened the cabin doorway that was just aft of the cockpit. Standing at the bottom of the ramp was an Air Force Sergeant wearing a bright green, glow in the dark safety vest.

"Sir, welcome to Frankfurt. We couldn't believe it when ground called us saying that you were taxiing off the active for the south ramp. I haven't seen the soup this thick in years. Anyway sir, a Major Nellis from your flight operations called us. He would like you to call him as soon as you can. They have the number inside." The ground crew sergeant said, his speech rapid, indicating a little too much caffeine.

"Thanks Sergeant, be right there..." Seth turned back and shouted into the cockpit as Mike was finishing the checklist. "Mike, I guess now we'll find out why they stretched us a little too long and ran us out of fuel, be right back. I'm going in to give Nellis a call."

Priority one was seldom used during peacetime reconnaissance missions, it meant to remain on track as long as possible. The pilots needed to maintain complete coverage throughout the designated time.

Every one knew why, the analysts were listening to some electronic emission or seeing some imagery that was essential to National security. However, this did not fit. They were conducting validation testing, not real mission support. Seth's mind wondered from one reason to another as he rode in the crew van to the airfield base operations to call his Operations Officer, Major Nellis. He couldn't even imagine why they'd asked him to remain on the surveillance track well into his reserve fuel status. Seth was now collecting his thoughts to make sure he asked the Major the right questions. He'd have his answer in a few minutes.

Seth was about to dial up Wiesbaden on the secure military phone system when he was heard Mike's voice over the base operations radio. "Yeah, ask my Colonel, he should be inside, if he'd wants me to put the airplane away for the night."

"Sergeant, tell him to standby until I talk with our home base." Seth said to a young airman at the radio.

"Roger sir." The young airman manning the radio said. Seth noticed that he seemed anxious to do something. May as well put him to work, Seth thought.

Seth finally made it to the phone in the military transient crew lounge.

"This is Colonel Stephens, is Major Nellis handy?" Seth said to the soldier that answered the telephones. "Yes sir, standby..." The soldier put the phone on hold to transfer the call.

"Sir," Seth recognized Major Frank Nellis' voice immediately. He was one of those characters you could imagine being a General someday. Nellis had a terrific sense of detail and was very thorough.

"We have received tasking sir, from the Joint Chiefs of Staff (JCS). Soon after the mission began, we received some very interesting radio signals. The National Security Agency (NSA) passed a request over to the JCS for mission assignment and the Chairman; General Woodsen assigned the Priority One. He signed the orders himself. I've never seen anything like it boss." Nellis said.

"Okay Frank, we'll refuel and be back at Wiesbaden within the hour. Get everyone together for an ops briefing. Have Jeff Pulls there with his analysis." Seth said. There were a thousand thoughts competing for attention in his brain right now. He needed to get back to Wiesbaden and have all nine of the RC-680s prepared for this mission.

Seth walked back into the main lobby where the airman operating the radio sat idly by. "Can I borrow your radio?" Seth asked as he reached for it assuming that the airman wouldn't object. Seth called the Sergeant that was standing next to Mike Thomas on the radio.

"Sergeant, can you please tell Major Thomas that we'll need to refuel and return to Wiesbaden as soon as possible at the request of General Woodsen." Seth said trying to imagine Mike's expression about now.

"Roger sir, I'll pass the message." There was a short pause.

"Better yet, Major Thomas is standing right here." The sergeant said handing the radio over to Mike.

"Mike, don't get settle in too quickly, we have to go back to Wiesbaden tonight." Seth said.

"You want to fly back boss? Tonight? In this weather?" Mike asked. Seth could almost see Mike scratching his head quizzically. "What a kidder you are boss." Mike finished humorously chiding Seth.

"Don't worry Mike. Wiesbaden is only a fifteen-minute flight from Frankfurt. We'll have plenty of fuel for instrument approaches until the weather clears." Seth said trying to sound as equally humorous.

"All kidding aside Mike, we have a message waiting for us back at Wiesbaden. Frank Nellis said that I need to personally review it tonight." Seth said into the radio's microphone trying to be vague on the unsecured radio.

After Seth had given the microphone back to the airman, he thanked him for his help and headed out the door to walk back to the aircraft. The cold, fresh, night air felt good against his face. The moisture that hung close to the surface of the airport shrouded the lights in an eerie glow and muffled the sounds. He walked and was wondering about the reasons for Priority One mission. This mission was used in an environment that had many emitters on the air for a short period. Its primary objective was to soak up all of the electrons that the analysts had been receiving. They would have to stay in the collection area mainly because the emitters were perishable and wouldn't be around for long. Seth dismissed the idea as being an evaluation mission completely now. The RC-680 had been assigned it initial operational mission tonight. Something was out there that the National Security Agency wanted more information on.

Seth wasn't surprised to see the refueling complete and Mike barking instructions at the transient crew. If there was such a thing as a born leader, Mike Thomas was it.

"Boss, we can still get home in a cab from here. This way I'll save ten years on the end of my life and we can see a little of Frankfurt tonight." Mike said as he stopped talking to the line crew and walked over to meet Seth walking towards him.

"Normally Mike, I'd agree with you... Frank Nellis received a message form General Woodsen, who thinks that it is necessary for us to get back in the air for a Priority One. You have been around long enough to know that if a Priority One is called, it is a matter of National Security. If we can fly, we will." Seth said, the humor gone from his voice.

Mike's face turned from humorous to dead seriousness. He knew the significance of a Priority One. "Roger boss, she's ready to fly." Mike said as he looked at the aircraft.

Seth called in to the ground controller over the radio for engine start permission and then checked the weather over the aircraft Flight Management System or FMS as he called it. He typed in his flight plan. It would be transmitted over a radio link, directly to Flight Operations in Belgium. The FMS would call up the weather forecasts and the weather would be returned on a separate page in the FMS display. Seth and Mike worked in silence to prepare the aircraft for the return flight to Wiesbaden. The emergency at Wiesbaden that had caused them to land in Frankfurt had been cleared. The C-120 transport on approach in front of them earlier had skidded off of the icy runway.

It had been a long day that would not end. Neither Seth nor Mike knew for sure why the Priority One had been initiated by the JCS. They would soon discover that it was unlike any mission that they had ever been assigned.

They would never look back on this day without remembering it for as long as they lived, if it were very long at all.

3

The Briefing

Frankfurt International Airport, Germany, February 14, 2110 hours

"ARGUS niner-niner, Wiesbaden advises that the airfield is open and you are cleared for immediate recovery. Are you ready to copy your clearance?" The technician working clearance delivery said into the radio microphone.

"Roger, Rhein-Main, ARGUS niner-niner requesting clearance to Wiesbaden, information Quebec." Mike Thomas requested the clearance and acknowledged that he had the latest weather information, which was getting a little better – what a difference of few degrees makes.

"ATC clears ARGUS niner-niner to Wiesbaden direct, after departure climb to 4000', and maintain heading 270, radar vector for Ground Controlled Approach with Wiesbaden Radar. Contact departure on 120.15 and squawk transponder codes of 6207." The controller continued without skipping a beat.

"ARGUS niner-niner copies all." Mike replied after jotting down the clearance in his personal aviator shorthand.

"Roger, taxi to runway 27L contact tower holding short, you are number one for takeoff." The controller finished his part and was already thinking about the Condor Flight 747 that was preparing to be pushed back from gate 17. Condor Flight 747 was a special contract flight that was delayed by the weather.

"Frankfurt, this is ARGUS niner-niner, Thanks for your help today, see you later." Mike said as he pushed the throttles of the RC-680 up to breakaway-thrust and began to taxi the big jet toward the active runway.

"Seth, I don't like it when we get a priority clearance. That means something is up. Usually like a long deployment to some place I can't even pronounce." Mike said over the intercom as he watched the taxi lights appear magically ahead of them.

"Yeah, but look at it this way, we may get another tax break on the first $400.00 dollars we earn." Seth said as he programmed the FMS.

"Funny boss, very funny, sir." Mike said interjecting a little feigned insubordination and then ending with sir. Like it would have helped if Seth were so inclined.

"Okay, the suspense will be over as soon as we get back to Wiesbaden." Seth said looking down at the FMS to verify the coordinates that he had just placed in the flight plan.

Mike aligned the aircraft on the runway and pushed the throttles forward to set the engines to takeoff power. The turbines spun up with a deep throaty howl, which was the characteristic of the 680 on the big ship's engines. Mike released the brakes.

The short flight from Frankfurt to Wiesbaden did not leave much room for conversation. The two men were back on the same instrument approach that they were on less than an hour ago into Wiesbaden Air Base.

The weather didn't improve much over the past hour and one-half. But, at least the ceiling and visibility improved to above minimums.

'This was going to be on of those weeks where the weather just hangs around and stays the same...low ceilings and poor visibility', Seth thought.

"Nice landing Mike. I liked the second one better." Seth said as he commented on the way that Mike had let the airplane skip back into the air because of Wiesbaden's wavy runway.

"Thanks boss, coming from you that means a lot." Mike said countering Seth friendly sarcasm.

Seth was busy completing the after landing checklist as the aircraft taxied into the ramp. Both of them were anxious to get to the briefing room after they had touched down at their home base of operations. This was very unusual for an evaluation mission turning into a priority mission.

The visibility made maneuvering the big, gray jet tedious. The runway and ramps weren't originally designed for an aircraft as large as the RC-680. Wiesbaden still had some small and narrow taxiways. After all it did start out as being an open field where ME-109 fighters and JU-27 attack planes defended the Third Reich during World War II. It was now used discreetly as a base for one of the Army's premier intelligence units.

Mike was at the controls and they taxied to a lone hangar and clamshell looking buildings that housed the aircraft. The guard force that surrounded the facility was larger than the size of the unit that operated the highly automated aircraft. The Military Intelligence hangar was restricted from everyone assigned to the base, except the men and woman that had a definite need to know. Seth knew them all. Many times the guards would escort people that would ask too many questions or hang around too long away.

Most of officers in his unit were the top 5% of the army aviators that were selected for the fixed wing transition and subsequent military intelligence assignments. They had two very technical jobs in which to remain proficient. Along with everything else they had to be sharp technicians and soldiers. The best among America's finest

They taxied closer to the hangar and followed the signals from the ground guide. The lights in the guide's hands gave an eerie glow in the fog that surrounded them. The ground guide signaled the aircraft to stop and Mike smoothly applied the brakes to bring the 15 ton aircraft to a gentle stop.

"Okay, engine shutdown checks." Mike requested. Seth and Mike completed the checklist. They paused a moment in the silence of the dark cockpit before they unstrapped and headed for the door in silence and turned the aircraft over to the ground crew. The fatigue from the long day was beginning to set in.

"Tough mission tonight sir? Looks like she still in one piece though." The ground guide said as he opened the door of the jet and carried their gear for them to the open cargo Humvee that would take Seth and Mike to the operations room. Seth walked around the airplane to look it over one last time before he patted the sleek, tapered nose of the jet.

"Yeah, she's a good ship. Take care of her. Maybe an extra bucket of oats!" Seth said to the young crew chief that had his name painted on the side of the aircraft.

"No problem, sir, we spend so much time together, there are some times I think I actually hear her tell me what's about to break." The crew chief said enthusiastically. Seth smiled at him. He couldn't help but think that these young men and women were the glue that held everything together. Here it was nearly 2200 hours; this crew chief had been on duty since 0600 hours this morning and still was ready to go with enthusiasm and energy. Ownership and the philosophy to not ask your men and women to do something that you wouldn't do did that for soldiers, not a fifteen-page operation order telling them how they should do it.

Seth understood exactly what he'd meant. He patted the aircraft on the nose once again whispered thanks to her. After all she did bring them home. Funny thing about aviators, they do things like that.

He met Mike coming from the opposite direction after finishing the post-flight walk around. "Ready for the big surprise?" Seth asked as they climbed into the open cargo area of the Humvee and found a seat on the wheel wells.

"Sure, you know me... I like surprises, especially if they make me fly an approach below minimums." Mike returned.

The short drive through the fog and over the cobblestone paved roads of the Air Base held enough nostalgia that Seth could almost see things as they were living it almost 70-years before. The cold chill in the air settled with the fog on his exposed skin on the back of his neck. The halos that formed around the dim yellow old-styled street lamps reflected off of the damp cobblestones. Each cobblestone produced its own reflection of the light that struck it. The base hadn't really changed that much since after World War II. The stucco and timber exterior finish on the old buildings and barracks were the same, even the street lamps were the same design as they were circa 1940. Seth imagined that not much had changed in fact, the maintenance hangar that his unit occupied still bore the holes made by the .50 caliber machine guns mounted on the allied fighters during their strafing runs.

The only thing that was different as they pulled up to the operations room was their modern mode of transportation.

It was like reliving a scene from days past. The nostalgic atmosphere was so thick that it seemed that you could grasp it in your hands. Seth was snapped back into the present day as the Humvee pulled to a stop in front of his headquarters.

The sergeant of the security force assigned to guard the headquarters greeted him and Mike as they climbed out of the Humvee.

"Sir, welcome back. Major Nellis has everyone assembled for you. Quite a lot of chatter going on upstairs Sir."

"It's great to be wanted." Mike said with a bit of Thomas' patented sarcasm readily noted in his response.

They walked in the briefing room to find that they were the last ones to arrive. An orderly called the room to attention as Seth entered, Seth quickly returned an at ease command. Frank Nellis had already called everyone that would be part of the decision making team. The clock said that it was nearly twenty-three hundred hours and the entire leadership team from Seth's company was assembled. This was something big. Seth immediately assumed command of the meeting.

"Ladies and gentlemen, grab a cup of coffee if you don't already have one and find a seat. I am anxious to see what we have here." Seth said as the gathering hushed and took their seats.

Major Frank Nellis dimmed the lights and cued the computer image projector up. On it was a map of Europe centered on the western portions of Germany. Three elliptical patterns were highlighted. The patterns showed the starting point of the RC-680 tracks at Bad Hersfeld, Wurzburg and Ingolstadt. The southern track started at a location near Ingolstadt, Germany and that was where Seth and Mike flew for nearly the past seven hours.

"Sir, while the aircraft were on track this evening, the Processing Facility targeted some signals emanating from right here in Germany, and another off of the coast of France near the Channel Islands. As you can see the intercept in Germany is centered on the Harz mountains. Now here's the amazing thing, we had no information on these signals in our database. They aren't anything that we have seen before, so the computers earmarked them as new signals. We sent the Top-Secret report immediately to NSA based on Jeff's recommendation and they immediately returned an RFI (Request for Information) trying to collect more data. It turns out that these aren't new signals at all. The fact is that they are very, very old signal characteristics. Not used in the last half-century or so. We received the Priority One order signed by General Woodsen. Jeff has taken a few minutes and has done a little analysis on the signals himself, Jeff I'll turn it over to you." Frank gave the projector's remote over to Jeff Pulls.

Jeff took his cue and proceeded without so much as a skip in the momentum of the briefing.

"Sir, what we are seeing are typical low band intercepts, on a specific power setting, broadcasting at regular intervals. Not enough power to be picked up by our orbiting satellites and the perfect frequency to use the Tropo-skip. It turns out that we don't have these signal parameters in our databases because they went out with Sherman tanks and Stukas after World War II. Our console analyst that thought it was strange ran a few in-depth checks and called in his supervisor. Turned out to be exactly the thing he should have done. Now a small portion of the signal is encrypted. But it is mostly sent in the clear. The encrypted part is where it gets interesting. I'll get back to that part. Anyway, NSA wants around the clock surveillance on this signal. The signal's repetitive; there is no discretion at all here. Based on the information that we pulled out of the messages, there is no doubt that this is a broadcast specifically for US Military forces. Whoever is sending the emission wants someone in the U.S. to know about it. I've listened to it sir. It is odd. It has signal characteristics from radios used in World War II." Pulls concluded abruptly almost slapping the remote in his other hand and looking at Seth tight-lipped. The meeting paused tensely for a moment as the information soaked in.

Seth knew that Jeff was keeping something from him. He and Frank Nellis shared some unsettling looks as they traded the remote one more time. Seth could tell that he wasn't giving up the full story.

"Just a second Jeff, before you pass that remote off like it is a hot potato or something. Let's calm down a little and catch our breaths." Seth looked around the room. He and these people had worked on this and other missions before, yet they looked as tense as if he was a stranger. Frank Nellis and Jeff Pulls looked as if someone was caught with a hand in the cookie jar but weren't willing to tell whom.

"Okay," Seth said as he got up from his chair at the head of the table.

"Frank, tell me what is going on here. You guys are acting like this is your first intercept. Why the tension? So some guys have a couple of surplus WWII radios and are sending out broadcasts. What is it that has everyone so knotted up here?

Frank looked up from a head tilted down stance. "Sir, it seems that the signal was also picked up less than 5 kilometers from the IPF. In this area just above the village of Nieder-Olm, the transmitter at this location is acting as a repeater. Its transmission cycles are cued on the main transmissions from Jersey and the Harz Mountain site near Goslar.

Frank continued. "Sir, our mission is to continue to fly surveillance over these two primary targets of the Harz and Jersey sites, monitor the emissions and stay alert for other signals similar to these two. NSA has tasked us and this operation is classified as secret. Because we are working friendly territory, the government of Germany will have an observer in the IPF at the request of the State Department." Frank handed the order from the Chairmen of the Joint Chief of Staff, General Woodsen to Seth.

Seth took the cue and stood up. "Okay folks, we have been assigned around the clock operations. Post your people's schedules and get them ready for a long surge. Our only mission is this: Support the National Security Agency's objectives and collect data on these signals. Folks, this is really a hot one so our full effort will go into around the clock surveillance. We haven't received an expected termination time, so as far as we know it may last awhile. I want all sections to provide me with a briefing of the personnel estimate for this specific operation. Remember we have changed from an evaluation mission to an actual collection operational effort. No matter how strange this may sound, we have all been here before. Frank get your people spun up, do as much research as you can. We want to run this signal to ground. I want every position in the IPF manned. We'll ask the ground brigade for people to augment our analysts if needed. Mike, work with flight and get the airplanes in the air and prepare for surge operations as soon as you can. I don't want any lapse in this effort." Seth paused, "Ladies and Gentlemen, this was a rather fast and unusual briefing. I hope you got everything. Are there any questions?"

"Yes sir, why can't they just use the satellite signals collectors for this one?" Said one of Seth's technicians responsible for programming and updating the database.

"Like Mr. Pulls briefly covered, these transmitters are using a frequency that causes it to skip off of that portion in our atmosphere that changes to a more consistent temperature and density. The signals main lobe never actually breaks through into space. NSA doesn't want to risk losing one of the intercepts because of. This type of emitter can't get through the stratosphere, they kind of skip around just under it. But believe me, NSA probably has all collectors working overtime on this one. Our job is just to find out as much information as possible." Seth finished that answer before moving to another question.

"Sir, are there any ideas as to what this is?" A young lieutenant assigned as a shift leader in the Analysis Division asked from the back of the room.

"NSA hasn't said anything else. I don't know if they have a clue." Seth said as he looked over to Frank Nellis who sat with his head down avoiding a prompt. Seth paused and scanned the room for other questions.

"Okay, have your section sergeants turn in the work schedules, by name to the First Sergeant. He must clear any change. Everything else in life is on hold until we sort this out. Let's get to work and get to the bottom of this. What better way to validate a new system than with a real mission? Major Nellis and Master Sergeant Pulls, please remain here for a minute. Folks, we are going to need everyone's best effort on this one." Seth paused to observe the reaction. He was answered with an atmosphere that fed complete professionalism. "Let's get to work."

The room came to attention as Seth closed his briefing. They all offered a snappy salute as is customary upon the conclusion of a meeting with a commanding officer. As they filed out into the foyer, Seth approached Jeff Pulls and Frank Nellis and steered them toward a small office just off of the main briefing room.

"Okay, what is going on that you haven't told me? We've worked so long together I can read you two like a book, why the games?" Seth stood there looking at the two. They knew that one of them would have to tell Seth, as he was fast approaching intolerant.

Frank was the first to look Seth in the eyes. Seth knew that he was about ready to talk. He stayed quiet and changed his expression from one of being stern to one of understanding.

"Sir, Jeff was the first to hear the signals contents. There are only two supervisors that know about this and we are keeping it as quiet as we can." Frank said as he fumbled with the briefing papers. He continued, "Sir, whoever is sending the transmission is looking for you." Frank said with a heave, relieved to get that out in the open.

Seth stayed silent, waiting for more, and then his mouth fell opened indicating this was as surprising to him as it could've been. Frank and Jeff watched his expression turn from complete understanding to complete surprise.

"What?" Was all that Seth said in reply. "What, do you mean, they are looking for me?"

"They asked for you by name, Colonel Seth Stephens." Pulls quickly interjected.

"How do you two heroes come to that conclusion?" Seth said searching for answers. "You guys tell me that we are listening to a transmission from World War II era equipment, NSA is asking for us to give this a Priority One, and you give me a line that somewhere in all of this, you think someone is looking for me. Who is looking for me and how can you possibly deduce that? How do you know?" Seth began to get visibly agitated at their reluctance to tell him.

Jeff Pulls spoke next. "Sir, in the transmission, they are asking for Colonel Seth Stephens. That's part of the encrypted transmission. Right in here, plain as day, after we deciphered it, they are asking for Colonel Seth Stephens."

Seth rubbed his hand over his face and paused while staring at Pulls and Nellis before he spoke. "This, this, I can't wait to hear more of."

Jeff Pulls reached in his brief case and took out a small digital recorder. It was not in accordance with procedure and way out of line to listen to Top Secret media in a room only cleared for Secret, but Pulls knew that his boss would have that reaction. He would have had the same reaction too! Seth took the recorder and placed the headphones to his ears and pressed the button.

Seth's eyes grew wide as he listened to the recording that Pulls made of the transmission. He sat; almost fell into the chair behind him in surprise. His mouth dropped slightly as he listened. When he had heard enough, he slowly reached up and removed the headset from his ears.

"Sir, do you think that they said something else." Frank Nellis asked.

"No, no, there's no mistake." Seth said with in a slow, contemplating tone, looking in their direction, but staring straight through them. "You're one hundred percent accurate. Whoever they are, they are asking for Colonel Seth Stephens."

Seth paused, refocused and looked at them again rather than through them. He focused on each of them and almost drawing from a memory nearly as old as the transmission and said, "It is like listening to a voice long since buried."

The recording added more mystery to the situation than it did answer any of Seth's questions.

One thing that they all knew was that their long day was going to be even longer.

4

Receipt of the Mission

**Wiesbaden Air Base, Germany, Intelligence Flight Operations,
February 15, 0025 hours**

Seth shook off the surprise after hearing the voice in the
mysterious radio transmission ask specifically for him. Seth was trying to
rationalize that it had to be a prank. Seth approached Frank Nellis.
"Frank, do we have the exact location for the emitter antennae?"

Major Nellis was looking back at the charts and maps he used
for the briefing. "There, just north of this town, Nieder-Olm, the grid
location is latitude 49 degrees, 55 minutes north and 08 degrees 12
minutes east, one here in the Harz Mountains and one in Jersey, in the
Channel Islands. Our accuracy wasn't textbook because we were using
the side lobes of the signal in our calculations. The emitter could be
anywhere is that grid square. It appears to be a very elaborate system of
repeaters and transmitters tied into one another. Whoever put this
together didn't just set up some old World War II surplus antiques boss.
This took a lot of thought."

A soldier interrupted the two with a flash message from the
communications center. Jeff and Frank stood, waiting for instructions.
Seth lifted the Top Secret cover sheet and read the message.

"What is going on here?" Seth said still reading the message to
himself. He proceeded to the world coverage map and was looking at a
point on the Greek Island of Rhodes in the Mediterranean. "A navy
communications aircraft intercepted another signal in the Mediterranean.
Another off the coast of Venezuela." Looks like it has the same

characteristics of our signal in Germany. Jeff what to do think?" Seth asked.

"Sir, this goes back to those days when I was building amateur radios in my father's basement. We used to bounce low power signals all over the world using repeaters. I think that is what we have here, another repeater network being cued up by the main transmitters either here in Germany or in Jersey. There isn't much doubt that either one of those two is the main transmitter. My guess is that they are both primary sites and each can cue the others repeaters. That was cutting edge technology before the days of satellites. The Russians and Sputnik made that all obsolete. Now we bounce a signal off a satellite to an earth station or another satellite, depending how far over the horizon you want to go. In World War II, they just used a bunch of towers with repeaters to keep the signal strength up. It is the same principal, different method. We'll probably get a lot more signals waking up now since these two are active." Pulls said referring to the two sights in Jersey and Germany.

"Jeff, let's see if we can find out if, in fact, there is a network. If we can find some of this hardware, we can find out where it came from. Make sure we've got the emitters covered closely. It probably doesn't come up often, and we don't want to miss the opportunity when it does. Also, have everyone look for the characteristics that this is a ruse. If it's some terrorist organization, or some other covert operations, we don't want to tip our hand. Do whatever we can to cover the area. Finding the hardware is on the top of the priority list." Seth finished.

"I don't think we'll find anything more important out there than either the Jersey or the Harz site. The more I see the data, the more I think that even the Jersey site is a repeater. It's a very powerful repeater though. The power and low frequency response are very penetrating. They could probably have talked across the Atlantic with it. Still it looks like it is just a repeater. Reply patterns are too close to the originating signal coming out of the Harz." Pulls said as Seth listened.

"Keep me up in the loop on your theories Jeff." Seth said to Jeff Pulls sending him off with a slap on the back. "And keep me up to date Jeff." Seth added as Pulls walked through the doorway. Pulls waved his hand over his head as an acknowledgement as he walked out with his mission.

"Frank, make sure that the entire surveillance effort is air tight. We need to find a transmitter location and send in a team to find out what is going on. It seems that the entire DOD has more than just a casual interest." Seth said.

Frank replied, "Sir any guess as to why they are asking for you?"

"Frank, that ranks high on the mystery list for me right now. I honestly don't have a clue. But we are going to find out what in the hell is happening here, I'll tell you that."

"I'll head out to Mainz-Finthen to the processing facility to make sure that we have a solid game plan. Mike and I will coordinate the flight schedule to keep birds in the air around the clock. If it comes up again, we will nail the location." Frank said as he saluted and left the briefing room to drive across the Rhein River toward the south of Mainz.

Seth went to his office and broke out his maps; he plotted the coordinates that he received from Nellis. They were located on some high ground between the towns of Klein-Winternheim and Nieder-Olm in Germany. Not too far from the IPF complex or the old Mainz-Finthen airbase.

He let his mind wonder for a minute. Mainz-Finthen Air Base was an old fighter base in World War II. The Germans flew the ME-109 out of there. It was a good location from which to launch planes to protect the industrial town of Mainz during World War II. Most of the pilots lived in the neighboring villages. That was one of the key ideas the senior leadership of the Luftwaffe had, the men would fight harder if they had personal ties to a town or region, so they kept their officers and men close to their homes to compel them to literally fight for their lives.

Mainz-Finthen, was once just like Wiesbaden. It was a fighter base for the Luftwaffe. The type you'd see in war history books. The times that he was there, he paid particular attention to the building's styles and architecture. Most of the buildings were the typical German stucco exterior with two floors and high-pitched roofs. A very proud atmosphere was still evident as he walked through the buildings and hangars.

He wondered what the connection was with the emitter. Did someone place an emitter this close to their facility to make sure that they didn't miss it? Maybe there was no relationship at all. He knew the area was scattered with farmland and was used as a major source of food supplies during the war. Most of the native Germans still remember working the farms as children after school. He could remember hearing one of the town's elders talk about how the Mainz area fed Germany during the war. A lot of food was stockpiled underground in large storage areas. Toward the end of the war, the Germans practically moved everything underground to avoid the constant bombing by the allies. Who knew what was beneath the peaceful countryside still today?

He picked up his Secure Telephone Unit or STU-5 and placed a call into the Chief of Staff, General Maxwell Woodsen. It was late in Germany, nearly 0100 hours so if he figure it correctly, General

Woodsen would be just finishing his evening run and coming back into his office about now. The watch officer's answered and Seth asked to be transferred to General Woodsen. While he waited for the phone to ring in the pentagon, he jotted down some thoughts. He thought that a detour to the Mainz Stadt Bucherei might illuminate the situation. The library would probably have a few old photos and maps to look at. The history of World War II intrigued him. It was a conflict that involved nearly everyone in the world. The magnificence of everyone united against aggression was tremendous. The last few wars in the Gulf and Afghanistan also had that effect; so many were united against one evil individual. It was inspiring to know that there were still good and decent people that shared a common goal.

The communications went through to the duty officer. On the other end was a friend that Seth attended Command and Staff College with a few years ago.

"Seth Stephens, to what do I owe this unexpected pleasure?" Colonel Todd Murphy saw Seth's name and number appear as calling in using a secure line.

Seth saw the same as Murphy did when he answered the phone. The name, number, and security status was displayed on the computer monitor. "Todd, how have you been? Are you still hanging out in the bowels of the Pentagon? How is your supply of crackers and cheese stuffed in that bottom drawer?"

"Go ahead, make fun of me. There is something to be said about those cheese and crackers though. The damn things never go bad. They are stuffed with so many preservatives that when I die I won't need embalmed. It's a new kind of mummification. Thousands of years from now, when archaeologists excavate what is left of the Pentagon, they'll find me sitting in my chair, still in pristine condition." Murph replied.

"Murph, you need to get out a little more buddy. Go lay on the beach, get some sun, see some different scenery." Seth said as he laughed. Murph was always a little eccentric.

"Sun? It'll kill you quicker than a nuclear blast. Where else can a man work 18 hours a day buried five stories underground and never see the sun. Think about how much lower my chances of sunburn are down here. Anyway, when you are as in demand as I am, you don't need a healthy tan to attract women." Murph said laughing. "So, what can I do for you Seth?" Murphy asked inquisitively.

"Hey Murph, connect me to the old man's office." Seth said.

"Do you think he's there? It's late back here." Murph said looking at his watch.

"I know he's in there. Hell, any half-witted terrorist could plug him just by knowing his schedule. He is as regular as a Swiss watch, probably finishing up his post-run bottle of water now." Seth said sitting back in his chair and putting his feet up on his desk.

"Hold on Seth, I'll put you in there. Good talking with you man. Here you go." Murph transferred the call into General Woodsen's office. The Chief rarely took calls that someone didn't screen first, unless it was his wife scheduled to call.

General Woodsen had just hit his computer's enter button to bring up the watch officer's action log for the day. He noted the time where he had authorized the priority one for the new RC-680. He had half-expected Seth Stephens to call by now. The secure line beeped. Woodsen picked up the headset and slung it over his head. He read his computer's communications centerline; the call was from Colonel Seth Stephens.

"Seth, I was just wondering why you hadn't called. How are things going over there? What have you found out?" Seth could tell that Woodsen had thought about nothing else besides this mission.

"General, it is good to talk with you again Sir. I just wanted to ask you the same question. I know that there is more to this than just some errant signals being picked up. We'll get to the bottom of it sir, I was just hoping that I didn't have to learn what you already know the hard way." Seth said with complete respect for this Chief of Staff.

"Seth, Joshua McAdams, from NSA and I heard about this about the same time, earlier this afternoon. Rather than me spend the time here, I'll have McAdams send you the files over the network. Seth, something big is happening over there and I am told that this began at the end of World War II. This is something, something that we have been working on since the end of World War II. I don't know the complete story Seth, but Joshua McAdams says that the file was opened in 1943 and remains active. The frequencies and emitter parameters that you intercepted have remained on the high priority target list for nearly seventy years. That's what put the wheels in motion for the Priority One request for information. Tell me one thing Seth, how did your name get in the transmission Seth?" Woodsen finished.

"Sir, I was just as shocked. I have no earthly idea. We'll find out what is going on Sir." Seth said with determination.

"I know that you will Seth. That is the other reason that you got the job. I'll see you in Washington after you find out a few answers. Seth let me know if you need any additional resources for this mission. You have a blank check son. This is Woodsen out." With that General Maxwell Woodsen signed off.

41

Seth closed the communication and waited until the screen gave him an acknowledgement that the link was terminated. He pushed himself back in his chair and opened his desk drawer. On the top of his stack of black bound notebooks was a picture. It was a picture of Elizabeth Woodsen, the daughter of General Maxwell Woodsen. They had met when he was working out at Moffet Naval Air Station as a Test Pilot for the Army and Woodsen worked in the glass house as the Senior Intelligence advisor with Space Systems near Mountain View, California. He sometimes wished that things had gone differently with Elizabeth, but their careers got in the way. Right out of school she founded a charity for mothers and young children. Her whole life was devoted to that. They both realized that relationships were for other people not so driven by their hearts in other directions. She never knew it, but she was his inspiration. He replaced the photo in the file and pulled out another notebook. It was his notes on some research for an article that he had been writing while here in Germany. He leafed through the pages and stopped at a particular story told to him by an old German World War II pilot.

He had stopped by a small glider field near the town of Butzbach one Sunday afternoon. The scene was just as picturesque as you can imagine. Right there in the middle of the forest, filled with atmosphere and nostalgia sits an airfield. The motor glider aircraft were all lined up, some landing, others waiting for takeoff. It was there that he met an older man standing next to the fence watching the planes. Before he knew it he was in one of the motor glider with him for a short flight over the storybook countryside near Giessen and Butzbach. The old German gent was a magnificent pilot. Although he was aging and shaking at times, it didn't translate through the flight controls into his machine. He maneuvered the aircraft with such grace and smoothness. The airplane was an extension of him, not a machine. It became flesh, bones and blood.

Seth made mention that he thought that he was a good pilot and asked how long he had been flying.

"Since the war," was the old pilot's reply.

"What did you fly?" Seth asked.

"Stukas and Messerschmidts, I shot down 70 allied airplanes. It wasn't hard toward the end. There were allied airplanes everywhere. You had to try hard not to hit one of them there were so many in the skies." The old pilot replied.

It didn't take long for Seth to realize that an American or British airman either piloted most of those airplanes. This man was one of the great German Luftwaffe Aces that he had read about. Seth hoped to himself that that he wouldn't be this old German pilot's last American kill. He chuckled to himself at the thought.

After the flight, the two pilots had dinner at the small guesthouse near the glider field that evening. The evening offered the old German pilot the chance to tell Seth his story. He was just someone that battled with his enthusiasm for nostalgia and his regret. The two ate Jaegers Schnitzel accompanied with Licher Bier, a local brew from a nearby town. Seth wrote down one of the stories that the old pilot had told him in his notebook. Seth took a few minutes to re-read the story.

"Our dive-bombers had taken off in the early morning, just as the sun began to rise. The airfield was covered with a light September fog. Not enough to impair our plan, but perfect weather to hide an attack. No one knew about it. It was the perfect surprise attack. The tanks and infantry where lined up on the bordering areas waiting for the word to advance. The coordination and planning was fantastic. The integrated ground air, lightning fast attack was the root of modern strategic doctrine in the United States.

Our airfield was about twenty miles to the west of the Deutsche-Polish border; the target area was just inside of the town of Szamotuly. A military facility for the Poland's Army was there. We lined up on the airfield and launched the gruppeflug, a massive air armada. The roars of hundreds of our German built fighter-bombers drowned out the other peaceful sounds of morning. I'll never forget the day, September 1st, 1939, my birthday, I was so proud to be part of it then. Now I can only try unsuccessfully to hide my shame.

We flew low over the countryside of Germany and Poland. I could see many of the farmers; both German and Polish startled by our roaring aircraft making their way to the target. They all knew that this only meant one thing of course...WAR!

This was the start of the fighting that began the battles on the scale of the entire world. No country would be isolated. Everyone would be involved.

We had no idea that the entire world would soon unite against us and the atrocities caused by this one evil man. We called him the Furher; he was the master of our people. He had come to us in our time of need. How easy it was. He picked us up after we had lost the last war against the Frankreich, (France). Our economy after that war was in total shambles. No one had work. Poverty was everywhere. We couldn't believe that this was happening to our once proud country. How could it? Hitler, he was a man from modest beginnings. He had no special birthright to the country. The people could easily identify with him; after all he didn't come from a wealthy or powerful family. But, he had help with his plan. Don't you believe otherwise? He was a puppet for another man that was the mastermind. The first part of his plan was to set the stage. This happened in the First World War, after the allies were pacified and created their treaties and laws. They did not watch our broken and humiliated country. While they turned their backs, he was working to bring the country back to power. He started with his social programs of mass construction. Our famous autobahns, many thought that this was just a form of roadway for commercial gains. Hitler saw them as high-speed avenues of approach for his envisioned Army. His airfields were not only for commercial transportation, but also for waves of fighters and bombers to launch from.

I remember our briefing. Our flight commander came in to the briefing that evening with the Furher. We were to begin the reclamation of the fatherland. He spoke of things that made our blood hotter than fire. We were proud of our land and our people. Standing behind Hitler was a man, dressed impeccably. He said nothing and watched us, watched our reactions. I noticed his presence right off. I was uncomfortable at his stares. I watched him as he watched our Furher. He must have sensed me looking at him and we made eye contact. I tried to look into his eyes, but couldn't. The hate seemed to burn into my soul as he looked at me. I quickly averted my attention back to the Furher. He finished and we all stood as he and the man left the briefing. I'll never forget the sensation that I had when I looked into his eyes. I had the same feeling the next day.

The JU-27 Stuka dive-bomber was a perfect machine for its task. We were proud that we would launch the Fatherlands blitzkrieg, lighting war, by bombing the border cities and areas in Poland.

We streaked in low out of the cloud cover. The sleepy Polish Army camp was just stirring. The leader of the first wave of attackers led us with surgical precision over to the armory. At just the right moment, correcting for altitude, velocity and wind resistance, the leader released his deadly bomb load. We all followed. Four two hundred-pound bombs dropped toward the armory.

At an altitude of 500 feet it only took about 10 seconds for the bombs to hit their mark. I was so low that I could see the faces of the Polish soldiers walking from their breakfast that morning. They knew what was happening, but refused to let it register in their minds. They saw the bombs released and time must have stood still for them. Each bomb fell in slow motion. They watched as the first of the two hundred pound bombs fell through a dormer on the third floor of a barracks. In an instant, flames appeared, followed almost immediately by the thunderous roar of the explosion's concussion. They immediately dropped to the ground as shards of splintered metal and wood screamed and whistled through the air around them. The white-hot flames from the explosion torched the wooden framed barracks and armory instantly, engulfing it a blaze.

The men inside didn't have a chance. Our flight of five Stukas each dropped four two hundred-pounder bombs. Each scored a direct hit. The building was reduced to rubble before the last plane dropped its load. Inside the men knew what was happening as soon as the first bomb detonated. The armory-detailed guards scrambled to unlock the weapons secured to the racks. These would be needed to fight back, against the attackers. If only there was more time they thought. The bomb's explosion had the effect of killing several of the men inside as the force ripped arms and legs from their torsos. The force of the explosion was too great for the resistance offered by flesh and muscle. The men that survived the first few seconds could not function. The blast shattered eardrums and dazed them to the point of incapacity.

When the remaining bombs impacted, they were just stumbling around in amazement; some opened their mouths to scream. They wondered why they weren't. They heard nothing. Their deaf ears didn't hear anything, didn't even hear their own screams. The men running toward the armory would never forget the screams of those men that were already dead or dying. It would have been a blessing to them if they too, were deafened by the concussion of the explosions.

The would-be rescuers could not do anything now. In moments the armory was totally engulfed in flames. The secondary explosions from the small caliber ammunition were now cooking off from the heat of the fires that raged. The screams once heard from the men inside were now silent. I could almost hear them ask, was it over? Just as they did, the roar of our Stukas once again fell from the skies above.

For we pilots flying the Stukas, it was like a turkey shoot. We had expected some resistance, but yet, there was none. Just those poor fools running around like cattle, running from everything to nowhere.

All of the aircraft leaders had the same priority for targets. Weapons and ammunition storage points where first, followed by motor parks and repair facilities. Each wave had successfully taken out their primary targets and where running in for the secondary targets.

The soldiers on the ground now had no means to fight back. All weapons and ammunition were destroyed. The fighters and bombers had free rein now.

Our lead pilot once again lined up on his secondary target. The motor parks, with all the vehicles completely full of fuel and lined up neatly. His parallel flight path across the rows of parked vehicles made it an easy target for his 20mm cannon. Our flight lined up behind him, we would continue our strafing run until all of the Polish armored cars and tanks were burning.

I can remember squeezing the trigger on the control stick just as I lined up on the first vehicle. I felt my aircraft shudder as the recoil from the 20mm guns vibrated through the craft. I watched the first few tracer rounds tear through the thin-skinned vehicles and find the fuel cells. Explosions followed by thick black smoke bellowed from the targets. I continued until we reduced the parked rows of vehicles to burning hulks.

The flight rejoined at the rendezvous point to and head back to the forward bases, rearm and refuel. Not one of the aircraft was damaged so no repairs were necessary. I could remember almost acting as if it weren't me toggling the bombs off of the racks, as if it weren't me squeezing the trigger. I felt sadness for myself that I have never felt before. How could I, in anyone's name be part of such death and destruction? I saw my reflection in the instruments and I saw my own eyes. I couldn't look at myself just as the night before; I couldn't stand to look at the man that accompanied my Furher. His eyes held hate in them, just as mine now did. I knew that I would never be the same again. I too, had become the image of hate now and couldn't stand to look at myself. We would talk about the destruction that we had caused long after that day.

Immediately we heard that calls from the Polish embassy in Berlin were placed to the bundeschancellory. They fell on unsympathetic ears. No explanation for the attack was given, only silence was offered as a reason. Calls were also placed to the governments of the west asking for assistance. The polish people were the first to experience the full lightning attacks to be used by our fatherland.

It had now begun. That man that accompanied the Furher must have been pleased. He only had to plant the thought and the rest was following in perfect order. One by one, he continued, the century of evil was now here. He would finish this battle and be triumphant. We knew that good didn't have a chance unless someone would unite us against this man. I would see the man again in photographs with the Furher, always standing behind him. His hate for all of humanity was the greatest that I or anyone could ever imagine.'

Seth closed the notebook and thought about those words that were told to him by the old pilot from Butzbach. His clerk's voice broke over his intercom and snapped him back to the present.

"Sir, Major Nellis would like to talk to you." The clerk said.

Seth picked up the headset. "Frank, what have you got?"

"Sir, I just arrived here at the Processing Facility. I am sending you some information over the secure network. You may want to read it. We finished the analysis of the first few intercepts. You aren't going to believe this Sir." Frank finished.

"Right Frank, let me read it and I'll give you a call back. Stephens out." Seth closed the connection and turned to his terminal and brought up the message file that Frank had just sent over the computer. He read the first few lines and forced himself back into his chair in disbelief. 'What was going on here?' Seth thought as he stared at the words written on the screen.

Seth pulled up the screen that contained the message that Frank Nellis had sent him from the processing facility across the river. Seth pushed back away from the screen in near disbelief. The message intercepted stated that whoever they were, they were asking to talk to him, by name. Frank Nellis had rerun the intercept and had several of the analysts review it for accuracy. There was no mistake, but why? Why were they asking for him? How did, whoever they were, know about him? It had to be some hoax. There'd certainly be a more rational explanation for this.

Seth read the summary of one of the intercepts. The message announced the location of the installation and that they wished to meet with Seth. There was no mistaking it. They practically gave him an engraved invitation and wanted him to come to a complex located in the Harz Mountains, near the old city of Goslar. It was also surprising that a portion of the message was transmitted, encrypted in a code that the United States Armed Forces used worldwide to send secret and top secret information and orders. It was even correct for the date and time. If they knew that code, they knew much, much more. Whoever they were, they were highly organized and were accustomed to this way of doing business. If it weren't for NSA's message, Seth would have thought that it was a joke played by his friends from the Pentagon. He also had many friends at NSA but they wouldn't compromise National Security to joke about a Priority One. Especially when people could get killed in the process. No, he was sure this was no joke. No matter how incredible it may have sounded.

Seth was about to leave the office when his communications terminal beeped, to let him know that a Top Secret message had just arrived. He quickly logged on and downloaded the message. It was from the Joint Chief, General Woodsen. He quickly scanned the message:

TOP SECRET

FROM: JOINT CHIEF OF STAFF, UNITED STATES FORCES//USMFJCS//MW//

TO: WORLDWIDE FORCE DISTRIBUTION//WWFD-RAR//TO-SWB//

SUBJ: TASK FORCE VICTORY MISSION SUPPORT

1.   WOODSEN SENDS, ALL COMMAND LEVEL DISTRIBUTION.

2.   THE JCS ASSIGNS TASK FORCE VICTORY UNDER THE COMMAND OF COLONEL SETH
STEPHENS. COLONEL STEPHENS FORCE HAS AUTHORITY TO OPERATE WORLDWIDE AND
REQUEST ASSISTANCE FROM ANY RESOURCE.

3.   TASK FORCE VICTORY HAS THE HIGHEST PRIORITY. ALL COMMANDERS WILL
ENSURE

THAT THEIR RESPECTIVE UNITS SUPPORT THIS OPERATION. COMMANDERS CAN VERIFY
MISSION VALIDITY THROUGH FORCE OPERATIONS, WASHINGTON D.C. TASKING NUMBER
JCS-05-0212.

4.   POC FOR THIS MESSAGE IS THE JCS. DSN 812-0909.

WOODSEN, GEN

JOINT CHIEF OF STAFF

Seth was sure of it now. He wasn't even sure what his mission was and General Woodsen was giving him full authority to request support from any military unit, anywhere in the world. Whatever it was, it had the full attention of the National Military Command.

Seth left his office and checked out with his First Sergeant on Wiesbaden Air Base. He got in his car, a classic 1995 Mercedes-Benz SL500 and sat back in its comfortable leather seats. He savored the drive to his apartment, especially tonight. He could concentrate better if his mind was mundanely occupied by driving. The smell of the car's interior was as unique as the cockpit of an aircraft. The smell of leather and steel aged together was as unique as a fine French fragrance. It was an older car but it had been well cared for. He had purchased the car from a private owner that lived near Stuttgart. Seth had always wanted one and made finding one an objective while he was assigned to the European Command for the testing of the RC-680. Even though he had just recently purchased it, the car felt like it was as familiar as an old friend was. He loved older cars. There was a nostalgia about them that couldn't be explained. It was also one of the things in his life that he didn't change very often. Most men would buy a new car for the thrill of it. Seth kept his cars longer than some of his friends had kept their wives. It was a permanent thing with him. Once he made a decision, he stayed with it. Why not spend the time driving something that you liked.

The drive from Wiesbaden to his apartment in the sleepy little village of Klein-Winternheim was about 25 kilometers away, mostly autobahn driving. It was closer to the Processing Facility than the Air Base. Seth would spend just as much time there as he would at the flight line. He'd observe the results of the aircraft on track when he wasn't flying one of them. Seth would go home, shower, change eat something before he headed over to the Processing Facility. Tonight, he couldn't sleep so he thought that he might as well drive home first, this way he'd get a little more time on the autobahn. There was nothing better than the SL500 on Germany's autobahns. He usually covered the distance in less than 10 minutes, averaging 160 km/hour on the autobahns. The car handled it superbly. It was an older car but it didn't show any signs of old age. He passed through the guard point and returned the rain soaked guard's salute. Before the guard lowered his salute, he was shifting to fourth gear and accelerating toward the autobahn on ramp. He hated to waste his time and others; travel time to him was a big waste. His feeling was to spend as little time as possible during travel and then only in comfort. His car tended this feeling so he didn't mind that it would take a little longer to get home tonight because of the weather.

It was indeed a bad weather night; he hadn't seen it this bad in a while. The lights of his car could cut through the fog and mist only 25 meters or so before they were diffused into a glow rather than illuminating beam. The mist covered everything with a light coating that reflected any light off in millions of divergent directions. The sheen on the roadway reflected the streetlights and signs so clearly that it was difficult telling which was real. As he drove, the oncoming cars appeared out of the mist shrouding them in a mysterious glow. The night reminded him of a night long ago. He was nearly asked to resign his commission from the Army then during a time when he was assigned to the same unit that he was fielding the RC-680s to now.

Seth had been reprimanded by a commander for repositioning a reconnaissance flight to the area to detect the Emergency Locator Transmitter of a French Airbus airliner that went down near Strasbourg in 1991. The Airbus crashed into some high terrain while attempting to land. The crash was so severe that the emergency locator transmitter on the aircraft was damaged and would not send a powerful enough signal out to reach the search and rescue satellites in orbit. Seth was at the Processing Facility while they were conducting a surveillance mission on some ground maneuvers in the area formerly known as East Germany. He and some of his soldiers heard a faint ELT. They kept hearing the ELT and called the civil authorities to confirm it. The authorities told Seth that they suspected that an airliner had crashed but couldn't find it. Seth had sent three aircraft west and positioned them on his calculated surveillance tracks to get a more definite location from the airliners suspected ELT position. Seth sent the location of the ELT to the rescue units and they found the aircraft within meters of where Seth had told them they would.

The battalion commander wasn't aware of the circumstances because he was trying helping his overbearing wife sell cookies or art at the Officers club that night. When Seth tried to call and tell him, the club manager sternly told him that the colonel had left instructions not to be interrupted for any reason. The battalion commander found out the next morning that Seth had authorized a deviation and relieved him until the Commanding General relayed the commendation from the President of France. Seth's actions were credited for saving the lives of 22 people that barely survive the crash. Experts on the ground said that they wouldn't have begun to look in that area until 16-24 hours later because it was on the fringe of possible areas of which the aircraft was likely to have crashed. The doctors said that those surviving wouldn't have lasted two hours in that kind of weather, with those injuries.

A few months after the incident, the battalion commander was relieved for actions unbecoming an officer. Seems his wife was too overbearing and intent on wearing his rank and under-bearing in other performances. The poor man stated in his courts-martial than he was forced to seek the company of another because of her inadequacies, and that one of his subordinate female officers was eager to oblige him. The female officer's husband thought otherwise and complained to the commanding general about the incident, who in turn appointed another colonel to investigate the incident. Seth wasn't saddened to see him spend some time at Leavenworth.

5

The Transmission Site is Located

Frank Nellis' Intelligence Processing Facility, February 15, 0310 hours.

"Supervisor, pull the high accuracy location plots on this signal. Mark it and make sure that it is labeled. Let me know the size of the error ellipse when you've completed." Jeff instructed his supervisor.

"Roger sir, shouldn't be that bad, the signal isn't that far, I put it at just over 135 kilometers." The supervisor responded.

The RC-680 could plot a location with refined state of the art technology. Most of the main system in the Ground Station operated by computing the lines and angles these lines formed. The system would then triangulate the position from multiple lines of bearing. The more intercepts from many different positions of the aircraft would continually refine the location. This would work fine if the emitter would stay on the air long enough.

The RC-680 system added one more advantage to determining location. The computer would set up an internal graph and plot all of the energy it was finding. Pulls would simply ask for the correct frequencies and the computer would sort out the others. Using a Doppler principal to fix and graph the electromagnetic energy was far more advanced than the other line of bearing intercepts. The result was a very refined location.

"Mr. Pulls, I've found it!" The supervisor exclaimed. "Grid November Bravo 3347118163, just south of Goslar."

"Tag and record location and signals, positions two and three back it up," barked Pulls. "I don't want to miss one characteristic during the analysis."

A ten-digit grid coordinate is a very accurate location, within 10 square meters. They could direct search teams to the exact location of the transmission.

"Call Major Nellis over here, tell him we've correlated the data and the refined locations." Pulls couldn't wait to get the report out to the National Security Agency, NSA; he was going to do it himself. The supervisor paged Frank Nellis.

"Roger, tell Pulls that I'm on the way now." Said Frank Nellis rushing over from Analysis.

Within minutes, NSA knew everything that Jeff Pulls knew. In fact, the entire command structure of the US Forces had received the report through the secure Intelligence network and the report Jeff Pulls up-linked from the Processing Facility.

NSA responded as they always do, by placing a top secret compartmented clearance on the issue. From now on it was strictly on an as need to know basis.

"So what have we got now?" Nellis asked Pulls.

"We got two emitters that we are actively working. One at this location is near the processing facility and the other near Goslar. The transmissions have the same characteristics and it looks like they may be communicating with each other. It is a repeater system, just like I thought." Pulls reported.

"Excuse me sir." interrupted a young woman dressed in military issued BDUs. She was one of the processing facility's analysts that handed Pulls a message. Pulls took it non-chalantley as he was in mid-sentence to Major Nellis. Pulls looked at the message beneath his glasses reading it while still in conversation to Nellis. He stopped his conversation in mid sentence and focused more intensely on the message.

"Brother, what is going on here?" Pulls said as he turned on his heels and proceeded toward one of the analyst stations. Nellis followed him through the narrow corridor that connected the Facilities modules together. They turned into the narrow compartment that contained twelve workstations. Pulls headed over to the young woman that handed him the messages earlier.

"What have you got Specialist Eavers?" Pulls queried with intensity.

"Sir, our analysis shows another emitter located at near these coordinates." The analyst said

"Give me a 1:250 scale view of that area." Pulls commanded. The 1:250 scale really was a 1:250,000 map scale meaning that every 250,000 inches on the earth's surface was condensed into one inch on the computers 28" monitor.

"I don't believe it," Pulls said had he rubbed his chin quizzically. "I think the one in Jersey has been also responding to Goslar. There's not much doubt about it. Goslar is the only primary site." Nellis and Pulls looked at the computer generated map of the earth's surface covered with computer generated intersecting lines representing the calculated location of the radio intercept by the aircraft.

"Good work folks. The sequence of the transmissions was measured in milliseconds. You guys broke the code. Good work. Let's take a break until the aircraft are back on station. We have and hour or two." Nellis turned to Pulls. "Thanks Jeff, that was quick work."

Seth made it home quicker than he thought he would. The kilometers slid by in the SL500. Before he knew it he was pulling of the autobahn and onto the small narrow road that led to his house. He quickly showered, changed and ate before dashing out once again. In no time he was parked at the Processing Facility on Mainz-Finthen Airbase.

Seth walked through they heavy iron-gate that separated the secure area from the outside. Only after being challenged by the guards.

Seth handed over his security credentials to the gate guard. The guards knew Seth very well, but could not by pass protocol to check the credentials. They hadn't had a security breach in the last 9 years. The MP on duty that night knew that it wouldn't end while he was on shift.

"Evening sir." Said the soldier guarding the entrance to the Processing Facility.

"Good Evening Specialist, busy day today. I think we had more business today that we've had in the last seven months. Is Major Nellis still here?" Seth asked as the Specialist checked Seth's thumbprints in to allow him access to the top-secret facility.

"Yes sir, he and Mr. Pulls have been at it all day. Looks like we all are in for the duration. Just as well, it is nice and dry inside here. It is days like this when I don't envy the officers flying those machines." He handed Seth back his badge. "Have a good evening sir." The Specialist concluded.

Seth headed off to the analysis cell. That is where he'd find Pulls and Nellis. "Gentlemen, have either of you had anything to eat yet?" Seth asked almost startling the two, bent over pointing at a map display.

"Oh no, don't tell me you two have joined the cheese and cracker crowd." Seth said sarcastically as Nellis offered him an unopened package. "What is it with the Army, haven't you guys heard of the effort to raise nutritional standards lately. I have got to get you out more often. Not more than three kilometers from here is a fine little Italian restaurant. Great stuff; it absolutely beats cardboard and synthetic cheese." Seth said as he squeezed in to get a closer look at the map display.

"Sir, you give us a live mission and expect us to take time to eat. This is genuine excitement! Really, look at this technology." Pulls said as he waved his hand toward the screen.

"Okay, what have we got?" Seth asked.

"I'll tell you what we have sir, sheer genius. Nestled in the peaceful German Harz Mountains, just south of Goslar we have an intelligence operation buried there that rivals the CIA." Jeff Pulls, who considered signal intelligence more of a hobby than a job, listened hard to the signal's characteristics. He was bathed in the faint orange-red light that illuminated the control board at an Analysis Station in the Integrated Processing facility.

"I have been pulling data from every source since we received the location. I have put together this overlay of the area where the message sender identifies the location with the intercepts predicted location and some density sonagraphs from the area. Look at the digital terrain analysis here. The mountain is made up of hard basalt, the typical foundation rock of older mountains. It should give us a maximum read for density if we assumed it was solid. Look here just to the south of this lake, Lake Granestausee. The lake forms a horseshoe with the open-end oriented south. The density of this large area falls off to less than half of what the surrounding areas are. Sir, right in the middle of this area are where are target is located. The emitters are on the highest elevations off the cusps of Lake Granestausee. The location that they describe in the transmission is right in the center of this horseshoe." Sir, I think you are going to go underground." Jeff Pulls said moving away from the screen, straightening himself.

Seth remained fixed on the map displayed on the screen. "It is no secret that Germany moved most of their strategic capability underground during the war. We are still finding entrances to tunnels and underground hangars, command posts, and storage facilities. Frank; remember last year when they found a tunnel that ran from under Giessen to the factory near Niederklien. There must have been a squadron of ME-209 Messerschmidts there. All they had to do was blow the dust off of the equipment and they could have continued fighting a war with them. I wouldn't be surprised if what we see here is an old underground facility that has been taken over by some one else. The big question now is who?" Seth said pulling away from the screen and looking at Frank and Jeff. Frank and Jeff looked at each other as if the other had the answer.

Seth moved over to the communications console and picked up a handset. He pressed the touch screen that would give him a secure channel with Mike Thomas' handset. The speaker sounded like the brief version of an old fax machine's handshake with another. Mike voice came alive over the speaker. "Thomas." Was all Mike said over his handset.

"Mike, how's the flight schedule going?" Seth said not identifying himself. Mike knew the sound of Seth's voice. Seth would have only wasted time by identifying himself.

"Sir, the schedule is complete. We'll be able to cover the skies for the next 120 hours non-stop. Then we will have a 6-hour lapse in each day for three days before we can surge for another 120 hours. These RC-680s are the best aircraft I have seen. Maintenance is easier than anything. They are ready when we are. If all goes well, we'll have an answer to this mystery by the week's end." Mike said confidently, like he always did, after looking at his palmtop with the schedule that he had worked out.

"Mike, keep the flights on track. You and I need to do some ground reconnaissance the next few days so take us off the schedule and put your assistant on authority orders. I'll meet you at the supply room in three hours." Seth said.

"Roger boss. We'll have it covered. I'll see you then." Mike confirmed.

"Stephens out." Seth said as he closed the channel. Turning to Frank he continued, "Frank, maintain surveillance over the area just as we have planned for the next 120 hours. Mike and I are going up to the location to try and find out what is happening here. For the next 48 hours you're in command. Keep the surveillance up and listen for us on the radio. Jeff, keep the research effort up. Tomorrow evening, Thomas and I will try to meet with the senders. We need to find out if they have receive capability on that frequency." Seth said and was interrupted by Pulls.

"Sir, that is easy. The frequency analysis has this carrier wave pattern." Pulls brought up another screen that looked like a three dimensional oscilloscope. "Sir, see this energy wave segment? That indicates that the frequency has duplex capability, meaning that they can send and receive. See this segment here where it looks like the waveform flattens out significantly? That is the time segment where they, whoever they are, are keeping the frequency open for a reply. On older forms of secure radios, it's as good as you could be to being secure without having a wire connection. It was like the frequency was exclusive to only another radio that was tuned to those parameters. No one else could hear or talk back if they weren't tuned in. It is a good thing that we had the new RC-680 system in place here. We couldn't do this analysis with the old system. The RC-680 allows us to mimic any parameter and break in like we were an invited guest." Jeff concluded as Seth looked at him smiling.

Frank broke in…"Sir, what Jeff is saying is that we can talk back to them whenever we figure out what to tell them."

"Yeah I understood what Jeff as saying Frank; I just didn't want to interrupt. I like to here him brag about the system. He sounded like a proud father after he was describing how his son won the big game with a bottom of the 9th, two out, tie game, homer. I just didn't want to take that from him." Seth said laughing and patting Pulls on the shoulder. Pulls turned beat red and pushed his glasses up on the end of his nose.

"Let's send them a message gentleman. Tell them that Colonel Seth Stephens will meet them tomorrow at the specified place and time and send it using this encryption form." Seth wrote down the details on a scrap of paper and handed it to Frank while Jeff looked on. As soon as he handed it he turned to exit and was out of the door before they had finished reading and comprehending.

"Do you think that he was serious?" Pulls asked Nellis.

"About which part?" Nellis queried.

"Well…uh…the whole thing." Pulls stuttered.

"Yeah, I'm not sure why but he is. Who the hell is Marlene Dietrich and why does he want this sent in an old World War II encryption using Enigma." Nellis asked rubbing the back of his neck.

Pulls looked up like a light bulb just came on over his head. "He knows exactly what he is doing. I'll get this message prepped for encryption. I just need to make sure that we can find an old Dietrich recording somewhere. I want to make sure that it is authentic for the boss." Pulls said taking the paper and rushing off to the database console.

"I'm glad that you know. When you get time, explain it to me." Frank Nellis said heading in the opposite direction to check on the flight status information. "Marlene Dietrich…" Frank mumbled as he passed through the doorway of the tunnels that connected the modules of the Processing Facility in a barely perceptible volume, "Who is Marlene Dietrich?"

Seth was already heading back to his apartment to pick up some things before he left. One of the things was a small automatic pistol. Seth always carried his other personal weapon, in addition to his 9mm Beretta, which was against army regulation. His concealed pistol was a 1940, German issued, J.P. Sauer and Sohn, caliber 7,65mm from World War II. It was from an Uncle whom Seth never knew. His Uncle brought it back to the United States after he returned from World War II. Seth didn't remember all of the details, but he felt like it was one of his only remaining connections with a family that he never knew. He only knew that he had been born in Germany and was sent to the United States to live soon after he was born. His parents had died and he didn't know who or what they were. He found the weapon one evening when he was leaving for college. It was in an old trunk in the attic. It was sort of an odd good luck charm. He started carrying it on his first covert assignment to Central America years back and it has been with him since then.

He wheeled back into his parking area at the flight line shortly after 0300 hours. He could barely make out the outline of the protective clamshell hangars that housed his RC-680s. The fog still hadn't lifted. Seth could hear the jet engines starting and smell the thick smell of jet exhaust hang low to the ground as the aircraft were preparing to takeoff. He met Mike in the hallway that linked the clamshells. Mike was shouting orders to a junior soldier over the roar of the jets running up in the hardened structures with his back to Seth as he approached.

"Take that database over to the lead aircraft, sergeant. Hustle up now, we've a schedule to keep. Don't want to be late. You know how cranky the old man gets when we blow a wheels up, takeoff time." Mike said as the soldier noticed Seth approaching first. Mike turned and without skipping a beat said. "Sir, go on tell him how cranky you can get."

"No, no, by all means, you finish Major Thomas. You were saying it better than I could." Seth said winking at the young sergeant. The sergeant smiled, took the database and was off on the double.

"Old man, huh Mike? This old man can still beat your best time in two miles by three minutes." Seth said laughing.

"Boss, that is just one of my many endearing terms that I have for you." Mike said as he and Seth walked to a quiet office. "I thought I was to meet you at the supply room anyway." Mike returned. "It isn't good to sneak up on me, you may hear one of the more colorful terms if you aren't careful." Mike added.

"We'll just use my car and drive up to that location. Dress is civilian clothes, but carry your sidearm and as much stuff that we can in a small civilian backpack. I want to get up there before noon so we can do some surveillance on the area. Don't want to jump in with both feet without checking for bear traps first. I have also put the Brigades special response team on alert. They'll be covering us from the low hills. I have no idea what we are up against. But it is better to go loaded for bear when you're fishing for salmon. I'd rather be pleasantly surprised. Get some sleep Mike and I'll meet you at 0700 hrs at my office."

Seth said as he left the clamshell just in time to see the first RC-680 charge off down the runway in a thunderous roar and rotate into the foggy early morning overcast. The other two ships took off to the sky in rapid succession. As one broke ground clawing into the sky, leaving vortex trails of in the air the next began its takeoff roll.

'Magnificent,' he thought as the last RC-680 lights disappeared into the darkened sky.

6

The RSVP

"Boss there is nothing more enjoyable than a road trip with you. It kind of reminds me of those college days. A couple hours sleep and we were hard at it again. I wonder how I survived that. Come to think of it, not much has changed. I'm startin' to think that my chances of survival were better back then." Mike said as he shrunk down into a reclining position in the passenger's seat.

"Yeah but Mike, you weren't getting paid for dangerous living in college." Seth said as a witty comeback to Mike's comments. Seth accelerated the SL500 onto the A-66 autobahn heading toward Frankfurt. The autobahn paralleled the single east to west runway for Wiesbaden Airbase for a few kilometers. He brought the machine up to 180 kilometers per hour effortlessly. He shifted the transmission through its five speeds and the machine smoothly accepted the shift almost coaxing the driver into the next gear. The deep growl of the engine offered reassurance that there was plenty more power in reserve. The tachometer barley reached 2,500 RPM. Seth glanced at his watch and noticed the time. They kicked off right at starting point time. Their covering force formed from the Brigade's Special Response Team would be infiltrating discretely in an hour to covered positions in the low hills near Goslar.

They reached the autobahn's interchange and took the exit to get on the A-5 autobahn that would head north toward Giessen and eventually toward Goslar. The drive would take them about three hours. Seth thought about using a helicopter for the trip but that would attract too much attention. He wanted to draw no attention to this mission simply because he didn't know what he was dealing with. The mission was to go to where he was invited and that was it. After that he would need to de-brief General Woodsen and Joshua McAdams from NSA before he could take the mission the next step. If indeed there was a next step. Seth didn't want to tip anyone's hand on this first step so he and Mike would conduct this as a near covert operation, just like when they were assigned together in Army Operations. Some things never change.

Seth and Mike were dressed in typical casual attire. Seth had his palmtop, GPS navigator with him and his handset that he would use to communicate back to the Processing Facility with Frank Nellis. After the signals reached the Processing Facility, it could be beamed anywhere in the world via satellite. If he needed, he could contact Joshua McAdams and General Woodsen via a secure link as long as he used the RC-680s as an up-link relay. Otherwise, the small handset would be limited on power and antenna size to reach an orbiting satellite. Seth made a quick comms check with Frank Nellis at the Processing Facility while he cruised at nearly 200 kilometers on the northbound autobahn.

"Frank, we are just heading out of town now. Check the DF position and I'll verify it on my GPS." Seth said as he talked with Frank as clearly as if he were standing there. Seth opened the palm top GPS display as he drove the Mercedes effortlessly down the smooth road surface.

"Roger boss, standby." Frank returned. Seth could hear him hammer on the computer console's keyboard.

"Frank, how is the mission going? Have you transmitted our reply?" Seth said as he waited for Frank to give him his location.

"Okay, sir. I have you at 50 degrees, 15 minutes, 00.0 seconds north latitude and 8 degrees, 39 minutes, 55.7 seconds east longitude. Your Circular Error Probability is 4.23 meters." Frank replied verifying the readout that matched Seth's GPS perfectly. Even if Seth could only manage to press the transmit button for a second, the RC-680s could find him within 5 meters.

"Sir, Jeff transmitted the message the way you specified in the alternative encryption. He even transmitted your authentication and challenge method. Boss, why 70 year old music?" Frank confirmed and questioned.

"I'll explain later Frank. Has there been any reply?" Seth asked switching into the far-left lane to pass a slower moving BMW like it was standing still. The driver saw Seth's lane change and dropped his foot on the accelerator trying to keep the SL500 from passing but the seemingly underpowered 740 BMW was passed like it was standing still as Seth accelerated to nearly 230 kilometers per hour.

"Negative sir. I think that you scared them off with Marlene Dietrich." Frank said. Seth could hear him laugh as he finished.

"Okay Frank, just keep an ear opened for us. We'll report when we get to the site. Hey, send a SITREP back to General Woodsen for me. My copilot has fallen asleep, besides he can't type on these palm tops anyway. His hands get in the way." Seth said as he glanced in the rearview mirror at the fading lights of the BMW going all out but not even coming close. Seth pushed the button on his handset to terminate the communications link and replaced the handset in his inside coat pocket. He shifter his weight slightly to move his 7,65mm Sauer and Sohn pistol out of the way strapped to his side.

The gray overcast was trying to lift as the sun came up, but it still hung less than 100 feet off of the road surface. In about thirty minutes the second set of three aircraft would be launching to trade places on track with the three RC-680s orbiting over Germany. Seth hoped that the weather would lift a little to give the crews an advantage on recovery. They were all top picked crews and could handle the weather easily. Seth had no worries. They'd all do fine. He turned his attention to his mission. He'd find out tonight as they went up and knocked on the front door. Not a very discreet way of entering the clandestine facility, but then neither was the way their invitation was delivered.

Seth drove to the halfway point for about another 45 minutes. Just as if he had a built in timer, Mike started to stir. "Hey boss are you going to let me drive for a little or do you want this beauty all to yourself?" Mike said rubbing the sleep from his eyes and stretching his arms forward.

"I was just about to wake you, but thought if anyone needed beauty sleep, it would be you. Now that you're awake though, how about taking over?" Seth said slowing down for the exit of a rest area. "We have about another hour to go Mike before we make it to Goslar. Some breakfast will sound good then. Maybe we can find a nice little Gasthaus, eat something and then head off to the meeting coordinates up into the hills near the lake." Seth said as he braked the white Mercedes to a stop near the curb. Except for a red Mann diesel tractor and trailer, the rest area was empty. Seth and Mike switched seats and Mike closed his door first while Seth stretched for a moment.

"No ham fisted control touch Mike. All you need to do is think about it and she does it. Smooth please, be smooth with her." Seth said as Mike stretched his arms and fingers as if he were a concert pianist preparing to play.

"Boss, I am going to thoroughly enjoy this." Seth closed the door and strapped the seat belt and shoulder harness across him.

"Mike, it may be short lived. We may be switching again here in about 100 meters depending on how you do." Seth said as he pointed to the end of the rest area ramp, which was only about 100 meters ahead of them.

Mike was every bit as smooth of a driver as Seth as they covered the last 200 kilometers toward Goslar. Seth reviewed the coordinates sent in the message and looked at the plot on the GPS. Seth zoomed in on the digital image map and looked around the area. Frank Nellis had sent him a file using one of the RC-680 to downlink the transmission as the jet was coming off its surveillance track. It passed over the area and captured a Doppler image map and infrared image of the area. Seth could see nothing remarkable in the photo. It was typical mountain and forested land. The map coordinates where he was supposed to go was located near a rock out cropping. There were no structures, no caves, nothing. This would be a neat trick, Seth thought. I wonder what I am supposed to find when I get there.

About an hour later, Mike was pulling into Goslar and heading toward the south end of the old city. Seth spotted a gasthaus on the left side of a narrow street and Mike brought the car up along side the curb, just across the street. It was just after 1000 hrs and it still smelled as if breakfast was being served.

"Mike, don't salivate on the leather. Wait until you're inside." Seth said as he heard Mike's stomach growl. Mike pulled his coat from behind the driver's seat as quickly scanned the street up and down. Seth looked for any signs of observers in the second floor windows.

They both acknowledged of their quick surveillance to each other and walked toward the gasthaus. The smell of freshly baked kase brotchen hit them before they were in the door. The heavy smell of fresh sausage and coffee filled the room. Seth sat down first at the table farthest from the door and facing the entrance. Mike sat opposite covering the only other doorway. An older woman approached, clad in cotton dress and spotless starched white apron.

"Bitte Schon." She said as she placed the china cups on the freshly laundered clean white tablecloth.

"Guten Morgen meine Frau, Die Speisekarte, bitte." Seth responded in German. The woman presented Mike and Seth with two menus smiling at them all the while.

"Danke." Mike said, thanking her for the menu.

It only took the two men seconds to scan the menu and order. Seth went first. "Bitte, Ich hatte gern eine Bauernomlett und Kaiserschmarren."

"Etwas trinken?" The Frau asked as she wrote down his order for the bacon and onion omelet accompanied by pancakes with almonds and raisins.

"Einen kaffee mit sahne, sucre und einen grosse frischen Orangensaft.

"Gut, und Ihnen?" Said the Frau looking at Mike for his order.

"Zwei mal bitte, zu sammen." Mike said ordering the same as Seth.

"Veilen dank. Moment bitte." Said the Frau as she disappeared into the kitchen and reappeared with their coffee and a basket over flowing with fresh bread, rolls and preserves.

Seth and Mike discussed the weather, the nice gasthaus and the town's scenery in German to not attract attention to the fact that they were Americans.

The both blended well with the town's people so no one really noticed the two as they sat and ate in the gasthaus. As they finished, Seth told the Frau that he and his friend were visiting the lake in the Harz Mountains. For the next thirty minutes the woman told of her town and the lake and welcomed the two whenever they visited Goslar again. Seth figured that it might be sooner rather than later, but had no idea of really knowing. They paid their bill and left the money on the table for the breakfast. With a cheery send off from the waitress, the two made their way south out of Goslar into the Harz Mountains, driving up highway B241. With one last check in the rear view mirror, Seth punched down on the accelerator and sped out of town like a formula one driver at Monaco. The Mercedes was just as much at home on the smoothly paved forest road as it was on the autobahn.

It only took fifteen minutes to cover the distance up near the point adjacent to the lake. Seth wanted to park far enough away as to not attract attention, but close enough to get back to the car if they needed. They parked off in a little camping area next to a small, four-door Opel sedan. They used a parking area frequented by hikers and campers that came to enjoy the outdoors and the tall pines that the mountains offered. Seth pulled his leather rucksack over his shoulder and donned his sunglasses. He checked the time on his watch. They were 45 minutes ahead of schedule. They would approach the horseshoe section of land separately. Arriving from the west side, making a large circling approach from over the top and back around the west side, always checking behind them to keep their six cleared. Seth figured that he would be in position by 1400 hours and Mike would stay in a loose over watch with his M-8 at the ready.

"Mike, I'll head out now and you follow to keep me in sight. You take the over watch position in this location Mike, just above this out cropping of rocks. The security force from Brigade is in position at their location. We'll rally there at any sign of compromise. Stay there in the over watch position while I am meeting whomever and stay sharp! We'll survey the area until dark. By the way, here's an extra set of keys for the SL just in case we are separated. Monitor my communications on your palm top. Let's keep voice communications minimal unless we absolutely need it." Seth said to Mike.

"Boss, we've done this so many times before, I'll just follow your lead. If I see your hands go up, I'll come out guns blazing. You drop to the left side. The rounds will be coming up the middle." Mike said with the 110 percent confidence that Mike exuded.

"I know Mike, it makes me feel better though, you know every mission need a good recap right before execution." Seth said as he slapped Mike on the shoulder, smiling as he headed off toward the top of the mountain.

"Funny how I always thought that good stiff drink would help me…" Mike said to Seth as the two walked in different directions.

They were in place in less than two hours. The weather stayed overcast and cold all day. They watched and observed. Nothing out of place happened in the least.

The only things that moved about were the deer and long-eared rabbits that scurried in and out of the wooded thickets. Seth felt the vibration of his palm top that he had linked with his handset. He looked at the screen, a message had been sent by Frank Nellis. Seth moved the cursor to the message and clicked open to read it.

SIR, YOUR MEETING PLACE REMAINS THE SAME. HERE ARE ADDITIONAL INSTRUCTIONS:

PROCEED TO THE OUTCROPPING AT THE GIVEN COORDINATES. PASS INSIDE THROUGH THE GAP ON THE NORTH SIDE THAT IS FIVE METERS ABOVE GROUND LEVEL. ONCE INSIDE, PASS INTO THE INNER CHAMBER AND WAIT FOR THE MUSIC. PLACE YOUR RECORDING DEVICE UP TO THE EAST ROCK FACE IN THE FURTHEST CHAMBER BACK AND PRESS PLAY. STAND CLEAR AND THEN WAIT FOR THE LIGHTS TO SWITCH ON. WE WILL EXPECT YOU AT 2000 HOURS.

Seth read the message again before he sent an acknowledgement back to Frank Nellis. It read like some far-fetched fiction novel. Mike read the same message and typed a message back to Seth.

LOOKS LIKE SHOW TIME AT 2000 HOURS. I'M READY. MT

Seth looked at his watch, three more hours to go. He waited and wondered. What was he getting himself into?

The countryside was shrouded in total darkness by 1800 hours that evening. The damp gray overcast didn't allow much sun in through it, so darkness seemed like it came even earlier. Seth kept his surveillance keen. He watched for any movement in the area. There was nothing there. Everything was deathly still and quiet. The moonlight started to peer just over the horizon and cast an eerie silver glow on the wet mountain. He could see the lake to the north down the slope of the hill. A few lone lights from a single cabin offered the only light other than the illumination from the moon's dim light. Seth pulled his night vision goggles out of his pack and kept watch. He checked his watch and at 1940 hours he sent a message to Mike telling him that he was heading to the rendezvous point specified in the instructions. Mike acknowledged and prepared to move into a different over watch position after he saw that Seth was set in the well-camouflaged entrance.

Seth slowly got up from his hide position and moved cautiously to the rock outcropping. He looked up at the north rock face and saw the opening described in the message. He climbed up the near shear face using handholds created by natural fissures in the exposed basalt. The rock felt icy-cold to the touch. The north face lacked any moss or lichen growth, which would have made the surface more difficult to scale. Seth quickly negotiated the five-meter climb up the rock face and was standing just inside the ledge, using his night vision goggles to help him see the entrance.

He checked around every corner in the dark cave as he made his way to the back wall described in the message.

Only after he was certain that this was it did he call Mike up to his position. Mike traced Seth's route and was climbing up the rock face within minutes. He moved in on Seth just as Seth stood at the aft rock wall and checked his watch. It was 1956 hours. Seth pulled out his palmtop.

"Mike, I hope no one sees us playing music to this wall, they'll think we have definitely departed reality." Seth said as he pulled up a selection from Marlene Dietrich's 1930 movie, 'Blue Angel'.

Seth checked his watch, 2000 hrs. They were right on schedule. He could hear his breathing so loud now that he wondered if he'd hear a freight train let alone a music piece coming from…he wasn't sure where it would come from. He strained his ears to listen, hearing only his own heartbeat and breathing. Suddenly he heard it. Mike looked up at the rock face at the same time. They tried to judge just exactly what trick would be next. Marlene's low, sultry voice could temp the men of her day like nothing else could and the low frequency sound waved also passed easily through the dense material. He fumbled briefly in the darkness with his own computer and hit the key that would let the recording play over the small conical speakers that he fastened to the rock. He pressed the play arrow on the device and let his answer vibrate into the rock from where the music seemed to originate on the other side.

Marlene's voice faded off to silence as Seth quickly pulled the speakers away from the wall. He and Mike stood ready, weapons drawn. Mike watched the area just outside the rock wall. Nothing or no one approached. Who ever it was they were supposed to meet wasn't there. Seth took a step away from the wall and looked for a void, a wire anything. There just wasn't anything there. He took a step away and secured his computer.

Just as he was about to call Mike, he watched in disbelief as the rock wall began to move and slide just wide enough away from its sides to let him pass. 'This is getting a little more bizarre each second,' He thought to himself.

Seth took a deep breath and practically threw himself into the darkness on the other side. Mike saw what was happening and followed colliding with Seth through shear momentum as he plowed into the darkness on the other side. He was no more than clearing the rock doorway when the rock slid back into place. Seth realized just how vulnerable they now were. As he stood in the complete darkness, he saw nothing. Not even a hint of any ambient light to be amplified by the night vision goggles was apparent. It was completely black and silent. Seth began to feel his way around the chamber. The floors and walls were smooth, almost as if they were polished.

"Mike, you take this side, I'll take the other." Seth said commanding Mike to look for a switch or anything that would clue them to what would happen next.

"Agh!" Seth and Mike both let out an almost silent grunt as the lights came on blinding him temporarily with their brightness. They were standing in the middle of the chamber looking at three other people. Each had an automatic weapon leveled at their mid sections.

"Please put away your weapons Colonel Stephens, Major Thomas. I am Wolfgang Heinrich, please follow us." The one standing on the left side of the other two said faintly smiling. His mannerisms were very cordial but delivered in a typical not very warm German style. He led the way into the elevator, Wolfgang, Seth, Mike followed by the other two, guns still leveled at them. They were ushered into an elevator that was lined with dark marble and highly polished brass. They all avoided eye contact with Seth and Mike as the elevator cab descended.

Seth had no idea where they were taking them other than down. They could have killed him and Mike earlier if that was the plan. There was no need to drop into the depths of this place to do that. Although they didn't seem hostile, they certainly didn't volunteer any information. They quietly looked at him and Mike as they descended. He did the same trying to assess their capabilities. They were oddly dressed in black wool uniforms with highly shined black boots. They had no rank insignia present and Seth drew a comparison with the uniform worn by the Nazi SS officers. Although they didn't disarm them, they just asked he and Mike to holster and secure their weapons. That was a good sign. Maybe they just wanted to avoid a confrontation at the entrance foyer. Maybe they would wait until he was too far below the surface to try and escape. Seth thought any hostile scenarios were highly unlikely but he kept his suspicions active. The leader of these three would be the first target if any action started. Seth and Mike avoided any discussion but they had been in these situations before. Mike would take his cues off of Seth. They both knew the play and all Seth had to do was call it out. The elevator slowed to a stop.

The cab stopped after the descended to what Seth estimated over 300 meters. The doors of the zug finally opened and Seth emerged on the main floor of the cavern. The elevator doors opened to a magnificent foyer. The floor was made of Italian rose marble, as were the walls. Each piece was inlayed with the designs of the different crest of the cities and towns throughout Germany. In the center of the foyer was a compass inlayed with each point marked with a different colored marbled piece. It was marked with the directions with heavy brass letters, nord, sud, ost, und west.

Karl Linder had been a high-ranking intelligence officer for the Reich. During the last year of World War II, he was charged with developing a series of underground shelters to provide a refuge for the Reich's officers in the event that the war was lost and Seth was seeing first hand what Karl Linder had accomplished. Karl would later explain everything to him. The elevator ride from the entrance chamber room seemed no more than a five-minute trip down to the main cavern of the underground complex. The elevator or zug as his hosts called it, was state of the art when first built in 1941. The Otis Elevator Company had patented the high-speed cabs that used an internal motor on the cab itself system to travel at speeds up to 5 feet per second. Seth and Mike took in all that they were seeing. Seth thought about Jeff Pulls analysis of the area. Seth would tell him that he was more correct than he had thought. The mountain had to be nearly hollow. The cavern was so immense.

The underground shelter complex was completely self-sufficient. It was meant to withstand a direct attack from aerial bombing. It was powered only by geo-thermal energy that heated water to steam in the basement rocks beneath the Harz Mountains. The steam heated and turned the turbines to drive a pair of 500-kilowatt generators. The system would power the cavern for an indefinite period of time as long as the main steam tunnels, of which there were four, didn't become obstructed. These tunnels, two that sent the water down to the depths that had temperatures greater than 250 degrees centigrade, and two that transported the steam or water under pressure back through the turbine systems. This created enough power for every task throughout the extensive cavern.

The total volume of the cavern including storage, living, work, and recreational spaces was nearly 175,000,000 cubic meters, which had a greater area than most small German towns. It was designed to support 500 inhabitants for at least six years total time completely with food, fresh water collection, and other essential supplies without the need to leave the shelter. It was one of 8 designed shelters to keep Hitler's staff officers and leaders safe until they could infiltrate out leaving Germany in the event the war was lost.

Food, power, water, and shelter...everything was thought through in perfect detail. Some fruits and vegetables were grown in the greenhouse. Through the perfected technique of freeze-drying foodstuffs and storing the contents in hermetically sealed containers, the German scientists would compact the food's volume and attain an indefinite shelf life for foodstuffs. The menu of cuisine would have rivaled the finest restaurants. Menu items such as beef roulade and kartoffeln, sauerbraten with gemusse, spargel und sahn mit zweibeln, and swienenschnitzel mit karoten to name a few were available. After it was reconstituted and warmed, the chef, after years of experience, could make it taste almost fresh.

Even finer beverages produced and stored. The cavern even had a small brewery, but the taste lacked the robustness of a good Pilsner because the ingredients weren't fresh. Nonetheless, it was available and would keep the quality of their lives bearable until they could escape. Other beverages included some of the finest wines that were taken from the vineyards in France and throughout the Reich's occupation areas. Beaujolais from near Dijon, Champagnes as well as some of the finest table wines that had truly improved with age.

At first, the scientists were concerned that the lack of sun would inhibit the synthesis of vitamins and that would induce health problems. The combination of supplemental UV light and the water source, which came from deep in the basement rock of the Harz Mountains more than made up for the lack of sun. The freeze-dried cuisine contained just as many vitamins and minerals as the fresh foods did.

Many of the original fifty officers and people that inhabited the cavern were approaching eighty to ninety years plus. Because of the controlled lifestyles and habits they were accustomed to, none appeared to have aged past 50. Free of the toxins that were abundant on the surface, they weren't exposed to the chemicals that were carcinogenic as well as the constant attack by airborne viral and bacterial infection. The CO_2 scrubbers continually recycled the air and improve the oxygen content to just over 19 percent, a little less than on the surface. It was thought that a less saturated oxygen environment would slow the cellular metabolic rates and the anti-oxidant rich food prevented a flood of radical ions in their bodies, which slowed the aging process significantly. It was the perfect environment, conducive to long life.

Each of the inhabitants knew the complex extremely well. They had become comfortable in its warm and secure confines. They had lived in it since 1943. They had come in quite young men, and were now very old.

Karl Linder walked up to meet Seth. Karl was nearing his 87th birthday but he resembled a man of a very young fifty years old. "Colonel Stephens, I can't describe to you how wonderful it is to see you. I am Karl Linder." Karl Linder said and sharply turned to Mike. "You must be Major Thomas, I am so pleased that you both decided to visit us. It has been a long time since we have had outside visitors." Karl said as he looked them over and studied their faces. Karl could tell that they were indeed puzzled.

Seth watched Karl and his actions closely. Although he felt that they were in no danger, he still maintained his readiness for anything. The man that greeted them seemed more glad than suspicious of Seth.

Seth was just about to speak to break the silence as they studied each other, but Karl beat him to it. "Colonel Stephens, you have now idea how long I have waited for this day." Karl continued to say as a woman walked up and took hold of Karl's arm looking at Seth as if he were a miracle. Her eyes glistened with happiness and a most elated smile shone from her face. Seth looked at the two; somehow they looked very familiar. It was as if they had met somewhere before. He dismissed it as a coincidence and developed the pleasantries that they exchanged.

"It is my pleasure to be here, although I must say that I am at a loss. I have many questions for you sir. I hope that we clear up some items that the United States government is most interested in." Seth finished.

"Of course, of course, it is the least that we owe you an explanation and we will get to that. I would first like you to get to know our situation and our way of life first before I also ask you the many questions that I have." Karl said. "Come, let me show you our complex on our way to the operations center were I can properly brief you and then we can discuss my invitation. Please be assured that you are our guests and you are welcomed. I only hope that you and Major Thomas will allow me to brief you on our discoveries over the past years." Linder finished as he and his wife led the group quickly and spryly through the complex.

Linder led them across the large room adjacent to the foyer where they stopped at what looked like a small train station. Linder explained that they would be taking the electric Unternbahn, a type of underground railroad, to the operations area. It was more efficient than walking and would speed their trip to the operations room. They sat four to a car; two per seat facing each other and Seth guessed that they were proceeding in a northwest direction. He was fascinated with the facility as they rode past the ornate designs that decorated the walls of the complex. It was literally an underground paradise from what Seth could see. To his hosts though, it was simply making the best of a bad situation. They couldn't leave; it wasn't as if they had the option. This was a prison to them, a place where they no longer enjoyed the freedoms that some of them knew once. It was a place where the original 50 of them had rotated their watch over the world for many of the passing years. One at a time they kept a constant ear to the outside world gathering intelligence and developing some very impressive technology of their own.

The unterbahn slowed to a stop after their ride and they exited to the north side of the complex. At the speed they moved, Seth judged that they traveled about 8 kilometers on the unterbahn. Karl opened two large beautifully crafted wooden doors that opened to the operations area. The room was efficiently constructed. Map images were projected on large display screens surrounding the room showed the earth in four views, northern, southern, eastern, and western hemispheres. Overlays showed areas under current study. Seth was very surprised to see projection displays that showed the intelligence update board focusing on subjects common to any other intelligence agency. Seth could see analysts scanning radio frequency's looking for intelligence through traffic intercepts. Frequency ranges from 12 megahertz to 24 gigahertz were monitored and each analyst would post the most recent intercept that answered an intelligence requirement on the projected situation report. Several radarscopes were in the room, but none were currently active. Seth looked at Mike, there wasn't much different here than they had seen at Fort Meade. Only it was a much smaller scale.

"Karl, your government has done a very good job keeping your complex well hidden." Seth said as he and Mike realized that they were on the top of a new finding.

"That is because the German government knows nothing about this complex. It was a very closely guarded secret back in 1943. Only we, the current occupants and Hitler's immediate personal staff, knew of it. Hitler himself had no idea of the details for this location. He only knew of another located off of the French coast in the Channel Islands." Karl finished. Mike seemed confused but Seth looked as if he had known all along.

Linder briefed him on all the operations and covered every area thoroughly. Karl knew that he would not only have to prove to Seth that the operation was authentic, no matter how much like science fiction it sounded. He also needed to make sure that Seth was convinced that his cause was valid enough to invite the help of the United States government. Karl was proud of the accomplishments that he and his team had made but Seth could tell that he had something else to tell them other than show them their accomplishments.

"Karl, your accomplishments here are nothing short of tremendous." Seth said as he walked over to a map and situation board that showed the status of his RC-680 aircraft-orbiting overhead. Seth paused and turned to look Karl directly in the eye. "Where do I fit in here? What is it that you are asking? Why is it that you need my help and the help of government of the United States? Seth asked. He realized that Karl was showing him his intelligence collection capability to gain his confidence.

Karl looked at Seth; he was so much exactly as he had imagined. Seth was very matter of fact and didn't stray from the main point of an objective. Karl thought that he was very much like him when he was as a young man. The thought made Karl smile. He continued, realizing that he knew what would make Seth believe in his cause and take the message back to the United States leadership.

Karl sat on a comfortable leather chair and pointed to the two others arranged seated in the semi-circle.

"We haven't left this installation since we arrived in 1943." Karl paused. "My brother Robert and I began collecting data back in 1941 on a man that we believe engineered World War II for his purposes. This man's motives were to bring all of humanity under one rule, his. He was without a doubt the man behind Hitler's rapid rise to power. This man and his ancestors have methodically created a subculture of chaos among us. He has been subtly moving humanity in his direction through strong influence in order to bring the world's people under his rule." Karl paused to gauge Seth's comprehension.

Karl continued seeing that Seth maintained an open mind. Seth kept a straight-unalarmed expression on his face. "We have remained here partly out of fear but more out of a devotion to our cause. We believe in these facts so strongly that we have given up our lives and our children's lives to prove this. We have deeply researched each human conflict that has occurred since World War I. We have concrete proof and we can show the facts that cast suspicion on the many other dark times in human history. The most convincing argument is that we can and will prove this linkage. Our research and intelligence substantiates that he has strayed from his timelines. He has fallen behind his schedule and he is planning to create yet another major disruption in the world's order on a large and devastating scale." Karl began to feel that Seth doubted his conclusions as Seth consciously shifted in his chair to give Karl a subtle clue that he needed more information. Karl perceived this immediately and changed his approach.

"Seth, there isn't a day that we don't often think about the days before we entered this complex. The simple things that you experience such as sunshine, rain, and the wind elude us here, except for brief ventures outside. Everything that we had taken for granted through everyday

71

experiences we missed the most. We have not left our compound or the immediate area above it since we began to collect intelligence that concluded that a man named Hesbulah was behind the plan for the Reich. Hesbulah thrives on the frailness of man, our primary flaw of self - preservation. Make any man feel that his very existence is in danger and he'll jump to a conclusion to fight ruthlessly to defend himself. Hesbulah was nothing more than an instigator on a very large scale. Pit one of the world's people against another and they'll do the dirty work for him." Linder stood up and moved from the operations area into a small alcove just inside the operations center that functioned as a dining area for the people at their stations.

Seth and Mike followed as he talked. Karl motioned to the chef that was attending the kitchen that evening and as they sat at an immaculately clean and crisp white tablecloth complete with silver and china. The chef brought out the first course of their meal.

Karl continued. "Seth, toward the end of World War II, your government was interested in our discoveries. My brother, Robert went to America to brief President Truman and the Chief of the Army Security Agency on our findings." Karl paused to take a bite of the fresh green salad that was placed in front of them.

"What was the outcome?" Seth asked as he and Mike were completely captivated by Karl's story.

"No briefing was given. My brother died in an accident as he was traveling by automobile to Camp Meade. I never would see him again." Karl said reliving a time before when he and his brother discussed his leaving. "We discussed the dangers but he felt strongly about presenting the information to expose this man. Your government sent liaisons to escort Robert back to America. We felt that the information would persuade your government to look deeper into the world's events. America to us was like a very powerful child, still concerned with its own problems rather that the impact of the world on its development. We knew that if we could tell the American leadership what was happening, it would re-focus the attention of President Truman."

Karl continued, "Our first message was when we sent the information that allowed your intelligence operators to break the Enigma Code. You probably remember the story of how it seemed like the allies suddenly and mysteriously broke the code, but it was us. On every message that we sent to tell the allies exactly what was happening, we also sent a message of who we were and what we were working toward. We eventually attained credibility with General Omar Bradley when we sent several messages that divulged Nazi positions for a counteroffensive in final days of the infamous Battle of the Bulge. There was no mystery of how the American's most inexperienced division, the Battle Babies of the 99th

Division beat Joachim Pfeiffer's SS Panzer Division in Belgium. Afterward Bradley's staff wanted to arrange a meeting, but we knew that it was too dangerous. The Reich's leadership knew that certain factions, highly placed in the Reich were against them, but they lacked the information to expose us. We sent Bradley detailed information about staff planning and headquarters' locations as well as Hitler's location. The Allies acted rapidly on the information and the final blow to Hitler's rule and Hesbulah's subversions were halted."

"We had two major underground complexes at our disposal, this one here and the other on the island of Jersey, in Britain's Channel Islands. Robert was charged with setting up the Jersey complex and I the one here in the Harz Mountains. We used the Jersey location as our main depository for all of our data and information because of its location and the ease of access for the allies. All of our information was and still remains stored there. Robert left Jersey by a United States submarine that took him directly to the Pentagon's underground dock along the Potomac River. We suspected that someone knew of Robert's arrival because we intercepted messages originating from the United States that discussed the secret briefing that Robert was to give. The briefing was to be conducted at Camp Meade; an Army base just north of Washington D.C. Robert never gave the briefing. He and four other men that were the center of the operation were killed in an accident where the car in which he was riding was struck by a train near Greenbelt, Maryland. The explosion was so violent that Robert's remains had to be identified by your doctors in Washington."

"We continued to send the results of our intelligence collection efforts. We saved the world from a very different ending of the war effort by telling the Americans about the atomic weapons that Japan planned to use on your country. We continued to make several attempts to communicate with your government afterward but Hesbulah's forces continued to look for us. He realized that we knew and had proof. One by one those that we contacted were killed. We have continued this effort since then, waiting for the correct time to again try to let your country know. We have continued to provide your government the answers to some of their most difficult intelligence questions."

"We were somewhat fortunate however in 1943. Robert was a very suspicious man by nature. He took none of the data with him. Everything, all of the data and information that we collected was left in Jersey." Karl finished.

"So you lost none of your information when Robert was killed?" Seth said as he sat back in his chair.

He was about to play a hunch that he had thought of a soon as he had met Linder. It was along the same reasons that he used Marlene Dietrich and the Enigma code to send his reply. The authenticity of this man was becoming more difficult to doubt. Seth decided to give him another subtle hint that he was not completely convinced. "Excuse me Karl." Seth said as he reached around his back to move his pistol. Karl took notice and stiffened in his chair.

"Did I say something that offended you? It wasn't my intention Seth." Karl said as he saw Seth holding his weapon.

"What?" Seth said not sure… "Oh, Karl, I apologize. My weapon was a bit uncomfortable and I was just moving it to under my shoulder. Please forgive me."

The move had its intended effect by allowing Karl take notice that Seth was edgy. Seth said hoping that his move would give Karl a sense of discomfort. Karl caught a glimpse of the 7,65 mm pistol that Seth carried. Even a glimpse of the weapon gave away the design to Karl.

"Seth, what type of a weapon is that and where did you get it? May I see it?" Karl said eagerly while trying to look at the pistol under Seth's jacket.

Seth produced the pistol and unconsciously ejected the 8 round magazine from the handgrip. He placed it on safe and with the utmost respect for a firearm, handed it muzzle down and away, to Karl.

"It is a J.P. Sauer and Sohn, Suhl, 7,65mm semi-automatic pistol, German issued in 1940. It was a gift from my uncle. I never knew him, but the people that raised me gave it to me. I was told that my uncle captured it at Remagen. It was supposed to be just a battlefield souvenir but it is the most accurate weapon of its size that I have ever fired. I found it in a steamer trunk in the attic. It has been with me ever since. I never knew my family and this is as close as I ever got." Seth said as he and Mike began to feel more comfortable now.

Karl took the weapon and looked at it. His eyes stared at the engraved portion of the handgrip base, just below the receiver. An inscription written on the side read, *Robert Linder, Berlin 1941.*

Karl could hardly believe his eyes. He held the pistol as if it had to be cradled with both hands and traced his thumb over the inscription as gently as if he were caressing a newborn's skin. Seth and Mike looked at each other. Karl acted as if he had just been snapped back to the present after being transported back to 1941.

"Seth, this weapon belonged to my brother, Robert." Karl replied as his mind drifted instantly back nearly 60 years to visions of his brother.

Karl motioned to one of his men manning the supervisor's console in the operations center. The man appeared to be closer in age to Seth rather than Karl. Obviously he wasn't one of the original 50 people that started out in the facility.

"Bitte, go to the armory and have Johannes bring my sidearm here." Karl said and the man silently nodded and left the dinning area. Karl turned back to Seth and Mike.

"This was the same type of weapon that I received in Berlin 1941. There is no mistake. These were presented to us by Hitler himself under the Brandenburg Tor." Karl pushed his glassed gently further up on his nose as he examined the serial number. There is no mistake Seth. The serial numbers were in succession. Mine was the number after Roberts! Robert had this weapon with him in Washington D.C. I thought that it was lost in the explosion." Karl stared at the pistol and examined the damage that the pistol sustained in the fire after the crash with the train.

"I am surprised to see that you have it Seth, but very glad that you do. I know that it is in good care." Karl handed the pistol back over to Seth as if he were handing over a delicate and fragile piece of crystal. A man closer in age to Karl came into the dining area and handed Karl his sidearm that looked exactly like the one Seth had presented, sans the fire damage that Seth's displayed. Karl presented both weapons to Seth.

"Please see for yourself, especially the serial numbers." Karl said with almost uncontained elation.

Seth looked at the two weapons. The possibility of this being a coincidence in his mind was dwindling fast. The serial numbers were in succession. Seth looked at the inscription on Karl's weapon; it read exactly as his except for the different names. Seth looked at the two and then handed them over to Mike, who sat wide-eyed in disbelief.

"You are sure that your brother had this weapon with him in Washington D.C.?" Seth asked, now more convinced than he was before of Karl's story.

"Oh yes, there is no doubt." Karl answered folding his hands in front of him on the table. Seth read the signs of confidence that Karl displayed. Seth turned the conversation back to the data.

"Karl, you were saying that you were fortunate because your brother didn't take the data back to the States with him." Karl took his sidearm as Mike handed it back to him and Seth replaced his in the holster just inside his coat as Karl continued.

"That is correct. The data was not with Robert. He secured it in the complex near St. Hellier, Jersey. We are hopeful that it is still intact." Karl said with optimism.

Mike was as enthralled with the conversation and realized after he began that he was probably speaking out of turn. "What do you mean hopeful that it is intact?" Mike finished looking at Seth. Karl looked at them both and took a deep breath before he began.

"We believed that Hesbulah discovered the complex in Jersey through an employee from Jersey that worked in the Middle East. She worked as a geologist early in her life for a company that provided oil-drilling information to Hesbulah's interests. She moved back to Jersey, but after spending most of her life in the Middle East she developed many ties with the people there. We intercepted several transmissions from Jersey to Socotra, an Island where Hesbulah claims as his country. In those transmissions, she describes the site of our complex. Hesbulah acknowledged that he would visit the island and once we confirmed that he was enroute, the occupants destroyed the complex and themselves. There was no other way. We realized long ago that we couldn't escape him forever. Our only hope was to continue to gather information that would expose Hesbulah and his objectives." Karl explained.

"How do you know that the information hasn't been destroyed or captured by Hesbulah?" Seth asked.

"We don't know for certain. We only know that the information was stored in a vault that was designed to be inaccessible. We also know that Hesbulah did not stop at the island but only requested more information from his men as he flew above it on his way into London. We are hoping that the information can be retrieved and presented to the world now as evidence that Hesbulah exists and has worked for generations to subject the world to him." Karl finished and looked at the two men sitting crossed from him. He considered himself to be an excellent judge of character and he knew that these two men would see the next step.

Seth and Mike said nothing initially. Seth looked into Karl's eyes, looking for any sign of doubt or suspicion. He saw none. He saw the same intensity that he would offer to anyone when he was totally committed to an operation or mission. Karl's piercing, green eyes deeply set, looked back at him with an intensity that nearly magnetized his eyes to them. They were so familiar, but how, why?

Seth thought it through and spoke. "We need to go to Jersey and find the data Karl." Karl let out a sigh of welcomed relief. He knew that Seth would help him. He knew that their relationship would begin with a difficult task, but based completely in trust.

"Seth, I can speak for all of us here. We know that we can trust you and we our willing to place our life's work in your hands." Karl said as he reached out to warmly grasp Seth's hand more as a father than as a colleague does.

Seth continued to look into his eyes and couldn't explain the comfort that he felt by touching his hand and looking into this man's eyes.

He had never experienced anything like it before, or had he?

7

The Seduction of the Orient

Belgrade, Yugoslavia, May 1999

Hesbulah threw the paper down on the desk as he finished reading the Statement from the American Ambassador in China, dated yesterday, May 9, 1999.

He reviewed the words over in his mind. 'The Ambassador and the entire staff of the American Embassy and consulates express the profound sorrow to the people of China over the NATO bombing of the Chinese Embassy in Belgrade, and offer deepest condolence to the families of the innocent victims of this deplorable accident. As Our President has said, it was a tragic mistake. We must not let this mistake impede further progress in developing stronger US - China relations. That is so fundamental in the interests of both our countries.'

"An accident. Who can they fool? They knew of this meeting Sinovic. They knew."

Hesbulah was furious. "You are failing me Sinovic, I have given you everything that you needed…money, power and a chance to become one of the most powerful men in the history of man. I have painted the picture for you, and have given you the script, complete with every ingredient for success and you are failing. How can this be?" Hesbulah said with the false humility and a sincerity that he mastered so well.

"I have worked hard to align China with your cause. Your cause Sinovic. That meeting would have netted us more resources than you could have imagined. Now they will be skeptical of our offers. It will take me years to develop the relationships necessary to unite us against

NATO and the west. You had better find out who has betrayed us and deliver his head to me on a platter. With China and Russia behind us, we could have defeated NATO and its weakening alliance. NATO is torn over what should be done; the smaller countries would have turned and ran from a NATO alliance if we had Russia and Sino support. That meeting would have sealed it and our resolve to create an alliance that would have once again tested NATO's resolve. Now all I have are these damaged files from the embassy. Your leak must be stopped before it ruins my efforts."

"I only need more loyal men, the ones that I have under my lead are weak, they bolt and run and the first sign of an obstacle. They promise me that they will succeed, but they cannot follow through." Replied Sinovic Irratitch."

"I have made you the Prime Minister of Yugoslavia, Sinovic Irratitch. Have you forgotten that? You are the most powerful man in your country. You were to create a country full of despair and havoc. An example to the leaders of all countries that have been subjected to the will of these infidels, this mockery called the United Nations. Our plan would allow the frail and impoverished countries to band with you, rise up and challenge the wealthy countries. You were to develop a plan to rise and fight the members of NATO, The United Nations and The United States. I'll tell you what you must do. You must gather these weak country leaders, meet with them and unite. We must continue our struggle and we must not fail. You will be a great man Sinovic, but you must stop tempting my patience. You must trust me. Look to me for your inspiration. If anyone gets in our way, I will make them suffer. It is for a greater good. We can have what we seek. You shall report to me on your progress in the next day. I will be returning to Socotra this evening. My assistant Marek Elamesh will remain with you. Consult him, he will help in your successes." Hesbulah finished his angry torrid sermon by shaking Sinovic by his neck.

"I am always thankful for your leadership and opportunity. I am your humble servant." Was Sinovic's reply as Hesbulah turned and walked away.

Hesbulah's entourage gathered around him on cue and escorted him away from the dampened halls of the puppet Prime Minister's offices now damaged by intense NATO bombing. He couldn't wait to leave the damp, bone-chilling climate that the dreary skies of May had to offer in Belgrade. As he walked through the courtyard of the Prime Ministers Office Complex, the wind and pelting rain that fell even in May made the temperature feel colder than the two degrees centigrade that registered on the shrapnel scared digital clock and thermometer that hung, remarkably still working, on the side of a building that should have been bulldozed after the first series of bombing attacks.

It would take many years to recover from the aerial punishment inflicted by the UN recommended bombing campaign conducted by NATO. But it had achieved its effect. The Russians and the Chinese were pulling further and further away from any peaceful discussions. They realized that they must be able to match the force and power available to NATO to be considered a true player in this game.

But the gray skies gave Hesbulah hope. When the skies were gray, people were easier to persuade that all was hopeless. They seemed much easier to intimidate. They seemed more vulnerable. This reinforced his beliefs. He let his mind drift as the ruble-strewn streets of Belgrade drifted by the window of the armor plated Bentley. The drive from Sinovic's palace to the hardened bunker at the airport would take another 20 minutes on these roads.

"Marek, I refuse to let yet another opportunity to seize power be thwarted by NATO. It has taken me too much time to plan and set this plan into action in the Balkans. This region had been a root for instability ever since man began to move farther than his legs could take him during a day's walk. It is the meeting point of many cultures, all living closely, all unwilling to change or compromise. All of them believing that their way of life, their culture and their religion are the greatest. Even the slightest disagreement results in an inhumane combat between many, many differing cultures. Even the cultures that don't live here directly in the region realized its importance. It was the primary trade route between the European continent and the Asian continent, a bridge for barter and a major line of communication. It was a prominent meeting point. Thousands of people had either lived there or had traveled through there. The influence of the region was vast and far-reaching. My ancestors have always thought this to be a strategic position. No matter what the world has thought, I hold the region under my banner. It offered the beginning of instability and it brings out the greed in every leader. They all believe that the key to successful world leadership is the ownership or influence of the Balkans. It had expanded their empires before and that is what makes the terrain of the Balkans the most strategic position for leadership of the world. Territorial rights to the Balkans means a control over nearly every major cultural belief in the world. I will take advantage of this motivation. The destabilization of Europe and eventually the world is founded in the Balkans. The thought of world stability being reality was influenced by the successful foreign policy of the United States. Ever since the unification of east and western Germany, people began to believe that there was more to life than greed. They began to realize that they all wanted the same things. They wanted a life of freedom and a life without chaos. Peace was rapidly becoming the ideal of the fast approaching twenty-first century. I don't have time to wait this out Marek; I will rapidly lose momentum. There is no more to continue after me Marek. I am the last of Hesbulah. I plan to take full advantage of the instability within Yugoslavia and bring together the masses of China and Russia under our banner. Yugoslavia sets our stage. Russia, or the Commonwealth of Independent States as they now call it, is still in turmoil and experiencing an unprecedented economic disaster. I will use their misery to destabilize the actions of Yeltsin. China is now the new emerging world power. They are the biggest threat to the United States and NATO. Their strength in a new world order means that they won't buckle to the pressures from the Europeans or the Americans for that matter. If there was to be a new world order, China was going to be at the negotiating table and be there with a big stake. They would not be passed off as easily as the other puppet Asian governments. There is too much distrust between the CIS, China, the United States and the Europeans. I'll use that against them. I'll take advantage of this position and leverage it to my advantage. I must advance daily or take as many steps backward Marek. We face intangible losses if we can't capitalize on this plan soon. Nothing will compare to this. Our reign of chaos and negativism will be over; my ancestor's dream of human domination would be over. I will refuse to believe that it would be over. This empire has been passed to me by my father and his before him. The entire bloodline of Hesbulah has worked for world domination and I will not give up this position no matter what. That is my objective Marek. That is my objective. I will be the leader of this wretched population, to make everything controlled by my hand. I will gain this or they will all suffer, no matter the cost." Hesbulah stopped his tirade. Marek could see his festering anger as the veins on his head and neck bulged and his face grew red as his tried to restrain his anger. Hesbulah looked out the window and saw the suffering caused by his hand.

'So what,' he thought, 'human life is cheap; it was designed only to serve me. After all, there were five humans born every second.'

"Marek, you must see to it that this fool Sinovic doesn't further delay my plans. We need to find out what else NATO and the United States knows. NATO found out about this meeting somehow and sent in their bombs. Now they tell the fools of the world that it was a mistake. How utterly ridiculous that sounds. Now the Russians and the Chinese run scared, even in their own country. I should have carved out that fool Sinovic's heart while I had the choice. I do not expect him to take the lead on anything. He is useless and when the time comes, he will meet with a cruel turn of fate. Now that we have made the nuclear weapons from the Russians available, we will begin to transport them to China. We must capitalize now on the instability that exists between China and the US. I fear that the window may be open for but only a short period of time. The alliances between the United Nations, the puppets for the United States, NATO and the Russians are strained to the break point. The Russians will have no objections to the sale of their nuclear weapons to the Chinese now since the Americans didn't honor their attempt to broker peace in the Balkans. The diversion that I have created here has kept the United Nations too busy to watch China. The time is almost here to begin the final part of this process. Make sure that the meeting between the Russians, Chinese and the Yugoslavs is prepared for me. This time we shall meet in the United States, perhaps Denver. Maybe there we will be safe from their bombs." Hesbulah gave his instructions to Elamesh to ensure that the meeting to be held in the United States was firmly in place.

Elamesh didn't attain the position of right hand man to Hesbulah by chance. He had the intelligence to stay ahead of any complex situation, the self-discipline and initiative to maintain his focus and determine the course of action that kept all on track. He would make sure that the meeting to strengthen the secret ties between China, Russia and the other governments that were invited would indeed happen.

"Your insight once again makes me realize your greatness Hesbulah." It was all that Elamesh could muster up as a response. Time was growing short and Elamesh would have to follow through on this without doubt.

The drive from the governmental center of Belgrade to Belgrade's Airport was filled with detours and bone-jarring thuds as the Bentley's tires fell into water filled holes cratering the streets. Elamesh noticed Hesbulah's demonic smile as he looked over the destruction surrounding him. Elamesh smiled as he looked over the examples of a chaotic world and took pleasure knowing that he was part of it.

The motorcade drove through the airport perimeter fence on the south side of the airport. The lone arched hangar made of solid concrete was one of the few buildings that weren't damaged in the bombing. The escort vehicles pulled around the sides of the building and Hesbulah's sedan pulled through a entry way in the larger hangar doors into the even darker than outside hangar interior.

Hesbulah's Dassault Falcon jet was the only thing that showed any sign of activity. The sedan stopped a few feet from the entry stairs of the jet and a female attendant perched atop them wearing a tight fitting black sweater and tight slacks that showed every curve of a very voluptuous body. She was one of three attendants that would service every desire of Hesbulah's on the flight returning to Socotra.

The Falcon departed Belgrade's single usable runway to the north, off of runway 30. It climbed through the gray overcast and broke into sunshine and clear skies before turning to the south for the five and one-half hour flight to Socotra, just to the south of the Middle Eastern Country of Yemen.

Hesbulah was pleased to see that his three attendants had since removed their sweaters and slacks as they prepared for their performance. They knew the routine all to well by now. Their acting and modeling careers had brought them to this. They sculptured their bodies and neglected their minds. For this reason, Hesbulah's assistants selected them. They had aspired for nothing other than to be at the center of man's desires. They were receiving it. They all had initially objected very strongly to the proposition made by Hesbulah, but were convinced otherwise after their families were arrested and imprisoned on false charges made by Hesbulah. Not only were their lives dependent on each performance but, so too were their families. They would fulfill his every desire and offer no objections to anything that he might suggest.

Hesbulah settled into a comfortable position on his lounge and prepared to enjoy the feast and "activities" prepared for him by his attendants. Out of habit he reached for a briefing book prepared for him. He was immediately thrown off by the headline of the briefing. He didn't fully understand the implications, but this headline more than annoyed him.

American Satellite Reconnaissance Capability and Resolution Allows Unrestricted Observation On Any Target.

He picked up his satellite phone and dialed Elamesh. The connection was flawless, "Elamesh, I want you to find out more about this new reconnaissance capability that the Americans have. Find out what their target areas are and report back to me. Our efforts along the Althais may be in jeopardy. What is this about?"

"I will have the answers for you by morning," was all that Elamesh could muster as a reply. He hadn't seen the brief. He would find the answers for Hesbulah. He had never failed.

The attendants were delivering his dinner, a feast so extensive that it took all three to deliver it. Hesbulah turned his attention form the phone to his servants. Even the most powerful must take a break for pleasure. The first servant saw the expression on Hesbulah's face as he glared up at her body. He motioned for her to come closer to him. His eyes fixed on her. He reached up to her shoulders and pulled her toward him. She knew from his expression that this would be a very long flight back to Socotra for her.

8

Recalled to Washington

Leaving Goslar Enroute to Hannover, Germany, February 16, 0830 hours

"Frank, have two of the RC-680 that are coming off track divert into Hannover. Mike and I are enroute to the Hannover Airport right now. Mike and I will fly a RC-680 back to Washington. I need to get back ASAP to brief General Woodsen. Be prepared to move the operation and flex, as we need to in order to keep ahead of this mission. I will know more after I meet with the Chief." Seth said as he spoke into his handset as he and Mike cleared the entrance to Linder's complex just before sunrise.

"Roger boss, your hosts did a good job keeping us appraised of your status while you got a little sleep last night. Sounds like you were in good hands." Frank Nellis said as a technician handed him a confirmation about the RC-680s diverting into Hannover. "Sir, the RCs are leaving track now and diverting into Hannover."

Seth continued talking to Nellis as he and Mike made it to the SL500. Frank, the other RC-680 will bring the crew with them back into Wiesbaden. Have Flight Operations coordinate the flight and notify Hannover, Shannon and Saint Johns for military landing permits today. Keep the surveillance operations at the current level. Mike or I will brief you as soon as we can. Have the Executive Officer cut your command orders, effective immediately." Seth said as he and Mike secured their equipment in the trunk. Seth glanced at his watch; they spent nearly 24 hours with Karl Linder. Linder offered substantiated facts that Hesbulah was behind many chaotic and destructive events throughout the course of human history. From terrorist bombings to the destabilization of nations to

84

incite wars, one thing was clear, they had to do something. To do nothing after they had this information was wrong. Hesbulah had to be stopped.

Mike had already shifted into fourth gear as the Mercedes cleanly accelerated down the mountain road. Seth signed off with Frank and organized his thoughts before he contacted General Max Woodsen.

"Seth, what was the reason for using Marlene Dietrich and sending the reply encoded with an Enigma code?" Mike said as he negotiated a narrow bridge on a turn down the mountain. He downshifted the transmission and eased the car into the turn at nearly 85 kilometers an hour. The car followed his commands effortlessly and tracked through the turn like it was on rails.

"Any one could have sent that message. After Jeff Pulls did a little analysis and told me that the mountain may have been hollow, I thought about the underground complexes that we discovered near Ruppertsweiler." Seth said refreshing Mike's memory.

"So you actually had a hunch that someone may have been using some old Nazi equipment to lure us there?" Mike questioned.

"After we concluded that the frequency band checked and the signal strength was a match, I thought about all of the equipment that we had discovered abandoned by the Germans at end of World War II. All of the equipment that we found worked when we turned the switch on like the day it was turned off, nearly 60 years ago. What would have kept someone else from finding equipment somewhere else and just turning it on and then transmitting? I wanted to make sure that it wasn't a prank, or some mistake. Marlene and Enigma were just discriminators. I needed some form of challenge and password but had to pick something that was unique yet common. Only someone that used Enigma before and was familiar with the patterns could have replied as fast as they did. Marlene just bracketed their age for me. If they knew Marlene, they would have had to have been old enough to realize what an impact she made on millions of men fighting the war." Seth completed as he pulled out his phone and prepared to dial General Max Woodsen.

"So it was the same as me asking you who won the 1999 World Series as a challenge and reply. You never cease to amaze me boss." Mike said as he pointed the 500 toward Hannover. The weather had changed drastically in the last 24 hours. The morning looked to be a beauty. The temperature was a crisp five degrees Centigrade and the skies were clear. A slight breeze out of the south promised to keep the skies beautiful and the weather promising.

Seth punched in the number for the Joint Chief's office. The Operations Center in the Pentagon received the call and rapidly put him through to the Chief's home duty number. "Woodsen." The Chief answered after being awakened by the phone.

"Sir, this is Stephens." Seth said into his handset while pointing to Mike the correct turn to take onto the autobahn ramp.

"Seth, Where are you? Can you give me a SITREP?" Woodsen said as he left his comfortable bed and moved to his desk in a room beside the bedroom.

"Sir, Thomas and I have just left the complex. We are enroute to Hannover to meet one of the RC-680 crews. Sir this is bigger than I believe any of us originally thought. Thomas and I will fly in a RC-680 back to Washington. We should arrive early afternoon your time. I can present the information that Karl Linder has given me then." Seth said as he nodded to Mike as they sped up the autobahn toward Hannover.

"Seth, we'll plan an evening meeting with the Director, NSA, Joshua McAdams. Plan on coming into Davison Army Airfield instead of Andrews. We'll head up to an offsite meeting location a little more secure. Seth, I'm leaving you on this mission. Frank Nellis can handle the mission for the RC-680. We may roll up the support for this mission into the validation. Do you think that'll work?" Woodsen said as he pressed the Top Secret meeting key description into his calendar and sent it off to all that were concerned. The electronic distribution list for the meeting looked like a who's who in United States Government leadership. He hit the send button. In a few seconds the meeting would be scheduled on everyone's calendar and set up. He had chosen an offsite location for security purposes high in the Shenandoah Mountains near Paris, Virginia.

"Roger Sir. Nellis can handle it. Mike and I will look forward to seeing you again. Please give my best to Mrs. Woodsen Sir." Seth said in closing.

"Just get here safely Seth. It'll be good to see you again son. Woodsen out."

They arrived at Hannover in just under an hour. The RC-680 crew had arrived about 40 minutes earlier and had refueled and had the aircraft serviced before Seth and Mike arrived. Seth looked at the stealthy RC-680 aircraft as it sat on the ramp adjacent to a Fixed Base Operator, the business that served transient crews and serviced aircraft that landed in Hannover. Seth noticed that the manager fashioned his service to be comparable to any other FBO that you'd find in the United States. Mike pulled into the parking area after he left Seth off at the entry. Seth met the crews that brought both aircraft in as they were talking to the owner of the business. He approached the Captain that he recognized as the flight's leader for today's mission.

"Gentlemen, thanks for bringing the airplanes here. I hate to steal her out from under you." Seth said as he made his rounds with greetings and handshakes with his pilots.

"No problem Sir, glad to be part of the mission! Sir, this is Wegner Hoag. He retired from Army Aviation as a Sergeant Major in 1995. He owns this fine establishment." Said the Flight Leader.

Seth turned to face a man that still looked like a Sergeant Major. The only thing that changed in his athletic stature was a little paunch that developed after a break from years of running with his troops at early morning training formations. His haircut was still in strict military standards and his white shirt and tie, with dark blue wool pants were smartly starched and creased. Seth recognized him as a crew chief that he met at Fort Rucker long ago.

"Sergeant Major, you probably don't recognize me. We met at Fort Rucker when I was back there for the fixed wing transition. You were a Tac Sergeant with the Air Assault Course there." Seth said as he shook the older man's hand.

"Come to think of it yes. I still remember those late evening racquetball games. You were the only officer that kicked my ass Sir. I think I still owe you, sir." Wegner said.

"How is it that you decided to stay here Sergeant Major?" Seth asked.

"Sir, my wife is from Hannover. After I spent a career dragging her from one garden spot to another, I told her she could pick the retirement spot. We came here and I couldn't give up aviation so I bought this franchise and set up shop here at Hannover. I figured Europe would evolve eventually and modernize. They are actually flying quite a few business jets here now." Wegner said. He turned the subject back to where Seth really wanted it. "Enough about me Sir, how can I help an old Army buddy? Wegner said sincerely.

"Sergeant Major, we will probably fly in and out of Hannover a few more times and we need a hangar and a lot of discretion." Seth said looking deeply into the Sergeant Major's eyes.

Without skipping a beat, the Sergeant Major replied. "Sir, you just tell me what you need and you got it."

"We are flying back to the States this morning and need to lease a hangar for about a month. Do you have one that is out of the way? Somewhere, where we won't be in your way and tie things up?" Seth asked trying to cover some of the requirements that he anticipated.

"Sir, I just built three new hangars and all my customers wanted to move into them. They left my big hangar just off the end of the runway empty. It is back from the ramp area a ways, can't really see it too well from here because it's back in those trees."

Seth cut in before Wegner finished. "Is it that one back there near the highway, the one that doesn't even look like it is part of the airfield?" Seth finished.

"Yes Sir, I apologize but that is the only one I've got. If you were here about a week earlier, I could have put you into a new one. If you give me a few minutes, I'll call some of my corporate customers and make them an offer to move back into the old hangar for a month." Wegner said almost sorry that he wasn't prepared. He was shocked at Seth's reply.

"Sergeant Major, that old hangar is perfect. Sign us up for a month-to-month lease. Send the paperwork back to this fax number and my Executive Officer will take care of the arrangements." Seth said to Wegner as he bent over to write down the fax number for the Executive Officer.

Wegner was obviously relieved that he was able to satisfy Seth's needs. "Sir, you got it! If there is anything else that you need, you just call. I'll cover the paperwork so that it looks as if it has been leased back to the franchise here. No paper trails make it a little harder to track down." Wegner knew the deal. Seth wondered if he hadn't been involved in some covert operations in his past.

Seth saw Mike talking with the crews as he dismissed them. The flight leader waved a high salute to Seth as he and the other three pilots headed out to the RC-680 that they would take back to Wiesbaden. Mike walked over to Seth and Wegner and Seth made the introductions.

"Boss, we are ready to go. Those guys even ordered catering for us. We are filed for a quick stop in Shannon for fuel and then we'll hop across the north Atlantic. Weather looks good. Should be smooth flying." Mike said.

"Wegner, I have one small favor to ask of you, would you have one of your people take my car down to the hangar and park it inside?" Seth said putting out his hand and taking the keys from Mike.

"Is it that sporty white SL500 over there?" Wegner said as he craned his neck to look over the hedge in front of the window.

"That's the one Sergeant Major." Seth replied. "Consider it done sir, we'll even put a shine on her for you and store her away safe while you're gone." Wegner said comfortable with the arrangement.

Seth smiled. "Wegner, it is a pleasure to see you again. Thanks for taking care of us this morning." Seth said as he shook Wegner's hand.

He and Seth shook hands as Seth turned to accompany Mike out to the waiting RC-680 jet aircraft.

The weather was as Mike had said, perfect for flying, except for the weather in Shannon. The still cool early morning temperatures covered the west coast of Ireland in a dense sea fog, not unlike the fog that shrouds San Francisco in the early winter mornings.

After seven hours of flying time, they touched down on familiar space at Davison Army Airfield, near Fort Belvoir, Virginia, and runway 25 just past sunset.

They taxied the RC-680 as instructed adjacent to a VH-60 helicopter waiting with her engines running. The ground crew towed the RC-680 into the classified hangar while Seth and Mike were still seated at the controls. The twenty-minute helicopter flight seemed too brief as the lights of Washington and northern Virginia faded out the right windows. The ridge of the Shenandoah's looked like a black void when contrasted with the lights of the small towns to the east and west of it. Seth recognized the mountain top helicopter-landing zone. A few small red lights illuminated antennae that were jutting into the night sky. The landing zone was void of buildings. The tall birch and locust trees were bare and lined a field that measures 300 feet by 200 feet. It was the perfect size for a flight of five helicopters to land in. In the days of the cold war and the months following the September 11th attacks, the military would rehearse evacuations of the civilian and military leadership of Washington D.C. They would land in the middle of the night on school yards and parking lots in the middle of Washington DC and pick up their loads of high ranking military and civilian leaders practicing an all out evacuation of the national and military command structure.

The VH-60 landed. Mike and Seth exited out the right door as the crew chief opened it. The helicopters navigation lights and beacons were turned off, as was the standard practice once the descent into the site was initiated. The star lights from the clear Virginia evening eerily reflected off of the crew chiefs helmet visor. Seth saw the parking lights of the vehicle in the tree line as the crew chief silently pointed toward it. Although the rotor blades continued to turn high above their heads, the two men jogged bent over to clear of the rotor's spinning disk as they made their way to the vehicle in the tree line. No sooner than they were clear of the rotors, they felt the blades increase in pitch and claw back into the air. Seth looked back and watched the shadowed craft climb into the sky and turn toward the east.

"Colonel Stephens, I'll take you down into the site now if you are ready Sir." The driver said as he took Mike and Seth's bags from them.

"We are ready whenever you are." Seth replied.

"Very good sir." The driver said opening the door.

The driver turned from the tree line south skirting it as they passed a hardened ventilation shaft and turned down the East Side of the mountain on a winding narrow road. The driver used only the dim parking light to move along the roads boundaries marked by reflectors. Within minutes, they were at the entrance of the complex that looked like a one-lane tunnel entrance. The van stopped at a guard's post on the north side of the entrance. The driver handed the guard a pass and the guard cleared the passage without a word. Seth was familiar with the complex. He had been here before during operations briefings for missions in South and Central America. It was Mike's first time.

"Wow boss, so far this operation has been not only under cover but, underground. My suntan is going to fade." Mike said as he glanced out the window as the van descended into the underground complex. They stopped after passing through two large heavy steel doors at an entrance near the underground motor pool.

"Here's the end of the line gentlemen. The specialist on the inside of the doors here will escort you to the briefing room." The driver said as he stood by the door he opened for them.

They were escorted to a briefing room that was surrounded with theater size screens on the walls and several rows of computer consoles. The room was already filled with military generals and well-dressed civilians. They were mingling around the room in small groups engaged in steep discussion. Seth saw General Woodsen as he was pouring over several charts laid out on a map easel at the front. An aide saw Seth and Mike enter the room and moved to let General Woodsen know. General Woodsen shook his head and turned to look in their direction. He recognized Seth immediately and moved in his direction. Seth met him as they covered half of the room.

"Seth, good to see you! How was the flight?" General Woodsen asked.

Seth replied. "The RC-680 makes the trip easy sir, Mike and I could fly a few surveillance missions now. The fatigue factor is negligible. It is going to be a definite force multiplier sir." Seth said as they shook hands.

"How has the automation been performing?" Woodsen asked referring to a hiccup that the Flight Management System had earlier.

"Perfectly sir, we programmed the entire flight. It flew and even taxied to the chocks at our fuel stop at St. Johns. It is a hand's off machine. Mike and I could have slept the entire way here." Seth said elaborating a little on the system.

"Mike, how have you been? I haven't seen you since we left Moffett." General Woodsen asked as he grabbed Mike's shoulder.

"Colonel Stephens doesn't let me out much sir. You know how he is, a real slave driver." Mike said as he looked over at Seth and smiled.

"Well I am glad that you are taking the lead on this mission. Our planners have been developing the situation and we figure that we will need four operators. We have added one man from the UK. Seth you can pick your fourth man." General Woodsen was saying as the briefer from the National Security Agency interrupted him.

"Gentlemen, if you would please move to your seats. The sergeant will verify clearances before we begin. Admiral McAdams will be here in approximately twenty minutes and we will begin as soon as he arrives. Thank you."

"Seth, you and Mike are next to me. Seth you are the third briefer after McAdams finishes. You may be surprised that NSA has as much information on this operation as they do. According to McAdams they have working this theory for several years now. Ever since Pan Am Flight 800. McAdams and the rest of us are concerned with your professional impression of the complex that you visited near Goslar." Woodsen said as they reached their seats.

They were seated at a briefing table made of thick mahogany in the operations room that was overlooked by a control and communications room. The smaller control room was partitioned from the control room by thick sound and ballistic protective glass. Seth sat on the end farthest from the room's entrance and was astonished at the meeting's attendees. All of the Nations top decision-makers were here. The President's National Security Advisor, Mr. John Elliot was seated next to The CIA Director and the White House Chief of Staff, Allison Davies. The hushed murmur of one-on-one discussion continued as the sergeant verified security clearances while the attendees waited. The door opened and in walked retired Admiral Joshua McAdams. Seth recognized the tall; slender built, man as the NSA Director. McAdams had a reputation as a tough and direct man that would exhaustively track down the facts relating to the problem. He was relentless and wouldn't stop when confronted by an adversary, nor did he stoop to placation. Seth and Mike were the only ones standing as the Director entered. Seth knew protocol and he was definitely a lower ranking officer than the Director was.

"Please, sit down Colonel Stephens, Major Thomas. We all have been waiting for your arrival. You've had a very exciting past few days. And the next few days will probably be even more exciting." Joshua McAdams was a man a very few words. Each word was carefully chosen to convey the point as efficiently as possible.

The Director took his cues from the briefing slides projected in front of them.

"Seth, you've come across something that we've suspected for a very long time. Your intercepts from the RC-680 system are intercepts from equipment that was made in the Third Reich in 1938. We have matched the signal's parameters and have unmistakably verified the authenticity of the signals and even the 1930 recording from Colonel Stephen's genius of an idea of using Marlene Dietrich as a challenge. Even the enigma coding was authentic and couldn't have been replicated by computer simulation. When we received and analyzed the reply to Colonel Stephens message we maintained a 99.9% confidence interval that the signals were from authentic equipment using authentic devices and recordings. My compliments to you Colonel Stephens for your logic."

Mike looked over at Seth with a snicker, shaking his head. The man was incredible, Mike thought.

McAdams continued. "Let me back explain further. What I'm about to say is of the highest classification. Everyone read-on to it has been rostered by the NSA. Some of the names go as far back as 1944."

McAdams showed a chart on the computer projection that listed everyone from 1944 to now that has been read on as a need to know. Seth found it interesting to see his name and President Truman's on the same chart. On the cover of the classification read-on chart was the project's name, Victory. The director was circulating the printed copy of a leather bound roster that contained the information covered by the chart. Seth opened the cover and scanned the names. The first few pages were beginning to yellow and he had to look twice, the first name, signature, and prints were those of the President of the United States in 1943, Harry S. Truman. The list of signature's and prints were those of nearly every person in high leadership of the nation since 1943. Those that were deceased were clearly marked as INACTIVE.

McAdams continued, "The United States began Project Victory in 1944 after a General, a member of Hitler's Intelligence Service, Field Marshal Robert Linder, gave a very convincing testimony that he was secretly fighting an underground war to defeat the Reich. His claim was that Hitler was a puppet for a man that was using Hitler to implement his plan for World War II. His preliminary testimony was so convincing and substantiated that President Truman called the then Director of the Army Security Agency, Edison Clearmann and directed that Project Victory be initiated. The project was to uncover the full story behind the man that supposedly started WWI and WWII. Field Marshall Linder was to testify before the investigation committee and show conclusive evidence of the man's identity.

On his way to the investigation committee's docket at Camp Meade, Maryland, Linder was killed in an accident when a train near Greenbelt, Maryland struck the car, in which he was riding. The car burst into flames and the heat was so intense that the bodies of Linder and the four Army officers closest to the project were completely emaciated. We later discovered that the accident was staged. The car was found chained to the track and the explosion that followed couldn't have been that powerful without the aid of some explosives. During the investigation, we discovered that several dozen agents working for a man from Egypt were suspected of being responsible for the accident. They fled the country before we could act on our findings."

Joshua McAdams went on. "After the tragedy, the investigation committee continued and tried to put together the story of Project Victory solely based on the testimony already received by Linder."

McAdams paused to gauge the acceptance of the members in attendance. Everyone sat open mouthed in disbelief at the factual substantiation given by the Director. After he judged that they were still with him, he proceeded to go into even greater detail. "Linder had stated that there were several other officers of the Reich that discovered that Hitler was being influenced by this man. These officers of the Reich worked toward the same objectives as the Allies and didn't support the Nazi war effort. They worked methodically to convince others that Hitler's objectives were neither in the interest nor in the welfare of the German people. He had already subjected them to extreme hardship without any clear purpose. There were several attempts on Hitler's life. There were the meetings in Hamburg and Berlin when the officer from Hitler's staff tries to sabotage the meeting and kill Hitler himself. Then there was the attempt at the Eagle's Nest in Betchesgaden, Hitler's retreat and the assassination attempt on the train from Frieburg to Stuttgart. We didn't know about the last few until Linder told us, but they were all substantiated by independent testimony gained at the Nuremberg Trials. In all cases, Hitler was uninjured and miraculously was missed by the would-be assassins. Linder gave us some sketchy and unsubstantiated facts about the movement to kill Hitler going underground after several of them were killed by horrible deaths, accidental electrocution, decapitations, and poisonings. They all feared for their lives and disappeared from the face of the earth and literally lived underground, until the allies had hopefully won the war. They waited until it was safe to re-emerge and tell the world all that they had learned about this incredible plot."

Seth was more than intrigued by this account since he had just left Karl Linder's complex near Goslar.

McAdams added more. "It wasn't a coincidence that NSA had responded so rapidly to the report forwarded by the Processing Facility.

Ironically, the analyst that had received the report was on the original technical analysis team in the 40's. The man is nearly 90 years old and does this as a hobby. He remembered most of the details from when he received the original report. He was so excited that he gave himself a tranquilizer to calm down before he could speak slow enough to tell the watch commander about the report." McAdam's description got a laugh from the attendees. The watch commander now had to be read on and we doubted him at first until he described Project Victory verbatim. The clincher here is that Field Marshal Linder told the date and times that the radio transmissions would be sent, only he meant it to be over some sixty years ago when we relied on their reports to track the Japanese naval movements. They would always be sent at 1944 hours, local time Germany. These intercepts match those times that Linder told us about 61 years ago to the second. I briefed Mr. Elliot, the President's National Security Advisor as soon as we put together our recommendation and the President has authorized us to reopen Project Victory and work expose the man that Robert Linder strongly believed to be behind nearly every horrific plot against humanity. Gentlemen, in my many discussions on this matter with the Joint Chief, we have decided that Colonel Seth Stephens will lead the four-man covert operation in the field. The Joint Chief has already issued a message giving Colonel Stephens full authority over the resources of the United States to gather information to bring this man's identity out in the open and locate him. Colonel Stephens has already contacted members of Linder's original group and has verified their capabilities. Gentlemen, while we have been treating the symptoms that have affected our world for the last 100 years, Linder's people have been working to identify the disease. Colonel Stephens, I'll turn the floor over to you."

McAdams moved to his seat as Seth stood and moved to the podium. He looked at the members in attendance and swore that they as he did, were holding their breaths.

"Gentlemen…" Seth began as he looked out over the members. "Not more than twelve hours ago, I left the brother of Field Marshal Robert Josef Linder. What he has accomplished is no less than incredible…"

Seth continued to recap the events that he had experienced and witnessed over the past two days. It took him 85 minutes to field every question offered by the attendees. After he had completed, every one in attendance overwhelmingly agreed with the recommendation of Admiral McAdams, General Woodsen and Mr. Elliott. They agreed to the fact that Colonel Stephens should proceed, using every resource held by the United States to identify the man that had negatively influenced and prevented the harmonious relationship between the world's governments and their people.

Seth knew that his life would never be the same after this day as he looked at Mike Thomas and General Maxwell Woodsen after the vote of approval was overwhelmingly accepted.

9
Karl Sends

Cabin John, Maryland, February 21, 1730 hours

Seth had spent the past five days gathering as much historical intelligence information on the idea that Karl had presented. He used just about every background resource available. Karl's direction had taken Seth to the Naval Surface Warfare installation located northwest of Washington, the location of the National Photographic Intelligence Center's secret satellite receiving facility. The intelligence collected by the Harz Mountain cell indicated that Hesbulah was stealing refined uranium from warheads dismantled under the SALT agreements and transporting them from Novosibirsk into China. Seth would use the near real time satellite imagery to refine the intelligence.

He sat at one of the consoles that had the satellite mosaics of the Althai Mountains assembled on the large monitor. Another had a live video imagery of the Shenandoahs just to the west. He was reviewing an INTSUM that Karl Linder had sent only a few hours ago. It was an old INTSUM from Karl's archives that his people had prepared in 1996 and it was indeed puzzling.

'Why did the Chinese and the Russians plan to get involved in the Former Republic of Yugoslavia (FRY) and Kosovo peacekeeping efforts?' He thought as he pulled up any archives from the database maintained by NSA. He read the old headlines, INTSUMs and Analysis Reports trying to determine the motive.

He was familiar with Russian and the Chinese operative's methods and their directives from their superiors. They simply did not get involved only for humanitarian reasons. Their countries were humanitarian wastelands with more human tragedies occurring in one day than would have occurred in an entire year of conflict in Yugoslavia. Their motivation was always centered on their ability to influence the world toward isolation and uncooperative attitudes. They wanted to be the bullies on the block and rule by brute force and terror.

The old report of a Chinese-Russian cooperative approach initiative toward peace and stability in the Balkans had to be a front for some other operation. They were using the headlines there to turn the world's attention from what they really had as an objective.

Neither the Russians nor the Chinese trusted each other. Their motivation for cooperation spawned strictly from fear. They were two large countries that had shared a common border for centuries. Yet they never openly cooperated with each other on the slightest endeavors. Their common border issues held much more importance than Kosovo. Seth was almost sure that the effort back in 1996 was a diversion. The logic of it was all wrung out. There were too many holes in it. All of the patches he could mentally apply wouldn't help it hold water. There was something deeper happening here and he would find out.

Karl's message about the Chinese-Russian involvement was significant. The site in Jersey had done all of the current situation tracking and analysis. Karl's site was more of the fusion and deep analysis center. Without the information collected by the Jersey site, his picture was incomplete. Seth would need to retrieve that data soon and let Karl and his people work on the reduction if they were to stop Hesbulah. One thing for certain, He knew that Hesbulah would try other avenues since his plans in Yugoslavia had lost momentum.

"Boss, these were all of the summaries prepared by the Sino-Russian Intelligence Fusion Cell," Mike said as he delivered the INTSUMs that Seth had requested. Seth paused and turned to the window overlooking the Potomac River Valley just south of Cabin John, Maryland as he read one INTSUM in particular.

INTSUM – March 3, 1996

Chinese workers have completed repairs to the rail lines between Quitai in northern China to the Althai Mountains pass. The new rail line from the village of Burquin through the Althai pass has been completed. Inaugural service will begin in six days.

Russian workers have completed repairs to the rail lines between Gorno-Altaysk and the Althai Mountains. The new rail line will connect in the Althai Mountains and be used to transport Siberian crude to the Sino market.

Russia will develop oil exploration east of the Urals to boost the already existing exports to China. China is looking for a more reliable source of energy and cash starved Russia is looking for a market for their Siberian crude. The big detractor was always cost of bringing the oil to market. There is even talk of a Sino-Siberian pipeline in the making, one that will follow this Trans Althai Railway.

"Mike, the Russian and the Chinese friendly? What did the Russians have that the Chinese didn't? I don't believe that they have completed a Trans-Althai railway for oil exports. That is absurd. The cost of that line development means that they'd have to keep the trains moving night and day for 30 years just to break even. The pipelines to the eastern coast of Russia could have handled the volume with minimal costs, load it on the tankers for the trip to the markets around Beijing. This doesn't make any sense, Mike. No, there is something else out there that the Chinese wanted. I'll even bet that if we moved the new imagery satellites into position we'd see a little more."

"Lets see, caviar, vodka, bad weather, mostly unattractive women with poor dental hygiene and a few thousand old nuclear warheads." Was Mike's humorous response.

"It's scary Mike, you and I are beginning to think alike." Seth quipped. "I think you hit the nail on the head."

"What? Do you think it is the unattractive women?" Mike said quizzically.

"Nuclear warheads." Seth said as he got up from his picturesque view of the sun setting over the Shenandoah's. "It is a straight line from here to there and deep in the interior. I think that the Russian's used the rail line to move old nuclear material to the Chinese. Let's see if we can get a look at where the rails go." Seth said.

"Why doesn't Karl just give us the answers Boss?" Mike asked as he poured over the reports. "Karl is smarter than that. He only gives us fact and no suspicions. His effort doesn't include speculation. If he isn't sure, he sends us the facts and we draw the conclusion of what information we still need." Seth explained.

Seth left his office with Mike in trail. They headed down the corridor and turned into the secure area where they stopped at a heavy steel door. Seth and Mike passed their ID cards through the magnetic code reader. The monitor adjacent to the door blinked on with Sam's, the security manager's, face profiled in the screen.

"Raymond, what's good for dinner this evening in the cafeteria? Seth said as he and Raymond Sam traded niceties. Raymond and Seth had worked on several covert Central American projects together.

Raymond was considered the best imagery analyst in the country. He could take a family photo taken in the back yard, developed at Wal-Mart and tell you what the people in it had for dinner. He was that good.

"Seth, you know I would never tell a secret, even the menu in this place is classified. Anyway, they don't know until 5 minutes before it opens. Come on in Seth, but leave that undesirable out there." Raymond joked referring to Mike.

"Why don't I get any respect?" Mike feigned a saddened response.

Seth and Mike passed through the first door, waited for the door to secure and the interior door to open. The temperature was noticeable cooler in the highly secured area. It was darkened and hummed with computers. Technicians studied the screens and typed commands into the systems. They walked around the control center, which was one of several in the DC area used to view information on the CIA secure INTRANET. The control room was created to monitor the world's hot spots after the SR-71 was retired. Technology had advanced to the point where manned platforms for strategic photo surveillance were no longer necessary. Geo-synchronous satellites carried microwave illuminators that would flood an area with microwave energy and absorb the returns, decode the energy absorption and give a picture that was digitally enhanced to re-create a picture compatible with the human eye. The energy's wavelength was small enough to pass through some building material and foliage. This allowed the technicians to see things conventional imagery couldn't. The latest technological development was the concept of infinite zoom. The grocery store tabloids would have loved to have the imagery of Bill and Monica taken by the satellites. Those were some of the most classified images held by NSA, those taken when Bill and Monica decided to have a secret meeting at the Springfield, Virginia Sheraton's top floor penthouse arranged by Betty one evening. The low angle, oblique imagery penetrated the thin draperies and made Bill's definition of *is* a little more meaningful. The Whitehouse said at the time that it wasn't Bill and Monica, but the facts spoke for themselves.

Seth liked to think that it just proved that no one was safe from the watchful eye of the CIA. If they wanted to know, they would. Nothing was done to less than a 99.9 percent confidence interval.

"Raymond," Seth said as he rounded the cell for Satellite Number 6, positioned over the Althai Mountains. "Can you give me a look at the Althai pass? I want to see a close up of some rail networks."

"Seth, there's about an 20 degree difference on that area and we are at the maximum area scan capability right now. Why don't you buy

Mike dinner somewhere nice? By the time you finish, the timing should be about right for the satellite move into a better position and have a better look." Raymond replied.

"Do you have any imagery from previous looks?" Seth queried.

"Yeah, but we haven't gone to that magnification in that area. It'll take less time to get fresh imagery, rather than query and enhance what we have on file anyway. Besides, I'd rather move these high flyers around a little so the bad guys don't get to comfy with our aspect angles." Raymond said as his hands moved over his keyboard typing in commands to reposition the satellite. "Why the interest on the Althai Pass region? That area hasn't been a fertile area for imagery, just a lot of scenery. There's tons of snow and ice around. The only thing man-made is that rail line that the Chinese built a few years ago. We normally only take a look once every 20 days when we follow the preplanned satellite flight profile." Raymond added to his answer.

"Ray, we may have discovered a nuclear smuggling route if my suspicions are correct." Seth said looking over Raymond's shoulder. I can tell that we are being a little overbearing here. We'll get off your back for a little while. We'll see you after dinner." Seth said as he and Mike left for a break. Seth knew that there was nothing worst than someone breathing down your neck with anxiety as you were doing your job. He and Mike quietly left for dinner.

Seth and Mike left the Cabin John facility and decided on having dinner at the Fort McNair Officer's Club. Seth could use the drive. It was always a way for him to focus on problems more intently and besides, it was just great fun driving down the George Washington parkway towards Roslyn. The road snaked along the valley carved by the Potomac River. The trees had a frosty luminance to them and the evening air was crisp and cold. The long since setting sun cast a grayish tint to the now darkened landscape and the illusion created by the shadows on the south turns made the perception of speed greater and almost dizzying.

By the time they had reached the Memorial Bridge the evening was complete. The sun disappeared behind the mountains. The city came alive with the lights of the monuments and the government office buildings. The traffic through the city was light by this time of night. The majority of the weekday commuters now were out of the city. He and Mike practically had the streets that passed the beautiful buildings to themselves as they pulled off the street onto Fort McNair's drive. Seth turned into the gates at Fort McNair and slowed as he approached the guard. Out of habit he reached up and switched the car's headlights off. The single light suspended overhead from the guardhouse illuminated the soldier, a member of the Army's elite Old Guard. The soldier snapped to attention and motioned Seth through, offering a most precise and perfectly executed hand salute. Seth returned the salute and followed the street of Fort McNair to the right around the parade field.

"Wasn't this the parade field where the conspirator's of Lincoln's assassination were executed?" Mike asked while craning his neck to see the center of the field past Seth.

"Hard to imagine isn't it, that our country was involved in such a conflict that it almost divided itself before it was even one hundred years old." Seth offered his thoughts.

"We face issues every day now that could easily have an effect nearly as catastrophic." Seth added.

"Why do so many people now think that the Constitution guarantees that someone should make your dreams a reality, whether it is the government or a corporation? Have you ever heard of so many ridiculous law suits?" Mike questioned.

"No, and if people don't stop and realize that all America offers is a place where you can dream and work hard to make dreams come true, we will be in the midst of another civil war. The constitution only guarantees an environment of freedom. It doesn't guarantee that some one will give you the opportunity. That has to come from each of us." Seth said as they pulled into the parking area crossed the street from The Officers Club.

"Speaking of opportunity, I hope that there is the opportunity to have a huge steak here tonight or that civil war may begin sooner than you think." Mike stated in a matter of fact expression.

Seth and Mike walked crossed he street from the colonial styled brick building that housed the Officer's Club at Fort McNair. Fort McNair was a perfect location inside the beltway and the military officers that temporarily resided there while they were assigned to any number of locations in the Capital were very fortunate. It was once rumored that a developer had offered the Pentagon a billion dollars for the location. It would have easily returned twice that when developed. The pentagon firmly replied that the property was not for sale for any price. The property was located at the point where the Anacostia and Potomac Rivers met just to the south of the Government Center of Washington, D.C. Seth felt fortunate that he could enjoy the exquisite surroundings for dinner.

Just as Seth opened the door to the Officer's Club he looked up to follow the noise of a fast approaching jet preparing to land at Washington's Ronald Reagan Airport. He stared at it for a long while trying to see the tail number or markings. The dark night and speed of the jet made it nearly impossible. Still, it was odd to see a private jet on a final approach path arriving over Fort McNair after they had selectively reopened the airport for private or charter aircraft some months after 9/11.

The airspace was very close to P-56, a prohibited area around the White House and Capitol area. Someone unfamiliar with the arrival procedures probably piloted the jet. Although the thought momentarily disturbed him, the secret service and the Air Defense Batteries had him locked up miles away. Any moves off course and he would have been a ball of fire over the Potomac.

His attention quickly turned to the menu, as he smelled the freshly baked bread and apple pie, just some of the wonderfully prepared cuisine inside the Officer's Club.

They had just approached their seats when they noticed the Joint Chief of Staff and his wife, General and Mrs. Max Woodsen seated near the fireplace. Seth had always liked Woodsen and his methods. It was a very agreeable senior to subordinate relationship. They were so much alike. Both Seth and Woodsen had reputations of being firm but fair officers as they developed during their Army careers. They were both fast trackers that didn't follow dogma. They lived by their own mantras. Both were forward thinking Army Aviators tired of the Army preparing to fight past wars over and over again. He liked to learn from history, not relive it.

Woodsen was credited for moving the Army out of the role of security force for the Air Force and modernizing it to stay ahead of the major threats out in the modern world. The old organization of the Army left it too heavy and reliant on the Navy and Air Force to get it to the battlefield. He was famous in the halls of the Pentagon for his speech to the congress during the 1998 Department of Defense Bottom Up review. He told the congressional committee that he could save a lot of money by disbanding the Army.

"Hell," he said, "I can't get my force to the war in less than 30 days and then it is at the whim of the Air Force planes or Navy boats. The war will be over by then. If you want an effective Army, I need air power with the capability to self deploy anywhere, at anytime. I need to take the Army to the next level of mobility. I don't need more tracked personnel carrier and tanks. Don't waste your time on that part of the budget, just fold us up and split up our share with the other salivating dogs." Woodsen said.

A democratic Representative from Georgia could stand his comments no longer, "Well General, you're spending a lot of our time telling us what's wrong. Until you can tell us what we should do about it, don't waste our time. We need solutions not an amplification of the problem." The speaker paused giving Woodsen a dramatic smirk that he practiced hundreds of times in front of his office mirror. He waited just long enough for the press to capture the image of a seemingly stumped General before he proceeded. "Well, General...do you have any ideas to fix this problem?" The Representative from Georgia finished, smirking like he had the final word.

He couldn't have been more wrong. Maxwell Woodsen would not be outdone by some pudgy, never served his country, slick talking, backwoods, buy a vote, elected official. General Woodsen was waiting for the opportunity; he had captured the audience and had played them like a sharp intelligence officer would play an old second string Soviet battalion commander.

"Distinguished Ladies and Gentlemen, Thank you for asking. As a matter for the record, I do have a strategic outline." Woodsen said with the enthusiasm of an eager lieutenant. The doors of the congressional meeting room burst open and in walked a squad of officers carrying small hand held computers. They immediately linked them to the audio-visual system as General Woodsen stood up and prepared to present the plan that he had been developing for the past year. He had involved the brightest minds of the military's Acquisition Corps and Industry. He had done his homework well and was now presenting it to the congress at the most strategically precise moment.

"The Army's force structure needs mobility..." In the two hours that followed this statement, General Woodsen outlined the modernization plan for the Self-Deployable Army. It centered on the small, two-man, turbine powered HAWK. Combining the mobility of an F-16, firepower and survivability of an M-1 Abrams tank and automation that was inexpensive and state of the art. It could act independently or be massed to provide concentrated firepower. It could hover, stop and hold terrain, or self deploy at near supersonic speeds. Its automation allowed it to be manned or unmanned, depending on the scenario. The Democrat from Georgia acquiesced and stood to start a standing ovation when General Maxwell Woodsen finished. It was the only time that anyone could remember having congress give a standing ovation to a military officer. General Woodsen not only for upstaged him, but also saved billions of dollars on the defense budget with his intelligence and insight. General Woodsen received full funding for his initial test battalion and had four more battalions fielded within two years. His plan for Army 2020, had more destructive power at it hands in one battalion of Hawks than it had in two Brigades of M-1 Abrams tanks and AH-64s.

Seth was part of General Woodsen's briefing team that day. He was assigned as a test pilot at Moffett Naval Air station when he was asked to brief General Woodsen on the Army's newest aerial intelligence gathering platform at Fort Huachuca, Arizona. General Woodsen liked his presentation and asked him to stop in his office. He laid out his plan to Seth and told him that he was looking to develop a skunk works of a few officers to develop the United States Army of the future, Army 2020. Seth finally saw the opportunity to move the Army out of the muddy boot era, as he had termed it and begin real war fighting. One year and too much effort to describe, General Woodsen, along with Seth and the other members of the skunk works, completed the design of their vision. They were ready to build and needed funding. It was during that briefing to congress where General Woodsen received full congressional funding approval and they began to build the Hawk. General Woodsen offered Seth the first battalion. Seth declined. He was an officer that worked better behind the scenes and independently. Fame and the spotlight that came with it weren't motivation for Seth.

General Woodsen developed an even greater respect for Seth because of his honesty and values. Mrs. Woodsen once told Seth, "the General likes you because you are the man he wanted to be when he was younger." They had been good friends ever since. Seth was always eager to share a table with the General and his wife. Many assumed that the relationship was because of Elizabeth, the Woodsen's daughter. It didn't have anything to do with Elizabeth. Both relationships each stood on their own merits.

"Seth, come on over here and join Mrs. Woodsen and I. Let me buy you dinner." General Woodsen said. Seth walked over to the General's table. Mrs. Woodsen asked the waiter to set out two more places for Seth and the Mike who was with him.

"General Woodsen, what a surprise sir. Ma'am, do you remember Major Mike Thomas?" Seth said to Mrs. Woodsen. Mike was immediately flustered and was on his best behavior.

Mike managed to stammer out, "General Woodsen, Mrs. Woodsen, it is wonderful to see you again."

"Please, sit down, sit down," General Woodsen said and turned to give instructions the waiter,

"Herman, bring another bottle of the Rombauer Chardonnay. I trust that will meet your approval," the General said to Seth and Mike.

"So tell me Seth, have you had a chance to call Elizabeth yet, she would love to see you."

"Maxwell, you are putting Seth on the spot." Mrs. Woodsen said smiling sternly.

"Hell, Barbara, Elizabeth keeps wasting her time on these Washington Beltway losers." General Woodsen said laughing as he winked at Mike and Seth.

"Maxwell Woodsen, you will be dining by yourself in the bar if you don't contain yourself." Mrs. Woodsen said losing some of the implied humor.

"You're right, I do apologize, and I shouldn't be so matter of fact." Woodsen said to no one in particular, crossing his heart as a sincere gesture with a grin on his face.

"Sir, I for one, certainly appreciate your frankness." Seth interjected as he looked over at Mike for a response. Mike responded by slugging back a full glass of the Chardonnay in one swallow.

Mrs. Woodsen knew it was time for a rescue operation. The General had stuck his foot in his mouth a little too far this time.

"Well Seth, I'm sure you and Mike are starving. Why don't we order dinner?" After years of experience, Mrs. Woodsen knew exactly when her husband was mentally going back to work. She valued their time together and tried to keep General Woodsen's life balanced even if he was too abrupt at times. Work could be all consuming for him, so she kept the edge off of his life after he was home with her.

The four enjoyed a few more laughs before the waiter, attired in crisp server's whites, appeared at the right time to take their dinner orders. He recommended the Chicken Provencal, which was the house specialty that evening. All four seemed to unanimously arrive at the same fare. Dinner was an enjoyable event for them. Seth couldn't help but think about Elizabeth as they dined. Mrs. Woodsen was much subtler about Elizabeth than the General. She must have mentioned a dozen times that Elizabeth was 37 and still single. They talked about the latest Washington events, and managed to keep their distance about the political events, religion and sports. The Chicken Provencal was the best they had eaten on this side of the Atlantic and the Rombauer Chardonnay was a perfect compliment to their dinner.

For desert they all decided to keep the trend going and ordered the Bread Pudding with rum sauce. It was a much-needed break in the very tense and tedious events of previous days and offered a welcome respite.

They were just about to adjourn to the lounge when Seth's handset signaled an incoming call.

"Seth, this is Raymond. We have the satellites in position to look at the Althai Pass. You may want to see this live." Raymond said.

"Roger, Mike and I will be there in a few minutes. Seth concluded the conversation, let out a big sigh followed by a hearty smile.

"General Woodsen, Ma'am, we must excuse ourselves, some information has just arrived." Seth said as he apologized to General and Mrs. Woodsen.

"I certainly understand Seth, I hope that we can see you again before you leave Washington, perhaps you can come over for dinner.

The general is right, Elizabeth would love to see you." Mrs. Woodsen finally admitted.

"You have my promise Mrs. Woodsen. General, I look forward to seeing you again." Seth said with sincerity.

"You are always welcome. I enjoyed dining with you and Mike this evening. Mike, make sure you watch each others six." General Woodsen said as he stood and shook hands with each of the men.

Seth gave polite instructions to the waiter as he and Mike turned towards the door. "Waiter, please bill my account for the dinner this evening and don't let the general convince you otherwise."

The General and Mrs. Woodsen watched as the two headed for the door.

"He is a wonderful person, Max, you wouldn't mind having him as a son-in-law would you?" Mrs. Woodsen commented.

"Barbara, I'd give my right arm for that." The General paused in thought. "Seth has other things he has to take of right now. He has the weight of the world on his shoulders. And you know what? He is probably the only man alive that could succeed with that mission."

General Woodsen watched as the door closed behind them and he and Barbara proceeded to finish their bottle of wine before the General went back to the Pentagon to finish up his after dinner reading.

Mike and Seth walked silently out into the cold night air that seemed even more chilling since they had just left the warmth of the Officer's Club and good company.

Seth spoke first. "Mike I just had a thought, give NSA a call and try to get with the experts in the Chinese cell. I need a list of every item China has imported from Russia in the past decade. Also get a list of China's oil production capability and their demand. Find out if there is a reasonable need for oil imported from Russia. Also find out about any orders for durable goods that they have placed in the last 5 years. Try to look for a pattern and try to find out where the deviations begin. Then get some sleep; tomorrow's going to be a very hectic day. I'll meet you here, tomorrow for breakfast at 0630 hours." Seth said as he was climbing into the car as Mike called the duty driver for a ride to NSA.

"Hey boss, I try to stay a step ahead of you. I am still a little lost right now." Mike said with a pained look on his face. "I did however, coordinate with Army Operations and our transport has been replaced. I think that you'll be impressed. Any word on who our third man is yet?" Mike said as he turned back to talk with Seth through the open window of his car.

"He should join us tomorrow, I'd tell you but I'd rather wait until I'm sure." Seth said as he waved to Mike and turned out of the parking lot and headed for the main gate and return to the Naval Surface Warfare Lab near Cabin John.

He would cover the distance back to Cabin John in 20 minutes or less with this pace. The traffic was almost non-existent now and he could open up on the Parkway. He only passed two vehicles on the way back; one was a US Custom's suburban and the other a dark ford sedan. He laughed at the diplomatic license plate on the sedan; there were more diplomatic plates here than anything else. He slowed down just in front of the two vehicles; his natural suspicious nature told him there was cause for concern. He watched the two vehicles in the rear mirror. There was something just not right about this although everything appeared like it was in order.

The two vehicles turned off onto the road that led to several government buildings south near the Clara Barton Parkway. They were probably heading to the CIA annex near Carderock, he thought. He dismissed and attributed his thought to an overly suspicious nature.

Within minutes he had parked at the secure lab where Raymond Sam had the images ready and was past the secured areas, making his way into the monitor room.

"Raymond, what do we have?" Seth said approaching Raymond from behind as his eyes were riveted to the monitor.

"Seth, we've have Chinese military engineers and soldiers, still working to maintain those rail links on the Russian side of the Althai Pass." Raymond said with an astute matter of factness.

"The other thing is that they have gone through an awful lot to make them not look like Chinese military, they also know when are satellites are passing overhead. All work stops and they go underground. They still think that we rely on the old imagery satellites. They don't know yet about the low observance angle satellites that we have co-located with the geo-stationary Global Positioning System satellites. Seth, look at this one thing in particular. Look at how these rails pass through what appears to be snow sheds. It is one thing to keep the snow off of the tracks, but it also looks like they can store a hell of a lot of trains in those sheds." Raymond said.

"Or they could be using them for warehouses or work areas. Raymond, you do good work. What'll it take for me to even things up? You saved me a lot of leg work here." Seth said as he reached out and pointed to the details of the image on the screen.

"Nothing' Seth, you just keep up the good public relations so that congress keeps our funding intact. It seems like every freshman representative wants to cut the deficit during his first term. Hell after we beat back the terrorists in 2002, you'd think that they believe the threat is all gone. They always look at the CIA and NSA as number one budget targets. Lawyers and finance geeks, they'll be the ruination of civilization." Raymond said.

"Raymond, they're just trying to do their jobs and get re-elected. They can't help it if they think that everyone in the world lives like we do here in the states. We are like the watchdogs, if the thugs of the world know we're around, more of them will consider an honest job. It is less painful."

Raymond began toggling the receiver through the automated search list of Priority Intelligence Requests or PIRs as he called them. It was a completely automated system. The intelligence requests came in from every field station, CIA operative, Analyst and military organization. The Deputy Director of the CIA also doubled as the Director of the NSA, the CIA's military side. He decided on the areas that were hot spots and assigned priorities to the requests. The satellite system would then produce the imagery to satisfy the Intelligence Requirement. Raymond was scanning the systems parameters when he noticed that several of the Error Ellipses were close to tolerance. Seth watched Raymond expertly enter a few keystrokes to bring the system into alignment.

"Raymond, really how long did it take you to become one with the machine here? Seth asked with a bit of implied satire.

"Oh after a few nice dinners together, a bottle of Mosel Valley wine, and some flowers…no time at all actually." Was Raymond's equally satirical reply. "Now we can check the alignment by commanding Satellite Number 34 to look right at us. Smile Seth, you may be on the CIA's camera."

Seth watched the large monitor over Raymond's shoulder begin to focus. He recognized the long cylindrical shape of the Naval Lab become recognizable. "What amazing clarity." Seth commented.

"You haven't seen anything, let's see if we have any "parkers" over on the service road. We can get up close and very detailed." Raymond quipped.

"Raymond, I'm surprised at you, they drive all the way out here to find a little privacy and here you are pointing your camera at them." Said Seth. Raymond increased the magnification. Seth and he both saw the black sedan on the service road.

"Seth, here's the amazing part. Watch the clarity with full microwave illumination." Raymond said as he typed in a command. Raymond's eyes froze on the screen. Seth was just as astonished. The image on the screen was straight from a Hollywood movie, only this was real and they saw it as it was happening. The side window of the sedan shattered. The car's safety glass offered little resistance as the high velocity projectile transferred too much energy too quickly for it to remain intact. On the inside, they watched a woman's head fly apart as if it had exploded from the inside, outward.

"Holy Christ! Seth, did you see that?" Ray said in disbelief.

"Raymond, go to a wider area view…right there, magnify." Seth urgently spoke.

Raymond now stunned, responded only due to Seth's urging and zoomed in on the two vehicles that were positioned to the north of the other sedan. Seth could hardly believe. Right there were the two vehicles that he had passed on the parkway when he was returning to the Lab.

"Raymond, how do we contact your security officers?" Seth asked with an urgent tone and tempo in his voice. Raymond handed Seth a small transmitter that was placed next to the terminal.

"Security, this is base, over." Seth transmitted over the secure radio. He repeated, "Security, this is base, over." Nothing was heard.

"Raymond, give me a wider view of the area." Seth commanded. Seth saw the images of the darkly clad men on the monitor as they ran from the valley. They were headed toward the Custom's Suburban and the dark sedan that he had seen earlier on the parkway. Seth could plainly see the diplomatic license plate that he had seen earlier that night.

"I should trust that little voice inside me." Seth said thinking about earlier that evening when he had seen the same two vehicles on the parkway. Seth tried another call to the security force and realized that no one would answer. He also knew that if the security team for the Lab was down that there wouldn't be any stopping these guys without a blood bath. There wasn't a police force anywhere that would be able to match their firepower.

"Raymond, keep an eye on those vehicles and keep me posted on the security radio." Seth dashed out of the room heading for the security checkpoints. He passed the front entrance the security station. It was unmanned just as it usually was after the shifts had changed. The security officers would have periodic check around the building. As Seth moved around in the darkness outside of the building, he confirmed the worst scenario. He had found a guard face down; he plainly saw the large entrance hole of the bullet. The bullet taking off everything of the guard's head from the ears forward marked the exit. He didn't have to confirm anything else. He knew that all the guards were probably in the same condition.

"Seth, the vehicles are leaving, they are heading southeast." Raymond said over the radio.

"Roger, Security is non-existent. Keep following the vehicles. I'm on my way back in." Raymond could tell that Seth was a few thoughts ahead of what to do by his tone over the radio. Seth burst into the room.

"Raymond, those fellows dressed in black didn't come here just to kill the security guards. You can bet that they were here for something else. I suggest we plan on evacuating the site. We need to do it a few people at a time. I don't want to tip an observer off. Can you transfer control of the satellites to another location?" Queried Seth.

"We'll try boss, we barely had the funding to put this operation together. It'll take some time to orchestrate that. Why, what's going on here?" Raymond answered as his hands wrung nervously as if he were trying to forecast their fate.

"I'm not exactly sure but, it probably isn't a bad idea to begin transferring the controls to another location." Seth said as he left the control room. He was headed back outside to do a quick recon while the building was being evacuated.

It took a few minutes for his eyes to adjust to the low ambient light of the Maryland woods. The sound of the Potomac sounded louder than ever. He forced his senses into there most acute state. He wasn't sure what he was looking for but anything out of the ordinary would provide a clue. He was suspecting sabotage and was counting on the fact that this well rehearsed attack would follow the typical terrorist pattern. The terrorists had evolved rapidly since 9-11. No longer did they fly jets into buildings. The learned that working smarter paid bigger dividends and reaped better rewards.

That 70-virgins thing couldn't motivate them forever. Whatever they had planned wouldn't happen until they had left the area or the country. Seth rounded the first corner of the long cylindrically shaped laboratory and saw something reflecting off of what little moon light that was ahead of him. The ground was disturbed adjacent to the building and the upturned sheaves of mica, a mineral that had the same reflective qualities as thin sheets of glass, which was fairly common in the ground near the river, was acting as a mirror. Seth examined the area closer, being careful not to disturb it. He pulled out his sheathed ceramic knife that he carried in his boot and began to probe the disturb ground. He held the knife flat in his open palm so that if it had contacted something it would simply slide upward and not disturb any device that may be buried there.

Seth was thinking that he had wished this were Hollywood's version where he'd simply locate the explosive device and disarm it or move it. He could save the day instantly and be a hero just like in the movies.

Seth knew otherwise. Most modern sophisticated explosive devices are tamperproof. Inside the case are electronic microchips that are built in to the devices. They vibrate at millions of cycles per second and will detect the slightest movement. Any detected motion will detonate the explosive. All of the casings are sealed and once the timer or detonation device is activated, you can't remove a panel to see the inner working to even attempt disarming it. The only option is to try and limit the damage the device does when it detonates. The only way to prevent a saboteur's intent is not to allow them to position the device. Seth knew that he was more than a little late on preventing that.

"Raymond, I have found some evidence that suggests that we weren't alone here tonight. Someone left us a few surprises. Tell me, is everyone almost out?" Seth said with hardly a hint of anxiety in his voice.

"Just the four supervisors remain inside Seth. We feigned a computer shutdown and told everyone to go home for breakfast this morning." Raymond reported. He was proud of his inventiveness but was still trying to hold back his feelings of hysteria.

"Meet me outside in the parking area now! Seth commanded. He knew that the building would be a total loss and was now just worried about how he could save lives.

As he made his way back to the parking area, Seth contacted Mike on his handset.

"Mike, how's the hunting going?" Seth asked in a false enthusiastic tone. That was Mike's first clue that something was wrong. Seth, almost always, was more direct and to the point.

"Great, I wish that you were here with me. How's your excursion going?" Mike asked.

"Not as well as expected. We had uninvited guests, I'll be returning early. Meet me as soon as you can." Seth said with complete calm.

"Roger, I'll be there in 30 minutes." Mike replied.

Seth made one more call on his cell phone. "This is Colonel Seth Stephen's at the Naval Laboratory, I'd like to call an emergency. Can you arrange for an officer to meet me at the Cabin John exit?"

Seth rounded the corner of the building and could see Raymond and the others waiting near his car.

"Raymond, is everyone clear of this building and the area?" Seth asked in a rapid fire speaking voice.

"Roger Seth, everyone is clear." Raymond responded.

"Raymond, you're going to lose your building. There are a string of explosives planted around the perimeter. I think we have less than 60 minutes, but I can't be sure. Those people that we had seen on the imagery were setting the explosives. My guess is that they would give themselves enough time to leave the area so they couldn't be linked. Raymond is there anyway that you can keep this capability going even with this building destroyed?" Seth asked.

"Seth, fortunately we had a little notice. All we did was switch the routing from this building to the old NSA downlink facility near the mountain by Paris, Virginia. We have the connectivity and all we need is the equipment. I think that we can be up and running within 24 hours, if we can get the equipment."

"I'll contact Joshua McAdams and make sure that you and your team have everything available to you to get set up. We had better clear the area now. Raymond thanks for your help." Seth said.

Raymond handed a disk over to Seth. "Here's the imagery that we talked about near the Althai region and the people that were visiting us this evening. You may need it." Seth and Raymond shook hands and parted company.

Seth waited until Raymond and the others left the parking area before he followed them to the Cabin John exit to meet with the Defense Department Uniformed Police officer.

As he rounded the turn he saw the unmarked sedan bristling with antennae. He pulled along side and identified himself to the officer inside.

"We have about thirty minutes to evacuate everyone within a mile radius from the Naval Surface Lab." Seth continued to briefly describe the event of the evening and left the evacuation in the capable hands of the officer. One call to the National Command Center verified Seth's credentials and the law enforcement officers quickly put everything in motion. There would be one hell of a fireworks show here in about 30 minutes Seth thought as he accelerated onto 495's Cabin John Bridge.

The folks that lived in near River Oaks would be rudely awakened, one-way or another.

10

The Assassins Arrive

Washington, D.C., February 21, 1836 hours

Marek Elamesh was certain that the American involvement would end here. Hesbulah's loyalists before had bombed the Americans. The World Trade Center in the early 90s, Oklahoma City was history, the World Trade Center and Pentagon destruction in September 2001 had already shattered the innocence that the Americans presumed. His task now was to destroy the satellite downlink facility that threatened Hesbulah's operations in China and Bhutan. Nothing could stop them now. First the idiot Sinovic, then Bin Laden and Hussein, Hesbulah would not tolerate much more. He had to find out who was inside his working inside his fabricated Al Qaeda network and find out fast. After he destroyed the American's facility, he would go to Paris to find out about the intelligence coming out of Germany. But not before he personally delivered this message on behalf of Hesbulah. Hesbulah had planned this finale for many years, first attempting it in World War II just after his Nazi scientists perfected atomic weapons. How the Allies had discovered it was now becoming clear. It would stop. Hesbulah would use the same plan and not be confounded. Everything was better now. The years that past allowed the technology to mature to allow the full effect of the attacks. He wanted to instill the fear of Hesbulah in their hearts. The Americans, he thought, were still so foolish, they think that they can retreat to the safety of their isolated country. He would deliver the message for Hesbulah. They would again prove that no place and no one are safe from their vengence or attacks.

The flight from Egypt had taken about 13 hours. Elamesh hated the long flights from the east to America. He hated the customs and immigration officials prodding and searching the airplane, while he was detained. The customs inspections were a laugh. Of course he had weapons. What did they expect him to say? 'Yes I have weapons and explosive on board and I am carrying illegal items.' He was a criminal. He killed people. What did the customs officials expect, for him to tell the truth because they were US Customs? He laughed at the thought. Stupid little people, while they continue to go through the motions and do their politically correct duties and not profile people that fit his image, he smuggled arms and money in and out of America routinely. He laughed out loud at his thoughts. His men looked at him surprised and began to smile. Obviously if the boss is smiling we should too, they each thought.

The Falcon jet had refueled once in Reykjavik, Iceland, then Toronto, Canada after it had departed Rome, Italy. The enroute stops would cloud the origin of the flight. It took the edge off of the customs inspectors. They seemed to let their guard down just a little when the crew claimed that the flight had departed Iceland or Canada enroute to the US. If they were to claim that they had departed Cairo, customs would be more suspicious.

Elamesh looked down at the Potomac River while the aircraft was on final approach for the runway to the south. The pilots had to maneuver over the Anacostia River as they approached from the east. Elamesh looked at the brightly lit city. What fools he thought. They have even given me diplomatic clearance to land at Washington National. What fools!

Lights were everywhere. It was as if the sun never set. He could look down and see the upraised hands of the sculpture on the lawn at East Potomac Park and Haines Point. He could see the White House and the capital building along with the mall and all of the monuments that were precisely positioned according to the plan originally drawn by the Frenchman, L'Enfant. He noticed the military installation that they were passing over. They were so low that he could see the two men walking toward a building and one in particular, illuminated by the street lamp, look up as if he could see the occupants inside of the airplane. Elamesh felt uncomfortable as this man stared at the arriving airplane. He somehow felt compromised. He felt that someone knew he was here. Elamesh quickly dismissed the thought. "I must be becoming paranoid." He mumbled to himself as the two men disappeared from view beneath the wing of the Falcon. A light sweat formed on his brow, he would be a little more suspicious during the customs inspection. Maybe someone had tipped off his arrival. Maybe they were waiting for him down there.

115

The jet's tires squealed in protest to the pilot's heavy-handed landing. His braking was equally rough as they rolled out on runway 18. They taxied to the customs ramp in darkness and saw the Chevrolet Suburban with US Customs marking waiting for them. Elamesh's thugs were ready for action.

Marek contacted Hesbulah by satellite phone. "Hesbulah, this Marek Elamesh. We are in position and prepared. On your command."

Hesbulah answered. "Marek, we can't afford to fail this mission now. The Americans are using their satellites to collect information. If they see any link between the rail lines and Urumqi, we may be delayed yet once again. It is ironic though isn't it, to think that the Chinese would use technology given by the Americans to deter a first strike. Still, Marek make sure that this capability no longer exists." Hesbulah said with a deep and commanding, nearly inhuman voice.

Elamesh had no sooner than secured the phone, when the Falcon's cabin door was opened. The first customs official entered. He was a man with a marine style haircut and shoulders as broad as the cabin door. "Welcome to Washington, D.C. gentlemen, we shouldn't detain you very long. I see that all of your arrival documents are in order. Have you anything to declare?"

Everyone on board the aircraft smiled and shook their heads side to side in a negative gesture. Some looked at the agent others averted his look.

"We will just look around if you don't mind." The agent stated as he moved to the aft of the cabin looking for the aft baggage entrance.

"Allow me to help you." Offered the first officer as he led him to the rear of the aircraft towards the baggage area. Elamesh noticed that there were only two inspectors. The clothing that Elamesh and his thugs were wearing under their suits was a perfect match to what the customs officers were wearing. He observed that the light coats with the customs emblems embroidered on the back and hats would fit them perfectly.

Elamesh's thugs wasted no time positioning after the customs inspector had gone to the rear of the aircraft. Elamesh kept a trained eye on the other agent standing by the front of the Suburban. Elamesh's men acted quickly. The floor panels of the aircraft were removed and the weapons and explosives were removed and the panels replaced. The first officer had finished the inspection and was signing off on the inspection form as the Customs agent radioed to the desk agent that everything was in order with the arrival. "178 cleared on the ramp." The Inspector announced to the desk officer.

As the customs official turned to make his way from the baggage compartment, Elamesh signaled to the first officer. The timing was perfect. Two of the men grabbed the agent's arms and secured the radio to prevent it from being dropped or transmitted. The first officer slid the wire garrote around the agents neck tightened the loop. It immediately restricted the air and blood supply to the agent's body. It caught the agent completely off his guard. The agent thrashed wildly for about 10 seconds until Elamesh's men wrestled him to the ground.

Elamesh called for the second agent. "Can you please come aboard, there is a problem!" Elamesh asked the other agent standing by the front of the vehicle parked next to the aircraft. The agent came immediately and as soon as he placed his back to the cockpit door two more of Elamesh's men quickly subdued and strangled him. Elamesh looked at the two bodies and smugly smiled at how unprepared the customs officials were to die. It was too easy.

"Quickly, we must proceed to the desk agent or he will suspect something." Said one of the thugs in a loud whisper. "Do not hasten and be stupid, the Americans will suspect nothing. They are on their own soil and he is probably watching one of the many stupid American television shows. Be thorough and hide these bodies so they won't be found until we have departed." Said another of the thugs who appeared to be more seasoned.

Elamesh's thugs acted quickly with rehearsed precision. Two of Elamesh's men posed as the two customs officials and moved out of the aircraft and waved back to the aircraft as they got into the Suburban. Elamesh watched them drive toward the customs officer's headquarters before he called for his sedan, courtesy of an Embassy staff member. The sedan arrived and backed into position near the Falcon's baggage compartment. Elamesh's thugs loaded the two bodies into the back of the sedan.

The two customs imposters made their way to the desk agent and came in the side entrance of the customs building. "Jerry, we need to contact McFrettle over at Dulles before we change shifts. He has just received email about a Falcon that departed Cairo this morning. Said we may want to really look it over." Said Ted Gerald; a 23-year veteran customs agent that was more interested in retirement than working. Jerry's imposter was leaning over the fountain getting a drink, seemingly oblivious to the desk agent's voice. "Jerry...hey Jerry, Jesus Christ Jerry are you gonna drink the place dry or what?"

Jerry's imposter looked up and Ted couldn't have had a more confused look on his face. "Sorry, bud...I thought that you were Jerry, Hey who the hell are you?" Ted said as he pulled his hands to his hips as a show of authority.

As Jerry's imposter turned and unbridled the machine pistol from under his coat. Ted took one hand off of his hip and held it up in a typical stop motion toward the imposter as he reached for his 9mm.

"I'm just the messenger bud...here to shoot you!" The imposter's finger squeezed the machine pistol's trigger and fired a burst of 15 rounds through the silenced weapon. The only noise was the breath being knocked from Ted's body, the dull slap of the rounds impacting his chest and the metal to metal knock as the bolt from the weapon slammed another round into the chamber on its automatic ride. The noise stopped as suddenly as it began. They calmly turned out the lights, just as the clock's hand went vertical. The only thing that appeared out of order was the wafting cordite smoke and it was quickly being removed by the buildings ventilation system.

8:00 PM time to close the customs office until 10:00 AM the next morning. After 8:00 PM, customs was on call and had to be requested. There were no requests made tonight. The timing was perfect. They had 14 hours to complete their task and be out of the country before the next shift of inspectors would arrive on duty. They were on schedule and would only need ten hours to let their terror reign.

"Plan to depart on my command." Elamesh commanded to the flight crew. "Let's go." He muttered, as he entered the sedan and headed toward the gate where the customs vehicle with the imposters was waiting.

Both vehicles passed through a gate for cargo deliveries and service vehicles. The customs vehicle had a remote opener that would allow them unhindered passage through the gate whenever they pleased. The two-vehicle motorcade headed north on the George Washington Parkway. They passed the Pentagon and Arlington Cemetery.

"Only the dead will not fear us after we show the Americans once more that Hesbulah can strike anywhere." Elamesh stated as they passed the rows of white markers in Arlington. The vehicles headed up the Potomac valley passed Roslyn.

Elamesh maintained his orientation and mentally transposed his position on the mental image of the map that he had studied of the city. Hesbulah's intelligence had traced the source of all of their compromised movements to the United States satellite surveillance capability. Whenever they had tried to cover their movements, it seemed that the United States had always known what was happening. He had even executed many of his men, sincerely believing that some were planted by US Intelligence agencies. All were murdered violently to provide examples of what would happen if one held contempt for Hesbulah. Elamesh suspected that the US was using satellites when after a US movie that he watched on a commercial flight from Europe showed the capability of the technology. He had suggested this possibility to Hesbulah and they moved their operations deep underground to avoid detection. Every other connection was sterilized so it did not cause any suspicion. This was but only one of the reasons that Hesbulah allowed Elamesh to assist in his operations. Elamesh had convinced Hesbulah to allow him to strike the "nerve' center of the US satellite surveillance effort. The risk was high but the payoff would be even higher. They had to destroy this capability before the Americans discovered the supply line of nuclear material from Russia to China. Hesbulah knew that the rail connection between Russia and China would draw suspicion from the Western Intelligence agencies. He would reduce their ability to use their high technology by turning it off.

His thoughts made the drive pass quickly. They were already turning west onto a small gravel road that served as an access road for the groundskeepers of the old research laboratory, the same lab that now served as the downlink site. He looked first for the antennae locations. The antenna were located in old water towers used to supply water to the small towns that were outside the city before the extensive water supply pipes were used to link the suburbs. He easily identified them from the photos taken by earlier by Hesbulah's loyalists working on diplomatic missions and living here in Washington.

'What fools,' he thought, 'they think that Hesbulah's efforts are to unite all of the Arab peoples. What incredible fools, Hesbulah's thoughts are only to make everyone servants. Hesbulah wanted to be like God. He wanted to be the object of worship.'

Elamesh watched as his thugs dismounted the vehicles and donned their night vision goggles and prepared their weapons and the explosives.

The sharpshooters were the first to position on the high ground surrounding the facility. There were very few lights and Hesbulah was impressed that this site was as well disguised. It would have been one of the last places that he would have looked if he hadn't received the information from an American ex-military Muslim that believed that foolishly believed that he was advancing the position of his people.

After they had received the information that Hesbulah had wanted. He was killed in a plane crash one summer as he and his family flew from their home in Chicago to Pittsburgh. The plane crash was arranged by remote control and was so completely devastating that nothing but small pieces were left of the craft that buried itself in a hillside. He was grateful that the man had provided the information in such detail, because it saved him valuable time.

As the teams left the area, Elamesh started his clock. They had rehearsed it in a setting that offered almost the same type of terrain at an abandoned military facility in Germany near the town of Neuhausen. They had worked the timing out to less than six hours. Move in; plant the explosives and egress. They would be on their way back to Europe before the explosion would take place. He timed it so that they could watch the chaos on CNN when they were refueling in Iceland just as they had watched the Trade Centers collapse years ago.

The guards of the facility routinely dressed as local hunters. They drove old pick up trucks, dressed in rag tag old hunting garb and carried weapons that looked as if they were handed down from their distant ancestors. They gave the outward appearance of the typical cowboy. No worries. Life was meant to be used for two things…huntin' and fishin'. The mind was a wonderful thing to waste. They had been living this charade for so long in a very benign environment that they actually started to believe it themselves.

Most of them retired from the military and were the sharpest in their professions. They were trained killers that had lost the edge. Their instincts were dulled by years of soft duty and they believed their duty was not important and they let their guard down long ago. They suspected nothing and were content acting like just a few beer swillin' good old boys out on the farm. They made their rounds and settled into the routine of the evening. They had no idea of knowing nor would they even suspect that tonight would not be as routine an evening as any other would.

Elamesh's sharpshooters were ready and in position and watched their targets through the rifles scopes. As soon as the guards separated themselves by a few yards proceeding to make their rounds, the killing would begin.

The sharpshooters were in position and were using a silenced 30.06 with a 270-grain bullet. It was a fast round with a relatively low trajectory. It was originally designed for the military because of it fast low trajectory qualities. At 200 meters, each of Elamesh's sharpshooters could put 10 rounds through the same hole in as many seconds with the 80 power night vision scopes. They would plan for two headshots each. One would more than do the job. Two would provide a little extra margin for assurance. Elamesh was listening on the secure radio as the sharpshooters called in position. He also heard the command to commence firing.

Johnny Volk, a retired Army Special Operations veteran from Culpeper, Virginia, had just started making his rounds. He and his buddies had been doing this for years and although he had been one of the best before he retired, he could no longer make that claim. He lived from day to day, remembering the days when was a player and not a has-been. He dulled the pain of his present life consuming too much beer. His once fit body now was fat and abused. His gut hung over his belt so far that he had to distort his spine to make walking comfortable. The only time his belt was visible was when he took it off. Each day, walking his beat became more and more of a chore. He vowed to get back into shape many times only to fail. Johnny rounded the northwest corner of the power station where he stopped, leaned back and tried to find his belt.

"Shouldn't have had that last cup of coffee," he said to himself as he fumbled with his zipper and tried to relieve himself in the darkness. Elamesh's sharpshooter laughed to himself. He was used to challenges and difficult assignments. This was easier than their target practice. This fat slob was standing there taking piss, not moving, not aware of anything, but his own urges. This was too easy. The sharpshooter squeezed off two rounds in rapid succession. Before Johnny Volk had hit the ground, the sharpshooter had moved to his next target and had two more shots off.

In less than 30 seconds, all of the sharpshooters had called in complete. Twenty of the guards were down. Their brains spilled all over the Maryland soil, crumpled into heaps of bloody flesh where they once stood. They never knew what hit them.

Elamesh listened as the lead sharpshooter called for continued surveillance as the explosives were placed into exact positions around the main building. The building was a long, over 750 meters, and narrow building that was used to test large caliber cannon projectiles. The naval research facility constructed it many years ago as part of the Naval Ordinance Research Facility at Cabin John, Maryland. The length of the building forced the men that were placing the explosives to cover the distance on the double. They had rehearsed it many times and worked without much thought. They placed the series circuit packages in shallow holes and recovered them to prevent premature discovery. The explosion would take place just after the first shift of analysts had arrived for duty. Over 600 pounds of high explosive shaped charges would be placed around the building. Each of the four would carry 150 pounds of the high explosive. This was about 4 times as much as needed to completely level the facility and destroy any trace of their deed.

"Vehicle approaching service road." One of the sharpshooters announced over the radio.

"Maintain surveillance and report," was the only answer from the leader.

Elamesh tensed. He was savvy enough to know that the simplest of overlooked details could compromise a mission's success. Elamesh waited for any hint of suspicion. He would order the sharpshooters to wait until the car had driven far enough onto the service road and out of view from the main road before he ordered the sharpshooter to kill the occupants.

"Two occupants, one male, one female. They are 300 meters from your location." The sharpshooter paused briefly.

Elamesh knew that placing the explosives would take another 30 minutes. His anxiety level was increasing.

"The vehicle is moving off to the side of the road now and is stopped." Announced the sharpshooter.

The vehicle was less than 200 meters from their position and Elamesh could see the headlights of the vehicle partially illuminating the valley's darkness. The rapids of the Potomac River in the distance masked its approach down the gravel road. Elamesh had no concern for human life, he thought about it for a moment and calculated what would jeopardize the success of the mission more, killing the vehicle's occupants or allowing them to live. His suspicious mind felt that it was security guards that had discovered their vehicles hidden in the trees on the side of the road. Elamesh commanded the sharpshooters to fire.

The two people in the vehicle were as equally paranoid. Phil had just picked up Lisa 20 minutes before. He was a congressional staffer that was in the midst of having an affair with a congressional aide. His job as a staffer was putting undue pressures on him as his senator was implicated in accepting payoffs from the tobacco industry lobbyists. The workdays became longer and longer and he saw less and less of his wife and family. He felt that he needed a change. He began to work closer and closer with Lisa, one thing led to another and he found himself betraying his wife for this other woman whom he knew nothing about.

She was as loose as they came. She would sleep with any man that gave her a second look and a chance to advance. She wouldn't even insist on a nice hotel room.

Phil had turned off the car's headlights and ignition. He slid next to Lisa. His hands worked their way up inside her skirt as she parted her legs to give him easier access.

"Is that what you want Phil?" Lisa asked as her head tilted back and her breathing became more rapid. Phil muttered something as he pushed his lips deeper into the hollows of her neck as his hands worked furiously. He was about to pull her closer to him when the two rounds came through the front windshield of his black Lexus and struck him in the left side of the temple. The second, unhindered by the windshield glass, struck just in front of his left ear. Lisa heard and saw the explosion of safety glass, flesh and bone. Before her mind could work out the details, two more rounds, fired by another sharpshooter came through the right side window of the Lexus and struck her in the back of the head. Their bodies fell together quivering as the nerves spasmed because of a sensation a little more different than they previously experienced. Their body fluids mixed, not as in the same way as they did the night before, but in a puddle of bright red, on the seats and floor of the Lexus.

Elamesh listened to the reports transmitted by the sharpshooters. "No movement, two confirmed." The voice crackled over the radio system. Elamesh would inspect the vehicle as they left, but commanded the sharpshooters to continue surveillance.

The ten remaining minutes passed quickly. The explosives were finally set in place and the thugs were running back up the trail to the Customs Suburban and Elamesh's sedan. They covered the distance much faster because they had left the heavy weight of the explosives around the building. They had perfectly positioned the shaped explosives to direct much of the explosion inward. The effect would amplify the force since it did not radiate in a full circle as a conventional charge would. Its effects were designed to focus most of the force toward the center of the building. The explosion would rip into the concrete cast building and completely gut its interior. Everything inside would be either destroyed by the overpressure or incinerated by the intense heat created by the 600 pounds of the composite explosive.

Everyone was accounted for and loaded quickly into the vehicles. They proceeded down the gravel path led by Elamesh's sedan without using lights. The drivers would keep their Night Vision Goggles or NVGs in place until they reached the main road. Elamesh saw the sedan that the sharpshooters reported 20 minutes earlier. He had his driver stop beside it and he held his NVGs up to look inside. There was no movement by the two bodies felled toward the car's center. He opened his door, got out and moved closer to shin a small light into the interior. The shapely legs covered with nylons and the short skirt of the passenger suggested to him that this was a female. He couldn't tell by the facial features because there weren't any. The driver had the general stature of a man minus his head. There weren't any other occupants in the vehicle and Elamesh was quite certain that they were both dead. As Elamesh turned to enter his car, he heard the cellular phone in the Lexus beep out a musical tune not familiar to him. He turned once again back to the car instinctively to make sure that it wouldn't be answered. As he looked inside, he couldn't help but notice the embroidered initials on the cuff of the driver, PLO. PLO? He chuckled; another complacent member of the PLO had just lost his head.

"I believe we have finished here, quickly, back to the airport." Elamesh commanded the driver. He keyed his radio transmitter on a different frequency.

"Prepare to depart in 40 minutes." Were his instructions to the flight crew of the Falcon.

"Have you had any difficulties at the airport? Elamesh asked.

"It has been very quiet here." Replied the captain.

"Wonderful, I can't say the same for us, but I expect that in approximately four hours, it will be much, much more noisy. Elamesh exclaimed.

It was approaching a little past 4:00 am in Washington. They were two hours ahead of their schedule. Elamesh fought the urge to doze as the vehicles moved through the dark road leading towards the city down the Potomac River Valley. 'They must be near the CIA headquarters,' he thought, 'located in Langley. For now it would be spared, but perhaps it will be next months target. Whenever, it will be a much easier assignment. A remote controlled Airbus 320 transport filled with explosives or perhaps a nuclear device would be much easier than bringing in one of his hit squads. The time would come when they would no longer need to operate like mice, sneaking around at night. As soon as Hesbulah's arsenal was complete, the reign of terror would begin.'

They approached Chain Bridge and were heading back towards the airport. Elamesh called the flight crew; "we are fifteen minutes out."

"Roger", replied the Falcon's captain, "We are ready to depart as soon as you arrive."

Elamesh could see the lights of the airport as they passed the park named in honor of one of America's first lady's. The customs vehicle passed to be in the lead. They entered the airport through the same drive and parked besides the Falcon to load their equipment into the waiting aircraft. The entire process took less than 15 minutes and they were soon airborne, enroute to Iceland.

Elamesh watched the lights of the city disappear beneath a thin layer of cirrus that formed over the city and turned his attention towards the first officer that was now up and serving the catered food that they had picked up in Iceland earlier. Elamesh had sent a message to Hesbulah. Mission completed. Downlink facility targeted successfully and execution within one hour and thirty minutes. No chance to de-arm the packages. Elamesh was looking forward to the seafood and wine that was being served and then some sleep. As they headed east and were climbing through 37,000 feet, the sun was breaking over the horizon of the Atlantic Ocean. Four more hours…then he would begin searching for the installation that the Americans had visited in Germany. After it was destroyed, Hesbulah's plan would be certain of success. He only had one last stop to make in Paris. There he would find out exactly where the complex in Germany was located.

11

Departing Dulles for Europe

Washington D.C., February 22, 0500 hours

Seth left the Laboratory and drove directly to the Pentagon. The men that he had seen would have to leave and Raymond's satellite views showed them heading toward Reagan Airport. He planned to use the North American Air Defense Radar network to locate the aircraft that was leaving Washington, D.C.

"These bastard aren't going to get away with this on my watch." Seth said under his breath. It would prove to be a difficult task.

He made a call to the tower at Ronald Reagan Airport. They would give him a list of all of the aircraft that had departed in the last hour. Then it would be just a minor matter of following the aircraft through the flight plans it had filed. He would then query any airports listed as a destination on the flight plan to retrace its steps. Air travel offers an unrestrained freedom to come and go anywhere in the world, but anyone can find out where you were and where you are going with only a little effort.

He pulled into the reserved parking area close to the Pentagon building and in a matter of minutes was in the Operation's Room. The room bristled with high tech equipment. It was designed as an intelligence fusion cell to track the requirements that were most important to nation's security. They had even used it to track the movements of various military leaders around the world. Data feeds came from a variety of sources. Seth wanted to use the tie-ins to NORAD or Space Mountain in Colorado Springs, Colorado. Seth was counting on this link to track the airplane as it flew from Washington to its destination.

As he entered the room, everyone's attention was turned to the breaking headline reported by the major news networks of the city. A reporter was covering the evacuation of the area adjacent to the Cabin John Naval Research Facility. Seth listened for one thing; he only wanted to hear that everyone had been evacuated and that only robotic devices were sent to survey the area for explosives.

The building itself was located in the center of a government complex of over 120 acres. He was sure that this would provide a buffer for the explosion and limit the collateral damage. Seth wasn't certain, but he thought that they would have a little more time before the explosion would rock the area. The "spokesperson" for the Naval Research Lab was commenting on the safety of the building and those situations like this are rehearsed. Seth knew the "spokesperson" was from the CIA public affairs office. They were experts on spinning a story. They could tie it in to whatever they wanted and the sensationalists working for the news organizations would trip and fall to be the first to broadcast the hogwash. There wasn't much truth to the press releases sometimes, but they'd say anything to prevent a public panic or loss of confidence in the government.

The camera panned the now deserted facility; the long shadows of the winter morning were just beginning to form. The troopers were watching, waiting, some were talking casually amongst themselves. They were taking a well-deserved break after scrambling earlier to clear the affluent neighborhoods that surrounded the facility. The reporter was telling the viewers the history of the complex, which was originally built in 1942.

Suddenly the building in the background, which used to be the long half-cylindrical, shaped building, erupted in an intense, rippling, white-yellow explosion. The reporter with his back to the facility continued to talk momentarily unaware of the explosion until the slower traveling sound waves and blast concussion reached where he stood. He instinctively dropped his head and turned toward the plume of flame and debris shooting into the early morning Virginia-Maryland sky. The camera's view was filled with fire and smoke. Seth noticed the split second timing of the explosives. There weren't several explosions within seconds. A central timer detonated this explosion. It only added confirmation to his theory that the bombers weren't amateurs; they were highly trained and professional.

As the smoke and dust began to settle, it became apparent that the total destruction was complete. It was highly localized and surgically precise. The reinforced 15-inch thick, dense concrete building that was over one-quarter of a mile in length and one hundred yards wide was completely destroyed. The rubble was piled with an eerie neatness toward the center of the buildings long axis. It was as if someone had taken years to level the building. Painstakingly dismantling and piled the pieces neatly into the center of where the now demolished structure once stood. Not a trace of its original shape remained. The blast was directed with such precision, Seth noticed, that trees and shrubbery planted within several feet of the building were untouched. It would be difficult for anyone in the government to claim that this was an accident caused by unfound, unexploded ordinance from years gone by, which was what the "spokesperson" was eluding to during his original disclosure.

This would be a headline on an even bigger scale than the first World Trade Center bombing. That first terrorist attack was traced to amateur, self-proclaimed religious fanatic using rental vans filled with fertilizer, the second with Muslim extremists flying passenger jets into it.

This explosion couldn't be dismissed as easily. Even with the high state of security that America was in since September 11, 2001, it would be apparent that now the terrorist could strike any target, anywhere with surgical precision. Seth believed that this was only their introduction. He was certain that something larger loomed on the horizon.

Seth waited a few minutes for the shock to wear off from the officers in the operations room. They too knew what this was and it wasn't an accident. When Seth noticed that they began to talk amongst themselves, he introduced himself to the Watch Officer.

"Murph." Seth said as Murphy slowly turned hearing his name unable to disconnect from what he had just witnessed.

"Seth, Seth Stephens, Jesus Christ, did you see that? What the hell is happening?" Murphy said as he turned back in shock and awe.

"Yeah Murph, I need your help tracking the aircraft that I believe is carrying the people responsible for that." He said as he produced the document authorizing his presence.

"Hell yeah Seth, what do you need?" Murphy said as he dived back down to reality.

"Seth, nice touch. I saw the message that General Woodsen sent out the other day. How does it feel to have a blank check?" Murphy said as he moved toward his desk.

"Murph, I'll need a record of any aircraft that have left the U.S. Air Defense Identification Zone within the last three hours. I'm certain that the aircraft would have left Reagan or possibly Dulles International and will be heading to Europe via the North Atlantic. They aren't that concerned with covering their tracks, so I don't believe that they will be heading south to take a more circuitous route." Before Seth finished, the watch supervisors that were directing the information requests were around him and Murphy trying to learn more.

"We should have the information in a few minutes Seth." Colonel Murphy replied. Seth turned his attention to the monitors that listed the top ten-intelligence requirements worldwide. The intelligence requirement list would make some piece of the puzzle fit. It would complete the picture that some section of the organization was developing. Seth's attention was drawn to the item that requested infrared imagery of the activity near the Harz Mountains located in Central Germany.

A young captain dressed in the Class B uniform of the Air Force handed Seth a printed list of all of the aircraft that had departed the east coast of the US during the past few hours. Seth noted the departure points and noticed that only one had departed Reagan. Its destination was listed as Reykjavik, Iceland.

"That's the one." Seth said confirming it not meaning to announce it. "Thank you Captain…" Seth was hoping for the Captain to fill in the blank, which she did.

"Feller, Sir. Captain Jill Feller."

"Thanks Captain Jill Feller." Seth said with a genuine smile as they made eye contact for a moment.

"You're more than welcome, sir." Was her reply as she turned to walk back toward her desk.

"Murph, what is the status of the number five Priority Intelligence Request or PIR up there? The one concerned with unfriendly message traffic tossed about looking for the site in the Harz?" Seth asked.

"We have intercepted a lot of traffic that shows interest in that particular area. Most of it comes from satellite phones around the world and feeds into this island, Socotra." Murph said as he looked at some correlation reports.

"Murph, if you get any ideas on that, let me know. Especially if you hear any traffic that talks about definitive action against it." Seth said as he continued to study the list while he was putting things together in his very keen mind's eye.

Murph looked over Seth's shoulder as he was talking. Mike Thomas entered the operations room and caught his eye while they were talking. Seth turned without skipping a beat to speak to Mike.

"Mike, we'll be heading out within the hour. I'll brief you on the way. We'll plan to leave and be at Dulles in 40 minutes." Seth's brevity would be vague to anyone listening to the conversation, but Mike knew exactly what he meant.

"Roger boss, the X is ready to go when you get there." Was Mike's equally brief reply.

"Mike," Seth interjected. "Do you remember Izz Deconcerio?"

"Remember him, I'll never forget him." Mike replied.

"You'll get the chance to see him again, He's on the team." Seth said confidently.

Mike's tone changed to absolute sincerity. "He's a good man to have on the team."

"He'll meet us at the hangar at Dulles. It's almost time to gear up buddy." Seth concluded.

Seth took the opportunity to close the loop with Todd Murphy. "Murph, Can you notify the operatives based in Iceland for me? Give them the tail number of that aircraft that left this morning and ask them to find out as much as they can while the plane is on the ground in Iceland." Seth wanted the operatives in Iceland to get as much information about the terrorists as possible. He knew that they had something more to give and he was in the frame of mind to get all he could out of them.

"Seth, no problem. Consider it done. Where are you off to now?" Murphy asked as he scratched out a note to himself on his tablet.

"Right about here Murph, the lovely Island of Socotra." Seth said as he winked made a large loop around the island just off the coast of Yemen on a computer image map on the monitor. No one noticed, except Seth that the female Captain had placed herself close enough to discreetly eavesdrop and write down every note that she could. There were always leaks in any operation. With any luck, his ruse would buy the team some time.

"Thanks Murph. I'll keep in touch." Seth said as he pointed over to Captain Feller. Murph knew what Seth was saying.

Seth headed out of the Pentagon parking area and made his way through the streets of Washington towards Route 50 west. The early inbound traffic was already slowed to a near stop by the emergency vehicles racing towards the Naval Lab on the Potomac. The local news stations were still recapping the morning's explosion over the radio as Seth pressed on to the west toward Dulles. He and Mike shook their heads at the reporter's description.

He accelerated onto the Dulles access road. Just a few miles ahead the lights of the airport complex shown brightly against the still darkened western sky as the sun was coming over in the opposite direction. The smoke from the explosion in the northwestern part of Washington D.C. was rising straight up in the calm, cold atmosphere which stained an otherwise near perfect sunrise.

"The bastards," he said more to himself than to Mike as he thought about the cowardly acts of all terrorists, "they just can't stand peace."

Seth pulled off the interstate onto the access ramp that stretched out narrowly ahead of him. A few years ago, he had remembered reading that this complex was an annex for the Udvar-Hazy portion of the Smithsonian Institution. Now it partially was a warehouse for the CIA. The huge ramp appeared unused and vacant with sparse patches of grass growing up between the cracks in the cement apron. The outer door of the hangar opened as Seth positioned the car directly in front. The door opened allowing him to pull into the small entrance alcove. The door shut behind and the inner door opened revealing a bright bustling interior. Seth pulled into the parking area along side of several other cars. Seth was always amazed at the extent to which the agency would go to cover its tracks.

"Well, we'd be hard pressed to do better than this." Seth said obviously pleased with their transportation arrangements. Before them in the hangar at Dulles Airport sat a plain white Citation X, the Roman numeral for a perfect 10, jet transport.

"Mike, I hope you can contain yourself. Seth said facetiously to Mike as they looked at the jet before them.

"No Problem Sir, not much here to get excited about is there?" At least they both had their sense of humor. They both realized the impact of this mission but worked to keep each from letting it affect their outlook.

"Sir, we're all set." Israel "Izz" Diconcerio said as he walked down the air stairs of the Citation X.

"Israel, it is good to see you again." Seth said as he, Mike and Izz traded small talk for a few minutes.

Izz would be on Seth's team for this mission. He and Seth had served earlier as covert operators in Central America. They had met at Vint Hill Farms during a rehearsal for a covert mission in Honduras. Seth trusted not many men unconditionally, but Izz was one of the few.

During the rehearsal at Vint Hill Farms, they were training for a High Altitude, Low Opening, or HALO jump as they called them. One of

Seth's teammates harness straps became caught on the tail boom as he exited the UH-1H "Huey" helicopter on his jump from 10,000 feet.

Without a second thought or concern for his welfare, Izz scrambled out on the tail boom of the helicopter with just inches separating he and the revolving blades of the helicopter and untangled his teammate. That teammate was Mike Thomas. Izz DeConcerio didn't know Mike at the time and was willing to sacrifice his life to save another's. In that one single act of heroism, Izz distinguished himself and became the man that everyone asked for and wanted on their side.

Seth spent the next 25 minutes doing his pre-flight check of the transport. He had flown it on a couple of evaluation flights while at Moffet at the same time that his RC-680's were being completed. It was a beautiful and functional one-of-a-kind machine.

The legendary aircraft manufacturer custom built this one for the Central Intelligence Agency and Army Operations specially designed this particular Citation X. It had the ability to sustain the crew with supplies and livable conditions for 5 days before re-supply. It was complemented with satellite data, video, and voice transmission capability via any location on earth through secure defense satellites. Multi-channel duplex links allowed for any method to be transmitted to any location capable of inter-operating with many other systems.

It was specially modified to military standards for aerial refueling and extra weight bearing capacity. It had a maximum takeoff weight normally of 38,000 pounds; the special modification allowed operations to up to 43,000 pounds. The engines of the aircraft would normally develop approximately 6,500 pounds of thrust, with a military extension of the engines to 8,700 pounds per engine. This gave the airplane the capability to climb to its service ceiling of 51,000 feet within 22 minutes. It could fly for approximately 4,000 nautical miles before refueling, or indefinitely with aerial refueling. It could do this at near supersonic speeds, or a cruise of .92 mach. It gave the team global capability in a minutes notice with minimal preparation. It could operate out of 6,000 feet of runways at it maximum gross weight.

The cabin was elaborately decorated for an operational aircraft. It was actually cheaper for the manufacturer to include these refinements rather than re-engineer existing designs and contract new suppliers for a less attractive interior. The seating surfaces were the finest Italian leathers dyed a light natural saddle hue. The sidewall and interior fabrics were covered with a tapestry that was imported from Scotland. The woodwork was finished with burled walnut veneers polished to a high gloss so high that the reflection seemed endlessly deep. The lighting was designed to enhance the working environment that was comfortable and gave complimented exactness and precision. The design and craftsmanship of this aircraft was second to none. The price of the interior of this aircraft would have bought a beautiful house with a nice parcel of land anywhere in the Silicon Valley. It was all designed to make the work of professionals, very professional. When Josh McAdams purchased the aircraft, some in his department were afraid of the perceived non-political correctness of this marvelous machine.

McAdam's viewpoint was simply, "If we want our people to do a first class job, we have got to supply first class equipment." Although the aircraft was an expensive tool, design by perfectionists, the cost paled when compared to the monetary value of the successful outcome to this mission.

Seth did his final walk around the aircraft. He patted her on the nose and traced the sign on it as he finished. "If you perform half as good as you look, we've got no problems," Seth said under his breath.

"Gentlemen, let's get going. We will brief in the air." Seth said as he hauled a small bag from the trunk of the car. The door squeezed solidly into position and latched. Seth looked around the cabin and the electronic control consoles were already up and humming and manned by Izz. Mike was strapping into the right seat finishing up the Flight Management Program sequence. The ground crews were pulling the aircraft into the outer hangar that had a similar design to the vehicular entrance. The inner doors closed behind them and the outer door opened. The tug was disconnected and the aircraft's engines were started.

"Argus 99, you are cleared to taxi to and takeoff runway 36 right, contact the tower 118.25 holding short."

"Roger Dulles Tower," Seth replied as he released the parking brake of the Citation X and eased the throttles forward. He responded to the directions of the ground marshaller that signaled him to move forward and left. The Citation X was loaded very near to its gross weight of near 43,000 pounds with all of the special electronics equipment.

The aircraft was in position on runway 36 right and cleared for departure. Seth pushed the throttles forward and Mike monitored the flight instrument and the instruments of the Rolls-Royce engines. The aircraft approached rotation speed and Seth applied pressure to the control column that made the aircraft climb smoothly and gracefully. They were level at 49,000 feet in 20 minutes heading for the Coast of England.

"One thing great about this airplane is that you feel comfortable immediately with it as soon as you get back into it, it doesn't matter how long you've been away from her." Seth said, revealing at how much he felt at home in the cockpit.

The aircraft was on its way, flying the plan that they had put into the Flight Management System. Seth switched on the autopilot and reviewed the cockpit instrumentation once more before he would begin the briefing to Mike and Izz. This aircraft was equipped with a REmote FLIght Monitoring System, or REFLIMS. This system would allow the flight crew to take care of mission requirements while monitoring the flight and critical systems from a small console in the rear of the airplane. It was especially helpful when there weren't many crewmembers on board and mission tasks were critical. Seth would brief the crew and then put the crew sleep plan into effect. It would allow them to get some rest before they had arrived in Europe.

Mike sat at the REFLIMS mission console in the back of the jet monitored the progress of the aircraft as he sat in the back to hear Seth's briefing.

"Okay, let me bring you up to speed here. Our mission has been expanded. We are working to stop one man. His name is Hesbulah and we must stop him before he alone, can control a nuclear arsenal that would challenge that of the U.S." Seth paused for a moment to let Mike and Izz refocus before he continued.

"We are first heading to Farnborough, U.K., there we will pick up an MI6 SAS officer named Sean MacLowre. Sean will act as our liaison to the British Government. Joshua McAdams had arranged this with British Intelligence. After a brief stop in Farnborough we will reposition to Jersey, which is one of the Channel Islands of the United Kingdom. We are trying to find out what has happened to the primary German intelligence enclave located on Jersey. Izz, Karl Linder, is the German officer that we had talked to at the Harz mountain site. He gave me information to pass to Josh McAdams. Karl had lost contact with the primary enclave on Jersey before we had received our initial intercepts from the Harz location a few weeks ago.

Karl referred to a group of people or a person by the name of Hesbulah. Now here is where Karl had me doubting until I received the briefing from McAdams. Hesbulah is the one family responsible for nearly every major chaotic event in history. Linder and the Harz mountain enclave have traced the intervention of this family to nearly every incident of war or civil unrest since the 19th century. To make his position solid, Linder briefed me on his intelligence process that undisputedly links Hesbulah's involvement with the war within the Austro-Hungarian Empire and the destabilization of the Balkans in the late 1800's.

The Austro-Hungarian Empire was attempting an annexation of Bosnia in the early 1900s. Linder and his group have evidence that a man named Heinrich Keuhl, a henchman of the Hesbulah Empire, acted to destabilize the empire by playing both sides against one another. Keuhl was taking advantage of a weak alliance between Austria and Hungary to foil the annexation attempts of the Balkans.

If you remember your world history, the Balkans is a critical region for world stability because it is a meeting point of many cultures and religions. A conflict between factions in this region draws support from countries throughout the world. Hesbulah supposedly worked against the unification of the region and the opportunity to build stability and peace.

He worked against the peace process while most of the governments of Europe and the Russians understood this need for stability and were involved in working toward peace. Hesbulah's plans were so detailed that they undermined the existing governments efforts at the time. To take advantage of a deteriorating situation, Hesbulah had hired a family of first generation terrorists, the family Elamesh, to plan and execute the assassination of Archduke Francis Ferdinand and his wife, Sophia of Hohenburg. The assassination took place in Sarajevo. This act only solidified the tension between the Empire and Serbia because Serbia was against the annexation of Bosnia and it worked to destabilize the entire Austro-Hungarian Empire. Austria-Hungary immediately declared war on Serbia on July 28, 1914, inciting that country sponsored sedition and assassination.

Hesbulah took further advantage of the situation by widening the gap between a delicate association between Croatia and Serbia. He was bent on chaotic development and fractionalization throughout Europe, which would destabilize the world. Divide and conquer seemed to be his motto. He had the Croatian Sabor, the political offices that represented the people of Croatia to the Austrian Empire close its doors. He filled in an information void, by printing his own papers and inciting contempt against Austria saying that the defeat of the Austrian's would be beneficial for the development of Croatia. He gradually drew every developing country on earth into the fray through a twisted and negative influence, further destabilizing the world's tendency toward cooperation. He continued his campaigns of negative influence and instigation throughout the 20th Century. The destabilization of Europe and ensuing depression that encompassed many countries demoralized the people. Hesbulah's next target was Germany. The Germans were a very hard working, intelligent and focused culture but the destabilization left them desperate and starved for hope. Hitler, a puppet of Hesbulah, was given the resources and influence to manipulate the German people. Hitler's war empire grew astonishingly fast. Hesbulah, using Hitler, focused the country on nationalistic pride and gave them hope. He almost succeeded in advancing his empire during World War II by promoting the rise of the Nazis in the west and the Emperor of Japan in the East. His plan was to divide the worlds into two hemispheres, each controlled by his puppets. They would answer to him and only him. After the worst was over, he would emerge as the World's Emperor as he assumed power from his two stooges, Hitler and Hirohito.

His primary flaw, the belief that humanity has no direction unless it is dictated to, was the weak point in his plan. As the Nazi scientists were developing a super weapon for him, he didn't believe that they would question their conscience. One by one they began their escape to America and leaked to the Americans what the intent of Hitler actually was. They also brought with them the results of their research and the developments that they made on designing atomic weapons.

Robert and Karl Linder were at the main core of this discovery. They had discovered secret meetings between Hitler, Hirohito, and Hesbulah. They discovered the plan. They vowed to work against it and not be part of holocaust. Gradually they gathered more people that were decent and wanted no part of the Reich's twisted view of world domination. They had seen Hitler and Hirohito's evidence of true evil in the concentration camps and the atrocities committed in China, Korea, and most of the Pacific Countries. They vowed to secretly join the alliance and destabilize Hitler's Nazi Regime.

They also attempted to contact officers highly placed in Hirohito's staff to work toward weakening the Empire's position in the east. Hirohito's grasp was so strong, that every Japanese officer that they contacted died a very violent death and their families were murdered. The German allies could not discover insiders strong enough to help the efforts in the east. They then decided to provide whatever assistance they could to defeat the empire and end the war with Japan. They also knew that Hitler was sharing the technology with the Japanese and feared that they were also developing super weapons along the same time lines.

Linder's enclave also tried to tie in with the Russians and the Chinese, but because of their lack of unity and leadership, it was difficult to reach out and pull them into the alliance. Linder explained that the diversity in each of those countries was too vast to resolve in that little amount of time. Time was a luxury that they could not afford to waste. Linder also discovered that Japan had nuclear weapons and was in the process of delivering it across the Pacific to Los Angeles and San Francisco when the Enola Gay dropped its bomb on Hiroshima. He passed this information to the War Department. The two fast, Japanese, stealthy attack cruisers carrying the nuclear weapons were sunk off the island of Midway by American torpedo bombers only days before the Atomic bomb was detonated on Hiroshima. Some say that the evidence that Linder provided sealed the decision. Most Americans don't realize how close we came to being the hunted rather that the hunters. If Japan had deployed the bomb they would have held the upper hand.

Hesbulah's organization rapidly discovered the fragmentation of the Nazi Regime, he tried to have them eliminated, but their numbers were too many. His greed and ignorance of the spirit of freedom and morality once again was his flaw. His atrocities were too bold and united the world against Hitler and Hirohito like no other cause could.

The end of the war came too fast for Hesbulah; his plan crumbled in his hands and he had to turn his attention to strengthening his hand in the east. He tried to gain China's confidence and form alliance between China and Japan. China wouldn't have anything to do with his suggestions citing recent examples of atrocities committed by the Japanese. He began promoting discussion with Russia and China to form an alliance. He played upon their unprepared conditions before and during World War II and used the cliché of strength in numbers alliance to form a communist rule. China and Russia were ripe for this discussion because of their lack of leadership. He paid off hundred of thousands of wealthy, politically influential puppets to form the communist pact. This alliance was his only saving act. It allowed him influence with the world when it came time to redraw the political boundaries of Europe and reduce his losses. Hesbulah tried to regroup and turned his attention now toward the east and began destabilizing small countries like Korea and Vietnam using his communist pact to draw them into the fold. His plans were to once again draw the world into a conflict. But he lost his momentum. He had no nuclear capability. We had taken that from him and were now using his own weapon against him. We held the threat of retaliation and destruction against dictators up to nothing but evil intentions.

Hesbulah, now realizing his folly, passed the baton to his only son. He had been trained as every other male in the generations of Hesbulah, to rest only when the reign of the world was complete. He would now carry on the legacy and continue. The Americans were now in Vietnam and we were keeping that conflict contained. Other countries were not joining the war to support Communism because of the fear that the Americans would retaliate instantly. The junior Hesbulah realized that he was failing his father's legacy. He also realized that he was the end of the line. There were no more after him. He had no sons because of his impotence. He was it and his desperation was increasing.

He planned to take the opposite approach. He began supporting treaties against nuclear proliferation, while secretly continuing nuclear development in Russia. Karl Linder continued to watch his every move. Linder's intelligence network was focused solely on the root of the evil that Hesbulah brought to the world. American, British, German, Australian, Canadian and Brazilian intelligence networks were given leads that discovered weapons development, anarchy in developing nations, and acts to destabilize commerce and trade. Hesbulah couldn't eat without Linder's group knowing it. Hesbulah became so inflamed trying to find out who on the inside of his tightly wrapped organization was seditious, that he had his thug's murder any one appearing suspicious. He'd arranged accidents within his staff to kill off his people with knowledge before he'd advance to the next phase of his plan, his crude method to keep information compartmentalized.

Hesbulah discovered the German Enclave's primary site in Jersey purely by accident. A young British woman, born in Egypt, to British parents from Jersey gave him some information. They were assigned to Egypt and she lived more in the Middle Ease than in Jersey. She worked for a company that unknowingly supported Hesbulah's organization as a researcher. She had briefed Hesbulah as one of his commerce staff on North Sea drilling operations. She had mentioned technology that the Germans used to create caverns in her parent's homeland during World War II. It was a self-sustaining drilling system that used geothermal energy to power drills that made the power sources more powerful the deeper the drilling progressed. Hesbulah wanted to visit the site interested in its technicalities.

Linder became concerned when they discovered that Hesbulah was going to Jersey. He contacted the Jersey site and told them. They transferred as much data as they could, using older technology analogue transmissions, basically text forms and some images. They couldn't transfer the data as fast using the schedules that hid their transmissions, so they encrypted it and stored it as safely as they could. The day before Hesbulah's arrival, the people at the Jersey site took their lives and tried to destroy as much of the site as they could after securing the data.

Korea, Cuba, Pakistan, Vietnam, Falklands, Grenada, Panama, Iraq and now once again the Balkans may be setting the stage for worldwide instability. We are up against the enemy of the world gentlemen. The goal of this family of connected thugs is to make the world subservient to their cause. They hold an immense wealth that has representation in every country. They are going for broke. Their leader, a man that simply holds his family name, Hesbulah, has no heirs. He is 59 years old and knows that he must succeed within the next ten years if he wants to see this objective of world domination pass. Even the world's terrorist at large, Bin Laden answers to him. He hasn't groomed a successor and the family will simply not trust someone not of the family's blood. They have pulled out all of the stakes and we are witnessing the complete resolve of this organization.

Linder and his people were preparing to bring this information to all of the world governments through NATO and the United Nations. The majority of their data has been stored in a site near St. Hellier on the British Isle of Jersey. They are afraid that without the proof contained in this indisputable information; we would further drive a wedge between any alliances formed. Hesbulah's infrastructure and support especially to the poor third world countries is so vast that those countries would simply not believe the charges if we didn't have undisputed proof. We must get to St. Hellier, locate the underground facility, salvage what we can of the information that Linder has said exists there. Then we help Linder present his case to the United Nations and discredit Hesbulah and isolate his infrastructure.

Recent imagery shows that the Chinese are using a rail line through the Althai Mountains establishing a direct link between Russia's western providence's and the northern areas of China. The purported reason is to expand trade routes. I believe it is where they are receiving nuclear material from the Russians. They don't want the junk that was designed by the Russians to deliver the weapon; they only want the plutonium. The old SS-20 ICBMs are falling apart and are antiquated. The Chinese know that actively mining plutonium shows up easily on our overhead surveillance systems. We can detect any new uranium mining quickly. The shuffling of previously processed material is more difficult to track. Weapons grade plutonium is heavily shielded and doesn't glow on satellite imagery as raw Uranium would.

Hesbulah is dealing with the corrupt Russians and Chinese. The guess is that he is buying the stolen Russian plutonium and passing it through the Chinese. The Chinese received the latest technology on our ICBMs from a spy scandal originating at Los Alamos more than ten years ago. Josh McAdams believes that they have our technology. They only need more plutonium to have a better first strike capability than we do. Everyone suspects that Hesbulah is behind the influence.

The old Soviet SS series ICBMs were being stored near one of the largest Uranium deposits in Russia, near a city on the southern end of Lake Baikal, Angarsk-Irkutsk. The latest START treaty listed a location to dismantle the ICBMs as Gorno-Altaysk. The rail line that connects Russia with China runs through Gorno-Altaysk. There are more than one hundred snow sheds along the route from the Lake Baykal region to Gorno-Altaysk. That is where I believe that the Russians are removing the plutonium and packaging it for travel along the new rail link between the two countries. Once Hesbulah has the weapons in place he can just about name his price. The world would be at his mercy. If we disagreed, he'd simply annihilate resistance."

"There wouldn't be much left to rule after the land was contaminated with radiation." Mike said from behind the console.

"Mike, remember the neutron bomb technology that made big headlines? It is alive and well and perfected to the point where a very big blast would be much cleaner than the Hiroshima style Fat Boy bombs. Drop the bomb one-day, wait a week, and then go in plant wheat, build houses, develop industry and ship in some live people. It would be a very safe place after about one to two weeks." Seth relayed.

"There are thousands of places in China that are harboring long range nuclear missiles. We had spent so much of our effort keeping a watchful eye on the Russians that we had only a few resources keeping tabs on China. They have had a long period of development that we are just now discovering. The NSA/CIA report leads me to believe that we may be further behind than originally estimated. Hesbulah has and is always doing his homework. We are behind and we are now playing catch up."

"Is that all we have to do Seth, I thought that we were going to have a rough assignment." Mike said through a half smile.

"Seth, I should have known that saving the world would be in this mission someplace. Tell me…have they ever given you an easy mission?" Izz said with an enthusiastic tempo.

"Tell you what, if we come through this, I'll buy dinner. I know a great little French restaurant in Paris near Port Maillot. Chez Clement, they serve an excellent E'ntrico." Seth returned the sarcasm.

"I love working for a boss with a sense of humor, how about you Izz? Don't you love this guy?" Mike laughed.

Mike and Seth made their way back into the cockpit of the X. "Mike, Izz, we've go about two more hours until we will descend into Farnborough. This would be a good opportunity to get some down time."

"What about you Seth, I know you're super human but I'd like to know that you're getting some rest in between detonations." Mike said sincerely.

"You go ahead and get some rest first. I'm just going to sit here and watch the sun come up over Europe and listen as the wind on the nose of this machine whispers sweet thing to me." Seth replied staring off into the darkness over the Atlantic. His body was racing through the air at nearly the speed of sound but his mind was already racing into the future much faster than that.

12

The Underground Hospital

Farnborough, United Kingdom was the first destination for Seth and his men. It would allow Seth's team to make their final coordination between the US and UK agencies before continuing the mission. They would also pick up the United Kingdom Liaison Officer.

The short flight to Jersey would take only minutes and there they would hopefully find some of the answers. When they found and met Karl Linder at the underground complex near Goslar, the site of the original transmissions, they had discovered that the central coordinating agency for the watchmen of the world, as Seth sometimes called them, originated from the site located on the Channel Island of Jersey.

"I think she'll take 5,500 liters tonight," Seth said as he shouted instructions to the aircraft refueler above the normal airport noise at Farnborough.

The evening sky was beautiful. He couldn't remember ever experiencing one more pleasant in the isles in the winter. The refueler seemed to be reading his mind.

"Lovely weather we have for you tonight. It isn't often that we have clear skies here in the winter." Said the refueler with proper English accented by growing up in the Scottish highlands.

"Beautiful," Seth replied as he inhaled the fresh crisp winter air.

He looked toward the north and even though it was nearly 1800 hours in the evening, in the winter, the sky showed with a red-orange glow from the sun not too anxious to set. Mike was just coming down the stairs and stretching his arms overhead and glanced at the refueler.

"Hey boss, I'll handle the refueling, you can take care of the paperwork." Mike said as Seth shook his arm overhead as a sign of approval as he walked toward operations.

"Think you can handle it, Thomas?" Seth asked jokingly. Mike turned his ear toward Seth and cupped it as a sign that he didn't hear.

"The refueling, think you can handle it?" Seth said as he felt like it was time to interject a little levity into the mission.

"I don't know boss, but when you put two Englishmen together, we can figure anything out." Mike retorted.

"Yeah but one Scotsman can do the work of two English." Quipped the refueler.

"Scottish, you are mate?" Mike asked the refueler in his most convincing English accent. Mike, being a dry humored Englishman by decent couldn't resist the opportunity for a verbal round or two with the refueler.

"What do they let you do, clean the windows on this beauty?"

"No, they keep me around to keep the Scots in check." Said Mike.

"I see, but why you haven't been able to do that for centuries. Both men laughed. They couldn't help but take up bantering one another just for the sport of it.

"Beautiful, here in my part of our country tonight, isn't it," egged Mike.

"Oh yeah, every once in awhile we let some of our fine weather come on down here." The refueler said.

"So how are you going to enjoy this good weather tonight?"

"I was thinking about going out after my work and giving a few English a good thrashing."

"Think you may be up to it?" Asked Mike.

"Come to think of it, I believe it's me wife's turn. This way maybe you might have a chance."

"I've heard about your wife, come to think of it, burly woman, six foot tall with huge biceps, hairy chest and big handle bar mustache."

"No that's my wife's sister. My wife doesn't have a mustache." Laughed the refueler.

Seth was walking out to the plane as the two men shook hands. "I'm Mike Thomas, I help out the boss when he needs me to," Mike said pointing to Seth as he was closing the distance between them.

"I'm Sean MacLowre, part time dispenser of aviation fuels and member of the team." Said Sean.

"What team do you belong to?" Mike asked, but before Sean could answer, Seth came up to them.

"Well gentlemen, let's be on our way to Jersey. Mike I hope that you have had time to get acquainted with Sean, Sean, I'm Seth Stephens, don't know what I did to be put in charge of this mission but it is certainly good to have you aboard. We seem to have assembled quite a team here. We'll have time to get acquainted tonight over dinner in Jersey, I hope you know a good restaurant."

"Of course Sir, said Sean, it's the only reason I've been brought on board."

"I wouldn't doubt that, laughed Mike, can't think of anything else a Scotsman is good for."

"Your right Mike, so did the Queen, she felt is was about time we taught you English a little about life's finer things, that's why she invited us to join your lovely country."

"Invited, Mike asked, I believe that we kicked your arse and made you the queen's subjects."

"You English, always such a mind for the little details." Sean smiled, he already knew that this team needed to work closely together and they ironically were off to a good start.

The X was airborne in 10 minutes heading south towards Jersey. Jersey's history was just as intriguing as England's, the birthplace of many of Jersey's inhabitants now. The Citation X covered the distance of about 100 miles, in about 12 minutes. The lights of Jersey appeared as they climbed through 10,000 feet. It shone like a jewel placed on a dark velvet background as the glow of yellow-orange streetlights illuminated its western shores. The lights of St. Ouen, St. Brelade and St. Helier offered the most concentration of light indicating a concentration of population. They would land at the Jersey Airport, located on the western side of Jersey and drive to St. Helier along the southern shores of Jersey.

The island was only about ten miles in length, east to west and approximately 5 miles wide north to south. Its terrain offered wave worn craggy cliffs near Portelet Bayan on the southern side and almost the entire northern shore to tide washed beaches gently curving near St Aubin's bay and St Ouen's. The island was formed by ancient volcanic activity that still rumbled on occasion beneath the island's basement rock.

The Citation X quietly approached the Jersey shore from the west and landed without attracting any attention. It taxied to a hangar pre-arranged by Sean and located on the southeastern corner of the airfield and when the doors were closed, it covered any trace that the team had arrived.

The black S Class Mercedes, arranged by Sean, was quickly loaded with the team's equipment. They had to travel light and with equipment that wouldn't attract any suspicions from on-lookers. Seth wasn't sure but he knew that they were only a few steps ahead of those trying to stop them from learning the truth. Seth gave his final instructions to the team, "As far as we all are concerned, we are tourists. Watch your activities and expect that everything has been compromised. We'll get checked into the hotel and have some dinner. Let's keep the discussions in the car or other places that I specifically approve of. Don't discuss anything in your hotel rooms or off on your own. We are doing one hell of a job keeping this mission balanced. We can't afford to run into any more problems."

"You know us boss, we can keep secrets." Said Mike.

"I certainly do know you, and that's what I worried about."

"Who has the keys?"

"I do," Izz said raising the keys over his head.

"Here you go Izz, I'll drive." Seth stated matter of factly. "The speed limits only 40 mph on the island, Izz. I don't want you to feel like you're in Monte Carlo. There's less chance of us getting stopped for speeding if I drive. If that happens, how would I ever explain what I'm doing with a Scotsman and an Englishman in the same car?" Seth explained.

They were out of the hangar and steering the Mercedes initially east out of the airport's drive. Making a left turn on Le Beau Mont would take them to the Island's south coast. Once there, they would follow La Route de La Halle and Victoria Avenue into St. Hellier.

"Sean, get us some information on St. Helier off the navigation system. The S-Class Mercedes had a color LCD display mounted in the center of the Instrument Panel. It controlled everything from the telephone, radio, television, and GPS updated navigation system, similar to the one in the Citation X.

Sean bought up the display and asked for the Pomme D'Or Hotel where they would be staying. "Right over there sir, on Liberation Square." Immediately a demure female voice began to give them instruction over the car speaker systems. "Oh, what I would give to have her give me instructions." Mike said sarcastically.

"Hey Mike, you can stay out in the car tonight while we have dinner and type in all of the directions you'd like." Seth said half laughing.

"Yeah, at least this won't cost you anything." Sean said.

"Unlike you Scots, an Englishman doesn't have to pay for the company of a woman. Our prestigious reputations make us very much in demand." Mike shot back.

"Oh is it deep in here, let's stop before we soil the interior of this fine automobile." Izz Said.

"What, no one believes me?" Mike asked rhetorically.

"I think we've all seen you in action before, Mike." Seth said as he maneuvered the S-Class around a turn onto Victoria Avenue headed toward St. Helier.

The weather was just as perfect as one could imagine on St. Helier. It was getting darker now, the sun finally disappearing over the horizon to the west. Seth always found that fascinating when flying at high altitudes in the northern latitudes in the summer months. The sun's orange halo really never leaves the horizon. The Northern sky has its band of orange gold as the sun sets in the west and reappears on the east. In the winter though, it just the opposite. There's hardly any daylight. The sunrises at 0930 and sets at just after 1600 hours.

The wind was calm and the quaint city of St. Helier was quiet enough to hear the waves breaking against the ramparts of Elizabeth Castle on the east of St. Aubin's Bay. The island was home to bunkers and gun emplacements from the first and second world wars along with the fortresses that dated back to the 13th century. The island was contained by a perimeter of magnificent rock cliffs, caves, garrison houses overlooking the sea and fascinating ocean vistas. The island enjoyed two in-exhaustible power sources, geothermal energy and the rise and fall of the great tidal flow of at least 40 feet. The rich arable land and the low temperatures of 8 or 10 degrees centigrade made it a perfect climate so near the European mainland. Seth could see Liberation square come into view, a famous site marked by the liberation of Jersey on May 9, 1945.

Seth pulled the car into a space just in front of the hotel. The team proceeded to the reception desk to check in.

"Mr. Stephens, welcome to St. Helier." The lovely receptionist, a young woman from Jersey with dark hair and eyes that matched said to Seth smiling as he handed over his credit card.

"Thank you, it seems that it'll be my pleasure to be here." Seth responded.

"Mr. Stephens, you are in room 305, I trust that it'll meet your expectations." Smiled the receptionist.

"Thank you, what do you think guys, about 20 minutes to change, meet back here for dinner." Seth said half-looking up to the receptionist for part of the message and looking over his shoulder to his team for the other.

"Sounds great," was all they managed to say while they intently focused on the young receptionist, eagerly awaiting their turn.

"Close your mouth Mike." Seth laughed as he glanced admiringly at the receptionist.

Seth was the first one back down stairs. He waited in the well-decorated reception alcove for the other three men on his team. The old photos showing the Nazis standing around the same lobby many years earlier intrigued Seth. They were taken when the hotel was the Kriegsmarine Headquarters in 1945. They had pressed the Hotel Pomme O'dor owners into service then against their will. He appeared to be looking in one of the display cases arranged by the Hotel Staff, but he was really focused on the plan for the next day. The display cases held a display of goods offered by the tiny island, pottery, wines, and jewelry, fresh preserves and jellies. He was hungry no doubt; he snuck in a thought of how good the strawberry preserve would taste on freshly baked and toasted French bread. He heard his team coming down a half of a flight of stairs behind him.

"Come on sir, you're noticeably salivating. I know the perfect restaurant. How does seafood sound?" Sean asked.

"Great to me, I'm just thankful that you didn't suggest mutton. Although come to think of it, that sounds very good." Mike interjected.

"No, just around the corner and straight away is a great little place, La Poste. It is right off of Metviers Lane. It is only about five minutes away. I asked the receptionist if she'd mind calling ahead for a table." Sean offered.

Within a few minutes they had covered the distance and were seated comfortably at a table in La Poste, a very nice restaurant on the second floor of a building at least 300 years old with a commanding look of the pedestrian shopping area of downtown St. Helier. The waiter offered the wine list to Sean, who passed it out of respect, to Seth. Seth took a few minutes and ordered the St. Helier Chardonnay as the wine while the others perused the menu. Seth ordered the fresh catch sea bass baked on a bed of rice, complete with freshly picked island crisp green beans. The others all ordered the Lobster bisque following Sean's lead. The Chardonnay had just a hint of oak with a full body and light finish. Perfect by any vintner's standards, including the standards of the French vintner that had migrated to St. Helier after World War I and trained his sons in the art. The food was well prepared and was complimented by the Chardonnay that Seth had chosen. As agreed the kept their discussion far from what tasks that lay ahead. They casually conversed about their favorite past times. It was inevitable that the conversation turned to aircraft. It was the one very strong background that they all had shared. As they sat and Seth glanced out the window, scanning the area out of habit, he couldn't help but notice the two men that he had seen at the airport security gate.

He casually looked away from the window and pretended to pick up on the conversation, just in case the table was prepped before they had arrived.

"Well gentlemen, I think I'm ready for a good nights sleep, we've a lot to see and do tomorrow." Seth said as he was getting up. He was also writing instruction on the back of the bill that had just been dropped by the table. The three others understood the instructions immediately. They appeared to wish Seth good night and remain at the table as he left. One by one they excused themselves until only Mike remained. Seth had picked up the watch from behind the two suspicious looking men. Only when Mike had appeared to leave did the two men move from their very conspicuous spot to look around the corner. The corner was dark and the two never saw what hit them. Seth came from the left side of the building and Sean the other. The impact with the two was timed to the split second. Both fell unconscious to the ground after quick blows to the temples administered by Seth and Sean's forearms. Izz had already entered the building and opened the door near the two and Seth and Sean dragged the two by their collars into the building. Mike followed up with the sweep to ensure that there weren't others.

"Sean, I expect you to be a little more precise next time. You did a little noticeable damage to this man's nose. He'd remember you for a long time if only he had seen you." Sean feigned the reprimand.

"Sorry mate, no excuse for ineptness. I'm just a little out of practice."

"Well if this mission keeps going the way it has for the past few weeks, you're going to get more practice than morning drills at Camp

Peary." Mike said commenting about their training at the CIA's base located in southern Virginia.

"Secure these two amateurs so that they don't interrupt us any further during the next two days." Seth said. Izz placed two capsules under each of the two's tongues. Within minutes the two were men that were tailing the team were unconscious.

"If the rats don't get you, maybe the high tide will. Sorry fellows, the boss doesn't want to be bothered." Izz said as he tied the two to a post in the dock's pilings.

Within minutes the team had secured the two and checked out the area in a search pattern designed to flush out anyone. They were very thorough at what they did. A few minutes later, they walked to the Hotel Pomme D'or to get some rest. If tonight offered a forecast of what the rest of the week was going to be like, they would need a little more than rest to get them through it.

Seth began rereading the document prepared for him by the team at NSA as he settled into his room.

In October 1941, Berlin ordered that work begin at once to create an underground bunker, large enough to maintain an entire division. This Division would be the foothold for the invasion of Britain. The underground bunker was completely encased in the granite basement rock that jutted up out of the Atlantic Ocean of the northwestern coast of France. Although its shores were much nearer to France than the United Kingdom, most of its inhabitants are of English heritage and descendants.

The German Army was extremely fragmented after a few years of war. Hitler tricked the decent people of Germany into supporting the war. After they had discovered his true intentions, they once again stood over tyranny and good and decency triumphed. They began to organize, using a system within a system to remain covert. It was difficult to trust anyone, unless you were absolutely certain that they weren't going to sway. The small enclave of German Officers that formed throughout the world was gaining momentum and helped the allies win the war. The enigma machine code breaking clues, were almost hand delivered by a German officer named Heinrich Sindel. Sindel discussed many other issues that were recorded and let the allies know of the attempts to topple the Third Reich from inside. The issues were very delicate.

Seth had read through the complete report when he was briefed on the operation back in Washington. He was also surprised at how organized the world's events actually were. His faith was completely restored by the fact that there were those that would guide the world to peace and prevent a rein of chaos.

Seth and his team made it down to the car park after a quick continental breakfast of fruit, fresh baked pastries and breads, yogurt and preserves. Eating even a continental breakfast in Europe was a delight to the senses.

The Mercedes was checked over quickly for any tampering and an electronic sweep was done to turn up any intrusions. None were found. Perhaps the two, unconscious now and tied to the pilings, from last night were acting independently and had no companions. Still, Seth thought, it is always better to keep your options opened. They drove to a warehouse just next to the Museum on the waterfront to pick up the equipment that had been arranged in advance. Everyone was extremely quiet and extremely observant. Nothing could be left to chance. Seth knew that each was just reviewing the plan and the silence just before an operation was good. It kept everyone sharper and focused. A compromise now would mean that that Hesbulah could organize more resistance and reduce their available time. They picked up the equipment that Seth had anticipated he would need after he had talked with Karl Linder from the Harz Mountains.

As they drove east out of St. Helier, the terrain rose rapidly into the surrounding hills. The sun was just breaking over the horizon. The island was a miniature study of a seascape, beach, sandy transition area, and bedrock layering and granite hills. It was difficult to imagine the diversity in such a relatively small area. It was a beauty that one had to actually experience. The fresh shore smells that accompanied the warm ocean currents maintained the island's moderate temperature all year long. It would have been easy for an untrained and undisciplined team to forget why they were here. Seth's team needed no reminder. This was the big event. It was an operation that would unite the world together as never before.

Their first plan was to tour the facility just as many other tourists normally would do just to get the general layout of the site. They knew that there was much more to this than an underground hospital based on the description offered by Karl's detailed report. Seth discussed some of the topographies with Sean, Izz and Mike.

"It looks like they have the perfect location here. The radio line of site is unrestricted towards the UK. The line of site would only be restricted by curvature of the Earth's surface. Many HF radios used during the war used atmospheric skip. It is a process from which the signal was bounced from the tropopause to anywhere in the world. In these northern latitudes the tropopause is actually quite lower and allows a signal to literally bounce around the world on very low power. This is a perfect location for that, other than Iceland."

Mike tossed out a new thought, "or to an allied ship or submarine offshore."

"Exactly, gentlemen, I think this is where we will find a few answers proving some of the claims that Karl and his men have proposed." Seth affirmed.

As they approached the site, they were slightly surprised with the view. There really wasn't anything there. The historical society of St. Helier and Jersey had improved a parking lot and a sign. Only an entrance gate and a fence like structure that surrounded the area marked the site.

"The entrance is large enough to drive a few tractor-trailer trucks in side by side. I didn't think it would be this big," commented Mike.

"The Nazis had cheap labor to build it, didn't cost them a thing, but the sweat and toil given by the prisoners was no small effort. The bastards worked them until they dropped." Sean added.

The team parked the car next to the only other car in the car park. The large S Class Mercedes dwarfed the small Peugeot that was parked next to them just under the sign that stated the days that the tours were opened.

"Today isn't a regular tour date is it Seth," Mike said noting the opened dates.

"What a coincidence, we aren't going on a regular tour." Quipped Seth.

"Good thing, I forgot the video camera." Mike stated rhetorically, "and you know how I hate to loose a photo opportunity."

13

Inside the Hospital

The temperature was noticeably cooler as they descended deeper into the granite that surrounded the tunnels of the underground hospital. Surprisingly, there was no evidence of ground water leaking into the cavern from above, but the team could definitely hear the sound of a lot of fast moving water coming from down below.

They had left their guide about 200 hundred meters behind while posing as geologists assigned by Her Majesty to conduct studies on the subterranean metamorphic rock structure of the Jersey Islands. After they had won the confidence of the hospital's only volunteer on duty, the very old, but lovely, Mrs. Perry, did offer to them the complete, unabridged history of her family, the island and the hospital completely and unsolicited. Seth had felt that he had given about as much time to the wonderful Mrs. Perry before he insisted on proceeding. He hoped that they could see her before she left for the day. He would have enjoyed hearing about the history of the island. She had made it to the 1930s when Seth had to excuse them. He figured that they did not have enough time for the lovely Mrs. Perry to recall the remaining 78 years before they were behind their schedule.

As they reached the end of the corridor that served as the main access to the tunnel, it formed a "T" intersection. Seth had asked Izz to estimate their depth and plot it on the small laptop computer that held the plans for the tunnel.

"What depth do you show Izz?" Seth queried.

"I have us at about 200 meters below the surface boss." Izz shot back.

"If I see any of Arnie's initials carved in a rock, I'll let you know." Izz added referring to the Jules Verne's novel, *Journey to the Center of the Earth.*

"We are in the exploring mode now guys, the descriptions given by Linder are from reports by the occupants and no personal experience." Mike was the first to notice the worn path that led to the seemingly solid rock on the left side of the path that they were on.

"Seth, look at this. It is difficult to see because of the ground water that was seeping and pooled around the area, but I think that we have something here." Mike said as he brushed the debris from the area.

"Sean, get a quick scan on that wall." Seth commanded sharply. Sean used an ultrasound device that looked like a small cellular telephone. The ultrasound would detect any voids behind the rock.

"Bingo, boss. We have a void about the size of a garage door here. Thickness is about 20 centimeters and then a void beyond that."

"This has got to be it, it fits Linder's description."

"What is the differing density on the other side of the rock Sean?" Seth wanted to know if they were looking at a passage or possibly the course of the strong ground water or subterranean oceanic flow that the geological maps showed cutting crossed the island.

"Negative Seth, it shows nil for density on the other side. I'll continue to scan it to get a better picture, while Mike drills to insert the camera into the area indicating the void."

Mike was already assembling the drill with a titanium sectioned drill bit. The bit was tipped with diamond cutting edges and had a hollow point to allow a water stream to cool it while it cut through the granite.

"I love this job, where else could I get such cool toys to play with?" Mike spouted. He always had the perfect statement to take the edge off of the mission.

It took nearly eight minutes to bore through the natural rock wall made of solid granite. It was more than enough time for the team to don their self-contained breathing apparatus and facemasks as a precautionary measure. Some "booby traps" in old German war tunnels were to fill the voids with a VX gas, a type of nerve gas that would kill instantly. Seth and his team took nothing as a given.

"Give me the five millimeter probe, Izz." Mike called over their team's radios that were part of their face -masks.

"Already set up Mike." Izz inserted the probe as Mike removed the drilling shaft and bit.

"Negative gas readings so far boss", Izz reported. Seth and the team were glued to the monitor except for Sean. He had finished taking the void readings and was now providing security for the rest of the team.

"I'll use the IR camera setting initially, to preclude tripping any photo-sensors. Everything will have that lovely green cast to it." Izz explained. Everyone had seen images from the small fiber optic camera at the end of the probe. The thermal imaging infrared system would translate differing temperatures into an image displayed on the 12-centimeter monitor the team was using.

"Would you look at that!" Exclaimed Izz. "That is the last thing that I would have expected to see here." The team was looking at the image on the monitor.

They weren't sure what to expect but it sure wasn't what they were seeing on the monitor. Their attempt to comprehend exactly what they were seeing was interrupted by Sean's alert over the radio.

"Seth, we have company! I count four targets moving fast down the corridor." Izz had the probe withdrawn in a split second and had it secured in the pocket of his backpack and was already lying prone with his 9 millimeter oriented toward the aggressors. Seth and Mike were moving to take up an offensive position toward the uninvited guests. Sean was oriented in the opposite direction and monitoring the sensors that they had placed in the corridors while they approached the site.

Mike was planted into a recess along the rock wall. He would cover Seth as Seth posed as a geo-physicist mapping wall density for the Royal government if any questions were exchanged.

"They are about 30 meters in front of you boss, their movement has slowed." Sean reported on the radio. Seth was crouched partly behind an outcropping of granite. He had placed his light to shine on the granite walls between himself and the aggressors. They had no doubt seen the fluorescent lights come on and had slowed their movements. That was a good sign. They were not well trained. They allowed themselves to be surprised by the lights coming on and slowed their advance. If they were professionals, they would have thought this through and anticipated the meeting. The aggressors were in the reaction mode now, behind the decision curve. Seth and his crew anticipated their arrival and new the course of action. Through this one indicator, Seth and his team had already gained ascendancy.

"I've got four clear shots on the bogies boss," Mike reported from his position.

"Roger, Mike, What are they carrying?"

"Number one has a machine pistol, two, handgun, three, unknown, four, unknown."

"Roger Mike, on my mark…three, two, one."

Seth proceeded with the plan; he tossed a small hand held light out into one of the shadows. The small confines of the cavern corridor were immediately transformed from silence to a loud chaotic, staccato of gunfire. The leader began firing into the direction of the light and sound that Seth had tossed.

'So much for the discussion.' Seth thought.

Mike dropped the lead aggressor with two precise bursts fired from his M-8. The first burst of automatic fire from Mike's weapon aimed at the larger target presented by the chest area stitched its way up across the body impacting slightly to the right of his nose on his right cheek bone. The impact of the bullets left him spinning wildly to the right as he crumpled into a heap onto the hard granite rock flooring. The other aggressors stooped and scrambled trying to find cover in the rock walls. The area that Seth's team selected as the kill zone offered no cover for the aggressors. They began firing wildly in the up and down the corridor and in both directions. The wildly fired rounds ricocheted off the jagged rocks making a variable high-pitched buzzing sound. Mike stopped their hasty retreat as he fired again. He fired a single shot this time. The shot bored a clean hole into the neck of the assassin that was bringing up the rear of the assassin team. He dropped to the ground immobilized by the paralyzing shot that severed his spinal column. The two in-between fell to the ground and continued firing blindly into all possible directions, not knowing where the shots had come from. Several of the bullets had ricocheted off of the rock walls and sent rocks shards spalling from the walls and showering Seth and Mike with razor sharp rock fragments. The second assassin boldly and brazenly jumped up and rushed where he had seen Seth's shadow in the darkness of the cavern. Izz had moved up from his position and supported Mike's cover fire.

Seth was in no danger in his position and was calmly directing the movements as he caught a glimpse of movement from his periphery when Mike called, "boss, check right side."

Mike could not get a clear shot at the assassin without risking Seth. The assassin had moved in a line covered by Seth's position. "No clear shot boss," was Mike's reply to Seth.

Seth was already moving to get into a better offensive position. The assassin had seen Seth's movement and began charging blindly, shouting and firing in his direction. The rounds sounded like that from a

9mm as they spun off in differing directions after impacting the angular shapes forged by the granite wall. Seth was glad that they still had their facemasks on; they offered protection from the shards of granite splintering from the walls. Seth did not need additional time to aim. His years of experience and training gave him the ability to use a weapon with the same precision as that of a skilled surgeon making precise cuts on the mark with a scalpel. Seth instinctively aimed at the assassin's frontal lobe and fired twice but not before the assassin had fired, one of the bullets from the assassin's weapon had deeply grazed a wound in Seth's upper arm. Seth's two rounds found their mark as the assassin's head exploded in a spray of blood, flesh, hair and bone. The two bullets impacted with maintaining relatively high energy because of the short range. The body continued on its momentum toward Seth, headless, and fell to Seth's feet as the blood spurted, unstaunched from the head now missing the upper half from the mandible on up. Seth noticed that his dress was very American, but his shouts were in a middle eastern language and dialect.

"Sean, move up to the alternate position and be prepared for our withdrawal. I'll have the incendiary devices in place in 30 seconds." Seth was placing the incendiary device that would destroy any evidence that the gunfight had happened. Flesh, bones and teeth, would be reduced to a white powder, similar to what remains of the human body after cremation.

Izz and Mike advanced about 5 meters to make quick work of the two remaining assassins. In about four minutes it was over. Mike and Izz quickly searched the four and taken fingerprint scans and photos on the Sony zero illumination digital camera.

"Gentlemen, the devices are set. Sean, call when clear." Izz moved to the position where Sean was and Mike accompanied Seth to the other end of the corridor.

"Boss the sweep is complete and the corridor is secure."

"Good man Izz, we wouldn't want the lovely Mrs. Perry to get caught in the middle of our small fire storm." Seth heard all of them check in just by saying their last names. The radios that they were using were the latest and incorporated GPS, voice identification features, satellite communications, frequency hopping, encryption and range finding. The GPS would give others a location of the team members instantly when queried and the information was displayed on a wrist mounted plasma display.

When Seth was confident that all was clear, he sequenced the detonator to fire the incendiary device. The rock walls absorbed the heat and light energy. The temperatures increased by only 10 degrees

Centigrade where the team was located. The energy quickly dissipated to about 5 degrees above normal within minutes after the thermal release. The device didn't really explode to release energy; its release was gradual enough to raise the temperature to nearly 1,800 degrees C in about 8 minutes. The rush of air into the chamber to support the combustion was the loudest noise. The team scanned the upward rising passage further beyond their position to make certain that no one else was approaching. Only then did they move back to begin their inspection of the caverns that held the origination of the radio transmissions. Several near 60-degree turns in the tunnel walls sheltered the area where the firefight occurred. These barriers created by the change in direction of the rock walls, similar to maize, contained most of the heat. The assassin's bodies were reduced to a thin film of white ash that was already being scattered by the airflow moving about the cavern as the temperatures once again equalized. One thing certain, they would never see the sunlight again. The granite walls were noticeably warm to the touch, but nothing else was unusual. Nothing remained. Nothing substantial that would give any indications that this was the final resting-place for four ill intentioned hooligans.

"Izz, let's get that probe re-inserted. I want t find the entrance to the inner locations before we call it a day. We are on a short time line here. Mrs. Perry will be closing up the main entrance before nightfall." Seth commanded.

"About 2 minutes is all I need boss," replied Izz. Sean and Mike were already scanning the areas using the ultrasonic device.

Izz had completed the sweep with the probe of the wall separating the cavern and the main entrance to the Underground complex from which Linder had spoke of. Izz had made a video of the entire sweep in both day and infrared. The probe also contained an ultra high sensitive microphone that would give them any sound indications along with the video.

"Let's go!" Was all Seth needed to say into the radio. The team was moving toward the entrance in a moment. It took them about 10 minutes to cover the distance at the double. Their run was slowed by the low rock ceilings that kept their posture at more of a crouch than a stand up run. Still the team would have rivaled any university cross-country team by covering the distance that quickly, especially with their added load of equipment and supplies.

"I shouldn't have eaten dessert last night," was all Mike kept saying under his labored breathing.

"If you would have had only one dessert, you would have been fine chubby." Sean fired back.

"I was just compensating for lack of company and affection." Mike replied.

"You must have to compensate loads mate." Sean quipped.

"When we get through with this Seany, I'll introduce you to a few of my friends, they'll keep you out of those clubs in near Piccadilly Circus."

"You two have too much energy. How would you like to carry my pack? Izz said.

"You sound like two fools."

"Izz you're just too tense. What do you think Sean, We can take Izz along with us, he'd have a good time." Mike wheezed.

"What do you think Izz, when we're finished, you want to head out with Sean and I?"

"Do you think you guys could stand me in our free time too?" Izz asked with false empathy.

"Sure Izz, you can be our bestest buddy." Mike said in a high falsetto.

"Gentlemen, do you think you might stop the chatter and get your minds on the task at hand? Seth asked without showing a hint at being out of breath.

"You know boss, I don't mind at all. Tell me though, how is it that you aren't even winded? Sean asked.

"Look at him, shot in the arm and moving like he was walking on the beach."

"That's were I do my best running, Sean." Seth said. "The beach, buddy, the beach."

The door's partition was about 15 meters ahead when they slowed to a fast walk. The incline had dramatically reduced.

"We have enough time for a small chat with the lovely Mrs. Perry and then we'll head back to the hangar and debrief. Izz run all of the info back to NSA with the download and have them work the identification on the goons in the tunnel. We'll also have them analyze the imagery that we have on the opening. We have to get back here tomorrow with the answers or all of the data that we have to get will be lost. Have NSA contact Linder and have him read in on what we have found. We have just raised the heat on this mission a little more." Seth's voiced was showing the intensity that Izz, Mike and Sean knew meant it was time for the foolery to stop.

When they opened the partition from the cavern to the tour area, they smelled the characteristic strong smell of cordite, the explosive chemicals used as a bullet's propellant. The lights were out and the darkness added to the eerie feeling that something was wrong. Seth made his way to the docent office. Mike, Izz and Sean set out local security and did a precautionary sweep to make certain that the area was not another ambush waiting to happen. As Seth rounded the last turn of the tour area before the exit in almost complete darkness, the glow of a computer terminal was the only ambient illumination. The feeling that something was wrong was irrefutable now as he drew his 9-millimeter and held it at the ready. He peered around the corner of the already opened door and saw what he had suspected all along. Mrs. Perry had been shot cleanly through the heart. Her body was had slumped forward onto the desk. Seth took note of the expression on her face. There wasn't a hint of surprise at all. Seth made a quick and almost completely accurate estimate of the final scene of Mrs. Perry's life. The gunman had sat in the chair just in front of Mrs. Perry's desk and had discussed a few items with his gun draw. There was a calm discussion and nothing frantic had taken place.

Seth spoke into the squad's radios, "Izz, pull the last 2 hours of time from the Hospitals security camera's and make sure that you introduce the appropriate failure codes that make Scotland Yards explanation more believable. Sean, give your contact a call a make sure that he knows what to expect. Gentlemen, I do believe Mrs. Perry had a part in what we had seen earlier in the bunker. Make a final sweep of the area, exit time in four minutes." Seth liked to keep the radio traffic concise. His team knew what to do. They'd make a final sweep of the area to cover or highlight any clues that would make it easier for Scotland Yard to solve the puzzle. The security camera's tapes would be engineered quickly by Izz to show only the things that supported what they wanted everyone to know right now. Izz would simply pull any time that showed them in the area and would insert a static typical video loop in its place. This would keep the timeline in place. Although the British Government was in the know through the liaison, their standard procedure was to leave the intact without any implications to their presence.

Seth knew one thing for sure. They were expected and now maybe even compromised. He headed for the exit to meet with the rest of the team. The exit doors were opened and he was sure that the goons that did in Mrs. Perry and had attempted the same for them weren't trained enough to put security outside the exits but, he didn't make any assumptions.

"Izz, make a sweep of the parking lot and the surrounding area with the FLIR and ambient light imagery. Seth commanded in a quiet calm.

"Already on it boss," Izz calmly and confidently quiet answered.

"Just a little tampering with the Mercedes, Seth, but I don't see anyone that would have a clear shot at the exit as we come out."

"We'll head back to the airport on foot gentlemen. Better not push a bad position by setting ourselves up for another amateur attempt.

We'll take the high road tonight through the lovely Jersey Countryside back to the airport," Seth stated. This time there was no token resistance. The boss had his game face on which meant that the joking lamp was out.

They cautiously moved in teams of two, in a bounding over-watch, where each team provided cover for the team that advanced through their position onto the next defensible position. Seth was right; the Jersey countryside even in the late evening was wonderfully pleasant. The temperature was near 12 degrees centigrade, Seth guessed. The light breeze signaled the nearness of the beach and dormant wheat fields. Seth found that the smell was very comforting. It was a combination that he hadn't ever remembered experiencing before. The dry sweet smell of winter grass coupled with the moist briny smell of the sea allowed for a full range of fragrance. The moonlight filtering through the high broken cirrus cloud layer softened the sun's reflected light and created ghostly shadows through the trees and fence posts. He quickly snapped his mind from this mental vacation and focused hard once again on the operation.

They were now skirting the hilltop just to the southeast of the airport and could see the airport clearly. The GPS said that they were moving at close to 18 kilometers per hour. The team was in great shape and not one of them would have disappointed any track coach. Moving around, especially cross-country at that pace was exceptionally good during the day. But while at night, under limited visibility, it made it just short of record breaking. Seth was feeling the sting in his arm from the wound that the bullet had created. He knew from experience that it was just a bit into the tissue below the skin. The bleeding had stopped even before he had applied the field dressing. It would be sore, but he summarized that it could have been much worse. No need to dwell on the past, he thought. Keep things on track. We'll have time to recover and lick our wounds later, after this was brought to closure.

The rotating beacon that identifies the airport's location to aircraft in flight was beaming in the clear air. It was such a pleasant hike that he almost wished that they had a little further to go as they negotiated the obstacle created by the airport's perimeter fence. It was just a short distance straight line to the hangar, but Seth took the convoluted route while Mike gave cover from a vantage point just below the crest of the hill. Mike heard the team discussing their movements and he would move in once they had made it safely to their secure hangar at the south end of the field. Sean and Izz were securing the perimeter until Mike came in from the over-watch formation. Once Mike came in, he would relieve Izz so that Izz could begin passing the data to NSA for analysis.

Seth had made his way through the locked doors of the hangar and kept his night vision goggles down and on to secure the hangar under the cover of darkness. He was satisfied that the security system codes showed no attempted entries. The security system was of a completely passive thermal and acoustical design. It would sense the heat of an intruder or the vibrations and noises that an intruder would present. Nothing had compromised the sensor's field.

"Gentlemen, we have a clean house," Seth said into the transmitter.

"Over-watch, recover." Seth said. It was the only command that he needed to say to bring Mike in to relieve Izz. Mike closed the distance down the hill and relieved Izz and Sean to take the first security watch. He along with the assistance of his thermal-acoustical sensor array would keep the team from being surprised.

14

Inside the Hangar

Jersey Airport, February 23, 2010 hours

Seth switched on the aircraft power systems. Mike could hear nothing more than a faint hum from the quiet power generating system as he stood his post just outside the hangar's thin metal walls. Anyone standing more than 10 feet from the hangar would hear nothing. Seth was bringing the systems on line, beginning with the aircraft power management system and the remote security monitor of the acoustical and IR sensors that would detect intruders approaching the hangar. Izz came in through the jets opened cabin door and secured it as he passed through it. The heavy door was balanced perfectly and took minimal force to open or close. The jet's door seals inflated and the environmental system conditioned and filtered the air to provide a pure breathing environment even if they were in a toxic environment.

Seth was collecting his thoughts as he waited for the systems to come up to 100% and on-line. Less than twenty-four hours on this mission and they had already been the targets of a hostile force. Seth had to find out who was following them so closely and eliminate the threat. With this record, they could hardly be considered a covert operation. They were at a critical decision point and had to act quickly to maintain their discrete status or the operation would require much more manpower. That would nearly elevate it quickly to become a full-blown military operation much earlier than anyone would have wanted. It was something that they weren't prepared for just yet. Seth had to find out who knew about them and he would have to subdue the actions.

"Izz, systems are on line. We'll need to up-link the data back to the National Security Agency quickly. Those thugs that attempted the ambush in the hospital worked for someone and we have to get to them before they realize that their intercept plan has failed. We are way behind getting inside the enemy's decision cycle." Seth said more thinking out loud than giving instructions.

Izz had the small laptop fitted into its docking device as Seth spoke. The power was up and the computer was ready before they both could get settled.

"I've got a good satellite signal, a signal to noise ratio of 37, not bad for this latitude," Izz commented under his breath. "Secure up-link initiated and transmitting data. 30 seconds to go."

Sean was making his rounds and distributing the evening's dinner; military issued, Meals, Ready to Eat, the famous MREs. They would rotate roles amongst them daily and integrate a rest plan which called for rotation through a 24 hour period where each of the team slept for six hours and ate at least twice a day. They all had a good night's sleep last night but now with the threat of compromise they had to initiate the secure plan that provided at least two of the team awake and ready to launch the aircraft, the Citation X at a moments notice.

"How does it look outside, Sean?" Seth offered as Izz up-linked the data back to NSA more to initiate conversation with Sean than actually check on anything extraordinary. It was his technique that helped him check his team's morale without being too intrusive.

"Looking great boss, except for the fact that I'm cooking dinner for the Englishman. I think I'll give him the beefsteak, he deserves it." Sean said with a little hidden sarcasm.

"You'll never have to worry about your guests beating your doors down for seconds if you serve them that. That has to be the worst selection out of the entire lot. We should have specified to supply no beefsteak." Seth offered laughingly to let them know that they could unwind a little. The mission had a long way to go.

"Still your beefsteak beats British field rations hands down." Sean laughed over his shoulder as he exited the hangar to deliver Mike's delicacy.

"Izz, last night we dined on the fresh catch of the day, sea bass. Tonight, it'll probably be turkey stew that is I don't know how old." Seth quipped.

Izz returned his reply while laughing. "Well at least we have some great atmosphere. I could be in a guard tower in Iran. You won't see me complaining."

The signs that his men were giving him comforted Seth. His team had worked well together in their first action. He gained more confidence in the fact that his men were showing no signs of stress at all. Only after he checked and made sure that everything was in order did he move aft to the small lavatory in the aircraft to examine the wound in his shoulder. The bullet took more of his clothing off than it did anything else. Fortunately, it looked much worst than it actually was. He felt for certain that he would be a little sore and nothing else. After a thorough cleaning with the betadine solution he applied a light bandage dressing and changed his sweat and blood soaked shirt. It was a good thing he thought that the environmental system changed the cabin air every 55 seconds otherwise the adrenaline-spawned odors may have gotten the best of them. He smiled to himself with the thought; 'brand new jet and we already have it smelling like a gym'.

"Mike, how's the activity?" Seth queried over the squad radio as he moved to the work area.

"Looks normal boss. There is nothing out there. I can only see a few cars passing by the airfield road heading to and from town. No one has entered the airport since we have arrived. Sean's on his way in to get some rest." Mike reported.

"How was your dinner?" Seth half laughed.

"You're hittin' low boss. Come on beef stew? Who picked that out? No matter what they do to the stuff, it still tastes bad. I think that they use pig's knuckles or something else, but it sure isn't beef. Not that I'm complaining but come on, do we have to use the lowest bidder for everything?" Mike finished his comical tirade.

"You're just not hungry enough yet, remember back on the Central America trip. We didn't eat for two days. The beef stew then was one of the best meals I've ever had. It's all relative buddy." Seth nostalgically reminded him.

"Hey boss, was there ever a negative that you can't turn into a positive?" Mike asked humorously.

"Not yet Mike." Seth replied. His words trailed off as he thought about the next phase of the operation and turned his attention back to working with Izz.

Mike stayed focused and went back to maintaining a close watch for anyone trying to approach the hangar. He monitored the remote thermal-acoustical sensors that were placed at strategic locations around the countryside surrounding the airport. Nothing out of the ordinary was happening, yet. It was a nice late winter evening on this channel island of Jersey. The breeze that came out of the west was bringing with it the fresh smelling Atlantic influenced air masses. The new moon was just about ready to clear the horizon as it contrasted with the blue-black, star laden heavens. As he looked out to the west, the crisp views of the heavens merging with the sea were unhindered by the shadowy outlines of the mountains that he could remember seeing on winter evenings in southern Arizona. It was wonderment as thrilling as anything that he could imagine. Mike settled in to a routine that would scan the avenues of approach nearly every fifteen seconds.

Izz spoke out first as the computer terminal beeped at the arrival of an incoming secure message. "Seth we are receiving the initial data replies from NSA," Izz announced to Seth. Sean was just coming out of the lavatory and heading into the bunk area when Izz spoke.

"I hope you don't plan on taking phone calls at all hours of the night. Don't they believe in calling during normal business hours back in Washington? Sean said with a humorous tone.

"How do they expect a growing boy to get the sleep he needs?" He asked rhetorically.

"Sir, this message was reviewed by nearly everyone, Army Intelligence and Security Command, INSCOM, at Fort Belvoir, the encrypted code on the from line indicates a multi-department interface for all of our transmissions." Izz said with a contemplating attitude as he reviewed the distribution list on the message heading.

"Yeah, it looks like they are routing this message simultaneously to over fifty different agencies right now. By using the system of systems and the network interconnectivity, we can get hundreds of people looking at the problems at the same time. Each of the agencies knows who would be the best focal point to bring the information together to make it actionable intelligence for us. In this case, INSCOM was probably best organized or may be working a key part of this problem." Seth said reading the message as it came over the secure satellite link.

Seth began to read the Intelligence Summary, or the INTSUM, which was the reply to his request for intelligence, or more commonly called the RFI.

^^^^^TOP SECRET^^^^^
PROJECT VICTORY - EYES ONLY

TO: CDR, TASK FORCE VICTORY, VINT HILL FARMS STATION, VA

FROM: CDR, INSCOM, FORT BELVOIR, VA

SUBJECT: (TS) INTSUM REPLY TO RFO 231940Z FEB

1. (TS) IDENTIFICATION OF THE FOLLOWING IS BASED UPON INFORMATION FORWARDED BY TF VICTORY, 231940Z FEB:

2. (TS) SUBJECT NUMBER 1, IDENTIFIED AS SHABIL MOHEM, BORN 27 DEC 1967, BORN IN ASWAN, EGYPT AND STILL MAINTAINS AN ADDRESS IN ASWAN, EGYPT. IS A KNOWN ASSOCIATE OF MAREK ELAMESH, ASSASIN FOR HESBULAH. LAST KNOWN LOCATION, RHODOS, GREECE. CLAIMS TOUR DIRECTOR AS A PROFESSION. WAS SEEN WITH JAMIL HARLEQUIN ON THE DAY OF THE CIA SNIPER INCIDENT. JAMIL HARLEQUIL WAS THE IMPLICATED ASSASIN BECAUSE WE COULDN'T IDENTIFY MOHEM AT THE TIME. SHABIL MOHEM IS SUSPECTED WITH A 98.367% CONFIDENCE INTERVAL OF BEING THE ASSASIN RESPONSIBLE FOR THE CIA ASSASINATIONS IN 1996.

3. (TS) SUBJECT NUMBER 2, IDENTIFIED AS JAMES MCNAUGHTON. BORN IN READSVILLE, U.K., 2 SEPT 1974. MAINTAINS AN ADDRESS CYPRUS. LIST OCCUPATION AS TOUR DIRECTOR. KNOW ASSOCIATE OF MAREK ELAMESH, ASSASIN FOR HESBULAH. UNDER INVESTIGATION BY INTERPOL FOR THE FIRE BOMBING OF TWO NIGHT CLUBS IN VIENNA, AUSTRIA WHERE 26 PEOPLE WERE KILLED, INCLUDING MILTON CLINE, THE DEPUTY TO THE US AMBASSADOR IN AUSTRIA. MR. CLINE WAS LEADING THE INVESTIGATION OF HESBULAH ACTIVITIES IN SOUTHERN EUROPE AND WAS SCHEDULED TO APPEAR TO THE HOUSE SUB-COMMITTEE ON ORGANIZED CRIME.

4. (TS) SUBJECT NUMBER 3, IDENTIFIED AS WAHOLM HURGHADA, BORN IN

TAMANRASSET, ALGERIA, 14 OCT 1964. LISTED ADDRESS OF ASWAN, EGYPT. FREQUENT ASSOCIATE OF SHABIL MOHEM. SOURCES INDICATE THAT HURGHADA IS THE RIGHT HAND MAN TO MOHEM. TRAINED WITH THE US FORCES AS A LONG RANGE RECONNAISANCE PATROL (LRRP) LEADER. DESCRIBED AS A MEDIOCRE LEADER WITH POOR SELF-DISCIPLINE AND A VIOLENTLY SHORT TEMPER. POOR PLANNER AND EXECUTOR BY THE US OFFICER IN CHARGE OF TRAINING LRRP FOR BRIGHT STAR EXERCISES.

5. (TS) SUBJECT NUMBER 4, NO POSITIVE IDENTIFICATION. GENETIC PROFILE SYSTEM USED FACIAL STRUCTURE AND BODY PORPORTIONS FOR COMPARISON. SUBJECT ETHNIC ORIGINATION FROM THE MIDDLE EAST, EGYPTIAN REGIONS, 86 PERCENT CONFIDENCE INTERVAL SUGGESTS EGYPTIAN NILE VALLEY. PASSPORT PHOTOS SCAN SHOWS CLOSE PROBABLE MATCH OF SHARM EL HESH, BORN IN LUXOR, EGYPT, 8 AUG 1967, ADDRESS LISTED AS ALEXANDRIA, EGYPT. OPERATOR'S REPORT FROM HUMINT SOURCES IN CAIRO LISTED SHARM EL HESH AS A SUSPECTED TERRORIST IMPLICATED ON THE JULY 1996 TOUR BUS AMBUSH IN CAIRO WHERE 12 EUROPEAN TOURISTS

WERE KILLED. NOTE: KILLED IN THE TOUR BUS ATTACK WAS HELMUT KAUFMANN, BUNDESBANK MINISTER RESPONSIBLE FOR LEADING THE BUNDESBANKS POLICY OF DENYING FOREIGN ORIGIN INVESTMENT WITHOUT SUBSSTANTIATED VALIDATION OF ORIGINATION BY THE GLOBAL BUSINESS RECOGNITION COUNCIL (GBRC).

6. (TS) SUBJECT NUMBER 5, AMANDA PRESTON PERRY, BORN 1 NOV 1933, LAAYOUNE, MOROCCO, CERTIFICATE OF BIRTH ABROAD, LISTS CLAIRISSE AND THOMAS PERRY AS PARENTS. BOTH WERE BORN IN ST. HELIER, JERSEY, THE CHANNEL ISLANDS AND WERE BRITISH CITIZENS ASSIGNED TO THE FRENCH-BRITISH COOPERATIVE COUNCIL BASED IN LAAYOUNE, MOROCCO. PERRY LIVED IN THE MOROCCO FOR 22 YEARS BEFORE RETURNING TO JERSEY IN 1955. U.K. VISA RECORDS INDICATE THAT PERRY HAS VISITED THE MOROCCO AND EGYPT EVERY YEAR IN MARCH SINCE 1955.

7. (TS) FROM COL TM, PENTAGON. MARAEK ELAMESH WAS IDENTIFIED BY OPERATORS IN ICELAND AS THE KEY OCCUPANT IN THE AIRCRAFT THAT DEPARTED WASHINGTON D.C.

8. (TS) MARAEK ELAMESH HAS BEEN IDENTIFIED AND LOCATED IN PARIS. LOCAL OPERATIVE'S OBSERVATIONS AND INTELLIGENCE CONFIRMS THAT HE HAS LEARNED OF THE LOCATION OF THE HARZ MOUNTAIN SITE. MESSAGE TRAFFIC INTERCEPTED EARLIER TODAY CONFIRMS THAT HE HAS BEEN DISCUSSING THIS INFORMATION WITH PARTIES ON THE ISLAND OF SOCOTRA, FEBRUARY 8. WE SUSPECT THAT THE MESSAGE IS DIRECTED TOWARD HESBULAH. BE ADVISED THAT THIS CELL ESTIMATES THAT THE HARZ MOUNTAIN SITE WILL BE TARGETED BY ELAMESH AS SOON AS HESBULAH APPROVES IT. HEBULAH CANNOT BE LOCATED AT THIS TIME. RECOMMEND THAT YOU TAKE ACTION IMMEDIATELY TO ELIMINATE THE CHANCE OF ELAMESH REACHING THE HARZ MOUNTAIN SITE. THE CHIEF IS STANDING BY TO IMPROVE THE DEFENSIVE POSTURE AT THE HARZ MOUNTAIN LOCATION BASED ON YOUR RECOMMENDATION. ANY ESTIMATE ON WHEN WE CAN EVACUATE PRINCIPLE FROM THAT SITE? WHEN DO YOU ESTIMATE DATA RETRIEVAL FROM JERSEY WILL BE COMPLETE?

9. (TS) POC THIS MESSAGE, MIDDLE EAST REGION CELL, DSN 772-1212 AND COL TM, PENTAGON FUSION CELL. THE CHIEF HAS BEEN APPRISED OF THE SITUATION AND HAS APPROVED THE RECOMMENDATION. GOOD HUNTING!

^^^^^TOP SECRET^^^^^

PROJECT VICTORY – EYES ONLY

Seth studied the message. His suspicions were confirmed. The Hesbulah organization knew of the Harz mountain site. They were also responsible for targeting the Naval Laboratory in Washington. Sean and Izz were silent as Seth thought about the actions required next. Seth also spoke into his radio for Mike's benefit.

"Gentlemen, the good Mrs. Perry was into this up to her neck. She obviously notified Hesbulah well in advance of our arrival. I don't think that they expected us so soon and sent in the amateurs. That would explain the arrival of the assassination team. The two that we met in St. Helier last night were just local inept goons that Mrs. Perry probably recruited. When they didn't check in, that raised a little suspicion and she notified Hesbulah. I'll bet that if we look around the airport. There will be a charter aircraft out there just in from the Middle East this morning. They had no time to set up, do any reconnaissance or checking. They made a big mistake of assuming that we were not expecting them and that we'd be sitting ducks. We need to get back there soon, before the reinforcements arrive. We have been successful at getting inside Hesbulah's decision cycle and we are briefly ahead of the game. Izz acknowledge the message. Tell them that we will move into to Paris and eliminate Hesbulah's point man before he can reach Harz. Tell them that we should have the information from Jersey within twenty-four hours. Here's the updated game plan…Mike you and I will head to Paris and find Elamesh. After we stop him, we should have a little more time to get the data back to Karl and get him back to the states. Elamesh seems to be pulling the strings for Hesbulah right now. My guess is that he is preparing an occupation team for Jersey right now. They made a big mistake, but that is the only one they'll make. We need to capitalize on it and do it quick. Izz, Sean, get back to the underground hospital and find out the secrets that it has to tell. Mainly, how do we get into the site and retrieve the data." Seth continued to outline the plans with his team.

"Mike how's the activity outside?" Seth prompted.

"Still quiet boss," Mike replied.

"Sean, you can call in the local authorities now about Mrs. Perry's misfortune, get the ball rolling with your contacts. That'll make it difficult for Hesbulah to do anything with discretion. There will be too many official investigators here for him to move about freely, especially now since he prematurely ended Mrs. Perry contract."

"Roger, Sir…I'll contact the local constables." Sean said without any hesitation.

"Izz, Sean, we'll let you make the trek over to the hospital. Scan the Mercedes and bring it into the hangar, use this as your base ops. We'll leave the remote sensor and communications package here inside. I wouldn't suggest using the hotel any longer. There are too many variables there." Seth concluded.

"Mike, you keep the watch. We'll unload in here and get the X ready to go. I'll give you a head's up when we are ready to open the hangar. Sean, Izz…let's get your base ops opened up."

It took less than 10 minutes for Seth and his team to set up the remote base inside the hangar on Jersey's Airport. They would now use Jersey as the base of operations because of the ease to monitor who was either on or arriving on the small island. Seth had filed the flight plans directly with the military liaison officer assigned in the Brussels's Flight Control Center. It was a direct and efficient link through his global satellite phone. The flight from Jersey to Paris would be less than 20 minutes. Seth did a quick mental time line and estimated that they would be on the ground in LeBourget in less than 30 minutes and heading for Paris' Quay de Louvre in less than 40 minutes. Marek Elamesh had about 1 hour left to plan his terror. But the plan would never be put into action if Seth was successful. And Seth's track record didn't leave much hope for Elamesh.

15

To Paris and Elamesh

"You are cleared for takeoff runway 27, maintain runway heading." The controller announced in a slanted British accent.

"Roger Jersey Tower, cleared for takeoff runway 27, maintain runway heading to 3,000 feet." Seth repeated over the aircraft VHF radio.

Mike was flying this leg and as Seth repeated the clearance, Mike was pushing the power up on the two big Rolls Royce engines that powered the X. Mike released the brakes on the strong, sleek machine. The rapid acceleration immediately pushed them both back into their seats as it shot down the macadam surface of Jersey's main airport runway. The aircraft climbed into the night sky heading toward the French coast. As it climbed Seth looked over his right shoulder out the side cockpit window at the hangar and the route back to the hospital. The tranquil, serene countryside of the seemingly peaceful island of Jersey disguised the actions that had taken place and offered no clue as to what was about to happen.

"Jersey Departure Control, we are level at 3,000 feet."

"Roger, climb and maintain flight level 210, you are cleared direct to destination."

Mike pointed the X skyward once again and directed the aircraft to 21,000 feet. Seth selected LFPB, LeBourget Airport, in the Flight Management Computer navigation system. The screen on the computer showed LFPB as their direct destination and computed time enroute. The X was level at 21,000 feet in less than 7 minutes and speeding toward

169

Paris at over 400 knots. Seth was on the aircraft's satellite phone arranging with the watch officer at the U.S. Embassy in Paris for logistical support originating at LeBourget. The short flight normally wouldn't have allowed for last minute coordination but every US military and state department office knew the code for immediate response.

Good Evening, United Stated Embassy, Paris, Major Plumb, this line is secure, may I help you? The aircraft was covering ground at the rate of 6 miles a minute. Seth figured her bureaucratic phone etiquette covered about 10 miles.

"Good Evening, Major Plumb, This is Colonel Seth Stephens, could you please arrange for a car for me at LeBourget in about 10 minutes?" Seth asked. He immediately summarized her type. She wasn't here for the right reason. She was an opportunist, one of the officer's that spent most of her time in and out of military schools "punching tickets" as he termed it.

She attempted to back pedal. This man Stephens, she thought, thinks he could call up here and get something. He obviously wasn't aware that there were procedures to follow.

"Who have you got on the phone Major Plumb? Asked the Director of Operations for the US Embassy in Paris, Colonel Pete Marchette.

"A Colonel…Stephens was his name I believe…he wants a car at LeBourget in 10 minutes. Can you believe this, ten minutes? It'll take me at least fifteen just to fill out the request." The overweight Major with a pretty face replied.

Marchette stopped reviewing the reports he held. He looked up over his reading glasses at Plumb. "If it is Colonel Seth Stephens, tell him it'll be there in 5 minutes." Colonel Marchette replied while he picked up the phone to call the duty officer at the motor pool.

"Sir, we don't have any paper work for this request and this is not the proper channels. If we set this precedent, everyone will expect it." Major Plumb replied.

"Tell him it is on its way Major and tell him now." Colonel Marchette said with a hint of anger in his voice.

"But sir…" injected the near insubordinate major.

"Tell him Major, tell him now! Directed Colonel Marchette in a more stern voice.

"Colonel Stephens your vehicle will be at LeBourget when you arrive." Sarcastically replied Major Plumb to Seth.

"Thanks Major, I knew you'd be very helpful." Seth replied with a little false excitement.

"Colonel Marchette, why did we buckle to this request, I mean a Colonel sir...I don't get that kind of handling when I make requests." Stated Major Plumb.

Colonel Marchette also knew the type of "officer" with which he was dealing. As a twenty-eight year Infantry officer, he had more experience as a war-fighter than this Major would ever imagine. He had commanded Ranger Battalions and Infantry Brigades in Grenada, Panama, Somalia, the Former Republic of Yugoslavia, twice in Iraq and Afghanistan. He had been wounded more times that he cared to recount leading damn fine soldiers. He knew what built character and it wasn't sitting in a classroom and being accepted to the French Staff College or attending Harvard on a military ride. He knew exactly how she had gotten where she was. It wasn't through her military aptitude.

He and Seth Stephens were cut from the same cloth and he had more in common than he and Plumb. He and Stephen's were the doers, the good horses that were worked because they achieved results; they were the men of action. Plumb, well, she was a sexual harassment or discrimination suit waiting for an opportunity. She'd play that card in a minute and he knew it. He also knew that he would not be the one listed as the defendant on that complaint. He was much smarter than that.

"Major Plumb you are a fine officer, but Colonel Stephens, he just happens to be the one with a little more responsibility than you and I right now.

The Flash message in the read file that we received last week, the one signed by the President, our Commander in Chief, in it says that his mission is of utmost importance and he will not be delayed, under any circumstances. It also says that every organization will immediately place prime emphasis to support Project Victory, which is led by Colonel Stephens. So no matter what you think because of all of your taxpayer bought education, you will simply have to be happy with sitting on the bench while the coach puts the best player in. Do you understand?" Silence and a contemptuous glare were all that he received from Plumb.

"Do you understand, Major Plumb? Colonel Marchette repeated his stern prompt.

"Yes sir," Plumb replied, once again bordering on insubordination.

Colonel Marchette felt good about all that he said; someone needed to start telling the truth, no matter how politically incorrect it was. The vehicle would be ready for Stephens and Thomas when they arrived and Colonel Marchette would make sure that they had all of the support they needed while they were in Paris.

Mike landed the sleek aircraft at LeBourget and taxied to the east side of the field were just as promised, their car was waiting in just under 25 minutes from the time that they had departed Jersey.

"Now that is service boss, what auto rental agency did you say that you were using? Mike said with his telltale sense of humor. "I like traveling with you Seth, I never have to wait in line and most of the time we get direct connection. Occasionally we do get shot at, but hey, it's a small price for convenience."

The aircraft was secured and Seth and Mike were on their way to the center of Paris. The traffic at this time of the evening was much lighter than normal and the covered the distance to the Hotel at Pont Nuef where Elamesh was staying in less than 15 minutes.

Seth and Mike checked into the hotel. As planned the operative tied to following Elamesh had done everything for them. The reservations were in rooms on both sides of and across from the room occupied by Elamesh. The keys to the hotel were left in the rear seat of the sedan left at LeBourget by the Embassy. It also had a recent picture of Elamesh and the current alias, a Mr. Indida Oran, the alias that he was using today.

"Our man is Monsieur Oran today, a.k.a. Marek Elamesh. We should have time to get there and prepare. The CIA says that he normally has dinner in the hotels restaurant at 2300 hours. That's one thing that we could get accustomed to huh Mike, dinner at 11?" Seth mused as he read the report.

"Yeah as long as it is followed by one I have already eaten at 1700." Mike replied.

"If we can bag him quietly, we'll turn him over to the CIA in Paris so they can ask him a few questions. We'll have to be thorough. If he has any chance to make contact with anyone, we could jeopardize the operation. If we could get information from him that helps us find this elusive Hesbulah, we could save ourselves a lot of time and effort. We have got to go through the wall on this side of his room to set up surveillance. That is our only option here, in order to make it as discreet as possible." Seth said as he discussed the option with Mike.

Mike got to work setting up the equipment in the adjacent room as Seth did the local reconnaissance of the hotel. Mike was working fast to install the surveillance camera. He grabbed the high speed, noise-suppressed drill. In less than 10 seconds he had gone through seven of the eight inches of stone and masonry that separated the two chambers.

He carefully re-measured the remaining depth. He couldn't punch through all of the way. That would leave drill dust on the holes other side and make it easier to detect. He wanted only a thin veneer of paint and plaster in place and he'd pull that through with a little suction. In less than ten minutes the micro-camera was in place and they had full view of the room through their monitors.

"He has pretty good early warning system on the doors and windows." Mike told Seth over the radio link between the two. "Seth you won't believe this, he even has the old empty coke can balanced on the room's door ledge."

Seth laughed to himself as well but out of all of the devices that he had seen over the years, it was one of the most primitively effective and very clever one. It provided a little extra assurance. Most techies used their infrared and sonic grids to keep a room secure. But most didn't think that the companies that designed them also designed the systems that would defeat them and allow some one unannounced entry to the room. It is just a part of capitalism. Why only capture half of the market when you can get both sides? The can balanced on the doors edge would fall after the door was jarred or even opened in the slightest. It was stealthy because electronic sweeping devices certainly wouldn't detect it and it was difficult to see because of the can's paint scheme when viewed through the black and white or green hued low light system monitor on the end of the hair thin fiber optic camera

Seth knew that he have to act soon and make this happen. The stakes in this game were too high. The people behind this didn't have cash flow problems and money was no object. This was the last fight; the winner would take it all. He knew that this man was a hardened killer and would do what was necessary to meet his objectives. He had been in similar situations before and didn't like it. He would have to make sure that this man didn't get the chance to kill innocent people again.

Time was a luxury that Seth and Mike did not have. They had to find Elamesh, take him and return to Jersey before dawn. Hesbulah would be finalizing his plan to get to the Harz mountain site. They had to take Elamesh out of the equation and get as much information about Hesbulah as possible. Then they would have to get back to Jersey, get the data and give it to Karl before Hesbulah could act.

Seth read the folder from the American operative in France. There were several weaknesses that this Elamesh didn't take care of. He was operating without a counterpart and that made him vulnerable. His success had made him complacent. He felt invincible and that would be his fatal mistake. Everyone had to go to sleep sometimes. Without someone to check your six, you could be seen. If you could be seen, you could be killed.

The plan was simply. Wait for Elamesh to return to his room and intercept the meeting between him and whoever was bringing the information about the Harz Mountain site. Then both would be taken into custody and interrogated 'How ironic. 'The hunter now became the hunted. The roles can change very quickly.' Seth thought.

Mike was watching the camera that they had positioned to survey the hallways in both direction and cued Seth as Elamesh approached. Elamesh was casually strolling down the hall in a careless gait with one hand in his pocket fishing for the magnetically coded key card that replaced the bronze cast keys that were once used by the hotel years ago. He appeared to not be aware of his surroundings, but Seth knew otherwise.

Seth appeared to walk from the opposite hallway and haphazardly strolled down the hallway. Elamesh had seen Seth but was not suspect. Seth kept his head down as if reading the card for his room number while walking down the hall. But he had to make certain that this was there target. A face-to-face encounter would be necessary. He couldn't resist, he let one shoulder drop and at the right time slammed it into Elamesh as if by accident. Elamesh was more than surprised; no one had come this close to him in as long as he could have remembered. "Monsieur, Pardon," was all that Elamesh could eek out because of his shock. Seth looked at him with laser like focused eyes, glaring through him, sending him a message with only eye contact.

Elamesh's expression evolved from surprise to contempt. "You should perhaps be more careful, your carelessness may bring you harm some day." Elamesh said with direct eye contact to Seth in the same manner that two heavyweight boxers would, as they prepared to fight.

Seth fought back the strong urge to take him then and there, but there were too many variables. Some guest unaware of what was happening could easily derail the covertness of the operation.

"My mistake." Seth said. He made sure that Elamesh's hands touched his briefcase to verify Elamesh's identity.

Elamesh's first instinct was to pull his pistol and dispose of this common idiot who couldn't watch where he was going. But as he looked into Seth's eyes, his aggressive, murdering instinct was replaced with a fear that he only felt when he looked onto Hesbulah.

Seth immediately gained the moral ascendancy. He knew it and so did Elamesh.

Elamesh could say nothing more. He was as stunned as if he were looking death in the face. Elamesh turned and walked away toward his room as Seth maintained his position, watching Elamesh as he went to enter his room.

Seth would have preferred a direct confrontation. He was in the right place and could have dropped Elamesh with no hesitation. He restrained this desire.

Elamesh felt fear; but he didn't know why. It oozed from his pores in a nervous perspiration. This made him more nauseated. It was a smell that he had experienced before, before he killed an adversary. But he himself had never experienced this feeling before. Elamesh hadn't pulled a trigger in many years. He only managed the terror and used others to do his work. He tried quickly to shake off the fear, reminding himself that he was a powerful man. He mentally tried to reassure himself. He tried to bolster his immortality. He was one of Hesbulah leaders, how could he be afraid. There was nothing to fear. It was just a cocky American that didn't know who Elamesh was. "I should have killed the pig where he stood." Elamesh said out loud to himself as he shut the door to his room, making sure that the door was locked and the security measures were in place. He even re-balanced the coke can on the door. He turned toward the chair near the window where he would watch for his contact crossing the bridge at Pont Nuef across the Seine River. The man that would deliver the information that exposed the Harz site. Elamesh settled in his chair but not before he made one last look back at the door.

Seth moved to the room where he and Mike planned to wait until Elamesh would give an indication of the contact's location.

Marek Elamesh was trained by the best that money could buy. It probably was the same money that lured many of Seth's former team members to the negative, chaotic lifestyles of terrorists and murderers. One flaw was painfully evident though; he acted through rote memory, without the application of trained intellect. He was too careless, by coming back to this hotel again. He should have never fell into a predictable pattern. It allows for easy compromise.

Elamesh let down his guard. He was certain that the team he had sent to Jersey had killed Seth and the rest of this nuisance. Seth had seen it coming though and played the game through to allow him and his team some extra time. It was enough time to let Elamesh report back to Hesbulah and for NSA to trace his communications.

Elamesh had just sat down in the chair facing the window above the Sein River adjacent to the Quai de Louvre. As he sat in the overstuffed chair, his body was perfectly silhouetted from the lights just across from the police station on the opposite street side. He too was waiting.

Mike broke the silence. "The route down Quai de Louvre may be too open, and still too busy, I recommend Boulevard Sebastopol instead." Mike said after scanning their egress route back to the airport.

"And here comes the man with the information. We won't have much time." Mike said as he watched the man that Elamesh waited for cross the bridge at Pont Nuef.

"That's about as ironic as it gets Mike. Leaving and going past the Palais de Justice down Boulevard Sebastopol," Seth said perceptively. "We are going right by the police station. We could probably just drop the two off there."

"Uh, he's looking at his watch Seth. He's definitely expecting someone. Look at that on the bridge, right there, second light post from the end. Could be the contact Seth." Mike said as he followed Elamesh's stare. "Seth, he's dialing his cell phone. If the person on the bridge answers, my guess is that is your man, er, uh my mistake, it's a woman. You seeing this Seth?

Seth was looking at the enhanced image of the suspected target on the bridge, he wasn't certain but it looked like the same captain that was in the Pentagon the morning that the Naval Lab was destroyed. "I see it Mike.

Seth made the call to the CIA team. "Your target is on the bridge, second street light from the end closest to the hotel. Make sure you have all egress routes covered – we can't let her get away."

Mike saw her answer her cell phone. "Seth, she's the one! I've got a link between her and Elamesh right now. We'll get this conversation completely on tape." Mike said almost at the same instant she began to speak.

"Outside exits are still clear, still no one in the hallways." Mike reported after checking the perimeter and turning on the system to capture the conversation.

"Roger, plan to move in 10 seconds." Commanded Seth.

"Perhaps today will be the day, Elamesh." Seth said almost loud enough for Elamesh to hear.

Elamesh turned his head and positioned his arms to push himself out of the chair. Seth was watching the monitor intensely, ready to make his move as soon as Elamesh was halfway to the door to walk out and meet the contact on the bridge.

Suddenly, Elamesh's head jerked back, almost snapping it from his shoulders. Seth saw the glittering and shimmering tiny pieces of glass fly around Elamesh's room. He new exactly what had happened.

"Team one, move now, move now! Seth shouted into the radio commanding the CIA team to move in and apprehend the contact on the bridge. It was too late, as soon as he moved his attention to the monitor that contained the image of the captain-turned-traitor on the bridge, he saw her head jerk back twice in rapid succession.

Mike was studying the image and saw her legs buckle from her. He too knew what had happened.

They both bolted out of the room to get to the contact that had just fallen on the bridge before the information fell into someone else's hands.

The projectile fired from the tower Saint Germain took less than one-half of a second to cover the distance. The entry angle was nearly 100% perfect to cause the most damage. As it impacted the outer layer of skin on Elamesh's neck, the skin responded by tightening to prevent puncture. The distortion gradually widens as the projectile applies it full force to the elasticity of skin and tissue. When the limits of elasticity are reached, a tear appears. The hole in the flesh first is small and then widening to accept the full dimension of the intrusion.

The next layers of muscle and visceral tissue also mimic the outer layers. Once the projectile has penetrated these barriers, it grotesquely distorted itself because of the impact. Now full of jagged and pitted edges, it spun and ground like a drill through the visceral barriers. As it bored its way into the carotid artery, it created a surge of high-pressure blood in the artery that forces the blood past the tiny tissue feeding arteries in the eyes, ears, nose and mouth. Blood and fluid immediately flowed from these any orifice. The tissue behind the projectile was irreparably damaged and could not constrict enough to contain the flow of blood. The newly created orifice accommodated most of the expelled blood and fluid and it arched far beyond what it is normally capable of under normal body induced pressures.

The projectile struck the body initially at a force of 8,000 pounds per square inch. Most of this force was transferred to the fluids as they moved from the localized impact area just as rapidly. The body could not contain the hydraulic force of the fluid's pressure. It simply sought the path of least resistance.

Elamesh'e eye sockets were one of the least resistant paths. The force of the increased fluid pressures pushed his eyes from his skull, while a cascade of blood and fluid erupted from the sockets. His eardrums expanded far from their normal position until the explosion sounded like a plastic bag being filled with air and slapped with a hand.

The projectile, still maintaining most of its force twisted and tore through the larynx about the same time Elates screamed out with agony. The nerve impulse commanded the lungs to let out a bellow of air past the vocal chords in the larynx. The already severed vocal chords could not vibrate to produce a scream. This blast of air only forced more of the free flowing blood into the opening as it splattered in an arc from the newly created wound. The projectile continued into the cervical vertebrate. The impact snapped his head over toward the entry point touching his shoulder and separating the vertebrates. This first high impact with the side of the cervical vertebrate created millions of tiny fissures in the projectile's metal and it retained only enough energy to cut the spinal nerve chord into two ragged and torn pieces as it spun widely out of balance. It finally met too much resistance on the opposite side of the vertebrate and shattered into tiny pieces.

Elamesh's brain maintained enough awareness to feel the explosion happening inside his head. At first he felt no pain. The body tries to delay the feeling of pain and it appears to take almost twice as long as other feelings inside the body because the impulses have travel to the brain, trigger another response and send it back to the area. Tactile or pressure sensations only have to make half the journey. They simply send the message to the brain. Elamesh only had an awareness of pressures that felt like his head was being heated and filled with high-pressure air. The grinding and penetrating of the projectile first felt like a hot, dull drill bit being pushed against his neck. He tasted the blood and felt the pressure on his eyes, from the inside out as they were forced from their sockets. The initial increase in pressure immediately caused him to see only a red curtain before him caused by the flow of blood through the viscous humor of the eye itself. This was followed by a shimmering distorted image as the cone shaped receptors lose blood flow we perceive and millions of shimmering lights twinkling inside our brains. He wanted to scream but never felt the vibration of the vocal cords. His brain began to shut down all activity by constricting vessels to maintain blood supply and pressure. All voluntary activity was first to go. He lost the ability to hold himself upright and slumped over in the chair. His bowels and bladder immediately relaxed. Urine and excrement flowed through their openings. His eyes, blown from the sockets momentarily regained the proper pressure balance and momentarily saw his shoulder from a completely new perspective as they dangled from their sockets, held only by the optic muscles and nerve. He wanted to grasp the side of his neck to pull away this incredible pain, but couldn't. He was no longer able to control his movements. He was only able to lie there, over the side of the chair. His body relaxed to form every contour that the chair offered.

Now in blackness, his last conscious thoughts were of his complete mortality. Unable to staunch the unconscious, last flow of thoughts, buried deep within the recesses of his mind, he experienced true pain. The thousands of murders, heinous human crimes and wrong doings, the victims of his evil and chaos, came to haunt him. These were the images he saw as he was folded over in this chair. Each and every one of his victims had their revenge. They all in an agonizing measure of slowness, in turn, hacked away at him causing pain that he couldn't imagine. He felt every part of his body burn with a heat-pain so intense that it radiated from his insides and gained strength only to burn deeper and deeper. In his subconscious, he laid, writhing in the intense heat-pain caused by an unforgiving subconscious that never forgets.

It was in this eternity of unconscious thought, where time is rational and does not belong. It has no bounds, no meaning. It was this, his personal experience of hell. It was an eternity he would not leave, as the evil played over and over in his mind, unchecked, because the conscious mind had no opportunity to tell him it was only a nightmare. He couldn't wake from this nightmare of hell. The endless sea of people hacking at him parted; they turned their attention away from him and turned to see him. They parted just enough as if to allow an unhindered view of the man standing their dressed all in white, holding a sword made of the most brilliant and gleaming metal, a thousand times more intense than the sun's reflection from highly polished gold.

"Perhaps today is the day Elamesh." Did this man, dressed in brilliant white holding the sword high above him speak the words?

"NO, NO, NO!" These were Elamesh's silent screams. The screams before the searing-heat-pain and hacking at his body started over and over again. There wasn't the conscious realization that this was an unchecked replay of events occurring in his life. Each face reflected the pain and suffering he caused that he had seen in agony caused by his design. It was an eternity, his eternity.

This memory would play over and over for Elamesh without end in his subconscious as his life faded. He no longer had any control over the events in his life. His eternal memories were made while he lived. These intense, heat filled, excruciatingly painful thoughts would last forever for Elamesh and as far as he knew now, there would be no relief and no end.

The marksman's bullet had done its job. This man, Marek Elamesh, was now experiencing the same painful and hideous death that he had brought to many. Only his would never end. It was justice for all of the suffering that he had caused the many men, women and children in his deplorable life.

16

Data Stored in Jersey

Departing LeBourget, February 24, 0110 hours

"Mike, we bought some time and that's all we did. Whoever assembled this information will be getting it to Hesbulah. By now Hesbulah has already chosen another stooge to find Karl and take him out. Hesbulah must have known that we were there. Jill Feller, our Hesbulah spy - Air Force Captain was in the loop and she knew may have known that we were heading to intercept Elamesh or did she? Unless her only mission was to collect the data about the Harz site and turn it over to Hesbulah. Mike, someone else is out here protecting the location of Karl and Harz Mountain. It is the only thing that fits; Feller would have been read on to classified information in the Pentagon only. We only knew that Elamesh was going to be here a few hours ago. There is no way that she could have found out about our mission to intercept Elamesh and get across the Atlantic into Paris to get the information. It has got to be someone sympathetic to Karl and his mission or else they would have taken us out too as we picked up the data from Feller's body. Would you mind taking this flight back into Jersey? I need to get some information back to Joshua McAdams." Seth asked as they pulled up next to the hangar at LeBourget on the north side of Paris.

"Not a problem, Sir. I'll get things rolling up front and you take care of that commander stuff." Mike answered sensing the intensity in Seth's voice.

The aircraft was rolling out of the hangar in less than 20 minutes. Mike called for the takeoff clearance and they were airborne soon enough and on their way back to Jersey.

Seth was in the back and reading the messages that were waiting for him as he logged on to the network.

DIRECTOR, NSA SENDS

TO: (TS) CDR, TASK FORCE VICTORY, VINT HILL STATION

SUBJECT: (TS) CHINESE-RUSSIAN-HESBULAH MEETING

1. (TS) MEETING BETWEEN DELEGATIONS OF THE CHINESE GOVERNMENT AND DELEGATIONS OF THE RUSSIAN GOVERNMENT MEETING WITH REPRESENTATIVES OF THE ORGANIZATION HESBULAH IN BELGRADE AGAIN. MAYBE IT IS POSSIBLE THAT THEY BELIEVE THAT LIGHTNING STRIKES TWICE.

2. (TS) OPERATIVES CONFIRM EXISTENCE OF THE TRANS ALTHAI MOUNTAIN RAIL LINK BETWEEN GORNO-ALTAYSK AND URUMQI. SUSPICIONS ABOUT THE SNOW SHEDS CANNOT BE CONFIRMED BY HIGH OBSERVATION TECHNIQUES. CONSTRUCTION OF SHEDS WITH HEAVY SHIELDING PREVENTS INFRARED SURVEILLANCE. WILL CONTINUE TO COLLECT INFORMATION ON TARGET AREA.

3. (TS) RAILWAY AND ROAD NETWORK SYSTEM FROM URUMQI CONNECTS 97% OF THE KNOWN MISSILE LAUNCH FACILITIES WITH THE RAIL LINE FROM GORNO-ALTAYSK.

4. (TS) YOU CONTINUE TO HAVE THE PRIORITY TASKING AUTHORITY BY THE DIRECTOR NSA.

5. (TS) SEND MISSION REQUIREMENTS TO DIRECTOR, NSA.

6. (TS) GOOD HUNTING.

JM

Seth talked to Mike over the intercom, "Mike, we'll be heading to Goslar and then Kazakhstan after we finish up in Jersey. If you have the time, put a flight plan into the Flight Management System from Jersey to Hanover. We have got to get that information to Karl Linder soon after we receive it. I believe that our time lines have just been shortened." Seth said as he reviewed the information carried by the

Fellers the woman that Elamesh would have met. The information was complete and described the location of the Harz mountain site near Goslar in detail. If Hesbulah had this information, they'd be racing against each other and whoever got to Linder first would win a major battle in this all out war.

The aircraft covered the distance in no time. Seth had just enough time to catch up on the events before the aircraft was on final approach to Jersey's St Helier airport. He quickly sent off a SITREP message to keep Joshua McAdams and General Woodsen up to date. He also requested that General Woodsen send a small covert defensive team to the area around the Harz Mountains. The information from Elamesh's contact would eventually reach Hesbulah and Karl and his men would need security unless they already had it.

As the near super-sonic jet taxied up to the hangar on the island of Jersey, Sean was opening the hangar door to permit Mike to taxi into it without stopping. The aircraft was in place and the hangar door closed hiding all traces of its presence on the island.

"I take it that you had a successful expedition." Sean commented as he entered the cabin door.

"It fell apart. Someone took out Elamesh and his contact before we could read the play. We have some work to do and we are racing Hesbulah to Harz Mountain. Let's pull in Izz from local security and brief the plan quickly, we haven't the time to waste." Seth directed.

The hangar was secured and the four headed off in the darkness toward the Underground Hospital. They moved in a loose over-watch formation, two up front leading and scouting and two about 100 meters behind providing surveillance with the Night Vision Devices. The communicated via the secure squad radios. Chances are that if Hesbulah had the information that was supposed to be delivered to Elamesh, he was already on his way.

"Sean, bring me up to date on the situation. Has MI5 maintained security on the site?" Seth prompted Sean.

"They have established local security and have local police have cleared the crime scene. The supervisor knows about the incident that we had with the gunmen in the hallway. MI5 has briefed him. They are briefing MI6 on the event as well, since MI6 has agents operating outside of the UK. The local Constable is an insider with the MI5 so he knows the protocol here. He won't leak the essential facts. The press has been reporting Amanda Perry's death as a suicide. She has no family left on Jersey. The press conferences have emphasized her despondency and recent visits to the clinic here for chronic depression. They have kept the area secured for us and I have verified that no one has entered the lower corridor through our remote seismic and acoustical sensors. Not even a mouse has been stirring through that lower hallway." Sean reported as they double-timed through the Jersey countryside.

"Good work Sean, alright gents, here's the situation recap. Hesbulah knows that someone is to close to his trail. Let's assume that he knows about us and is setting a few surprises out there. Move cautiously! The mission for tonight is to collect secreted evidence that the Enclave has been collecting about Hesbulah. We get into the tunnel, get the info, and get out. Here's what we can expect when get to the tunnel. Linder said that the people at the Jersey site have hidden the files and media that they used to record the information that they have been collecting about Hesbulah. They have destroyed the equipment in the cavern and themselves. The vault where the information is stored is cleverly hidden in one of the geothermal conduits. There are several valves that we must find and open them simultaneously. One of the valves controls the flow of super-heated water, the other the ocean water used as coolant. To keep one man from entering the vault, the valves are located in opposite ends of the underground complex. Mike and Izz will go to the one site and Sean and I to the other. Mike, your valve must be closed off initially to stop the flow of steam. Sean, our valve allows ocean water, which they used as coolant into the conduit. We'll need about 60 seconds of coolant flow before we can enter the conduit. Then we'll shut off the coolant flow and head down to the vault. The intense part is that we'll only have about six minutes to empty the conduit, cool it, get to the vault, open it, retrieve the data and get out before the super-heated water bypasses the shutoff valve and re-enters the conduit. The pressure building up activates a relief valve to allow the super-heated water by-pass the shut-off valve and flow back into the conduit. If anyone is trapped in there, they won't leave." Seth paused to think about what he said and shook his head in disbelief.

He continued, "We'll set up security and cover the east-west corridor entrances. Set up advance warning devices as soon as we enter the tunnel. I want to know if anyone is following us. I don't want this to take more than 30 minutes to get in and out. We'll use the knoll right here as an assembly point if we get separated. I set the security around the hangar to maximum. Do not cross the 50-meter barrier point without deactivating it. Any questions?" Seth finished his briefing as they crossed the knoll overlooking the underground hospital location and moved double time to the entrance.

Mike's voice broke over the radio, "Seth will we have enough time to verify the timing on the flow in the conduit? I've always felt a little sympathy for lobsters as they a dropped into the hot water. I'd hate to try and impersonate that act."

"You won't be in the conduit Mike, that's my job." Seth said as he commanded the team over the hill toward the entrance of the tunnel.

The team ingressed passed the local constable and made their way into the tunnel. The walls of the lower passage sealed from the public tours was coated with gypsum. The light played off the reflective surface in many angles casting an eerie reflection from the temple mounted halogen lanterns on their heads. Sean and Izz placed acoustic and seismic sensors at key locations as they proceeded into the passage.

They moved quickly through the passageway and were at the location where Linder had told them the entrance would be. Izz found the hole that they had drilled earlier and re-inserted the optic fiber. The view from the other side of the seemingly solid rock wall revealed the door slides area points and latch mechanisms that Linder told them about. A lever adjacent to the latch mechanism would allow steam pressure vented off the geothermal conduits to open the access. Izz traced the mechanisms latch point to a pressure plate on their side of the wall. Quick work with his survival knife outlined the plate that when pushed would open the door.

The team checked the airflow through their breathing apparatus before Mike pushed the plate inward. Seth gave Mike a quick nod. Mike pressed the plate.

The heavy, thick and solid granite door groaned in protest as the pressure increased to lift its mass upward. Izz reached around in his pack unconsciously to reassure himself that they had enough C4 explosive to open the door in the event the mechanism failed.

With the door opened to its fullest travel, the team verified what the horrible sight that they had scene earlier.

"The poor bastards." Sean uttered under his breath. Before them laid what appeared to be a several human bodies. Some were partially burned. Their flesh hanging from exposed bones. Some of the faces were burned on one side but seemingly untouched on the other. Seth and his team captured the images on digital imagery for later analysis. Seth surmised that the victims had happened on the passageway long ago as they explored the lower portion of the tunnel.

The bodies appeared to be relatively good condition so it was difficult to tell how long that they had been there. But the dust and accumulation around the entrance way suggested at least a decade. The microbe free air that supplied the tunnel in the same manner that supplied the Harz Mountain site would slow down any decomposition considerably. It was nearly as anaerobic as a hermitically sealed chamber.

"My guess is that they stumbled upon the passage and blindly entered it. If the team inside were suspicious for any reason they would have activated their defense systems. In this case, the vents of superheated steam, which would flood the airlock and cook the intruders trapped inside. The opening cylinders for the door probably couldn't build enough pressure because it was vented off into the chamber. The temperature of the small chamber was probably up to 500 degrees within seconds. The side of the bodies exposed to the vents cooked a little longer than the sides turned into the center. By the time they had thought about escape, they were already incapacitated." Seth guessed.

"Let's keep your head on a swivel gentlemen. I would rather us do the job well rather than end up well done."

As they proceeded through the inner door of the airlock system, Seth noticed how thorough the self-destruction was. The marble floors were now pitted and debris covered. The ornately chiseled and polished granite walls were chipped and cracking allowing the ground water to seep into the chambers interior. None of the hand crafted mahogany and teak furniture remained recognizable. The flame producing incendiary devices had done the job thoroughly. The passages were littered with debris that had fallen making their way through the rock-strewn passages slow. They were one minute ahead of their plan by the time that they had reached the intersection leading to the valves.

Seth looked at his watched. The team glanced at their watches to make sure that their watches were synchronized.

"This is where we part company gentlemen. It'll take about 3 minutes to cover the ground to get to the valve locations. If we can't communicate for any reason, plan on closing the respective valve in five minutes beginning on my mark." Seth and Mike started their clocks simultaneously.

Everything now would happen on a time schedule. Communications would only be needed if a contingency not thought about happened.

Seth and Sean moved quickly to the valve station next to the conduit. It was located in a recess that ran from ceiling to floor, about one meter wide and one meter deep. Sean was first to reach it. It appeared to be in good condition and undamaged by the self-destruct incendiary blast. Sean turned it a little just to make sure. Confident that they were on schedule, they glanced at their clocks. One minute and twenty seconds remained before Mike would have his valve closed.

Seth looked at the oval shaped hatch that entered the conduit. There was a very small site glass that contained an impeller that was spinning rapidly indicating the flow of the super-heated water coming from vents in the earth's crusts. The water was under tremendous pressure that allowed it to be heated far beyond the temperature at which it normally would boil. These conduits were the power source for the underground locations. They supplied the power that drove turbines for electric generators, applied force to hydraulic actuators, and heated the passageways closer to the surface. Mike's job was to close the valve that would shut the super-heated water off for several minutes. Sean would open a valve that would allow seawater in to cool the passageway to temperatures in which a human could survive. The super-heated water conduits could easily have reached temperatures from 800 – 1,000 degrees Fahrenheit and needed to be cooled before they could enter them.

Seth checked his watch the mark passed. Mike should have closed his valve now. Seth watched for the site glass turbine to stop spinning. It gradually slowed and then stopped.

"Great job, Mike." He whispered under his breath. Seth started his six-minute clock.

"Sean, open the cooling valve."

The site glass turbine slowly picked up speed and then spun rapidly indicating the flow of coolant. Seth had taken his hand and felt the conduit door. The temperature was noticeably cooler now that the coolant had done its job, but it was still very warm to the touch. He only allowed the coolant to flow for 40 seconds before he commanded Sean to shut the valve. He watched the turbine site glass stop and rapidly spun the screw type lock that sealed the hatch. As the hatch was opened, he peered into the conduit and immediately felt the blast of hot air that filled the conduit rapidly expanded to heat up the outer passage.

The temperature felt as if it had risen 100 degrees in the tunnel. He and Sean began to sweat. The sickening humid, hot, sticky air changed their environment so quickly that their bodies did not have time to physiologically prepare. Their pulses and respiration raced to maintain body temperatures. He forced the bile back from his throat as the nausea overcame him. Without skipping a step, he forced himself into the conduit. He could hardly see as the sweat poured into his eyes and around his mouth. The temperature of the oxygen stored in his bottle was beginning to rise. It no longer offered the cooling effect to his lungs that it did initially. The mask around his face seemed suffocating. The ambient air was so humid that it seemed that it did not contain enough air molecules. Seth switched his mask to 100 percent oxygen to stave of the hypoxic effects he felt. He checked his clock. He had four minutes and 40 seconds to go. Time slowed to an agonizing pace in the hellishly hot environment. He saw the outline of the vault recessed into the conduit. It was the only metal object on the right side of the wall.

He faced the vault and briefly studied the door exterior. The surface was covered with hundreds of drilled holes. To the right in a watertight box contained hundred of metal pins that fit perfectly into the holes. Seth remembered the instructions Karl had given him. He had taken four of the pins and outlined the Christian symbol of the cross on the drilled surface. He glanced at his watch; three minutes remained before the relief valve would open allowing the scalding torrent of water to flood the conduit. Seth grabbed the handle and pulled. The handle moved slowly but seemed to catch on something. Seth pushed harder. He would only have one chance at this. If he failed to enter the proper code with the pins the information would be lost forever. One code entry allowed one opening of the vault. He pulled harder, his body was pushed to its limits, and he would have to ask more from it. His heart raced and his respiration was coming in short, dangerously rapid, wheezes. He was staring directly at the door but could not see it. He recognized the impending indications of loss of consciousness. If he blacked out now, he would never see another day. The flooding super-heated water would boil his body until it dissolved. He was pushing human limitations to the absolute limit, far beyond those of a man with a weaker resolve. He never knew failure and he wouldn't let this win out. His head pounded in excruciating agony as he strained to open the door, maintain consciousness and his situational awareness in the suffocating extreme conditions of the conduit.

He felt the handle move centimeter by centimeter, until it was in the opening position. Seth reached in the blackness of the vault and grabbed anything that he could. He felt the three data storage canisters. In his mind, he felt as if he was moving quickly but in reality he was barely conscious. His body was now numb from the pain. His heart muscle was nearing failure, the electric impulses firing so rapidly now that they were on the verge of a chaotic unsynchronized pattern. He was stuffing the canisters into his backpack and was gradually losing his grasp of reality. Amidst the chaos that his body was creating, his eyes focused on someone at the end of the tunnel. It was a familiar face he thought, but he just couldn't connect the sight with a memory. He looked down and continued to fumble with the backpack straps. He was doing and undoing the straps. His mind was now acting on its last conscious command, repeating it over and over. He was beginning to become annoyed at this distraction. Why wouldn't she leave him alone? Why was she calling to him? Why wouldn't she... with the last ounce of reality gripping at him he forced himself out of the void of near unconsciousness. 'What was Elizabeth doing here in this hell?'

He snapped a look as if his mind was suddenly working again up in the direction where he saw Elizabeth. At the same instant heard the rushing torrent of water behind him. The temperature of the conduit began rising rapidly again. He glanced at his watch…he was over the six-minute limit. He began running as fast as he could force his atrophied muscles to move. His body was way over its limits. He was moving now on sheer will. He forced his mind back to reality and saw a light at the other end of the conduit. He kept moving toward it, away from the heat and hell behind him. He felt the pain as if thousands of razors sliced at his back. Pain brought on by the intensity of super-heated steam being released from water pushed too far above its boiling point. The steam rushed around him and was cooking him alive. He kept pushing his legs, one step after another, one after another. The light was getting brighter. He was almost there. He felt his last step and realized that he wouldn't take another. His mind had already asked his body to do what was far from possible.

Everyone is limited by physical abilities and Seth knew that he reached his. People distinguish themselves by how hard their minds can push their bodies. No other man could have mustered the drive to push his body as far as Seth did. With one last attempt, he pushed off his numbed legs toward the light in a superhuman leap. He stretched out his arms as far as he could to reach it.

Sean peered into the conduit and was shouting to Seth. He saw Seth fumbling with his pack. Sean could barely stand the heat coming from the conduit. 'This was it' he thought. No man could stand this. He felt for sure that this would be it.

Sean tried to reach Mike on the radio. The density of the rock walls prevented any reliable radio transmission. He couldn't imagine any man surviving this hell. The heat was so extreme that the rubber soles on his boots was softening and sticking to the rock floors. He couldn't touch the doorway any longer now; the temperature was burning his hands through the thick leather gloves that he was wearing. He kept his light in the tunnel and would until the last possible second. Maybe he could grab Seth's body as it was forced by on the torrent of water. Sean was beginning to feel the loss of consciousness effects wearing on him. He wasn't thinking clearly. He wasn't seeing clearly. He thought that he was watching, as Seth was half-walking, half-running, half-dragging his body toward the doorway.

The temperature was well over 180 degrees now in the corridor as the super-heated steam was blasting its way past the relief valve.

Izz and Mike felt the relief valve that allowed the super-heated water to flow back through open.

"Nothing more left to do here. Let's head back toward the intersection." Mike shouted. The ground rumbled as the steam and pressure building under them released itself. They moved on a run toward the intersection. Upon reaching it they did not see Sean or Seth and continued toward the conduit opening where Seth had entered to get to the vault. As they turned the corner, they felt the temperature rising rapidly. They sprinted toward the conduit opening, both imagining the worst. As they turned the last corner they could see the steam erupting from around the conduit opening and Sean lying with his head in the conduit. Sweat was pouring from their bodies as if they were trapped in a sauna on the surface of the sun. Mike grabbed Sean and pulled him from the opening.

"Make your way toward the surface with Sean, Izz." Mike commanded as he immediately looked back into the conduit and felt as if he was looking directly into hell.

He didn't expect to see what he did. Seth was in the air, arms out, flying superman style toward the opening. Mike reached in and with timing that was perfect, grabbed one of Seth's out-stretched arms. Seth felt the tug on his left shoulder as his numb body slammed to the ground. He felt the pull on his shoulder and looked toward the force pulling him.

Mike looked into the facemask and saw the wild, higher on one side than the other, characteristic smile that only could be Seth's looking back at him. With one last super effort, Mike pulled Seth from the conduit and slammed the hatch closed with the other in one complete motion. He was leaning with all the power that he could muster against the door and dogged the latch shut as the boiling torrent was seething around the hatch's edge. Both men's hearts were racing and almost synchronized with the wildly spinning turbine in the hatch's sight glass as it indicated the high-pressure super-heated steam flow.

They could only stare at each other without uttering a single word. Mike could see that Seth was alive but had taken the most that a human body could and still survive. Mike wasn't exposed to the life sapping heat as long as Seth was but it still was unbearably painful. Mike surveyed Seth's condition and took a canteen of tepid water from his pack and helped Seth drink several mouthfuls of the fluid. The heat from Seth's steaming clothes seemed to steam more as the ambient air now cooled and accepted the water evaporating from Seth's clothing. Seth's face and exposed skin around his hands were a deep glowing red. Mike knew that the flesh had been exposed to at least first or second-degree burns and hopeful nothing more. Seth began to show signs of life. Mike checked his pulse and respiration.

The pulse and respiration count seemed to reduce itself by half with each second passing.

Seth was moving his lips as if to speak. Mike listened closer. "Angel…an angel."

'What was Seth trying to say? What were the words Seth's hoarse voice was croaking out?'

Mike was taken back, and then it struck him. "I've never been called an angel before buddy."

Seth looked at Mike with a puzzled look. "Don't look at me like I'm the one who said it, you're the one that called me an angel." Mike corrected.

"You're not the angel! It was Elizabeth. I saw her here, leading me out of the conduit." Seth wheezed the words out. "She was standing by the hatch as I was losing consciousness. If it weren't for her, I'd have suffered a Maine lobster's fate." Seth smiled as he tried to get up. Mike offered his assistance to his weak, miraculously recovering friend.

"Easy boss, you've been nearly boiled alive. Wait until I get Izz back down here. We'll have you out in no time." Mike said as Seth pushed half against him and the wall to get to his feet.

"No time, we've got to get to Linder as fast as we can. Hesbulah is learning more about us with each minute passing. He may have already retraced our steps to Linder. We have got to go now."

Mike watched in disbelief as Seth regained his strength and stood on his own. He couldn't imagine any man surviving the hellish environment that existed on the other side of the granite that separated them. He shook his head in denial and tried to steady Seth as he made his way up the passageway toward the sun's light.

"Seth, you are driven like a man possessed. Slow down, we don't know how bad you've been hurt." Mike said with genuine concern for his friend's condition.

"No time to waste Mike, this may be the last battle we will fight. I don't want to be a no-show." Seth said. The conviction he felt was plainly evident in his voice. He remembered the thoughts of Elizabeth and smiled inside again. He reached around and felt the canisters that he had stowed in his backpack. He gave them a little pat for reassurance and hobbled up the passageway with Mike in trail.

They had cleared the granite slab that separated the lower passageway from the Underground Hospital and the Enclave's tunnels. Izz and Mike pulled the plate back into position and the heavy slab slide securely into place. They quickly covered any traces of the sliding stone and their entry tracks into what appeared to be a rock wall.

Izz and Mike watched with amazement as Seth and Sean checked their wounds and drank all of the water that they had with them. With each swallow of water Seth felt the strength returning to his body.

His face and hands stung like the worst case of sunburn imaginable, but he was alive.

He was alive because of the vision he had in the conduit of Elizabeth beckoning him toward the hatch leading out of hell. He knew one thing for certain; he'd call her when or if he made it back to Washington. If it was only for one thing, he wanted to thank her for saving his life.

17

Return to Goslar

Goslar, Germany, February 24, 1600 hours

The drive from the airport to an early dinner was uneventful and down time was what the team needed. It was one of those rare, late winter days in northern Germany where the sun was the only thing in the sky. There wasn't a cloud anywhere to be seen in any direction. Seth drove while his team relaxed, slumped over in the corners of the sedan. Mike, of course, was sound asleep. Mike could fall sound asleep on a moments notice. It didn't matter where they were, a five star hotel or an ambush position on the wait, this guy could sleep anywhere. Seth on the other hand was a light sleeper. He felt rested when he slept, if even for short naps, but would wake at the slightest noise.

They all deserved a rest. He had been driving them hard and they needed some rest and good food before they left for Kazakhstan. He figured he had about 48 hours before they would leave the peaceful German countryside that was offered by the vistas near Goslar.

"All right Gentlemen, we're here. Stand by for the best schnitzel that you have ever had. Schnitzel mit pomme frits und bier. You'll think that you have died and gone to heaven. For you Mike that is a probably as close as you're going to get." Seth said as he pulled the sedan that they had borrowed from the aerodrome's manager, Herr Sergeant Major Wegner Hoag, into the parking area of the Gasthaus Hildesheimer.

"Oooo, boss you're developing a fine sense of humor. That's encouraging, even if it is at my expense." Mike laughed.

"I don't think he was demonstrating a sense of humor Mike, I believe the boss was serious. Weren't you being serious boss? Izz said, while managing to keep a straight face.

"Seth, how did you know that this place existed? I can tell you from experience though that these hard to find, not well traveled places have the best foods. And judging by its remoteness, this place should be the best." Izz commented.

The four walked into the Gasthaus and were seated by the restaurant's owner. The restaurant was relatively empty. The few people that were there were undoubtedly from villages nearby. Seth purposely selected the location because it would have been a one in a million chance that someone would have known that they were going there to set up an ambush. They selected a window seat that allowed them an unrestricted overview of the approach avenues.

The head waitress approached their table. "Guten Tag, mein Gott, Du habe sehr schlecht sonnenbrand, mochten sie etwas… antiseptisches mittel?" The waitress greeted them looking at Seth's very red face thinking that he had a bad case of sunburn.

"Nein danke, Ich habe Mein personaliche Artze hier, veilen danke!" Seth replied, telling her that he had his personal doctor with him, putting his arm around Izz's shoulder.

The Frau laughed. He continued to order four beers and four orders of the schnitzel and pommes frittes. She took the coaster from Seth's place at the table and made four marks on the Licher Bier emblazoned coaster and disappeared into the bar and kitchen area.

The four made light conversation as they waited for their meals. They commented on the ornate woodcarvings that hung from the heavy timbers that stuck out from the plastered stucco walls and ceilings. The atmosphere of the Gasthaus was unmistakably German. It was the perfect atmosphere for a schnitzel and beer. Before the four had realized it, the waitress was around with another round of beer. Soon after, she delivered to them the largest schnitzel that they had seen. Seth swore that it was larger than he remembered. The meat hung over the sides of each of the four large platters. The French-fried potatoes were heaped in a single, family style, serve yourself bowl, placed in the center of the table. The seemingly fresh-picked green beans were served in the same manner and the bowl was also placed in the center of the table. Seth asked the waitress to keep the beer coming for his men. He would keep his senses and allowed his men to enjoy the schnitzel and beer. He felt relatively sure that they would make it to the Harz Mountains without any problems. If they had made it this far without meeting Hesbulah's men, whoever took out Elamesh must have delivered a reeling blow to

Hesbulah. It would take some time for him to recover. After they could eat no more, Seth asked for the bill from the waitress.

"Die Rechnung, bitte." Seth asked.

The waitress came to the table's side and tallied the total for the dinner for the four men. "Drei und neunsig, bitte." The waitress said as she finished her mental calculations.

Seth handed her one hundred and twenty Euros. The waitress instinctively dug into her small change purse strapped to her hip. Seth pushed her hand away gently and thanked her. He knew that no gratuity was required in the small towns away from the touristy stops in Europe. The old custom of the owner knowing that you enjoyed the meal was all that was required. The extra money that Seth insisted left the very traditional waitress blushing. She thanked all of the men and wished them well before she turned on her heels and headed back to the kitchen, loaded with empty plates and glasses.

The four left the Gasthaus almost unable to move because they had eaten so much. Seth took his place behind the wheel and the other three piled through the three remaining doors of the sedan. They headed down the two-lane highway that led from Hanover to Goslar. It would take Seth about 10 minutes to make it to the place were they would park the car on a street in Goslar and walk up the side of the mountain to find the entrance of Linder's cavern. Seth would wait until he was sure that no one was watching his moves before he would head to the entrance of the underground site.

It was late evening when they arrived in the town of Goslar. Seth drove in a convoluted route to a small side street where they pulled off the street into a small high-gated courtyard. Seth approached a farmer that owned the area and offered him 200 Euros to secure their car in his farm's courtyard. The farmer gladly accepted and shook hands with Seth. Seth and his team were getting the small backpacks out of the trunk as the farmer began pulling a large gray tarpaulin over the front of the Sedan.

"Now that is service. I've got to tell you guys, no matter where this guy goes he has people tripping over themselves to provide service even if it is the middle of the night." Sean commented.

"Now you know why I love to travel with him." Mike quipped, his quick wit unrestrained by a few tankards of German beer.

The team moved out of the courtyard through a different entrance and Seth called them into an over-watch formation.

"Sean and I will move first, Izz, you and Mike pick up a loose trail. We will double back a few times to make sure that our 6 o'clock is clear. I don't want to compromise the site's location. Stay awake and shake off the effect of those beers gents." Seth commanded.

"Roger boss, why don't we just call in the security force that Woodsen setup for us Sir?" Izz asked.

"Linder wants us to keep the site a secret until he has made his case to the United Nations and is sure that the information has been passed. He still remembers what happened during his brother's trip back to the states in 1945. Hesbulah got to him when they were under the strictest security. Basically if Hesbulah knows about you and can find you, you don't stay alive very long." Seth said straightening his back and reassuring himself that his 9mm and the canisters for Linder were still where he could get them, yet out of sight. "Linder and his group have given up many freedoms to keep their watch on Hesbulah. At the very least we can respect their requests." Said Seth as he adjusted his pack's straps and continued on.

Seth and Sean moved at a quickened pace through the village and out of Goslar up into the foothills of the Harz Mountains. There weren't any volksmarchers this late in the evening through the pine forest. Seth wondered if Karl and any of his group have ventured out into the local villages or if they truly had been secluded for the last 60 years. It would take incredible self-discipline to remain in relative isolation with so much natural beauty surrounding you. The fresh pine smell was carried by a light breeze. The feel of the carpet of pine needles that covered the sandy path made the walk effortless and silent. Out of the corner of his eye he caught a movement and froze so he wouldn't draw the same attention to himself. Out from behind a tree came a man and woman holding hands. They walked toward him not yet noticing them as they carried on their conversation. They were completely consumed with each other and did not seem to notice Seth until they came to within several meters of his position.

Izz and Mike saw the two people approach Seth. They maintained their watch with their weapons discreetly at the ready. Sean watched the approach from behind a small shrub and wasn't as concerned with the pair until they came closer. They nodded at Seth and continued on their way following the contour of the hill and not any path or trail. Seth returned the nod and pretended to review a map of the area. He cursed himself for allowing himself to be surprised. If it were an ambush set up, he'd have walked right into it. He reminded himself that although he had been here before and had met with Linder, this was not a safe area. The dangers were more real now than ever and couldn't let his guard down.

Sean approached Seth's position. "Something's not right about those two. Did you notice the shoes, the coat and scarf? They were straight from the 1940s; even the ladies gloves were something that I've only seen in my grandmother's attic. The two people weren't that old but, unless we have changed fashions in the last week, clothing like that hasn't been the trend in Europe since the end of the World War II."

"Sean, I can tell you all about it, but just wait. You'll see more than you'll be able to believe here in a few minutes. Seth said to Sean just before he keyed his transmitter to talk with Mike and Izz.

"Mike, Izz, do you still see the two that passed my position, they have got to be from the site. I'd say they are the reconnaissance element. Let them pass if they see you." Seth called over the radio.

"Negative Seth, they disappeared around the curve of the mountain. Do you want us to reposition to observe? Mike returned.

"Negative, position yourselves to provide a good over-watch." Seth commanded over the radio to Mike and turned to Sean, "Let's keep moving, the entrance is just over the north side. Hopefully we won't have any more surprises."

The moon was just breaking low on the western horizon and the tall pines reduced the amount of ambient light that was available as they reached the cavern's entrance. Seth and Mike remembered the place. The cavern entrance was near a huge outcropping of jagged rocks and large boulders strew at the bottom of a nearly vertical, but irregular face reaching over 25 meters high from the floor of the sharply contrasting gentle slope. Tall pines and shrubbery that seemingly grew from the sides of the rock surface masked it. Seth remembered the entrance location and climbed quickly to a ledge about 5 meters up that prefaced a crack between to large boulders. He pulled a small light from his pockets and pointed it into the area that disappeared into the void. He first examined the ground leading into the void. It was difficult to determine if anyone had been there recently because the surface was gravel covered and revealed no footprints.

Mike and Izz were just cresting the top of the outcropping by skirting it along the west side where the slope was somewhat gentler. They had established a commanding over-watch position and could see all approaches leading from the lowlands up the north side of the mountain.

"Seth, we're positioned. There are no signs of any observers. Not even the two we had seen earlier." Mike reported.

"Roger Mike." Seth acknowledged. Mike and he had discussed earlier the procedure that they would use to determine if they were followed. Mike and Izz maintain their over-watch until Seth returned to the ledge and recalled them from the over-watch. If Seth didn't return within 50 minutes, something was drastically wrong and they were to escape and evade back to Hanover and contact Joshua McAdams.

"Sean, cover the entrance while I attempt to contact Herr Linder." Seth commanded. We don't want to come here unannounced and turn up like our friends in the antechamber in Jersey, a little over done for me."

"Nobody more than I wants to make sure that we don't repeat that mistake. I have been overheated once too many times this week already." Sean commented.

Seth walked past the entrance where Sean was positioned just inside and proceeded about 10 meters to a point where the cavern narrowed to just a small opening about one meter square. Seth dropped down and crouched to make sure that the way was clear before he proceeded. He passed the restriction and was inside a small chamber with no other visible exits other than the one he just came through. The floor of the chamber was covered with gravel ranging from one to two inches in an irregular diameter. He switched his transmitter to a very low power setting and a designated frequency that would be picked up by a hair thin antenna that was running through a natural fissure in the rock face.

"Gruss Gott, Meine Damen und Herren." Seth waited for a response. The time seemed to pass slowly but he knew that he dared not open the outer passage without announcing who he was.

On the inside, Karl Linder was called to the transmitter. "Gruss Gott my friend, we have been waiting for you. I see you have three friends with you today. Please come in through the outer doorway once you have assembled your friends."

"It will be good to see you again Karl, please allow us 10 minutes sir." Seth responded over the radio. Now knowing where the man and woman that they had seen earlier in the forest had gone. Seth retraced his steps back to where Sean was covering the entrance. He switched his transmitter back to the squad frequency.

"Mike, move to our location." Seth directed.

"Roger, nothing observed." Mike returned.

"See anything out there Sean?" Seth asked.

"Nothing Seth, only a few hares are moving around out there. Everything cleared for us on the inside?" Sean asked.

"We have been cleared. I only hope that it still is Karl Linder on the inside and not just his voice." Seth answered.

It only took Mike and Izz five minutes to move down the hill above the entry point and climb to the ledge where Seth and Sean were located.

"Okay, just to be cautious, Sean and I will move into the inner chamber. Mike, you and Sean will stay out here to cover the entry and Izz and I will make sure that the Karl Linder and his group are still in control on the inside. We have come to close to take any unnecessary chances this far. If it isn't Karl on the inside, E and E back to Hanover and report to Joshua McAdams. Hopefully, we'll see you in a few minutes." Seth said as he handed Mike the backpack containing the canisters.

Mike moved to the entrance to continue covering the team as they passed into the Karl Linder's cavern.

Seth and Izz found the pressure plate that would open the outer door. They stood clear of the irregularly shaped outline that looked to be several connected cracks in the rock wall on the right of the plate. Izz waited for Seth's nod and pressed the plate.

"I always wanted to say this...open, says me!" Izz said with a wizard's deep-set falsetto. It took about 80 pounds of force to move the plate inward. The irregularly shaped outline to the right of the plate moved inward about 15 centimeters before it slid to the side.

Seth peered inside the chamber looking for any signs of a trap. "I guess this is our invitation Izz." Seth said looking at Izz.

"After you boss," Izz replied.

Once they were in the chamber they proceeded to the second pressure plate and repeated the drill. This time the outer door closed and nothing happened for several seconds. Seth thought that if it wasn't Linder and his crew in control of the site, Seth and Izz were about to be baked. Seth began to turn to the wall adjacent to the door about to depress the pressure plate that would re-open the door that just closed; the inner door began to move. Seth and Izz faced the door with their guns drawn.

Uniformed men immediately surrounded them with machine guns leveled at their midsections.

"Hand over your weapons immediately please. We are pleased that you have returned Colonel Stephens. Do you have the canisters?" The leader of the force said with a heavy German accent at the same time leveling his Luger pistol at them.

"Unfortunately, I don't. They are on their way to the United States as we speak for analysis." Seth said glaring at the pistol-armed leader.

The group was staring at the two Americans with their weapons ready to fire.

"Das genug, danke! Came a voice from the rear of the group. Seth expected the group to begin firing, but instead they lowered the weapons.

Seth was startled to see Karl Linder making his way to the front of the crowd. He had a somewhat look of surprise on his face.

"I'm sorry for the very rude welcome my friend." Karl Linder said as he was reaching around Seth's shoulder with one hand and grabbing Seth's hand with his other in an elated welcome. "I am very glad to see you Seth. Please understand that we cannot afford to be careless now. We are very close to disclosing the one family whom has been the foundation of everything counter to peace that we have experienced throughout the world." Karl was turning to take Izz's hand; Seth took the opportunity to introduce Izz.

"Herr Linder, this is Major Irizzary Diconcerio.

"It is my pleasure to meet you Major Diconcerio. Welcome to the Harz mountains. You have joined a great cause." Karl Linder said with a heart-warming smile and penetratingly sincere eye contact.

"The pleasure is mine sir. By the way, my friends call me Izz. I'd be pleased if you would." Izz said with and enthusiastic smile and equally warm handshake.

"Seth, I would like you to meet my nephew, Peter. Peter this is Colonel Seth Stephens." Karl said as he presented Peter to Seth.

"It is a pleasure to meet you Peter." Seth said with a quizzical look.

"I must apologize for the welcoming that I had arranged. We now know that Hesbulah knows of our existence and will stop at nothing to destroy us. My uncle has spent his life developing the intelligence background on Hesbulah and his family. If Hesbulah has found out about our research, I'm afraid he would direct all his energies to destroy all that my uncle has discovered. He would attempt anything to keep his mission and agenda intact, including an attempt to impersonate you." Peter said with a completely different look than he did when he was leveling the pistol at Seth's chest.

"It is understandable, for those same reasons I had two of my team mates remain outside while we verified the situation inside here." Seth said as he noticed the security force that had assembled for the welcoming begin to disband and move down through the central corridor. Izz was attempting to take it all in but was astounded by the details and materials used in the construction.

"Seth, forgive me for being so direct but the majority of the data that I require is contained in the canisters that you had retrieved from the Jersey site. The sooner I have my staff begin analyzing and translating the information the better. They can begin reducing the information while we have dinner this evening. My nephew and his wife will join us if you don't mind. I would like him to accompany me to New York when we present the information to the United Nations." Karl said. Seth noticed that Karl was beginning to feel the relief that comes from knowing that the end of the mission is in sight.

"Let me get the rest of my team. They have the canisters outside with them." Seth said as he proceeded to the pressure plate area.

"Of course Seth, with your permission, I would like to assemble the security force again. Please explain to your colleagues that I normally do not greet friends in this manner. Karl said as he turned with Seth to the entrance door. He quietly gave several instructions to Peter; they spoke in perfect English to not offend Seth or Izz.

Seth looked to Karl before he depressed the inner door control. Karl smiled and nodded in approval. He opened the door. It took less than five minutes for Seth to escort Mike and Sean back into the main corridor. They exchanged introductions and Seth took the backpack that contained the canisters from Mike.

"Herr Linder, here are the canisters from Jersey. The were contained in exactly the location that you described to me when we first met." Seth said as he handed over the canisters to Karl.

"I have since spoken with Mr. Joshua McAdams. He is standing by for instructions as to when and how you would like to move from your location to New York. There are only eight people that know that you will be going to address the UN The four of us here, Our President, Joshua McAdams, the Director of the NSA, General Maxwell Woodsen the Joint Chief of Staff, and the Director of British Intelligence, Brigadier Thomas Watson. I have met and know them all and can promise you that they will use any means necessary to bring the reign of Hesbulah to an end. As soon as you leave, I have a brigade of US Army soldiers staged to secure the compound here." Seth said as he handed the three canisters to Karl.

Karl accepted the canisters as if the were very fragile and Seth could almost feel Karl begin to breath again once he had touched them. Karl handed the canisters over to Peter who in turn walked with two assistants down the corridor to begin reducing the data.

"So, please, business is finished and now we shall eat." Karl said as he acted as the tour director while walking to the dining room. He covered as much of the history of the caverns as he could in the fifteen-minute walk and shuttle ride to the dining area.

Seth didn't tell him that they just stopped in a Gasthaus on the way to Goslar and gorged on Schnitzel and beer. The four listened intently as Karl described the underground paradise. Although Mike had been here before, he hadn't seen this part of the cavern and was astonished by the construction as well as the detail that had gone into the building of the cavern. The cavern was brightly lit in some areas with a light that was as close to natural sunlight as any of them could imagine. Plants and trees grew around marble finished pools. They swore that they could get a suntan in one of the recreation pool areas. Music and sounds of birds and nature flowed through a very sophisticated sound system that neither of the four could tell where the speaker systems were located. The polished marble floors and walls would gradually taper off to natural rock walls were wetted by the relaxing sound of ground water trickling down into a very well designed and ornate drainage system and more austere illumination. The transitions from one style of décor and ornamentation flowed perfectly. Everything was subtle, the detail perfect and intricate. It was an underground paradise, completely self sustaining and efficient.

"Will you be staying until we are ready to go to New York?" Karl asked as the turned into the dinning room. Seth was beginning to answer but stopped short when they turned through the large wooden double doors that opened into a palatial dining room. Seth tried to downplay his bewilderment and casually answered.

"With your approval Sir, I would like to allow my team the opportunity to rest for a few days. As you are probably aware, we are leaving for Kazakhstan. We have a difficult task ahead of us to help prepare for your briefing at the United Nations." Seth said.

"Seth, you are all welcomed to remain as long as you like. We don't have guests very often and we would enjoy your company for as long as you care to stay. What exactly do you plan for this mission Seth?" Karl asked with genuine concern and sincerity.

"We are going after Hesbulah Karl." Seth said. The gravity registered deeply on Karl's face.

The strained pause was broken by the food and drink delivered by young women dressed in dirndles and apple blossom hair decorations. "My home land is not Germany. I was born and spent the first twenty-two years of my life in Austria, near the village of Schaffenfeld, near Amstetten. We try to keep culture and refinement a part of our lives here. The women that you see are wearing the same traditional dress that you would have seen in Austrian dining rooms 60 years ago." Karl said.

"Forgive our stares, but we didn't see everything when we first met. The lifestyle that you have created here is magnificent. I couldn't imagine building what you have here. It is impossible to describe how fantastic it really is." Seth said that as the other three could only nod their heads in affirmation of Seth's statement.

"I must ask the question and forgive me for being so direct. We are seeing people that are very young. How many generations live here in the Harz mountain site, what is the population?" Seth asked.

Immediately the men seated at the table stopped everything and gave Karl their complete attention.

"There were initially many very intelligent people that were assigned to the site in 1943. Most considered brilliant savants by today's standards. We weren't all intelligence officers, as a matter of fact; there were only twenty-six intelligence officers. Others were doctors, nurses, educators, scientists, engineers, chefs, artists and musicians. We were sent to be self-sustaining and each of the enclaves was to carry the essence of Germany with them. Hitler wanted to preserve the best that Germany had to offer in puritanical groups. Hitler was a terrific optimist and also very pragmatic. He realized that if the allies won the war, German society would suffer. So he combined groups of people that could carry the essence of the German culture to a huddled populous after the allies had won and allowed Germany to begin its rebuilding. Hitler didn't want to leave to chance those who would remain. The program was very secret. Only Hitler and his top three leaders knew of the operation throughout its inception. Project Neutag, or New day, included 30 locations throughout the world. In Europe we were assigned to these underground locations. In other lands, people were sent to Australia, South Africa, America, South America, and Central America. Two thousand, one hundred young men and women, the modern day equivalent of Noah's Ark spread throughout the world in the spring of 1943. We were volunteers from Germany's heartland and we believed in the best that Germany could offer, not its war making ability. We were given unlimited resources and we prepared for what you see here. Our mission was one to survive and begin rebuilding. The isolation took on a different meaning though, once we weren't restricted to Hitler's propaganda, we began to see the world from a new perspective. We began to realize that Hitler was using Germany to advance not Germany but his agenda. He had the momentum and he had the enforcement. He crushed any ideas not loyal to his view of the world. The designated leader of the entire group of us was my brother, Field Marshal Doctor Robert Linder. He soon began to realize, as we all did how terribly corrupt Hitler's doctrine actually was. We realized it soon after he singled out the Jews for isolation and containment. We also discovered that he was secretly meeting with Hirohito and Hesbulah. That was what began Robert's redirected intelligence efforts. We used all of the resources that we had available, including a very advanced communications network that is still intact today. We aren't as fast as a modern digital system but we can link our enclaves, communicate requirements and situation updates overnight with an analogue system. Robert designated the Jersey location as the central location because of its data storage capability, isolation and accessibility. We could travel to any part of the world without drawing attention. A ship or submarine could pull up to an isolated shore or port on Jersey and we were within walking distance from the Underground hospital's location. The Harz mountain site was the most difficult for outsiders to get to. Since we were closest to Berlin, we received the most of the resources as the war started to turn against us. Robert naturally designated this sight as the secondary site.

Seth looked up as Peter and his wife were walking through the doors leading into the dining room. The four stood as the two approached the table.

"I do apologize for holding up your dinner gentlemen. I wanted to wait until our technicians examined the metallic ribbon to verify its condition. Wonderful news, all of the information is retrievable. It is in perfect condition. Helmut is re-printing it as we speak. He estimates that he will have all of it printed within 72 hours." Peter reported the news to his uncle.

Mike was the first to notice then everyone did. The eyes of the elder Linder began to well up as he smiled. "It is wonderful news. We are a step further to bringing peace to the world." He reached a crossed to Seth first and the all in turn, shaking their hands and thanking them for delivering the data to him. "You are the archangels of the world today, delivering news that will bring an end to over two thousand years of a designed evil present here on earth. Thank you! Soon we can all leave the cavern and live again in the sunshine and snow that only can exist in the mountains of Austria. It will be a great day, soon, very soon." Karl displayed the emotions of true joy and paused to clear his throat and wipe his eyes.

All were quiet and focused on Karl Linder. Seth and his team did not mean to stare, but they were only now beginning to comprehend the devotion that Linder held, along with all whom had worked on this project for so many years, to remain singularly focused on this, the problem of eliminating the influence of all evil. Peter's wife sensed the need to say something. It was an awkward moment for the men, not knowing who should break the tension of the moment.

"I would like to introduce myself, I am Elke Linder. Seth Stephens is it? I have heard many things of you Seth. It is my pleasure to finally meet you." Elke said offering her hand to Seth.

"Please forgive me. Elke this is Colonel Seth Stephens, Major Izz Diconcerio, Major Mike Thomas, and Major Sean MacLowre. Gentlemen, Elke Linder." Karl said regaining his social astuteness.

As the four returned the pleasure of the greeting they began to re-seat themselves once Peter had assisted Elke to her place at the table.

"Sean, your accent indicates Scottish heritage. How is it that you have come to join these Americans?" Elke asked. Her mannerisms and distinctly perfect English indicated only a glimpse of her intelligence and charming disposition.

"I would like to think that I was asked to join to help the team succeed. But, they need no help at all. I now have just taken the position to learn." Sean said, remembering how he almost caused a failure in the tunnel at Jersey.

The conversation remained light as they enjoyed their dinner together. Every subject under the sun was covered lightly. Seth enjoyed the discussion and couldn't help but think of Elizabeth when he looked over at Elke. She, like Elizabeth, was a perfect lady.

The meal was magnificent. As the conversation pursued the late hours of the evening, everyone realized that everything happened for a reason and their reason was plainly obvious. They must not fail in this mission.

"The hour is getting late. We should allow our guests some rest. Perhaps we can continue this conversation during breakfast." Karl said chuckling.

Seth remained with Karl as the others left the dining room. "Karl, we think we know how Hesbulah is going to conduct his next attack on his terror agenda. He has been sponsoring meetings with the Russians and the Chinese in Belgrade and Urumqi. I believe that he is buying Plutonium from the Russians and using it for high technology missiles that he has based in the remote regions of China. He has coerced many corrupt politicians into joining his side. There is a meeting scheduled tomorrow in Belgrade, with any luck Joshua McAdams will send a strong message that we make both sides reconsider, or at least delay their progress until you can brief the United Nations. Hesbulah has acquired the latest developments for warhead and delivery vehicles from the United States. We have tracked the stolen secrets to China. Satellite evidence shows that the corrupt Chinese sponsored a rail connection initiative crossed the Althai Mountains. My team and I will go to Kazakhstan, cross the border to Urumqi and Qitai and gather the hard evidence that we can use to build a coalition to launch strikes on Hesbulah's sites in China. We want to present this evidence simultaneously because we need to have the good people of Russia and China on our sides. If we don't, we could face the nuclear holocaust that we averted years ago with the Russians. I believe that after the meeting goes off tomorrow as planned, we'll have less than 96 hours before the Hesbulah makes his first demands from the world's government or launches several missiles as a demonstration of his capabilities. We need to brief the United Nations and gain approval of the legitimate Russian and Chinese governments in order to destroy the delivery vehicles and sites so Hesbulah can't use them for a launch." Seth shifted his position. He leaned forward in his chair, elbows on his knees, and looked directly into Karl's eyes before he continued. "Karl, can you have your briefing ready by tomorrow, sir?" Seth finished.

"Seth, I too have been developing what I believe is Hesbulah's timeline. In four weeks and a day from today it will be the Christian holy day of Good Friday. The negative family Hesbulah was completely usurped nearly 2,000 years ago by this one man, a man that sacrificed himself for the good of all humanity. Because of the Christian calendar, the exact date, time of year and location of everything, even the same alignment of the major heavenly objects that existed on that day, will be the same as it was 1,975 years ago. That exact physical situation happens four weeks and a day from now. I believe that all good intervention, inspiration and influence will end on that day. Listen to what I am saying. This may be difficult to understand. The Biblical description of Armageddon doesn't describe a certain cataclysmic event where the world physically ends. It is the day where we will lose unconditional intervention and prevention before evil triumphs, unless we finally defeat evil and its influences. Using our intelligence analysis of the writings of the Bible, the Koran and the Buddhist scrolls, we have determined the design of mankind and the role of the trials that we have experienced in these last two millennia. It was designed so that we would succeed in our quest for perfection. But, we alone are to determine that without continuous influence. We are to use the freewill that we are empowered with to choose harmony and peace, instead of destruction and evil. On the other side there is the chaotic influence of the world. The family Hesbulah is the embodiment of the negative influence. We have the ability to think and rationalize, to choose love over hate, to choose to work together peacefully or in chaos. We have been given every opportunity to overcome evil. We have been given 66 generations to continue the fight after we were sent physical proof that there is a perfect existence. Hesbulah stands against peace, harmony and our freewill. At the end of our time, if Hesbulah is triumphant, God relinquishes our souls. He will no longer provide the "miracles" that we see everyday. Humanity will continue to populate the earth, but we will be slaves for Hesbulah and his leadership. He will not allow freewill, because we still may choose harmony occasionally over chaos. He will be sure to inflict us with every opportunity to experience pain and suffering for his entertainment.

There is no doubt Seth; this is the last fight. If we defeat Hesbulah, the battle is over. We expose him for what he actually is and the world will know that it is not the true human condition to endure pain, suffering, starvation, wars, killing and extermination.

The people of our world see that it is because of Hesbulah's negative influence that we have chaos and the terror of the human condition. Once he has been defeated, pain and suffering will be eliminated and we will enjoy continued inspiration everyday. Miracles will be commonplace." Karl paused and smiled at Seth.

"But the good news for you and the entire world Seth is that we have a little more time than you believe. I suggest that you allow your men to rest here with us before you go to Urumqi. I will show the details tomorrow but here is the timeline that I would suggest." Karl paused to allow Seth catch up.

"So you have known about our plans to proceed to Kazakhstan. You've known all along what we have been planning." Seth said.

"It isn't as easy as that. We can't afford to be discovered until our work was completed. There are some exceptions however. Just recently, Peter had to lead a team into Paris to make sure that information of our location did not reach Hesbulah. We intercepted transmissions from Hesbulah's commander, Marek Elamesh to an American trying to arrange a meeting to exchange information that was taken from the Pentagon. We do what we must to protect our mission. Even the two that passed you in the forest this afternoon were from our local security group. We knew that you were coming, so we put out our local security team. They confirmed all that they needed to and allowed you to enter the cavern. Some have been unfortunate to not make it that far." Karl said matter of factly to Seth.

"Karl, I was in Paris as well trying to intercept Elamesh and his contact." Seth said and added. "I am only now realizing just how expansive your group is. Why did you involve us, couldn't you have simply destroyed the sites and taken care of Hesbulah alone? Seth asked realizing the answer to his question as he asked it.

"We have done that in the past. But, we have failed to expose Hesbulah. Our small interventions and preventative excursions haven't united the good in the world. We needed to include you, the Americans. Your tenacity to achieve objectives as a people is a true miracle. Never in the history of mankind has a social group achieved so much in so little time. Your focus and self-discipline and willingness to sacrifice yourselves for peace and harmony is unmatched by any civilization yet on earth. Your country has been blessed. The bad side of that is that you are not as open minded, as you should be. You have disregarded the big picture. Instead of looking for the sub-structure of the problems, you find ways to solve the problem that has been created, instead of looking for ways to remove the influence or cause. We had come to our impasse. We needed more power, power that could only be attained by the focus of the people of the United States of the America. You are the spearhead of the people of our time, Seth; we need to convince your people. We need to have the United States rally the world against Hesbulah in this final battle. That is why you must lead this charge. With President Abraham, Admiral McAdams, General Woodsen and Brigadier Watson behind us, the United Nations will not only allow me the time, but will assume my credibility to speak to them. Our proof is indisputable and we can provide hard examples, but we only must convince them to allow us to unite as the world did in the last great war sponsored by Hesbulah and led by your great American President Bush, and destroy Hesbulah's facilities in China without creating more antagonism." Karl finished speaking and Seth noted the weariness in Karl's eyes.

"You have done so much Karl. Don't worry, we will succeed. I don't doubt that in the least. I do believe now, however that it is time for some sleep. We can continue our planning in the morning." Seth stood first.

The two were silent as they walked, completely consumed by thought. Karl broke the silence as they stood outside his apartment's door.

"You have done a fine job Seth. Your family has been leading this fight for many years, it is only proper that you are the one standing here at the final victory."

Seth was completely taken back by Karl's statement. "My family?

"Yes, the family Stephens has led this fight from the beginning. Why do you think you are here right now? There is design in everything." Karl smiled and paused to look at Seth before he patted him on the shoulder and turned to walk down the hallway. Seth turned the lever to enter his apartment. Seth stood there, wanting to ask more. His mind began racing through history. He opened his mouth, but he couldn't speak, he couldn't select the words.

Karl knew that Seth was struggling and paused, momentarily turning back to him before he spoke. "Tell me Seth, have you heard of the celebration of the Saint Stephen?

Seth answered, "Yes."

"Why do you think it is celebrated on the very next sunrise after Christmas?" Karl said as he smiled and disappeared into the dimly lit corridor.

Seth stood there for a long time after the door had closed. His mind was full of thought, almost to the point of overload. He searched his mind for memories as he walked into his room. What was Karl trying to say? His mind raced and searched itself for memories, stories, bits and pieces of a puzzle that he couldn't put together. As he lay down on the bed, he was so consumed by thought that he didn't even notice the magnificently decorated chamber or the book placed on his nightstand by Karl Linder. His mind continued to race as his body succumbed to deep perfectly restful, pleasant slumber.

18

McAdams meets with Woodsen

Josh McAdams was confident in Seth's appraisal of the situation. He read with finality the message that Seth had sent as he closed his secure connection with Seth's aircraft after they had left Paris. It was unfortunate that Elamesh and the Air Force Captain, Jill Feller were killed, but it was probably better. The press would have had a field day if the CIA would have captured an American officer spying for a middle-eastern terrorist organization. If Elamesh would have found the exact location of Karl Linder's complex before they could get Karl out, they would have suffered a major setback. The information that Seth had taken from Jill Feller, Elamesh's contact outlined every detail of the Linder's discoveries. They may have bought a little time. But it was only a temporary stay. McAdams couldn't believe that Hesbulah was this bold about what he was doing, another meeting in Belgrade? He couldn't help but think of the word's that were written in Field Marshal Robert Linder's closing statement in the Project Victory file, One man, at the right time, in the right place, will make the difference. He knew that Seth Stephens was that man.

McAdams rang the secure line at General Maxwell Woodsen's home on Fort McNair at the intersection of the Anacostia and Potomac Rivers. "Maxwell, sorry to disturb your slumber. I just received a call from Seth Stephens about an urgent matter. Can we meet in the Pentagon Situation Room in say an hour?" Josh McAdams said as he spoke into the secure telephone.

"Not a problem Joshua, I'll see you there in 45 minutes from now." Woodsen said as he noted the time on his watch and terminated the secure connection. He was not much of a man for small talk when it came to business. His short, concise, well-chosen words were a trademark of General Maxwell Woodsen. He liked it that way. Many complained that he always seemed too gruff or impersonal. He liked it that way, especially in Washington where familiarity breeds much more than contempt.

"Barbara, I have to meet Joshua McAdams in a few minutes. He just spoke with Seth. I'm not sure how long I'll be. Why don't you get some sleep and I'll call you after I know more about the situation." Maxwell said to his wife. Barbara was a true night owl. She'd stay awake for hours after they had gone to bed watching old movies or re-reading novels that she termed the classics. He finished dressing in his full class A military uniform. Another one of Maxwell's trademarks, complete attention to details. It mattered not what time of day or night it was when he was called in. He was a soldier 24 hours a day and was proud of it. He once dressed down a Brigadier General for showing up for duty in the more relaxed Class B uniform and what he called "Pentagon slippers, a version of cheap spongy rubber soled shoes that officers who homestead in the Pentagon wore. He despised the ticket punchers that thought that the duty that they did in the Pentagon was tough. Some had let their military bearing go so far out of line that on his first day as the Chief of Staff; he conducted a Physical Fitness Test and a Weigh-in. The officers that scored less than a 270 out of 300 and even appeared overweight were reassigned to short tours and hardship tours where they could get in touch with what was really happening in the world. He continued with the famous Woodsen weigh-ins as the officers assigned to the Pentagon called it. If he noticed an officer that was pushing the limits of their military bearing, he'd invite them on a run with him from the Pentagon to the Capital and around the Washington Mall. If they didn't maintain his pace, he'd give them a PT test. Many officers were re-assigned within hours after that run. He was a leader that led by example and maintained the standards. He didn't care who you were or how well you were connected. His Iron Mike Motto, follow me and do as I do, simplified his leadership philosophy. He'd asked for input from anyone, from the lowliest private to the most brilliant civilian. But once good idea cut off time arrived and it was time to execute, you'd better succeed or die trying. There wasn't time to criticize or come up with a new plan. That complicated the operation by taking time to relay changes. He stressed the objectives, developed the intent, and came up with loose and simple boundaries. Above all he gave his subordinate leaders the authority to do what they thought was necessary as long as it didn't require extensive coordination with the man to the left or right. He praised initiative and did not tolerate inaction. He hated the staff process because it was bureaucratic and was self-consuming. One man, in the right place, at the right time made the difference. Not a bunch of bullshit pretty colored briefing slides. That never accomplished any mission. It was a support role. If an Operation Order had more than five pages, he was leery. Length leads to complexity. Complexity in combat killed more soldiers than the enemy. Woodsen was a tough man and a soldier's soldier. He was the favorite choice of the President of the United States. He and the President thought alike. They were God-fearing men of morality and duty. They were honorable and forthright. Characteristics that had been forgotten in the passé' politically correct Washington. Leaders, both elected and appointed that oscillated like the polls were voted out and replaced. The liberal thought, that anything goes, lost its place in the new leadership. The new millennium ushered in a return to core values of family and honor. What was right was right, the gray areas shrunk. People wanted leadership and steadfastness, not a man that tried to please everyone. There weren't any consolation prizes given for your family background, creed or skin color. You either were an American, which meant that you stood for the values that made this country great, or you didn't. Your ethnic background didn't matter. You either were part of the American Team or you weren't. You either liked our American God fearing values or you moved to another country. Americans grew less tolerant of those that tried to change the values that made the country great. Politicians were replaced at the rate of 50% per election. Maxwell Woodsen heard the President's campaign speech and stood up and clapped when the not yet elected President had proclaimed that the pendulum had swung to far too the left and he'd be the man to lead the push back to basics and balance. He was tired of special interests, political correctness, quotas, and affirmative action. Equal rights were decreed by the Constitution of the United States, nothing else. The thought of this country ending up like the once great Roman civilization sickened him. He wouldn't stand for it.

Woodsen would drive himself in to the Pentagon rather than wake his driver or Aide de Camp. He called and left messages for them with instructions to call as soon as they were on their way to the Pentagon. In less than 35 minutes from McAdam's call he was motoring through the front gate of Fort McNair on his way to the Pentagon.

He entered the operations room about five minutes before McAdams and was reviewing the punitive bombing campaigns on Yugoslavia. He looked at the Battle Damage Assessment charts and Target Accuracy charts. He noted that the targeting accuracy was greater than 97% and collateral damage to non-targeted areas was next to nothing. The extent of the collateral damage was due to bomb fragments chipping exterior surfaces and some glass breakage. Woodsen was quite content with the targeting list. The Watch Officer handed him the latest

SITREPS. He would receive a full briefing at the 0800 staff meeting and Operation Summary.

Josh McAdams walked into the operations room and was not surprised to see Maxwell Woodsen their reviewing a stack of papers.

"General Woodsen, Thank you for getting here with such short notice." McAdams said while reaching for Maxwell's hand. Although the two were old friends, they keep the protocol proper while on duty.

"Mr. McAdams, It good to see you!" Woodsen returned.

The two leaders moved to a glass paneled room that offered some security while they discussed the situation.

McAdams proceeded to brief Woodsen on his discussion with Seth that had taken place only hours earlier.

"So it boils down to us sending the Russians, Chinese and Sinovic a message with an impact." Woodsen said pausing before his next statement. "I know Seth and he doesn't make requests of this nature unless he is absolutely sure of the consequences. Everyone is suspicious of Russia and China and their attempt to broker peace negotiations once again in Yugoslavia, but we haven't been able to prove anything. Mainly because we didn't know about this character Hesbulah, the sooner we get Linder here the better. What would you suggest as saying in the message? Woodsen closed.

"As little as possible, they wouldn't take anything written seriously and I doubt that it would get t the senior leaders that are concerned anyway. Most of them have shot so many messengers that if it is bad news they simply leave it for the next guy until it gets shredded without a trace. Most of their claims are true when they say that they have never heard of something." McAdams continued.

"What I am asking is something more physical Max. I'd like to send a cruise missile into the Embassy where they are about to meet in Yugoslavia. Sinovic has taken over where Milosivic has ended. We have been in that country for too many years now to give up any ground. We'd be retracing our steps. Hell, we are now even bombing the same targets we did back in '98. We can't afford to lose anything more." McAdams stopped there to judge the reaction from Woodsen.

Woodsen reacted as if McAdams had grown another head. "Josh, you might want to say that again because I though that you said you wanted me to target the Chinese Embassy in Belgrade again."

"Max, that's exactly what I said. McAdams returned with the seriousness that Woodsen hadn't seen before.

"Max, we have reason to suspect that the movement of old nuclear warheads from Russia are making their way into China. They have completely circumvented the United Nations inspectors and are in the process of closing the deal. Seth is on his way to give the evidence to Karl Linder in the Harz mountains that will undisputedly link Hesbulah with this and many other major power plays throughout the world. Afterward, he'll proceed to Kazakhstan, cross the border into China and get hard evidence that the Russians are selling Plutonium from old SS-21 ICBMs to Chinese underworld leaders. We know that some of the corrupt leaders in China have our latest nuclear technology thanks to another administration. Put two and two together for God's sake. What do you think they are going to do with them? After the last bombing, Hesbulah is counting that we won't do it again. He has specifically decided to use that Embassy once again. He thinks that lightning won't strike there twice. What Seth is working on will help us present our case to the United Nations and will convince the world that just a few corrupt leaders in China along with Hesbulah are working to gain a dominant position in the world that will exceed even the capability of the US. While we have been tap dancing in these small diversionary skirmishes, Hesbulah has been gaining an advantage over us. Seth's reasoning is sound and we have the pieces of the intelligence puzzle in place to back his suspicions. What other reasons could there be? Tomorrow they meet again in Belgrade. All we have to do is ask what they are in it for Max. Hell, the corrupt old Soviets have committed many more atrocities in Grozny and the Chinese are ruthless customers themselves. Why would they be concerned with peace yet again in Yugoslavia? We have been in and out of there since, '92 and still have no resolution. Hesbulah has the only reason for keeping the conflict in Yugoslavia alive. Max, he's been using it against the world for 1,000 years. I'd like you to target the Chinese Embassy tonight, with the next wave of Tomahawks going in Max. I'll go to the President for this one but you know that will take more time, time we don't have. I'm asking you Max to target the Embassy. I'll take the fall for it, hell; I'll tell them that we used the old Air Force maps this time. Tell them that I told you to do it. I'll even have the State Department contact China and tell them that they may want to clear the embassy because the targets are close to the embassy. Name the conditions Max, but just target that embassy. We have to work together on this Max. We have got to send those corrupt bastards a message that says we know about their plans. A message that says we know about this and that we will take action."

Woodsen stared hard at McAdams eyes with a look that burned into McAdams soul. McAdams conviction for this mission ran deep. McAdams had more experience in intelligence gathering than anyone else. Woodsen knew that he best used that experience to formulate hunches and could "read" the situation with constant awareness.

McAdams was one of those men that had that natural ability to stay ahead of the adversary.

"Joshua, I have put my life in your hands many times based on your hunches beginning in Vietnam and not once did I receive so much as a scratch. I'll place the Chinese Embassy on the targeting list. I have no problems killing the bastards that are enemies of this country, but I won't intentionally kill non-combatants. Joshua, do everything to make sure that everyone is out of that building by launch time and I'll be your messenger. We'll dispel any of their doubts that we may or may not know. We need to stop that bastard in his tracks before he gets control of those launch sites. If we could find this clown Hesbulah, hell I'd give the authority to target him." Woodsen ended.

"Thanks my friend, Hesbulah's days are coming to an end. With the increased effort on finding Hesbulah combined with Linder's evidence, we'll turn the world against him so fast that he'll wonder who pulled his feet out from under him. Seth is on him hard and close Max. We'll end that sadistic bastard's family's 2,000-year-old terror sponsorship. We just have to give Seth all of the support we can right now. He's the spearhead and I couldn't name a better man to lead this effort in the field Max." Joshua affirmed.

"He'd be first on my roster for any mission. Seth doesn't know the meaning of failure." Whatever you need Joshua, just let me know." Max Woodsen patted his old friend on the shoulder and turned to leave the glass enclosed office in the situation room. Joshua McAdams had to make the call many times about life and death. Never in his life, did he feel more confident about any other decision. He knew and felt that it was the right thing to do.

19

The Day Before the Flight

Harz Mountain Complex, February 25, 0540 hours

He turned his head upward on every stroke taking in air as soon as his head cleared the water. The breaths were coming at a more rapid pace. He pushed himself and pushed himself harder. He made each reach count, trying to attain maximum efficiency. He grabbed for the water like each reach would be his last. His body moved almost machine-like. Each kick of his legs and each reach of his arms were perfectly timed. The water slid past his skin after being parted by his head and shoulders, cut by his forward reaching arm, his trailing arm tucked in neatly streamlined to create lesser drag. He saw the end of the lane approaching and gradually slowed his pace. His strokes matched the pace of the water gliding past; arms were no longer powered by the taunt pull of his muscles. He allowed his arms to streamline at his sides and glided gently, rolling over onto his back as he approached the lane's end. He relaxed and controlled his breathing as he allowed his heart rate to return its normal pace.

He couldn't help but notice the woman that was walking at a casual but demure pace toward the point where he'd exit the pool. She was an attractive woman, late 30s, wearing a one-piece bathing suit steeply cut up toward the hips. Her dark hair hung loosely about her face and she cleared one side of it with her hand not holding the towel, pinning it behind her ear in that nonchalant manner that would pull a smile from any man that noticed.

"Tell me Colonel Stephens, do you always train like you are fighting for your life or is that your normal intensity?" The dark haired woman asked as she stood at the end of the lane holding a towel out for him.

"No, it's just a good way to relieve tension. It calms the jitters a little too. Forgive me, I don't believe we have met." Seth said pushing himself up onto the deck surround the pool.

"No we haven't, I am Anneliese Schuler." Anneliese said handing Seth the towel. She couldn't help but look at his lean body as he toweled his hair briskly. Seth finished drying his hair and ran the towel across his back.

He looked at Anneliese, "Thank you for the towel. Do you make a habit of ambushing men in forests and swimming pools or are there other areas that you'd prefer?" Seth said with a smile in his eyes and voice.

"You recognized me. Very good Colonel Stephens, usually my sun glasses and hat keep me more discreet." Anneliese said.

"It was your walk. To me, the way people walk is as unique as their DNA. Some people remember names or faces well. I have an average aptitude to remember those distinguishing characteristics but the way a person walks really stay with me." Seth said in a humorous, dry manner.

"I'll remember to shuffle a little more the next time or perhaps be a bit more oscillating." She returned.

"Oh, I would suggest that you not change a thing." Seth returned.

"So did you come all this way to hand me a towel or just to ambush me again?" Seth asked.

"I would like to know when you have time for me…er…to brief you on the launch facilities in China." Seth caught her staring at his waist area as he knotted the towel around his middle. She continued somewhat embarrassed. "Uh, I will act as your liaison with the Operative Australian in Alma-Arty. They have succeeded in determining the route for the plutonium shipments and will help you locate the launch facilities." Anneliese said with a nervous quiver breaking in her voice. "Forgive me Colonel Stephens, but…"

"Please call me Seth. You've seen me half naked. I think that rushes the courtship along a little, don't you?" Seth said more laughing now than talking. They began to walk toward the pool exit door and into the main corridor.

"What? You are being a bit presumptuous now aren't you?" Anneliese said regaining her composure. Seth hoped that she would react that way; he was nearly as nervous as she was the way she was allowing herself to be distracted. She was a beautiful woman and he would have enjoyed the opportunity to spend some time engaged in stimulating conversation, but he wouldn't. He was beginning to have thoughts of another brunette but that too would have to wait. He had business here and that definitely came first.

Mike came in through the door just as the two were about to open it and looked at Seth and Anneliese. He smiled at Seth and then at Anneliese Schuler.

"Excuse me boss, I thought I was being a bit too eager by getting up early for a workout." Mike said. The surprise of running into someone at the pool this early showed on his face. Seth took the opportunity to introduce Anneliese.

"Anneliese, this is Major Mike Thomas. Mike this is Anneliese Schuler. She'll be briefing us later on the launch sites." Seth said in a cordial manner. The three let a few minutes pass in idle conversation before Seth broke in. "Mike get with Izz and Sean, we'll plan to spend the rest of the morning after breakfast in preparation and study the areas. Why don't we meet after breakfast and discuss a few things? Anneliese, how does just after lunch sound for your briefing?" Seth said.

"That is perfect." Anneliese replied still looking at Seth.

"Good, Anneliese, I'll leave you in good company. Mike, see you at breakfast." Seth said as he turned and left almost too abruptly as Mike and Anneliese watched him pass through the corridor.

"He is a rather rude and presumptuous man, isn't he?" Anneliese said.

"No, actually you won't find more of a gentleman. He just has the weight of the world on his shoulders and it isn't something that he takes lightly." Mike stood with Anneliese until she excused herself and exited through the same door as Seth. Mike thought to himself, 'maybe I don't know the whole story here.' He turned and plunged headfirst with a long low dive into the glass-like water's surface. The cool temperature and mineral rich water was very invigorating as he plowed his way through the liquid with broad heavy strokes.

Seth casually strolled through the magnificent corridors. It was still early and he enjoyed the ambiance of the complex and the slow pace this morning. It allowed him to collect thoughts that he allowed to pass as fragments through his mind. He thought more and more about Elizabeth and how she was the image that he had seen when he was in the conduit. He reached the heavy oak door of his apartment and opened it. He hadn't noticed it last night or early this morning, but the apartment had windows. The artificial light was illuminating the windows and bathing the apartment in light. If Seth didn't know any better, he would have thought that he was in an apartment above ground on a beautiful sun filled day. He moved closer to the windows and could faintly feel the heat when he stood in the light. He smiled at the detail that went into the design of the cavern. He spent a few minutes taking in the beauty of the decoration. It would have cost more money by today's standards to decorate one of these rooms than it would be to build and furnish an entire house. Fine linens, intricately woven tapestries; wool carpets detailed with interwoven crests and borders adorned the room. If one had to spend some time isolated from the world, this was definitely doing it sparing no expenses.

Seth sat in the chair next to the bed. He looked at the clothing he had worn in and he wished that he could have had it laundered. He noticed the wardrobe and wondered. He stood up and moved over to the wardrobe, just perhaps they…yes, they did think of everything. In it, was a complete outfit of clothes, even in his size.

He moved past the bed and was heading to the bathroom as a glimmer of artificial light caught the brass cover of a leather bound book. He stopped to look more carefully at the book set on the bedside table. He noticed it last night but didn't switch on the light to examine it further. He sat down on the chair next to the nightstand and took the book in hand. As he picked it up he thought about the discussion that he and Karl had in the hallway last night. The book was plainly bound in a thick brown leather cover. There were no markings on the cover. He opened it to the title page. It read, Family Stephens. The hair on the back of Seth's neck stood up, his skin rose like goose flesh. He was almost afraid to turn the next page. He did slowly. The page started out with year, 859 AD

Seth sat reading the story of his family's history unaware that an hour had past.

The sharp knock at the door that brought him back to the present was followed by Karl Linder's voice. "Seth, I was hoping that you would join me for breakfast. Seth scrambled to pull on the pants that should have been laundered first and moved to the door. "Good morning, Karl." Seth said looking at Karl with inquiringly.

"Perhaps you will need a few more minutes to finish dressing before breakfast." Karl said with a smile.

"Please, come in Karl. I have found that someone has done some interesting research and I lost track of time while I read through the book, marvelous, just unbelievably marvelous." Seth said.

"I was hoping that you would find it…" Karl briefly paused searching for the right word before he continued, "enlightening."

"Through our work here we have found most of the facts contained in that book. You, my friend have a great calling." Karl moved to sit at the table near one of the windows. Seth followed.

For the next hour Karl outlined the history of the family Stephens. Seth's interest was so intense that he felt as if he were eating and digesting each word. The words were not merely sounds that were coming from Karl's mouth. It was as if he were forming physical objects that he could hold onto and handing them to him. He could grab each one and take it inside him. Karl was recounting the legends that spanned history. His family was there throughout the crusades. His family was there during the revolutions of many countries, exposing Hesbulah plans. His family was at the Treaty of Versailles, Berlin, the Battleship Missouri, off the coast of Japan, the Convention in Geneva, P'anmunjom, Korea, Seth even at the elections in free Iraq in 2005 and the United Nations. He was the most recent descendant of a very long lineage of peacekeepers.

Karl outlined the details of how his family fought for peace at every turn. He seemed to draw an inner peace from Karl's words and at the same time the words made his intensity even more focused. He understood his passions and almost knew the outcomes of the battles that would lie ahead. He was armed with the weapons and inspiration that would help him in any time of need.

"Your family has been the spearhead of the force seeking peace since the time of Christ. The final battle is now soon to come. I wanted you to be armed with unfaltering confidence when you confront Hesbulah. Do nothing differently than you have in the past. Just know that you will be triumphant if you continue on your path." Karl ended by reaching out and putting his hand on Seth's shoulder.

Karl used both hands to push out of the armchair and turned to make his way toward the door. Seth couldn't see the pride welling in Karl's eyes. "Now we should eat breakfast. There should be some clothing for you in the wardrobe. I will meet you in the dining hall after you have dressed. I'm afraid that you have already become the main discussion of the entire population of women here. If you were to show up for breakfast half dressed; it may bring our operations to a standstill. Even heroes have to follow the dress standards here." Karl said laughing. He passed through the door and closed it softly as he did.

Seth sat down on the chair and caught his image in the mirror on the opposite wall. He didn't want to be a hero; he didn't want to be the main topic of a discussion. He just wanted to do the right thing.

Seth walked down to the dinning room with the same humility that he had before. Karl told Seth of his family's history and he knew that

Seth would be no different. He wouldn't change. Nothing could have been improved. He was ready and confident, without being arrogant. Karl's words reduced the anxiety somewhat but Seth was pragmatic enough not to rely on miracles. He had to make this happen, not rely on fortune, fate or mysticism. His faith and God-given abilities were all that he had. Seth rounded the corner and found the four of them, Karl, Izz, Sean and Mike seated and ready for breakfast.

"Lounging a bit this morning boss?" Mike quipped.

"Actually Mike, I found that I am a little sore after that swim this morning, needed to relax a bit more." Seth said winking at Mike.

Mike was shocked and thought, 'I knew it. I don't have a chance. There was something else going on there.' Mike shook his head and muttered something about never having a chance as breakfast was served.

The four of them enjoyed more of a brunch than breakfast. Small talk of life in the cavern was the topic of conversation. They were glad to be in the confines of the cavern for a few days, but none of them really could understand how the people here were so disciplined to stay for their entire lives. They had created an underground paradise and were free of many problems that life would offer. They remained completely focused on their objective to ensure Hesbulah's failure. Seth and his teammates admired their ethics. They would become much closer to many of them than they would think. The friends that they would make here would be life long. They all realized that once Hesbulah was exposed, Karl and his group would be free to make their own decisions as to where they would live.

They spent all afternoon in briefings and finalizing the plans for the trip to Kazakhstan. Seth found that the capabilities in the cavern's operation room were very efficient. They had developed a finely honed network of contacts throughout the world. Their system of requirements dissemination was perfected and followed simple guidelines. Seth could only imagine how efficient this network would be if it were coupled with modern day computers. With that technology, the research that Karl directed could have been finished several years earlier not cutting the timeline so fine. The only thing that Seth found inconvenient was the time waiting for a response. But he was used to the speed of light, where Karl was completely satisfied with the speed of sound. It was all relative, Seth thought.

Anneliese Schuler was handing out the briefing, which contained the locations of the missile launch facilities, dates and times that the plutonium would be ready for transfer and the contact information for the operator that would meet them in Alma-Altai, Kazakhstan.

"Gentlemen, if you are ready, we shall begin." Anneliese Schuler continued with the briefing. "We will plan your departure tomorrow at 1730 hours local time. There is an eight-hour time difference between Hanover and Alma Ata, so the four-hour flight will put you in there just before sunrise. You will be met by an operative agent who will expect your arrival at Alma-Altai. You can stay in contact with us via your secure high frequency radio on this frequency…"

Anneliese spent the next two hours covering the details of the mission. Seth knew what had to be done. Show evidence that the corrupt Russians and Chinese were transferring the plutonium and then destroy the facilities after Linder had briefed the United Nations four days from now. He knew one thing for certain. The next few days would be the test of his life. He would use every skill that that he had developed to help him complete his mission.

The team was quiet and introverted after the briefing. There was a lot of coordination that had happened but they had been on these types of missions before. The bad guys never play by the rulebook. They would have to make things happen and think on their feet to succeed. Flexibility and planning contingencies saved their necks before and Seth's team was the best. They were hands picked. If they couldn't succeed, nobody could.

Seth walked out with Karl, "Karl, Joshua McAdams is personally making he arrangements for you to go back to New York. He knows that you are the most important person in this mission. He'll get you back safely. We'll meet in London in a few days and we'll let McAdams throw the biggest celebration for you and your people here. Then you are going to show me a little about Austria. It'll be like going back home. It'll be a month of good food, good drink, and good company. Think that you'll be up for it?" Seth asked trying to lighten the intensity of the mood.

"When it comes to good food, good drink, and especially good company, I shall always be eager." Karl replied with his eyes shining as bright as the stars.

"If you will excuse me, I think I need to save Anneliese from Mike. She looks like she may need a diversion so she can escape." Seth said as they both looked at Mike talking away to the seemingly uninterested Anneliese Schuler. Karl gave a single nod of approval and blinked an affirmative with his characteristic smile.

"Mike, what would you say to one more swim in that fantastic pool before dinner." Seth said to Mike.

"Just a second, boss, I was trying to convince Anneliese to have dinner with me, er us tonight." Mike said trying to pull more information out about his suspicions.

"Anneliese, how can you resist? Won't you join us for dinner this evening?"

Anneliese looked at Seth and smiled, "You're right how can I resist? Dinner this evening, Now if you will excuse me, I must send a few messages to Alma before dinner. Please enjoy the water."

Anneliese walked out of the briefing room and looked back over her shoulder in their direction. Seth caught the smile on Mike's face as he watched her walk out. "You are quite the ladies man Mike, I was hoping to spend some time alone with Anneliese this evening. You beat me to it. I don't stand a chance now. You should give a guy warning just so the playing field is fair." Seth said with a hint of sarcasm.

"You know boss, just when I think that I have something figured out, you throw me a curve. You just need to spend more time around me. I'll show you how to drive the women crazy. Did you see the way she looked at me? Happens all the time." Mike said with dead seriousness.

"Mike, that is what I like about you, your tenacity and confidence buddy!" Seth said putting his arm around Mike's shoulder as they walked out of the briefing room.

20

Finding the Plutonium

Departing Hanover, February 26, 1730 hours

"Okay gentlemen, here's where we justify our existence." Seth said as he pushed the power levers up on the aircraft. The aircraft lurched forward like a true thoroughbred coming out of the starting gate. They had their full load of supplies and equipment on board the aircraft fully laden with fuel for the flight into Kazakhstan and it still responded to the throttle movements like she was empty.

"Hanover tower this is Argus 99, holding short of runway." Mike said over the VHF radio. "Argus 99, you are cleared for takeoff. Climb to 3,000 feet and turn to a heading of 130 degrees." Returned the tower controller at Hanover.

Seth ran the power levers up and released the brakes. The mission had begun. "Gentlemen, our flight today will take us over the lush garden spots of Warsaw, Samara, Orsk, the Kirshiz Steppe, Torghay, into the lovely ancient city of Alma-Ata, Kazakhstan, nestled in the foothills of the Tian Shan Mountains. In order to do this without being compromised, we'll link up with a chartered 747 out of Frankfurt bound for Beijing. We'll tuck up under his wing, turn off our transponder and ride in his radar shadows. We'll drop down to terrain flight after we pass the lovely River City of Torghay and take advantage of the no radar environment of western Kazakhstan and sneak into Alma-Ata just after sun up."

"Did Uncle Joshua charter that 747 just for us?" Mike asked rhetorically.

"He did Mike and they are carrying absolutely nothing into Beijing. They file the flight plan and all we do is follow." Seth returned.

"What is the condition of the airfield in Alma-Ata? I hope the accommodations there are similar to Karl's Place." Sean said from the back of the aircraft, already bunking in for his turn on the rest cycle.

"Izz, show Sean a picture of that airfield." Seth commanded. Izz brought the latest satellite photos up on the large screen mounted on the cockpit and cabin divider.

"Looks like a road to me Izz, where's the airport?" Sean asked.

"That's it buddy, we're heading to Alma to land on a road. Do you see that shanty over there off to the side? That's where will park this beauty." Izz replied trying to put on an old western accent.

Seth and Mike were maneuvering the aircraft into the airspace just south to where Rhein radar would vector them into position with the 747. "Mike, rendezvous time in 4 minutes. Why don't you give them a call, they're using a call sign of Condor 12." Seth said over the intercom.

"Roger boss, let's give them a try. Mike said preparing to key the secure UHF radio. "Condor 12, this is Argus 99, on UHF, radio check, over." Mike said and then listened.

"Argus 99, turn left heading 175 degrees. Climb and maintain flight level 450. Your flight lead will be at 12 O'clock when you roll out on your heading. Report him insight and advise MARSA." Reported a controller with a strong German accent.

Seth replied to the controller since Mike was attempting to contact Condor 12 on the other radio. "Roger Rhein, we will advise when Military will Assume Responsibility for Separation of Aircraft, MARSA, over."

"Roger Condor 12, Argus 99 has you loud and clear." Mike reported to the escort aircraft over the radio. "Seth, we are in radio contact with Condor 12." Mike said over the intercom.

"I have Condor 12 in visual contact at 12 O'clock and seven miles. Rhein would like you to advise when we can accept MARSA."

"Why don't you let them know that we'll accept once you get a visual on him, he's up ahead about five miles now." Seth stated over the intercom.

Mike looked ahead and acquired the aircraft. "Rhein, Argus 99, MARSA, over." He reported to Rhein Radar once he had a visual contact.

"Argus 99, you are cleared to maneuver with Condor 12, break, Condor 12, Understand that you will maintain the transponder code and radio contact." Rhein said talking to each aircraft without releasing his push to talk switch on the transmitter.

"Roger Rhein, Condor 12 has the lead." A deep professional voice said responding to Rhein Radar's inquiry.

The Citation X and the 747 formation was now established. The radar screens on the ground would only display one primary target if the flight kept their formation close to one another, as was the protocol. The CIA crew of the 747 had done this many times before. They had trained extensively in formation flights to allow other aircraft to operate discreetly in their shadows. Only a visual inspection would reveal that the single return on the radar screen was actually two aircraft. The night flight and the route over unpopulated areas, far removed from military bases would also help keep the flight elusive.

"Autopilot engaged boss, flight image director selected." Mike said to Seth over the intercom before contacting the crew of the 747 over the secure, short-range, radio link. "Condor 12, this is Argus 99. We are above your left wing, flight image director engaged." Mike reported to Condor 12.

"Roger, Argus. How's the ride?" Condor 12 asked, referring to the flight conditions.

"Great Condor, hope you're smiling, you're on camera." Mike returned.

Normally, an aircraft the size of the 747 creates turbulence in its wake that would make the flight in a close-following aircraft rough and turbulent. The positioning of the Citation X above the forward wing of the 747 allowed the X to operate in the margin of air that was undisturbed by the big 747's wing wake. The Flight Imaging Director would maintain the exact position. It was a system that used a digital video image to freeze the image of the 747 as viewed from the Citation crew's perspective into a computer that maintained the relative position by using cues from the digital imagery. The system fed the commands into the autopilot of the Citation X, which controlled the attitude, and speed of the X to keep it tucked in close to the 747. The two crews could now talk openly using a short range UHF radio transmitter that only put out enough RF energy to be heard from a distance of no more than 150 meters. Unless another aircraft or antenna closed to within that range, they couldn't hear what was being said. The use of these two systems allowed the CIA to mask flights into any region of the world when equipment or manpower had to be positioned.

Hundreds of thousands of thoughts were going through the minds of the men. This was the point where they mentally rehearsed the details of the mission. They tried to prepare everything and arrange contingency after contingency. Their biggest fear was being the one man that let the team down and failing in this mission. They would have sacrificed all else for the three other men sitting next to them. 'God, please don't let me screw this up,' was the common prayer that each would utter.

They reviewed hundreds of digital images of the area. Read the backgrounds and tried to find the weaknesses of anyone that operated in the area. They reviewed landscape models, escape routes, safe areas, pre-arranged supply caches. Everything that could be reviewed was reviewed. A mission like this wouldn't allow enough time to prepare if given a lifetime for any other group of men. But these four were unlike any other group. They had prepared for this for a lifetime. From the minute they were born, life began to hand out challenges and they had successfully had overcome each and every one of them. In senior military leader's circles, these four men were the top performers. If there was a difficult mission to undertake, leaders looked for men that could come close to matching the profiles of Mike Thomas, Izz Diconcerio and Sean MacLowre. These men did not understand what it meant to fail. They had the tenacity to hold onto something until they had beaten it. They would drive their bodies to the point where no more pain could be felt. They'd reach the pain threshold and keep going. They were unstoppable.

There was only one man that would exceed their abilities by far. Seth Stephens was the force that would lead this very able team to success. He led by example. His physical form was driven by a relentless desire to succeed. His trademark was to push the limits of human form far beyond normal limits. Mike had seen him injured and bruised to the point where most men die, but Seth would still come back fighting. There were men of larger stature, but none with more resolve or drive. His six feet, two inch frame was covered by a sinewy and muscular covering that pound for pound was capable of someone twice his size. His men thought that he spent most of his time in the gym but he didn't. He had the genes of a warrior, a thoroughbred's ability and toughness perfected through the years. But the one thing that made him such a magnificent leader was the fact that he always did the right thing. He was humble and forthright. He never used his ability for personal gain. His men were confident that he'd always lead them to victory and he maintained the moral ascendancy over any foe. If there was a man on earth that could defeat Hesbulah, it was Seth Stephens.

"Condor 12, we are six minutes from our descent. We will be breaking left in a descending left turn at the end of the count." Seth watched the clock as the remaining minutes passed. "3…2…1… off your wing. Thanks for your lead gentlemen. Have a safe flight into Beijing." Seth said into the interplane radio as the Citation X broke into a steep bank, descending to terrain flight levels.

"Roger Argus 12, Keep your head on a swivel and we wish you all the best, God speed!" Replied the crew of Condor 12 as they watched the ghostly silver-gray silhouette of the Citation X disappear into the darkness below their left wing. The crew of the 747 was not envious of the team aboard neither the Citation X nor the mission that they had ahead of them.

Seth took the opportunity to look skyward as the 747 passed overhead to the east. From his perspective he could look overhead into the darkness of night and the feathery contrails illuminated by the moonlight left behind the 747 and straight ahead into the sun, rising over the eastern horizon. The great dichotomy of sunrise and darkness was captured in one view over the skies of Kazakhstan. The realization that Seth was seeing the beginning and the end in one view astounded him and at the same time comforted him.

Seth quickly regained his situational awareness as the aircraft descended through 10,000 feet. The ground mapping radar and Ground Proximity System displayed the terrain on the Multi-Function Display in the center of the instrument panel. The Flight Imagery Director combined this data with its no light video imagery to give Seth the complete picture of the terrain over which they flew. Hills, trees, telegraph poles and wires, towers, antennae and buildings were displayed. Seth maneuvered the Citation X at 300 knots through the obstacles at 50 meters above the ground. Mike kept a constant eye on the desired navigation course and gave the distance and heading reading deviations from the true course to Seth as they maneuvered.

"The course line is 1.2 nautical miles to the right Seth. As soon as we pass by this peak we can turn further left to re-intercept." Mike suggested. The two worked as a well-oiled machine. Each knew the other's moves and intentions.

"Mike, I want to hit the final approach fix within twenty degrees of the final approach heading. Give me enough room to make the turn a little more shallow than normal. I intend to keep our speed up until the final approach point to avoid visual detection from someone taking an early morning stroll. At most, all they'll see is a blur and attribute it to a Chinese military trainer." Seth said almost thinking out loud.

Mike had his game face on and was definitely out of character. Seth stole a glance at him, just long enough to see that he wasn't having fun.

"Mike, don't peak too soon here buddy." Seth said smiling at him.

Mike saw Seth's expression and caught the words. "Oh yeah. Why did you smell something burning' boss?" Mike expressed, returning to himself.

"You were thinking a little too much over there. I didn't want you to hurt yourself." Seth said with his characteristic smile.

Mike returned to the navigation screen. "You're the only guy I know boss that can stay this cool at treetop level, 300 knots, at night, over some desolate part of Kazakhstan. What do you use the force or something?" Mike asked rhetorically.

"Something like that, Mike." Seth replied, turning introspective.

"Give me a one-half standard rate turn to the left Seth on my mark…three…two…one…MARK." Mike commanded as the aircraft passed the hilltop noted as hill 337 on the map display. Seth turned the aircraft at a bank angle of about 12 degrees. The Citation X sliced effortlessly through the cool early dawn air. Seth was almost visual now as the sun was still below the eastern horizon but bathing everything in a pink-orange cast of light.

"Passing final checkpoint Seth. Final approach fix four nautical miles ahead." Mike spoke intensely into the microphone.

They were flying so low that even in the dim early dawn light Seth could see the individual leaves on the trees of the sparse vegetation that they passed over. Their course would take them just over a small hill ahead. On the other side, the terrain would flatten for several kilometers and then rise rapidly to form the Altai Mountains to the north and the Karatau Mountains to the south. The crew was using these mountains to mask their approach from the radar sites located in Alma-Ata. The road that they would use as a landing strip was just to their right. Mike could see it out his right window. The map display showed that it would turn to follow the direction that they were heading as it crested the hill. Seth would plan to touch down on the sandy road just as it reached the base of the hill that they would over fly. He had three kilometers to use for a landing area before the road reached the large stone and wooden barn off to the left side.

Seth worked the controls of the Citation X and began a rapid deceleration. Slowing the near 44,000-pound aircraft from 300 knots to its landing speed would take unabbreviated skill. If he pulled the nose up too far the airplane would gain altitude rapidly and be visible on the radar screens from the Kazakh military. If he slowed too late he would overshoot the landing area and possibly compromise their presence visually. The timing had to be perfect. Seth brought the power levers to idle just as they passed the long stretching base of the hill. He deployed the speed brakes that would act to increase the surface drag and slow the plane. The airplane shuddered from combined effects of the speed brakes extension into a 300 knots air stream and the turbulence created by a crosswind flowing upward across the rising terrain. Seth judged the deceleration perfectly and commanded Mike to extend the landing flaps. Powerful hydraulic pumps forced the metal slats on the leading edge of the wings out into the airflow. The combined increase of drag created by the devices acted as if a cable had been attached to the rear of the sleek jet and was pulling on it.

The nose high attitude of the aircraft in its deceleration profile prevented Seth from seeing the landing area that fell away down a shallow slope under the nose.

"Mike, give me any heading requirements from the Flight Imagery Director. I can't keep the landing area insight and going around for another try isn't an option." Seth commanded in a cool clear voice.

"Roger boss, you're looking good. Maintain heading 110 degrees. The Radar altimeter is reading 75 feet. Touchdown point 1.2 kilometers ahead." Mike reported. Izz and Sean were facing the left and right sides of the aircraft with automatic weapons readied.

"Pretty exciting stuff huh Izz?" Sean commented as he watched the ground pass by in a blur. The sweat was starting to form on his brow in the cool dry cabin.

"Hey, if you've seen one landing in a hot landing zone, you've seen them all." Izz replied looking out the side window of the X. Both men were straining their eyes to see if any surprises were waiting for them.

Seth had the aircraft in the proper landing attitude and was waiting for the last second to lower the landing gear. "Gear down." Seth commanded as the aircraft started to lose its last bit of altitude. Mike responded by setting the gear handle to the down and locked position. The wind noise increased as the landing gear was set into the air rushing past the sleek body of the X. A solid thunk announced to the crew that the gear was down in the locked position.

"20 feet on the radar altimeter. Alignment good. The airspeed is 128 knots. Max lift/drag on the angle of attack indicator. We can't make her anymore efficient than this Seth." Mike announced.

Seth held the aircraft in the landing attitude as the peripheral visual cues told him that he was settling onto the landing surface at the right rate. Not too shallow, not too steep. Just about right. He wanted to let the wheels just skim the surface rather than plant themselves hard into the unstable surface.

"Last five feet to go boss." Mike announced referring to the radar altimeter. "Roger Mike," Seth replied firmly grasping the control column and throttles. Mike looked over at his boss just to reassure himself. Seth always looked confident, no matter what the situation. He may as well have been landing at Miami International's 13,000 foot paved runway. He was the picture of coolness.

Seth felt the subtle deceleration that let him know that the main wheels had contacted the hard sandy, Edwards Air Force Base dry lake bed-like surface. He felt it a second before the others. The three men tensed and waited for the sudden deceleration that followed the touchdown on an unimproved landing surface. It never came. The wheels accepted the weight of the airplane as the wings lost lift at the same rate that the dynamic loads from high speeds were reduced. The resulting smooth transfer of weight to the wheels could hardly be felt.

Mike looked out the side window at the moment of touchdown. The wheels kicked up the sand and dust into the vortices that were still developing as the wings were developing lift. The spinning cyclones that formed at the wing's tips were an awesome site. It visually showed the amount of air that was being moved by the 20-ton airship at the moment of touchdown.

Seth maintained directional control by using a combination of rudder and nose wheel steering as the airplane brushed along the compacted sand of the roadbed. As the speed slowed, Mike, Izz and Sean seemed to breathe again. The surface had a little more friction than Seth anticipated so he added power to compensate and keep his taxi speed up to reach the barn 200 meters ahead.

"Doors are opening on the barn boss. "Hope it's the good guys." Mike commented.

Seth saw the doors opening on the barn. From the distance it didn't appear that the opened doors would accommodate the 20-meter wingspan of the Citation X. Seth pointed and centered the tapered end of the X toward the barn's opening. "Well, it's not like we'll have time to call out a carpenter if we got the measurements wrong. Here we go." Seth said smiling, knowing that they'd fit.

The airplane fit in the barn like it was designed for it even thought it was at least two hundred years older than the modern airship. Seth applied a light touch on the aircraft brakes just to dissipate the last few foot-pounds of energy and pulled the engines into the fuel cutoff position. Sean and Izz had the door opened and rushed out to provide local security just outside of a 70-meter perimeter around the barn. Each of them noticed the person standing in the shadows of the barn's hayloft. Izz had the observation cameras out before Mike was at the rear console and had reported the presence of the person near the hayloft over the radios.

"Don't shoot him yet Izz, not until we verify who he is." Seth said.

"Looks either too surprised too move or he was expecting us." Izz replied on a full run covered by Sean's over-watch position.

"Satellite imagery clear boss, no fighters scrambled and no unusual message traffic detected. It looks like we fooled 'em again." Mike said examining the returns from the sensors positioned by NSA high overhead.

"Okay, Mike...give me a little security while I make contact with the owner of the parking garage, or at least the person that opened the doors for us." Seth walked down the steps of the X with his palms up too show that he wasn't holding the 9mm Beretta strapped to his side.

The dust had just begun to settle from their landing as he reached the point where their host was standing. Seth could just barely see that the person was dressed in the attire typical of the nomadic peoples that inhabited the area before the Soviets took over and forced farming after butchering thousands of the Kazakhs.

"Nice garage you have here. I don't suppose you could recommend a nice restaurant within walking distance." Seth said in a low unassuming and cool voice.

"No worries, after that arrival, you deserve a bit of breakfast." Came a reply that raised Seth's eyebrows. The hooded figure said removing the hood and confirming that the he that was to meet them was actually a she.

"Welcome to Kazakhstan Colonel Stephens, I'm McKensy Hod. I received your announcement from your NSA yesterday evening. Fortunately we didn't muck up the arrangements." McKensy said with a withering Australian accent.

"Right." Seth said, almost unable to mask his surprise. "Uh...if you don't mind helping close the barn's doors. I won't want anyone to think that I was born in here."

Seth and McKensy made it to the doors and hauled the heavy timbered doors closed. "Looks a little out of place here, doesn't she?" Seth said to Mike as he descended down the stairs of the Citation surprised to see Seth talking to, not only a woman but also, a very attractive woman indeed.

"Whaat?" Mike replied weakly.

"The X Mike, she looks a little out of place in a two hundred year old barn, doesn't she?" Seth said laughing under his breath at Mike's reaction to seeing McKensy Hod. If Mike had a weakness, it was beautiful women. "Ms. Hod, this is Mike Thomas, a man hardly ever caught without words." Seth said.

"Nice to meet you Mike." McKensy said as she held out her hand to Mike. Mike looked at Seth almost clueless as to what to do.

"Go ahead Mike, shake her hand." Seth said on the verge of cracking up. Mike looked back at McKensy and seemingly regained his composure.

"Oh yes, of course, I'm Mike Thomas, perhaps you've heard of me? World traveler and most eligible bachelor." Mike said laughing.

Suddenly, Izz's voice came over the squad radio. "Gentlemen, company's coming up the road from the village. It looks like two trucks in a big hurry."

"Okay men, time to go to work. Mike, pick out a good spot in the rafters overlooking the vehicles approach. Sean, provide security on the secondary approaches. Izz cover me, gentlemen if things start falling apart here take your cues from me. Hands raised mean weapons free. Take your best shot." Seth said scrambling for the side door to meet the vehicles before they could get inside the barn.

"Ms. Hod, are the vehicles we need here?" Seth asked as they reached and opened the heavy side door.

"Yes, we brought them in a few days ago. They are lorries from the Freemantle Company, a front company we use here in this region. Why?" McKensy asked.

"Just in case they start asking questions, follow my lead. I assumed that you are fluent in most of the dialects." Seth said.

"Of course, I have been here for eight years now. That's why I was sent to accompany you." McKensy replied looking at Seth as if he should have known.

Seth broke into view of the men of the lead vehicle at the same time Mike had the man seated in the passenger seat square in the cross hairs of his silenced automatic rifle.

Seth counted their numbers as they came closer. Two open bed trucks approached their position. The trail vehicle's bed was covered with a tarp. Each vehicle with not only a driver, but an armed passenger, plus one soldier manning a light machine gun in the front vehicles bed.

No radio antennae were showing on the vehicles. Seth couldn't see what was in the rear vehicle's bed, but assumed it was more men and firepower. The men appeared to be uniformed and not too happy. "I was hoping that we would have arrived a little more discreetly." Seth said in a half whisper to McKensy.

"They are local state police, a carry over from the days of Soviet rule. It is strange though; they rarely ever move the entire compliment of men at one time. It appears that their entire force has been assembled to greet you. They very rarely venture out beyond their local outpost. Fortunately though, we have bribed them before. They are very corruptible men. I can handle this matter." McKensy stated keeping her eyes on the approaching vehicles.

"Okay, Ms. Hod, we'll follow your lead. Please remember that I reserve the right to act independently." Seth said as he intently watched the approaching convoy.

21

Following the Ili

Alma-Ata, Kazakhstan, February 27, 0540 hours

"The trucks are from the local police force. They were trained by the Soviets before 1991. We shouldn't have any difficulties with them. They have seen the Freemantle Company here for many years. We are contracted by their government to provide survey work for the interior, the same as we do in China." McKensy said to Seth as they watched from an entrance door for the barn.

"Okay gentlemen, let's be ready for anything." Seth said, as the dust cloud from the approaching trucks grew larger. McKensy pushed opened the door a little more. She and Seth moved to where the two Freemantle trucks were parked as if she was just going about their planned business. Seth pulled his heavy jacket over his sidearm as they walked. The trucks pulled up closer to the two as they walked. The lead truck stopped within 10 meters of the Freemantle trucks, McKensy and Seth.

McKensy stopped as they approached and appeared surprised as she waited, watching. The convoy leader in the lead truck appeared to be talking on a radio. Seth watched and listened to his team check in with him using the earpiece mounted discreetly behind Seth's ear.

Izz was the first to talk. "There appears to be several more men in the back of the second truck boss. The grenade launcher is ready to give truck number two a surprise."

Mike checked in next. He had a funny way of letting Seth know that he had him dead in his sights. "The leader in the truck is already dead boss, I'm just waitin' to let him know."

Sean called last. "I've a clear shot on the machine gunner in the first truck."

Seth was confident that he and McKensy's moves were covered. All he had to do was raise his hands and the team would unleash their firepower on the uninvited guests.

Seth and McKensy watched the leader get out of the truck and stagger over to their location. The way this man was dressed was a disgrace to any man in the same uniform. His appearance summed up the capability of his force's potential. It too, would probably fall short of exactness. He was not a very large or tall man and the over extended stomach that fell over his trousers look hideously out of proportion. He was one of those that had watched too many cheap cowboy movies and tried to emulate the cavalier manner in which the cowboy would confidently stroll up to an adversary. He had the part just about right even the matted unshaven and tobacco stained stubble that formed a disgusting ring around his mouth. He looked confident but Seth had seen many confident "cowboys" die in his time. It never worked out in real life quite like the Hollywood version did. The man that thought ahead and planned for every contingency won the fight. Impulsive actions not thought through, well they lost.

"Your identifications cards?" The leader said in Russian, with a Kazakh dialect. He was barely able to stand and yet he made a good attempt at walking to where they were. He was either still asleep or still suffering the effects of last evening's libations. It was still early Seth thought, perhaps both effects were responsible for his lack of professionalism.

"Certainly." Replied McKensy as she and Seth produced the appropriate documents.

The half-asleep, half drunk, disgraceful, leader examined the documents in the dim morning light. He turned the documents at an angle to take advantage of the headlights from the vehicle. Seth watched him sway as a willowy tree would in a stiff breeze. The leader of the convoy seemed to take what seemed like hours examining the documents. Seth took advantage of the time available to observe the men manning the trucks. They fumbled with the buttons on their uniforms, rubbed their faces and could care less about what was going on. The leader grunted a few unintelligible words as he handed back the identification to Seth and McKensy comparing their faces with the photos on the identification.

"Several farmers reported that they had seen a military airplane crash into the road several kilometers up ahead. Have you seen anything?" The leader said barely able to keep his eyes open.

"No we haven't seen anything. We are traveling from Frunze to Alma-Ata. We stopped to examine a wheel on one of our trucks. The road is in horrid condition from Frunze. It is amazing that we have made it this far in two days." McKensy said in almost perfect Russian.

"Yes the road is terrible." The leader said as if passing the time waiting for something. He stood there shifting his eyes back and forth from Seth to McKensy.

"You and your men must be hungry." McKensy said as she walked to the back of one of the Freemantle trucks. She reached in under the rear window of the Range Rover and pulled out a large wooden box. Seth watched the men on the two trucks perk up and become curious. McKensy handed over the box to the ill-mannered leader.

Seth could see that it was filled with fruit, bread, cheeses and vodka. As she handed the box over to the leader, she also handed the leader a handful of Rubles, carefully so not to let the men on the trucks see the money exchange hands.

"I would normally not accept these offerings from you, but I did have to awaken my men very early. Perhaps this will make them a bit more understanding." The leader said lying through his rotted teeth.

"Have a safe journey and watch for the livestock crossing the roads. We were almost killed by a herd of water buffalo. The peasants here are ignorant. They aren't as educated as the rest of us. They think that the roads are for moving their herds."

"Thank you Sergeant. Good day to you and your men." McKensy said.

She and Seth watched as the leader got in the truck and shouted a few words to the driver. They tore off back down the road leaving a wake of dust to follow them by.

"Well so much for our surprise entry." Seth said as he moved back to the barn, McKensy followed.

"Gentlemen, we have about two hours to get moving. Mike we will have to fly the aircraft out of here a little earlier than planned. Those cowboys will be back here as soon as they report to their superiors that someone thought a plane had crashed and they ran into an Australian and an American near the area. It won't take long for someone with a little more intelligence to put two and two together. We can only assume now that Hesbulah has alerted his men all over the world. They'll be looking for any scenarios that could imply that we have arrived. Only then, they'll be more of them. Mike after we fuel the jet you'll fly it solo into New Delhi and standby for our pickup. McAdams has arranged for a support base there to cover our operations. We've already briefed the three pick up points that we'll use. If you don't hear from us in 68 hours, fly the route over the pick up points and look for the ground to air signals. Sean, Izz, grab the to-go gear from the aircraft and load it into the rovers. Mike let's get this fuel uploaded." Seth commanded. He knew that Hesbulah had to have put out some word for his intelligence operators to watch for anything strange. This would certainly fall into that category. As soon as stubble face sobered up a little, reported this incident to his superiors and realized his mistakes, he'd be back. Seth wanted to make sure that by the time he returned the team was long gone, along with any traces that they had been here.

The sun was full above the eastern horizon now. The cloudless sky and crisp temperatures would offer no cover for the Citation X's departure. Anyone looking skyward would see the aircraft in the clear skies. The sound of the powerful jet engines would travel farther than they normally would in the cold crisp morning air. Mike would fly the X at high-speed terrain flight through the mountains of Kazakhstan, along the borders of Tadzhikskaya, China, Pakistan and India. The 1,000 kilometer flight to New Delhi would take him about 2 hours at terrain flight altitudes.

"Good hunting boss. You know I hate being in the support role." Mike said as he climbed aboard the aircraft.

Seth nodded as he closed the door from the outside and gave the door two firm pats as it was secured into place.

Mike started the aircraft engines. The sound was deafening in the confines of the barn. Mike gave a quick thumbs up.

Seth and Sean opened the two doors and did quick scan up the road where they landed earlier. Seth returned the thumbs up to Mike as he confirmed that the roadway was clear. The overpowered jet leapt out of the barn and as soon as Mike lined it up with the trail, he applied full power. The wheels of the aircraft began to roll over the compacted sand, rapidly gathering speed. Seth saw the nose gear pull off of the ground and the rest of the aircraft followed. Mike accelerated the powerful jet while it flew in ground effect, just centimeters above the ground. The dust swirled madly about, forced in different directions by the downward flowing air off of the wings and the supersonic jet blast created by the engines. No one viewing the craft from the rear could see anything except a several large swirling tornadoes of dust and debris kicked up by the fast moving jet. Seth waited until he saw Mike gain altitude and turn down a valley to the south before he closed the doors and headed to the exit where Izz, Sean and McKensy were waiting in the two rovers.

"Stay close, heads on a swivel." Seth said as he passed the rover that Izz drove, along with Sean. Seth half-walked, half-ran to the lead rover that McKensy drove.

"You'll think we were your shadow, boss." Izz called out from behind the wheel.

He jumped into the lead rover, "I just want you to know that I don't believe any of what I hear about woman drivers, McKensy. On to Urumqi." Seth said as McKensy nailed the accelerator snapping his head back like a whip.

"I just want you to know that I never listen to chauvinistic prejudices anyway." McKensy returned.

They were on their way and had seventy hours to get the information back to the United Nations in time for Karl's brief.

With any luck, Karl would be safely on his way from Goslar to the states by tomorrow evening. So far, they had been fortunate to stay ahead of Hesbulah this far. They had probably been foolish to rely on fortune this long.

McKensy took a different road down from the plateau into Alma-Ata. They headed almost northeast toward Kapchangay. There, they would pick up the road that followed that Ili River and cross the border into China. They had 650 kilometers to cover before they'd reach Urumqi. Seth looked over at the speedometer on the rover. If they averaged this speed of 70 kilometers per hour, they'd reach Urumqi by late evening.

Seth examined the intelligence reports on his laptop. The plutonium was being moved by road and rail. After the transfer from Russia to Urumqi, it was being placed into heavily shielded piggyback rail cars for the journey to Bhutan. Bhutan was a small country about the size of the state of Massachusetts, between India and China. On a clear day, one could look down from Mt. Everest into Bhutan only 200 kilometers away to the east. It was surrounded by mountain ridges, and was impossible to reach without being observed. Socotra and Bhutan were practically owned by Hesbulah, as were the puppet governments installed to front his operation.

According to Karl, they were over two thousand delivery vehicles being stored in the mountains surrounding Bhutan. Seth's mission now was to document the plutonium transfer from the old soviet missiles in Urumqi, trace it movement to Bhutan, and confirm its loading onto the new delivery vehicles in Bhutan. And they had 72 hours to do it.

He would transmit the data and imagery back to NSA using a series of satellites to disguise the origination of his signals.

On the other road, the ragtag leader of the security convoy that challenged Seth was happy with his spoils. He would have much rather had the woman but he was in no condition to put up a fight. The food and vodka was just as good. He passed a few pieces of the food and a bottle of vodka to the second truck, but kept most of it for himself and the other two men in the first truck. He tore a portion of the bread off of the loaf that he was eating and passed it back to the dust-covered figure in the bed of the uncovered truck. He swilled down half of the vodka before passing it to his comrade driving next to him. By the time they had reached the run down and years neglected headquarters he was in the same condition that he was before he passed out the night before.

The trucks pulled up to the building and the leader thought that he would get some more sleep before he would call his superiors to report that there was nothing to report. No sign of a plane crash anywhere. He glanced at the two Mercedes off road vehicles parked across from his building on a side street. He staggered into his building and went directly to his seat in front of the pot-bellied stove that matched the contours of his own physique. He sat down, oblivious to the presence of the six men standing near the heavily curtained window, rubbing his hands over the stove to warm them.

"Comrade, what did you find at the top of the hill this morning?" One of the shadowed figures near the curtain said.

The drunken, stubble-faced leader spun around in his chair, quickly sobered by the surprise presence of the voice familiar to him. It was his commander. He hadn't seen him in months. The last time was during an inspection visit. He wasn't due here until next year, during the next inspection period. His commander never ventured from his lavish office building in the center of Alma-Ata to the outposts except for the yearly inspection visit.

"Colonel, I, uh, uh am pleased to see you this morning. I am not prepared for an inspection. My men have been busy with the border incursion from the south. We have had no time for preparations." The stubble-faced, cowboy clown said offering excuse after excuse.

"That is enough. Tell me exactly what you had seen on the hilltop." The commander said moving from the shadows into the dim light emanating from the fire in the stove.

"Nothing, nothing, I was preparing to send you my report. We stopped only a few herders and farmers that thought that they had seen a military plane crash onto the road. They had seen a huge dust cloud and loud noise, but no explosions or fires were seen. Even the Australian and the American from Freemantle Company did not see anything. And they had driven the same road from Frunze the evening before." The leader said trying to appear sober.

Another man stepped from behind the comrade colonel. He was a man of enormous stature. He was broad shouldered and his chiseled and jagged jaw punctuated his intensity. He was not dressed as a soldier of the Kazakhstanian Defense Force. He wore dark brown calf length riding boots that were un-scuffed and polished to a sheen that he couldn't imagine. The twill khaki colored wool trousers fit perfectly into the cuffs of the riding boots and bloused outward in perfect folds. His brown leather belted jacket was the same color as the trousers but was not adorned with any insignia or badge. He couldn't be a higher-ranking officer. This thought comforted the ignorant sergeant. The stubble-faced leader watched as the broad shouldered man removed a pair of perfect fitting kidskin gloves and tucked them neatly into the belt that surrounded his jacket.

"Tell me about the American and Australian, describe them to me." The broad shouldered Hesbulah calmly prompted the stubble-faced drunken sergeant.

The sergeant had never felt so intimidated. The deep voice was from a bellows deep inside a human figure. The eyes that looked through him were not full of life, but empty of it. They seemed to drain the strength right from him. He had to break eye contact. It was too painful to look directly into the eyes.

The stubble-faced Sergeant began to sweat profusely. He couldn't speak. His tongue seemed to swell in his mouth. He tried to form words but couldn't. He babbled in unintelligible grunts. Heaves were all that came from the tobacco stained stubble that outlined the mouth.

Hesbulah stood staring and waiting. The disgust grew inside him as he put on his gloves. Hesbulah moved closer and put a hand on the back of the babbling idiot standing in front of him.

"Tell me what I want to know." Hesbulah commanded with an eerie calm, ice-like deep whisper of a voice.

Stubble-face only stared ahead, afraid to look, trying to form words. Hesbulah stared and continued to tighten the grip on the back of the sergeant's cervical vertebra. The sergeant babbled more, he desperately tried to form words but couldn't. His half drunk and fear filled mind was racing too fast. It couldn't coherently translate the visual images that flashed across his mind's eye. The events of this morning were mixing in a jumble of images that he tried too quickly to explain. The result was incomprehensible mixture of grunts and heaves. Suddenly there were no more thoughts. Hesbulah's grip had crushed the cervical vertebra of the ignorant leader and stanched the flow of nerve impulses like a gardener would fold over a garden hose and squeeze to stop the flow of water. His body, now limp and lifeless was supported only by Hesbulah's grip.

Hesbulah turned to the comrade colonel and stared. Calmly, still holding one handed the limp and lifeless body, he said, "I want the American brought to me. Do you understand?"

Only El Hadin was not surprised. He had seen this display of intimidation before. Even if the sergeant had told him everything, the results would have been the same. The others stood staring at the lifeless suspended body as they replied in a stuporous unison. Hesbulah released the lifeless body and it crumpled into a heap onto the floor. The exposed flesh of the sergeant's body rested against the red-hot pot bellied stove. The smell of burning flesh filled the room. Hesbulah looked at them staring, motionless, too panicked to move.

"Now!" Hesbulah commanded. Jump starting some action from his thugs.

The two vehicles from the Freemantle Company made the turn eastward at Kapchangay. The range rovers were moving along at a good pace, lightly bounding over the frost heaved roadbed before them. The cold, sparsely vegetated, desert-like terrain offered no cover. They could be seen for miles. Their only hope was to make it to the mountain passes before someone started looking for them. Then, they could easily pull under a rock ledge or behind a hill to stay concealed. Seth looked at the Global Satellite System receiver. The GPS would tell keep him up to date on their navigation progress and allow him to remain more situationally aware. He scanned ahead, desperately trying to see ahead with more detail. Once they crossed the border into China, the threat level would be reduced. The concentration of soldiers and security personnel around the borders, just by sheer numbers increased the chances that someone would know about their arrival. The visit by the KDF this morning was unsettling. Stubble-face would be reporting to his superiors about now, Seth thought. Soon everyone would know that the American was here driving around in the Freemantle rovers. They had to shift to keep their advantage of surprise. Seth saw their new opportunity as they rounded a bend in the road.

'So far, so good.' Seth thought.

"Pull over into that warehouse McKensy." Seth said and then paused for a moment as McKensy turned the wheel, a question forming in her mind.

"How long have you been with Freemantle Limited? Seth asked.

McKensy replied, "Forever, why?"

"Well, its time for a career change." Seth said as McKensy drove the rovers into the open doors of a warehouse next to a truck impound lot near the Charyn Airport.

"This is a little different, Sean said to Izz as they followed Seth and McKensy into the open, abandoned warehouse.

"The boss is just staying a few steps ahead, Sean." Izz returned.

"Ah, so you know what he's doing." Sean said appearing relieved that Izz knew what Seth had in mind.

"I have no idea, Sean. I have no idea. But Seth does and that's all that matters." Izz said as he braked the rover hard to a stop next to Seth's in the far dark corner of the warehouse.

Izz and Sean saw Seth get out and walk to an open doorway at the south end of the warehouse.

"Sean, have you ever negotiated in Kazakhstan before?" Seth said to Sean as Sean walked over to the doorway where Seth was looking over the impound lot where a convoy of a brand new supply of Saratov diesel tractors were preparing to depart for China. Seth counted. There were about thirty-five of the new trucks lined up in the morning sun just off of the road pointed east. The blue-tinged smoke from the running diesels wafted in the calm air. The driverless vehicles idled as the drivers waited in the local dive for the convoy leader to head out to his truck.

"Never, boss." Sean replied as they both watched. There was a moment of silence as the two intently observed the activities going on in the impound lot next to them.

"Well, there's a first time for everything." Seth said as he patted Sean on the shoulder.

22

The Kara-Babau to Ining Highway

Near the Kazakhstani –Chinese Border, February 27, 0540 hours

"Boss, I would have been glad to negotiate for us, maybe we put Sean on the spot here." Izz said as they watched Sean leave the area where two of the drivers were standing.

"Sean doesn't feel like he is part of the team Izz, He thinks that he let us down back there in Jersey. He feels he needs to contribute. That is why he got the nod here Izz. I know how shrewd you can be Izz, for that reason and the fact that if I had sent you in there, you would have had them paying us to take their trucks. Here he comes now. It looks like a bit of good news, wouldn't you say?" Seth said as Sean and McKensy moved closer to them. Their smiles indicated that all was well.

"Yeah, things look positive from my perspective Sir." Izz replied standing next to Seth and watching the two approach their position.

"Two white ones." Was all Sean said as he handed the keys over to Seth.

"How did it go, no conflicts I trust." Seth said looking at Sean and McKensy as Izz unloaded the last container from the rover.

"You would have been proud." McKensy said. "He didn't even shoot anyone. He did drive a hard bargain. He paid two of the drivers twice the cost of a new Saratov Diesel and added the range rovers too. He probably could have got them with only a few bottles of vodka."

Izz winced. "You paid them how much Sean? We don't deal in pounds here do we?" Izz finished. He always approached things in a more economical fashion.

"I made them an offer they couldn't refuse. They were two single guys. I know the type. They jumped at the opportunity to live in the hills of Kazakhstan with more money than they would have made in twenty years driving around the highways of eastern China, delivering who knows what. They'll be lost in the hills of Kazakhstan in their new rovers in less than an hour. Our trail will be covered boss. They'll even bring the trucks in here in a few minutes. Talk about negotiations, actually, I'm proud of myself. I even had them change the registration papers in the dealer's office. We are almost legitimate. Imagine that." Sean said.

"You've a bright future ahead of you Sean. Izz, let's find a good hide point, just in case Sean's two fellows change attitudes." Seth said.

McKensy and Sean prepared to load the new Diesels with the mission gear as soon as the two drivers brought the trucks into the warehouse. As soon as Seth and Izz hidden high in the rafters and just as promised by Sean, two shiny new white Saratov diesels pulled into the warehouse. Seth watched as the drivers, both young men in their mid twenties, got out from behind the wheel.

They were as happy as if someone had just handed them a box of money and two new range rovers. Seth could tell that they were just as Sean said, two young single guys looking for a future. It just happened to be given to them as compliments of the United States.

"Sean, ask them to take the back roads and stay together for a few hours. Tell them there is an extra 50,000 in it if they stay together and deliver another box of fruit and vodka to stubble-face in Alma-Ata. This way if anyone is looking for us in the rovers, we'll be into the expanses of China before they realize that we're no longer in the rovers."

"Roger boss," Sean replied.

Seth and Izz watched as the two took the box of fruit and nodded their heads, smiling. Sean handed over the keys, the money, and even a handshake. If anything, he had the capability to be a salesman when he retired from Her Majesty's service. Seth smiled. They had been in Kazakhstan for almost four hours now and hadn't been in any situation remotely hostile. It had to be a record. But they had only sixty-eight hours left before Karl needed the information for the briefing. Seth watched as the two men left in the range rover and headed back to the east along the Kara-Babau to Ining Highway.

It only took them a few minutes to load up the equipment and move back into the line. The two trucks were placed in the convoy line to drive a crossed the border into China. The other drivers were just now coming out of the small shack along the road that sold food and drinks to drivers crossing the expanse into China. It was the equivalent of any truck stop in America. Fuel, food and rest, along with the women of ill repute, could be found here. Only the conditions here were a little more on the rustic side.

The Saratov diesels were magnificent trucks by any standards. A group of investors spun a division off of an American company. They used the years of research and development, saving those costs to develop a truck that could travel the terrible road expanses of western Russia. The same conditions existed in eastern China. Chinese companies realized that they could move more freight more economical with the Saratov's almost 50,000-kilogram tractor capability. That made the trucks ideally suited for the long brutal hauls that were encountered moving freight from the eastern and southern part of China to the west.

The trucks were equipped with extra capacity fuel tanks, a small living and storage area behind the two front seats. The streamlined body style coupled with two sets of steering tires located in the front and four sets of dual driving wheels in the rear. The huge mass of rubber and steel was almost unstoppable in any weather condition and mountain slope. The large 1200 horsepower Saratov Diesel engine developed the highest torque in the industry. It could maintain speeds of 200 kilometers per hour on level ground and pull its 50,000 kilogram loaded trailer up a 10-degree slope.

"Izz, try not to have too much fun with this. Stay close and follow me, especially if things get a little tense at the border." Seth said.

"Not a problem boss, hey its great they even labeled everything with pictures. It a shame Mike isn't here, even he could understand how to operate this truck. It is Neanderthal proof." Izz returned.

Seth left to jump into the passenger's side of the Saratov diesel that was positioned just in front of the one that carried Izz and Sean. He climbed the four-step ladder easily to find that McKensy had already occupied the seat.

"I thought that you were doing the driving today McKensy." Seth asked with a surprised look.

"I thought that maybe my driving was so bad that you decided to pick the largest vehicle that you could find to intimidate me. Perhaps I'll just watch you for the first 200 kilometers or so, just to make sure that I figure everything out." McKensy said.

Seth passed behind her seat and moved over into the driver's seat. It was like sitting in a small room rather that a vehicle. Seth took his seat. He looked ahead as he settled into the driver's station and saw the exhaust plumes from the lead trucks flare up, indicating that they had begun to move. The auto-hydraulic transmission simply had arrows for forward, neutral, and reverse. Everything else was as in a standard configuration. He continued to look out of the deeply tinted windows that would reduce the glare on the snow-covered roadways and also prevent anyone from seeing inside. He checked the engine gauges. Everything was operating normally. The fuel was at the full level, and the digital computer indicated that they could go almost 2,300 kilometers at this engine RPM. He knew that this would decrease as the engine developed power.

The vehicle in front of them began to move ahead. Seth depressed the accelerator and tried to maintain the same following distance that the vehicles ahead were maintaining. The truck was amazingly spry and required little additional power to start moving.

"Did you ever think that your career ladder would lead you Trucking McKensy?" Seth said with a smile.

He and McKensy passed the time talking about the mission requirements and her future. She told him that she'd always wanted to go to the United States, but her family had always been involved in covert operations. She was a dutiful daughter and worked hard at what she did, but her heart wasn't in it. She wished that someone else had the task of saving the world.

It would take about another 45 minutes before they would reach the border crossing point into China. After that they would leave the convoy and turn toward Urumqi.

Seth was distracted from their conversation as he saw the two old MIG-17 jets flying fast and low toward the border. Hopefully they weren't looking for Seth's team in the two new Saratov Diesels. The only way that they could have been compromised was if the two men that they bought the trucks from had stopped and told the authorities. Seth didn't know that the jets had already found their targets, the range rovers, moving back toward the west on the highway. The two combat jets had rolled in on the unsuspecting two drivers with 20mm cannons blazing. The armor piercing projectiles tore through the thin metal skins of the rovers and shredded the vehicles. The fuel spilling from the punctured tanks ignited as it mixed with air and exploded. The fiery wreckage and its driver were reduced to a twisted unrecognizable heap of scrap within seconds. The jets were returning now to their base in eastern Kazakhstan. The pilots reported their mission complete. Seth couldn't have known at this point that Hesbulah was satisfied that the vehicles that matched the description given by stubble face's men had been destroyed. Hesbulah and El Hadin would later inspect the wreckage, but were not in any hurry.

The border was crossed without any incident. They were just one of the trucks in the convoy. They weren't even stopped, only waved through. The next five hundred kilometers passed by quickly.

Just east of Ining, China, the main convoy turned south toward Aksu. The two trucks carrying the team proceeded straight through to the east and took a pass across the mountains to join a better highway that would speed their approach toward Urumqi. The Saratov tractors moved along at speeds of 175 kilometers per hour. They negotiated the rugged roadways effortlessly. Even though they were going through the snow-covered roads near the mountains peak, it presented no difficulties. Just after they had passed the city of Manassu they stopped in a remote area off of the roadway. The area was shielded with tall pines and small shrubs. Urumqi was now in sight. Seth glanced at his watch. The Saratov Diesels helped them make better time on the highways than he had originally planned. The team gathered in Seth's vehicle for a final briefing.

"The railroad switching yard is just to the north of Urumqi. The warehouse where the plutonium is transferred to truck is located here." Seth said pointing to the satellite photo.

Seth continued the briefing as the others gathered closer to see the map. "Izz, you and Sean will move further north of the warehouse and proceed to intercept a train that we suspect is loaded with the plutonium. Capture all of the imagery on the digital and we'll up-link it back to NSA when we move to the launch sites. Keep in mind that the intent is to link the plutonium to Hesbulah's operation. We must provide indisputable evidence that he is buying or taking the plutonium from a few of the corrupt politicians left over from the communist regime in Russia and transporting it with the help of some corrupted politicians in China. We suspect that there are only a hand full of people in Russia and China that would be part of this plan. The majority of the Russians and Chinese want the same thing that you and I do. Here is the satellite photo of the rail cars that the treaty inspector sealed as they left Irkutsk. The inspectors also verified the position of the plutonium in Novosibirsk where it was to be processed for final underground elimination. The numbers of the containers have been verified at Irkutsk and Novosibirsk. We know that they couldn't remove the shielding from this weapons grade plutonium anywhere in Russia without attracting attention or being picked up by our satellites. Urumqi was approved many years ago as the site for a nuclear powered electrical generating station. Anytime hot spots show up here, we disregard it as an event tied to the nuclear power station. Hesbulah's men have been breaking down the shielding here at Urumqi for that reason. It doesn't attract attention. He then simply ships it in the right packages and then uploads to his delivery vehicles in the sites near Bhutan. Your mission is to record the Geiger counter readings and get as much visual imagery from at least four opposite positions close to the rail cars, this way we can trace the approximate amount of plutonium in each container. Watch your personal dosimeter. The shielding was only designed to prevent detection from our satellites. No one can be sure how much radiation is leaking from the shielding at close range. McKensy and I will go directly to the warehouse where they are opening the shielding and verify that it is the Russian weapons grade plutonium from Novosibirsk. We also will see how they are moving it, record the transport to the launch sites and process used. Rendezvous point is this intersection in the city of Kuerhle in eight hours, at oh-one-fifteen, 0115 hours. We will wait no longer for each other at the rendezvous site. If things go bad, make it to either Yaertang or Namutso for pick up in 60 hours."

Seth paused and looked at his watch. "It's seventeen-fifteen on my mark, 5, 4, 3, 2, 1, mark. Any problems call over the radio to advise the other team, code word for failure is poor man. Izz, Sean, good hunting. Check your six and stay ahead. Expect anything!" Seth finished as they shook hands. He and Izz traded eye contact and smiles. Nothing more was said. They headed for their diesels and proceeded on to their mission objectives.

As they drove the remaining miles into Urumqi, Seth and McKensy were quiet. Seth looked over at McKensy and thought about what she said. He handed her a cup of coffee that he had prepared. She had no business being here. He wouldn't feel right putting her in danger. He thought about it one last time and then made the call to his contact near Urumqi as McKensy fell asleep quickly in the back of the cab after she said that she suddenly felt very tired. He'd make one more stop before he would continue on to his target area without McKensy.

The cold air was unsettlingly still. His breath clouded around his face as he walked toward the small sedan parked in the moonlit shadows of the evening. As he approached the sedan, the two men inside it got out and walked to meet him.

They appeared to be Chinese and were dressed in layers of heavy clothing that made them appear wider than they actually were. Seth stopped about five feet from them, just out of their reach.

"Good to see you again Seth." The agent wearing the black baseball cap said.

"It has been awhile, hasn't it? How is everything on the eastern front Nick? Seth asked.

"We've been very busy ever since the Alamogordo spy scandal. We've been running profiles on every agent that we know of here in China. You wouldn't believe how deep the scandal goes. Every corrupt politician in this country has a hand in our nuclear secrets. We've questioned these clowns and they all point to one man as the orchestrator. He's a phantom though and we haven't been able to pin him down. As soon as we get close and gain the confidence of the minions, they end up dead. A lot of bad accidents happen here." Nick said with apparent disgust in his voice.

"What brings you to Urumqi Seth?" Nick said trying to change the subject and adjusting his disposition more towards optimistic.

"Would you believe that I had some vacation time, Nick…didn't know what to do with myself and ended up in China." Seth said with a smile on his face.

"No, I wouldn't believe it Seth." Nick said half laughing.

"You're a smart man Nick, always have been ever since Officer's Candidate School. You still doing that bad Chinese Rodney Dangerfield impression?" Seth said as his characteristic smile began forming as he remembered Nick impressions from years back at Fort Benning.

"I tell ya, I get no respect, even in China…" Nick replied in his best Dangerfield. The three laughed and visited for another few minutes along the side of a dark road in western China.

"Nick, I have a young lady from Australia, she works as an observer for another intelligence agency. We need to get her back to Australia as quick as we can. She'll be asleep for another few hours. When she wakes up give her this note." Seth quickly scrawled down a few words, folded the paper and handed it to Nick.

Nick just looked as he received the message. No words were exchanged. Seth hesitated in thought as if to make sure that he was doing the right thing before he walked over to the truck. Nick and his driver followed.

Seth reached under McKensy as she slept, picked her up and handed her down to Nick gently. "It is about time that your life was yours McKensy." Seth said to her as if she could hear him. "Take good care of her Nick, she's a fine young woman, she has much more to offer to the world than risking her life here." Seth said as Nick and his driver took her into their arms and walked back to the sedan. Seth watched as they walked away into the cold night air. He pulled the door of the Saratov closed after he saw the Sedan drive off into to darkness.

Seth pointed the Saratov tractor towards the east. The roadway was starting to accumulate a trace of snow. He had a little more than seven hours to get to the transfer point north of Urumqi, get the intelligence and head back to Kuerhle, the rendezvous point.

The tractor covered the distance ahead of schedule. He pulled into the area that the satellites showed would offer the best approach on foot to the complex. The complex was located on the bank of a small river that drained the high mountains to the southeast of the city. The tangle of rail lines aligned north to south followed the river bed and passed through a valley between the long and linear Tien Shan Mountain range to the city of Hami, just south of the eastern edge of the Tien Shan Mountains. Seth parked the Saratov in a stockyard next to a few other tractors. Some already had their trailers attached. Others looked as if they had just arrived. The yard was empty of people except for the few drivers and yard workers that were just finishing up before their supper break that evening. There were no barriers surrounding the yard. The escape route out looked as clear as the route in. Seth made sure that all of the lights were out inside the vehicle before he grabbed his equipment from the to-go bag.

He quickly covered the distance from the stockyard to the high fence that surrounded the complex. There were three fence lines with about 10 meters in between each. Each was at least 5 meters tall, topped with triple strand concertina type, razor wire. The building appeared newer than those surrounding it did. Seth glanced at the GPS read out from the instrument strapped to his wrist and proceeded along the fence line to the drainage culvert that went into the complex. He placed several small explosive charges in and around the ditch. The next stop would be the riverbank as he moved stealthily across the ground. He found the first of several cameras that were scanning the riverbank and fixed explosive charges to the armored wiring bundles that connected them with the monitors in the security room. He checked the detailed plan that he received from NSA of the area and only had one more point to cover before he went into the complex. The two automated gun towers were within firing range of his exit point. He moved quickly to place the explosive charges and rewire the guns so that the commands from the controlled were reversed. His last stop was to place the small disposable mortar tubes in the areas that would cover his exit if he needed them.

He cut the wire in several areas and placed quick release fasteners on them that would hold them closed in the event a guard would happen by to inspect them. Satisfied that his escape route was complete, he entered the complex through his last wire cut, closing it behind him with the fasteners.

The kill zone was adequate he thought but just as the satellite photos had showed, there were dead spots in the areas. Spots where vegetation had grown in after the original surveillance plan was completed screened the kill zones. They may have had a professional design the security of the complex but a professional certainly didn't manage it. He wondered if any of the installed equipment even still worked.

He covered the distance to the building using the paths between the dead spots. The building had an exterior of corrugated steel siding, not unlike many warehouses or industrial buildings around the world. Its construction appeared to be within the last year, no more than two. He glanced at his watch. Plenty of time remained. He found a door where the light had been burnt out that wasn't yet replaced. The mounds of dirt and dead vegetation surrounding the entrance suggested that it hadn't been used in at least a season. The weeds that had grown around it during the summer were now dead from the winter's cold. He carefully cleaned the dirt and weeds from around the door to prevent the brush marks that would indicate that it had recently been opened.

He placed the small thermal charge around the lock and shielded the charge with ceramic clay to keep the light and heat from being seen. The thermal charge silently cut through the metal of the single dead bolt as easily as if he had used a cutting torch. The door swung open outward with protest from its rusted, unused hinges. Seth pulled the door closed behind him and fixed a small keeper rod in it. The keeper rod would pass a security inspection, but not prevent a man from breaking through it under the full force of his weight.

Seth was inside the dimly lit building. He took a few moments to orient himself. The transfer point would be at the midpoint of the building. He peered over a waist high brick wall that separated the working area of the warehouse from the walkways. He watched as men dressed in heavy overalls used a overhead crane to remove the piggyback trailers from the rail cars and swing them into the heavily constructed rolling platform that would move the trailers inside the steel and concrete building placed in the center of the steel sided complex. The inside of the complex was dimly lit except for the entrance and exits of the central transfer point. The intelligence given to Seth by NSA of the layout inside the building left much in question. He took a few extra minutes to study the routine of the workers and security men that roamed in no apparent pattern.

The temperature inside the building wasn't any warmer than the outside, but Seth felt the sweat forming on the inside of his clothing. He always counted on the adrenaline to rush and tonight would not be an exception. He moved around the supports of the building quickly and surely, remaining in the shadows and staying out of the observation areas. Stay low, he though to himself, no quick or jerky movements. He placed the timed remotely detonated charges as he moved from place to place. He covered the inner perimeter of the building, always scanning to get an accurate summary of the situation. He noted the place were the armed guards were located. They'd be the first danger encountered. He was now 180 degrees opposite of the place where he had entered the building and was approaching the transfer facility. Seth glanced at the dosimeter in his pocket. It still read zero. At least the shielding was sufficient at this distance. Seth saw the timing of the transfer from rail car to heavy rolling platforms. As one exited, a few moments later another entered. He moved quickly to the point were the rail cars approached the transfer point. He studied the list of numbered cars that had left Novosibirsk three days ago; the numbers from his list matched the sequence of numbers on the rail cars. Seth climbed on to the top of the trailer on the rail car. He lay on top of the center of the trailer waiting for his turn to move into the transfer point. He checked his dosimeter, still nothing.

The rail car began to move. The overhead crane began to swing into position. He heard the guide men along the sides of he trailer shout commands to the crane operator. The cradle approached the trailer. This is tighter than it looks from another perspective. He judged that the cradle would only clear the top of the trailer by no more than 30 centimeters. Seth made his body as flat as he could. The cradle passed over him, the heavy center brace resting above him restricting his breathing. It was so close that he could smell the steel and fell the icy cold temperature of the cradle. He couldn't take normal breaths. His short-rapid heaves had to make up for his normal respiration rate and expansion of his chest. The cradle clamped down on the lift point located on each corner of the trailer. Seth felt the trailer shudder as it was jolted upward by the cable tightening as the crane operator took up the slack. The guide men shouted to verify the attachment and the crane hoisted Seth and the trailer upwards. The load was moved sideways, where it was placed on the rolling platform. The crane was disconnected, the cradle that restricted his breathing removed and the platform was rolled forward by it own electric motors toward the concrete and steel transfer building. Seth kept his form as flat as he could, the trailer top would clear the entry with less than the 30 centimeters clearance from the crane's cradle. The smooth finished steel ceiling inside the transfer point building newer than the rest of the outer building. Seth could see the finishing marks from the factory where the steel was milled still apparent on the finish.

Seth could hear voices and see the reflections on the ceiling. He had to move closer to the edge of the trailer.

He moved close to the edge and turned his head. He could see crews dressed in protective clothing behind lead lined windows at a control panel. Men were still talking and verifying the trailer's integrity by checking the readings with Geiger counters. The men wearing full protective clothing and hearing protection were preparing to open the trailer with robotic devices and transfer the plutonium packages into the smaller casings that would be set in the delivery vehicles. Seth realized that he had to move fast. As soon as the heavy lead shielded trailer doors were opened, the compartment would be flooded with radiation. Seth slid back to the opposite side where the loading crews were leaving the compartment. Peering over the side he saw that half of the crew had their backs to him and were lined up to enter the doorway that led out of the compartment. The remaining crewmen were positioning the robots to open the doors by remote control. He slid off of the side of the trailer and drew his silenced 9mm. Seth came down on the back of the man's spine with pyramid shaped end of his 9mm. The unsuspecting worker fell unconscious as the well-aimed blow interrupted nerve impulses to keep him coherent. Seth quickly dragged the man under the platform carrying the trailer. In a flurry, he donned the protective gear and headpiece. In one smooth move, he was through the door and inside the control cab where the men watched the process from behind the thick lead lined shielded glass. The other part of the crew was passing through the outer door as the first half found vacant seats. They milled around uninterested in the process that they had seen many times before. Some sat resting their heads in their laps as if trying to sleep. When the doors were closed the control cab lights dimmed. It couldn't have been more perfect for Seth. Nothing seemed out of the ordinary for these crews that apparently had done this very monotonous drill everyday. Seth activated the small camera that he had placed under his wristwatch and leaned on the ledge near the window with his hands turned so the camera was pointing directly at the transfer.

The doors of the trailer were opened and the dosimeter placed on the opposite wall in the compartment flew off of the scale. If Seth had remained in the compartment he would have been exposed to deadly radiation within seconds.

A robotic device slid inside the trailer and pulled out the first plutonium package. It methodically transferred each to smaller casings and sealed them. Seth recognized the casings; they were similar in design to the RK-7 warhead casing used in the sea-launched cruise missiles used by the United States. The technology for that warhead casing was compromised years ago from a spy scandal at Los Alamos.

The robot continued to transfer the unshielded plutonium in a series of systematic motions until the operation was complete. Seth checked the integrity of the imagery that he had just received before he moved away from the window. He moved to the door as the others lined up and prepared to complete the transfer and move the small casings into another trailer that was on the other side of the door.

As the door opened Seth moved out and acted as if he were assisting the crew preparing to move the trailer and the casings out of the transfer compartment.

The exit doors opened and Seth moved too soon. One of the leaders saw his move out of the ordinary and came to confront him pointing toward the trailer. Seth shrugged his shoulders and looked around. He remembered a quote from General Patton's biography. Sometimes, any action is more appropriate than no action.

Seth grabbed the man's head in cross arm style and twisted his neck smoothly and silently. He fell to the ground in a crumpled heap. Seth began to shout for help in a high falsetto in Chinese as if his co-worker had fallen from illness. The other workers looked toward Seth's shout and came to the aide of the fallen worker. Seth moved from the fray and was unnoticed by the workers clad in protective gear but was seen by the crewmen still in the control cab. Seth could make out the shouts over the speaker system and looked over his shoulder. The protective gear clad crewmen moved slowly toward him at first and then moved faster toward him. He heard more shouts and then the security klaxon rang.

Seth had little time to react. With lightning quickness, he followed his escape plan. He could see the path to the door was clear but he'd need a diversion before he ran though the channeled escape path out the door. He'd be too easy of a target for the security guards as he passed through the doorway. Seth detonated the remote charges that he had placed behind him on the opposite side of the building. The explosion rocked the building's ironwork. It had created the diversion that Seth needed. The pursuing workers stopped and turned to look toward the explosion behind them. Seth detonated several more charges that he had fastened to the support structure near the transfer point. With a loud report the explosions reverberated through the interior of the building. Seth didn't plan on the demolition effect that the explosives had. With the center supports weakened, the roof of the building began to collapse. The twisted steel girders and supports fell to the floor. The hideous sound of crumpling steel and careening ironwork twisted from it attachment points followed the loud explosions. Seth made it to the doorway and looked back to see his pursuers diving for cover. They were no longer concerned with the pursuit but only to save themselves from the falling iron.

Seth paused by the door and opened it slowly. The entire complex was now bathed in a bright white light. He removed the white protective gear and drew his 9mm. Peering through the partially opened door he detonated several more charges on the opposite side of his escape path. This would give him the few moments that he would need to cross the open space between the building and the fence. Seth dashed from the door as soon as the explosion distracted the security force. He covered the open ground in mere seconds and dove into the small drainage ditch that offered cover before he passed through the open gates. His luck ran out. Two of the security team's members were running toward the explosion from the opposite side of the complex about 30 meters from Seth's position and saw his movements. Seth didn't see them but heard and felt the thuds as the bullets from their Chinese made AK-47 rifles slammed into the mud around his drainage ditch. They were running toward him and firing wildly. Seth rolled over onto his back and fired two well-aimed shots at his pursuers. The second of his shots hit one of the targets just above the sternum, squarely on the clavicle bone, and a little to the right. The shattered shards from clavicle bone tore into the man's carotid artery. Without pausing, he fired two more shots into the man just several steps behind the lead attacker. Seth felt the muck of the drainage ditch rebound as the large 7.62mm bullets from the attacker's rifles sprayed around his position. Seth's advantage was apparent; the attackers could not see him once he dove into the ditch. He exposed only several inches as a target to the attackers running toward him. They made the mistake of continuing to run toward him and fire while moving, instead of stopping and taking aim. They, on the other hand, were easy targets for Seth. The white lights that rimmed the compound illuminated them from behind. The second volley of bullets fired from Seth's Beretta hit the second attacker squarely in the chest cavity only several millimeters apart from each other. The combined impact force of the two bullets into the man's chest was the same as if a car traveling 60 kilometers an hour hit him. He was flung from his feet and catapulted through the air by the force. Seth had no doubts that he was dead before he had hit the ground.

Seth looked around and saw the automatic machine pistols in the acquisition mode. The guards had heard the firing from the AK-47s and assumed that one of their members had seen the intruder. Seth remotely detonated the remaining charges on the opposite side of the complex and broke into a dead run toward the opening he created in the first fence line. The radar that directed the guns caught his movement. The guns spat out 2,000 rounds per minute and had a dwell time of 8 seconds per firing command. Since Seth had reversed the firing command circuits, the more than 300 rounds that poured from the gun fired directly into the center of the compound near the positions of the advancing security force. Seth's moves were detected by the automated guns and but they continued firing their burst into the security force. The security force thought that they were being attack by at least 50 men. Seth fired the remotely placed mortars. They dropped six rounds of High Explosive grenades into the complex. The combination of Seth's detonation charges, the remote mortars and the automated machine guns firing in reverse created the effect that the complex was being over run by an invasion force. The explosions and staccato of automatic weapons firing was deafening. The muzzle flashes and explosions illuminated the night sky. The thought that he had over did it briefly passed through Seth's mind as he ran through the kill zone cleared between the two fences. The radar continued to track his movements and commanded the guns to continue firing. He rolled into the second fence and the fasteners that he had placed earlier broke away allowing him to pass through almost unimpeded. He continued in the same manner into the third fence and was out of the compound and out of the range of the radar that commanded the automatic machine guns. Seth fired the remaining explosives that he had set. The sequenced explosions looked like B-52 bombers were carrying out a small-scale carpet-bombing campaign. The explosions tore through the complex and created secondary explosions from fuel and ammunition stores. The complex was ablaze and smoke poured from the building in its center.

"Nothing better than a strong finish." Seth said to himself as he climbed into the driver's seat of the huge Saratov tractor.

He had safely cleared the area as the military convoys from the barracks in Urumqi closed in preparing to fight the invasion force reported by the security guards. Seth could also see the helicopters overhead prepare for their attack runs on the center of the invasion force. The smoke pouring from the compound multiplied the confusing effects that the early morning muster had on the arriving troops and aircraft. Even if this were a rehearsed response by the military, it would take hours for them to figure out what the hell was going on. The military was in the reaction mode, just as any force would be in this situation. It was nearly impossible to prevent an attack by one man. One man, in the right place at the right time, made all the difference he thought.

He joined several other civilian trucks heading from the area and steered the tractor south toward Kuerhle, where he'd rejoin Izz and Sean. He glanced at his watch and had completed his mission to gather the imagery in less than 6 hours. He pulled the imagery disk from his chest pocket and replaced it comforted that it was undamaged. Seth would up-link the data back to NSA at the rendezvous point near Kuerhle. Then he would proceed across the mountains into Bhutan to trace the route of the plutonium to its destination. Seth drove and realized that he was feeling tired and very hungry. He opened up a food packet and devoured the contents without noticing what it contained. He washed it down with a container of water mixed with electrolytes as he drove. He didn't even know, nor did he care what it was. It simply tasted like the best meal that he could remember in a long time. He allowed his mind and body to relax, to move from its energy consuming on guard mode to one of just relaxation. He felt confident that the military would be watching the routes out of China for the exit routes of the invasion force rather than one crazy man in a Saratov Diesel heading toward China's very inhospitable interior. Seth reached up and turned on the stereo that was mounted in the Saratov's instrument panel. He smiled. He never expected to hear a recognizable song sung by a popular western artist accompany him on the radio as he drove across the high plateau highway. He couldn't help but think that if he didn't know any better, he'd almost think he was driving up Interstate 17, across the Mogollon Plateau towards Flagstaff, Arizona. The drive, the terrain and the song on the radio brought back many wonderful memories. Memories that he would like to re-live again.

All that he had to do was survive the greatest fight of his life. That was all, just survive!

23
Hesbulah Catches On

The ornate and heavy wooden doors opened to the private breakfast. The commandant of the Kazakhstan Defense Force, Alma Ata Region, in honor of his guest, the most praised Hesbulah, was hosting the luncheon banquet.

The tension in the room was apparent to even the least perceptive. Hesbulah was annoyed at the stupidity and ineptness of the commandant. He glared at him as he gave his pre-breakfast address to those attending.

All forty-seven of the guest's eyes turned towards the officer that now approached El Hadin, fearfully, not knowing what next to expect. The officer approached with a message neatly folded over and written on thick parchment. Hesbulah watched with a very thin forced very rehearsed smile. It was a smile that projected more disgust than contentment.

The Commandant halted his address and also watched. The room was completely silent. The footsteps of the messenger were intolerably loud as he thudded a crossed the wooden floor at a quickened pace. Before they had started, they had left strict instructions to the officer stationed at the door of the dinning hall, to not allow any intrusions unless they were urgent and of critical nature. This had better be a good reason. The officer nervously presented the messages to El Hadin as Hesbulah watched out of the corner of his eye.

258

El Hadin scanned the message. The surprise registered in his expression. He handed the message to Hesbulah. "Perhaps you should read this Hesbulah. I believe the news will trouble you."

El Hadin looked at Hesbulah, as would a child as he admitted fault to accidentally destroying a prized family possession. Hesbulah took the note from El Hadin and stared at him as he did with a near fatal glare. Hesbulah read the note and the guests could see the veins in his temples and neck began to bulge as his anger increased with each word read. Hesbulah was reading the intelligence summary sent from his men located in Kazakhstan. They had completed the examination of the wrecked Range Rovers and were presenting the information to Hesbulah.

Hesbulah stood. He was barely able to contain his anger as he looked at the commandant. "I believe the party is over. I would like to thank you for your attendance and I am sure that we will be together again soon. The commandant and I do have some matters of importance to discuss. Would you please excuse us?" Hesbulah said, the anger crackling in his voice.

Hesbulah paused and waited for the room to clear. The guests left their incomplete breakfasts before them and mumbled in their surprise as they were ushered out the door by Hesbulah's deputy, El Hadin.

The commandant and his assistant stood as the last few guest left the room. He approached Hesbulah and stood before him nervous and sweating. He was unable to look Hesbulah in the eyes, afraid of what he might see.

"You have disappointed me commandant. Your soldiers disgust me. Your ineptitude sickens me. I have spent a fortune to secure your country and this is what I receive from you in return. My enemies operate freely and without impunity here in your country as the try to destroy me. You would have never enjoyed the success of independence from Russia without my help. I have funded your government's operations, your economic and industrial expansion as well as your personal wealth. This is the way in which you repay me. You have allowed the Americans to enter your country and make a mocker of your security. The Americans are alive! Your idiots acted on the reports of the drunken pig that should have initially recognized their arrival. We now know less than we did earlier." Hesbulah moved closer to the commandant.

"Hesbulah please, do not jump to conclusions. We haven't talked to our intelligence..." The commandant tried to defend himself.

"Enough!" Hesbulah said as he was within reach of the commandant. The evil anger was welling up from inside of him. Hesbulah slid the dagger from out under his coat and held it discreetly.

No one in the room noticed or expected Hesbulah's next move, except for El Hadin.

"You have failed me for the last time. I am removing you from your position." Hesbulah turned his head and looked at El Hadin, still standing in front of the commandant.

"El Hadin, Commandant Furin is no longer my authority in Kazakhstan. Please make the necessary arrangements to remove him. His assistant is now the authority." Hesbulah said with a deceptive calmness added to his voice. Hesbulah turned and looked at Commandant Furin's Assistant. "You are now my leader in Kazakhstan. You have been given my complete authority to maintain the country within the bounds of our charter." Hesbulah said with an almost reverent tone. Commandant Furin began to relax. He feared for his life only seconds ago. He was relieved; the roller coaster ride of emotion was near its end. He began to think about his future again now that the threat of his death seemed to pass. Hesbulah simply fired him, nothing else. Maybe Hesbulah did have some other use for him. Perhaps he could convince Hesbulah to allow him a small post in the government. He would make the best of it. The expression of relief washed over him as he rationalized his life's worth to himself.

Hesbulah moved from in front of Furin to the newly appointed commandant of the Kazakhstan Defense Force. "This is a proud day for Kazakhstan. Congratulations! My deputy and staff will make the necessary arrangements with your President. Tomorrow is a new day for you my trusted friend. I only ask of one thing. I demand your complete loyalty. If I don't receive it, the same thing that happens to your old commandant here today will happen to you. Be proud of your service. You shall have every resource that you need and anything that you desire. But remember I must come first, even before yourself. Do you understand?" Hesbulah said placing the weight of corrupt leadership upon the shoulders of the new commandant.

"Yes, Hesbulah, I will not fail you. You have my word." The newly appointed commandant said.

Hesbulah approached him and placed his hands on his shoulders while whispering in his ear. "I had better or I will have your life." Hesbulah pulled away smiling at the new Commandant.

Hesbulah turned and walked toward the door. El Hadin knew exactly what Hesbulah was doing. He loved to toy with the weak-minded emotion that some men displayed.

Commandant Furin looked at El Hadin, then to the new Commandant. That was it, he was safe, he thought. Hesbulah had no intention of killing him, but perhaps Hesbulah did overlook his next position appointment. A weak, trembling smile formed on Furin's face. "Hesbulah, I am at a loss about my new position." Furin said with a very humble tone in his voice.

With his back toward them, Hesbulah smiled. He knew that Furin would play into his misleading and deceptive action. He knew. Hesbulah turned sharply facing Furin. "Ah yes. We mustn't leave anyone out of a position. We have been through some difficult times together Furin. Perhaps it is time that we part company. Our association is complete. Tell me Furin, what is it that you believe that you deserve?" Hesbulah walked, still with his hand behind his back and under his jacket, concealing the dagger.

Hesbulah moved again in front of Furin, eyes glaring hatred and evil. Furin easiness was replaced with the nausea of fear rising again in his stomach.

"Perhaps, I may be appointed to your staff." Furin said with fear in a shaky and unsteady voice.

"Perhaps." Was all that Hesbulah said. Then he paused and stared at Furin. His face was so close that he could feel and taste the bile rising in Furin's stomach. Hesbulah said nothing more. He wanted to draw every ounce of fear from this man. Hesbulah stood there waiting, waiting for all of the energy to be drained from Furin's life. He absorbed it. Energy transferred through fear from the fearful to the feared. He waited and watched. Hesbulah shifted his eyes from feature to feature on Furin's face. Furin knew that he should be afraid, his eyes and mouth begin to twitch. Then his head began to shake uncontrollably. The sweat rushed from his pores. Furin's fear was paralyzing; he couldn't command a voluntary movement. Hesbulah waited longer. The fear flowed freely and Furin body was seconds away from being drained of all of its energy. Hesbulah sensed that Furin's fear was nearly at its crescendo, and then he struck. In one swift move, almost in a blur, Hesbulah pulled the dagger from behind him and stuck it into Furin's neck. Hesbulah knew the exact spot to strike. The nerves were bundled tightly together in a juncture from where every nerve ending in the body met to complete the circuit in the brain stem. Manipulated correctly, Hesbulah could achieve the same result as if every nerve in the body were tortured to the point when it sends it most intense pain filled message to the brain. He also cut several of the smaller arteries that would shut down the brain at the same rate as the brain commanded the release of endorphins to relieve the pain and slow the impulse. He knew exactly how to maximize suffering in the human body. Push the body to agony, while still allowing it to live longer in a complete saturation of agony. Furin's cry of intense pain was so shrill that the human ear couldn't hear it. The vocal cords drew so taunt that the vibrations were above human perception.

Hesbulah withdrew the dagger and Furin fell to the ground screaming and writhing in pain so severe that the mind was not meant to tolerate it. Furin's agony would last a very long time.

"Your new position will be in a very small hole in the ground only if the new commandant grants you that. I do not merely leave disappointed Furin. I leave stronger by the strength that I received from you, from your fear. Your place was to serve me. You seemed to have forgotten that. When I have taken all that I can from you and you no longer serve my purposes, only then will I grant you a painful death of the body. But your soul will agonize for eternity." Hesbulah grabbed a handful of Furin's hair as he lay on the cold stone floor and cleaned the blood from his dagger. In one last act of complete and total disrespect, Hesbulah stepped on Furin's chest as he headed for the door. He paused and turned to the new commandant.

"Do not move his body or touch him until his body is dead. Then feed him to the dogs. He is not worthy of even a peasant's burial. El Hadin, come we have important business to attend to."

Hesbulah left the hall directly for the airport completely energized and feeling very alive with El Hadin behind him.

"El Hadin, contact Socotra and get an update from my intelligence staff. I want to know exactly what the Americans hope to accomplish here." Hesbulah said staring out the window of the Mercedes at the passing city enroute to the airport.

"It is done, Hesbulah. We can review the information enroute to Bhutan." El Hadin finished.

Within the hour the car had passed the rusted steel gates of the airport and pulled up next to Hesbulah's jet. The crew had the engines running and was ready to taxi for takeoff as soon as Hesbulah boarded. The attendant's were already closing the door and preparing for their in-flight service. Hesbulah stared at them eagerly. The Falcon departed heading south toward Bhutan as Hesbulah stared, head resting on his hand, out the side window of the Falcon. For the first time Hesbulah allowed the doubts of his success to enter his thoughts. El Hadin perceived the deep thoughts that Hesbulah was engaging. He waited for his cue to call the attendants. With an expression of disgust and an airy wave of his hand, Hesbulah turned his attention now to El Hadin. El Hadin beckoned the attendants to begin the meal and personal services that they performed for Hesbulah. El Hadin excused himself and moved to a small galley and service area secluded from the main salon of the aircraft cabin. He turned to close the sliding door that would offer the salon privacy as the attendants began to disrobe. For a brief second, El Hadin felt sympathy for the attendants. Today, Hesbulah would be difficult to please. El Hadin sat and enjoyed his dinner and music, while he reviewed his notes. He would present the intelligence to Hesbulah after the meal and the attendant's personal service had been completed.

After an hour, the attendants returned to the galley area. As he looked at the beautiful women and the condition that they were in after taking care of Hesbulah, El Hadin knew that Hesbulah was now insatiable. He dreaded giving the intelligence briefing to Hesbulah but moved into the main cabin to present the information. Hesbulah studied the reports.

"I cannot believe it. Elamesh is dead? How could this happen?" Hesbulah said staring in disbelief at the summary while buttoning his tunic. "Has this been confirmed by my staff in Paris?" Hesbulah queried.

"Yes Hesbulah, it has been confirmed. It appears to be the work of a professional. We verified security. Elamesh's men had secured the floor of the hotel. It appears that he had been shot. The assassin fired from a tower on the site of Saint Germaine, just crossed way from Pont De Nuef. Elamesh did not meet his contact to receive the location of the complex in Germany nor did he meet his men the next morning. They were concerned and went up to his room and found him dead."

"I want answers. What is happening with the pursuit of the American, Colonel Seth Stephens?" Hesbulah said finishing his drink and raising his glass to the attendants for a refill.

"The man is a ghost. We haven't been able to track or find him. He exists on no records anywhere. Our servants in the United States Pentagon haven't found any information on him. We believe that he is the man that arrived in Kazakhstan this morning. The defense radar sites near Urumqi briefly picked up a target leaving from the area where the sergeant reported the detainment and discussion with the Survey Company. We have traced the trucks that were seen there and attacked by the MIGs to the Freemantle Company. Hesbulah, it is the same company that we had used to survey the areas for the transfer sites in Urumqi."

El Hadin waited for Hesbulah's indication to proceed. Hesbulah only nodded. El Hadin continued.

"The target that the defense radar only briefly tracked was moving very fast and low. The radar operators did not report the target. They have had several false echoes in that region and the air units have questioned the reports in the past when they have launched and not found anything. The radar operators believed that it was a similar problem with the old systems and did not report it. I believe that it was Stephens' aircraft departing after their insertion. There is no record of any flights that departed last night listing Kazakhstan as a destination. We have

263

tracked several aircraft departing from Europe to China last night but nothing that is unusual." El Hadin waited again for Hesbulah.

"El Hadin, I believe that this man Stephens must be the focus of our attention. Let us assume that they know everything. His moves would be to substantiate everything that has been reported. For whatever reason, let me call it instinct, I believe that Stephens has arrived this morning. He used Kazakhstan as his entry point because they could come and go without being detected by radar as they would in China. The security team responded because they suspected something. Perhaps I was hasty in killing the sergeant; he may have been the smartest person that we have encountered in Kazakhstan. Stephens was planning to use his aircraft to get him back out of Kazakhstan but after the security team suspected something he had it leave. Where do you think he is heading? What areas do you think are most incriminating to us? Where have we increased our counter-espionage efforts?" Hesbulah asked almost rhetorically.

El Hadin answered the questions without thought. "The rail crossing point into China, the rail transfer point in Urumqi and the Plutonium packaging point in Urumqi." El Hadin finished.

"'Exactly!" Hesbulah responded.

"We had Elamesh destroy the American satellite facility near Washington because they could see us with their technology. All of our other measures were very transparent and discreet except for the exposure we had to satellite observation. Now that the Americans no longer have that capability, they must send in agents. But the Americans know that we have an insider. They are keeping the circle of people involved in this mission very small. They will not allow an unknown into this circle. They are not following their normal protocol and releasing all of their information to the press. They have more information on this than they are letting out. Make sure that our staff in Washington is more probing. I suspect that Stephens will be moving on our facilities in China soon. Let our security near Urumqi know that we expect an intrusion." Hesbulah paused to look at his watch. It was 1418 hours.

"We will also plan to release our vehicles earlier, get me an accurate count of vehicles ready to launch from operations in Bhutan. Our last count was 68% of planned. Have our planners in Socotra re-prioritize the targets for maximum results with using only 65% of our planned vehicles. We will plan to release as soon as the headwaters of the Brahmaputra are accepting the melt water from the Himalayas. We will remain in Bhutan until the launch is complete." Hesbulah said regaining his confidence that he could salvage the plan, even if no more plutonium reached Bhutan.

El Hadin went to the rear salon of the Falcon where the office and communications equipment was located and transmitted the directives to Socotra and Bhutan. As he sat organizing his notes, the soft electronic bell rang announcing an incoming message. El Hadin read the message on the computer screen while it was also printing. El Hadin pushed back in his chair in disbelief. Hesbulah would not like it when he presented this information to him.

"Hesbulah, I have sent the directives. Socotra has updated our last summary." He said presenting Hesbulah with the message.

Hesbulah took the information and casually put his reading glasses up to his face.

INTELLIGENCE - SOCOTRA OPERATIONS

272300 FEBRUARY

A WORLDWIDE INTELLIGENCE ORGANIZATION HAS BEEN TRACKING HESBULAH OPERATIONS SINCE 1944. THIS ORGANIZATION WAS CONCEIVED BY FIELD MARSHALL ROBERT LINDER. ROBERT LINDER WAS KILLED BY IN WASHINGTON D.C. IN 1945. HERR KARL LINDER DIRECTS CONTINUING EFFORTS. THE GROUP HAS SEVERAL BASES THAT WE KNOW OF: 1) JERSEY, THE CHANNEL ISLANDS, UK; 2) THE HARTZ MOUNTAIN BASE, NEAR GOSLAR, GERMANY; 3) SAN CRISTOBAL, VENEZUELA; 4) PERTH, AUSTRALIA.

KARL LINDER HAS LEFT THE GOSLAR SITE AND HAS ARRIVED IN NEW YORK, USA. STAFF REPORTS FROM THE US INDICATE THAT LINDER IS PREPARING TO BRIEF THE UNITED NATIONS SECURITY COUNCIL, TIME AND DATE UNKNOWN AT PRESENT. HE IS UNDER STRICT MILITARY GUARD IN NEW YORK AT A SMALL MILITARY BASE IN MANHATTAN. THE DIRECTOR OF THE NATIONAL SECURITY AGENCY OF THE UNITED STATES, MR. JOSHUA MCADAMS HAS RE-OPENED THE FILE PROJECT VICTORY THAT WAS OPENED ORIGINALLY IN 1944 WITH THE DISCOVERY OF THE TREATY BETWEEN JAPAN AND NAZI GERMANY. THE ARMY SECURITY AGENCY CLOSED THE FILE AFTER ROBERT LINDER WAS KILLED IN AN ACCIDENT NEAR WASHINGTON, D.C.

AN AMERICAN REGISTERED AIRCRAFT DEPARTED HANNOVER GERMANY THE DAY BEFORE KARL WEBER LEFT GOSLAR AND MERGED WITH A GERMAN REGISTERED 747 THAT WAS ENROUTE TO CHINA. THE RADAR CONTACT WITH THE AMERICAN AIRCRAFT, TYPE UNKNOWN, WAS LOST AS THE TWO TARGETS MERGED. THE 747 LANDED IN BEJING, CHINA. THE UNKNOWN AMERICAN AIRCRAFT HAS NOT BEEN REPORTED AS LANDED IN ANY DESTINATION.

THE RAILYARD IN NORTHERN URUMQI, CHINA HAS COME UNDER ATTACK AND THE MATERIAL PREPARED FOR TRANSPORT TO THE TRANSFER POINT HAS BEEN LOST. CHINESE POLITICAL STRUCTURE HAS REJECTED OUR DIRECTIVES TO INTERVENE AND HAS RESPONDED TO CONTAIN AN ENVIRONMENTAL INCIDENT IN THE INDUSTRIAL RAIL COMPLEX IN NORTHERN URUMQI. PLUTONIUM DELIVERY RATE CAPABILITY FOLLOWING ATTACK - ZERO.

THE PLUTONIUM TRANSFER POINT IN URUMQI HAS COME UNDER ATTACK. CHINESE MILITARY INITIALLY RESPONDED TO AN ATTACK BY A LARGE CONTINGENT. THE ATTACK WAS AIMED AT DESTROYING THE URANIUM PROCESSING FACILITY FUNDED BY THE UNITED STATES TO PROCESS NUCLEAR MATERIAL FOR USE IN CHINA'S ELECTRICAL

GENERATING STATIONS. IT NOW APPEARS THAT THE OBJECTIVE IS TO CONTAIN ANY
ENVIRONMENTAL HAZARDS RELEASED DUE TO AN ACCIDENTAL EXPLOSION. THE
TRANFER POINT HAS BEEN COMPROMISED AND THE MILITARY IS INVESTIGATING THE
ISOLATION BUILDINGS BUILT BY HESBULAH. ALL HESBULAH PERSONNEL HAVE BEEN
KILLED IN THE ACCIDENT. PLUTONIUM TRANSFER CAPABILITY AFTER ATTACK – ZERO.

NINETEEN POLITICAL REPRESENTATIVES THAT HAVE BEEN ASSOCIATED WITH HESBULAH
HAVE BEEN TAKEN INTO CUSTODY AS CRIMINALS. THE DETAINED CHINESE POLITICIANS
ARE ALL OF THE HESBULAH CONTACTS IN NORHTERN CHINA.

THE CHINESE ARE COMMUNICATING WITH THE AMERICANS ON THESE ISSUES. THE
AMERICAN AND CHINESE AMMBASSADOR TO THE UNITED NATIONS HAVE BEEN IN
CLOSED SESSIONS WITH THE US NATIONAL SECURITY COUNCIL FOR THE PAST NINE
HOURS.

SUMMARY --- LAUNCH VEHICLES UPLOADED AND PREPARED FOR DELIVERY – 758 OUT
OF 1100 PLANNED. THERE IS ENOUGH MATERIAL IN TRANSIT TO BHUTAN FROM THE
TRANSFER POINT IN URUMQI TO UPLOAD 47 MORE VEHICLES. OUR ESTIMATES ARE
THAT 73.7% OF THE TARGETS WILL BE ACHIEVED WITH THIS NUMBER. 86% OF THE
WORLDS POPULATION IS WITHIN THE FATAL NEUTRON DETONATION CIRCULAR ERROR
OF PROBABILITY. ESTIMATES OF FATALITIES 4.3 BILLION PEOPLE. ESTIMATES OF
HABITABILITY OF AFFECTED AREAS AFTER DETONATION: 273 HOURS. COLLATERAL
DAMAGE DUE TO DETONATION: 6.5% OF INFRASTRUCTURE AND BUILDINGS.

EARLIEST AVAILABLE LAUNCH --- 64 HOURS.

EARLIEST NEUTRON DETONATION --- 127 HOURS, (5 DAYS, 7 HOURS, 27 MINUTES)

END OF MESSAGE

Hesbulah paused after reading the message and sat back. He
stated in a matter of fact tone, "El Hadin, we will plan to launch in five
days. I want all of our efforts to be re-adjusted to make sure that we have
100% confidence that the launch will happen. And, I want this Colonel
Stephens brought to me. He will sit at my side and watch how miserably
he failed before I kill him.

24

The Rail Yard

"Sean, I've got the data and I'm coming across the north side of this rail cars." Izz said over the radio as he scrambled under the rail car to cover himself from the automatic weapons fire.

"Detonation charges are set. Izz, get up here buddy. Things are heating up fast mate." Sean returned as Izz could hear Sean's weapon firing over the radio.

They had already retrieved the data that would confirm that the rail cars had passed through the snow sheds and traveled across the Althai Mountains out of Russia. They were in the process of egressing when a guard of the security force stumbled on Sean as he copied the number of the rail cars on the digital recorder. Sean acted hastily and shot the guard but not fatally. The wounded guard called for reinforcements. Izz was still in the center of the rail yard collecting information. The guard force responded instantly and was scouring the spaces in between the freight cars lined up in the rail yard. The force observed where Sean was covering position and had found Izz's position under and between the rail cars.

Izz detonated several small charges remotely to cover his moves. The guard force was too organized and too numerous. The distractions affected only a small fraction of their numbers and barely slowed them.

"Son of a bit...," Izz said as he had his head down ducking the weapons fire impacting near his position. The heavy rounds screamed past his head and ricocheted off the thick, grime covered frame of a rail car. Each bullet sent a shower of dirt, mud and other accumulated grime down onto Izz.

"Sean, keep their heads down to the north, I'll concentrate my fire to the south. I'm coming up the middle under the concealment of the smoke grenades. As soon as you see the smoke, pour it into that group coming from the north of my position." Izz said as he simultaneously fired his M8 with one hand and pulled the two smoke grenades from his ammo pouch with the other.

"Izz, it's now or never mate, I've got two more groups headed our way across the rail yard." Sean said firing into the security force that was moving more cautiously now that they were near Izz and Sean's position.

"As soon as I clear that last line of rails, I'll detonate the charges in sequence to cover our move back to the warehouse area. Keep the cover fire up hot, man. This is not good, not good at all, Sean." Izz said to Sean.

Sean could hear that Izz was beginning to sound concerned about their chances of success. "Hey Izz, the blokes are just making a lot of noise mate, they can't hit anything. I'm practically standing on the top of the hill. You'd think at least one of them would be a little jammy and hit something. Izz, I don't think that they have real bullets anyway." Sean said. Izz heard his English accent thickening under the stress.

"Yeah, right Sean. I don't think that luck has anything to do with it. Right now it is the quantity that has me concerned. The guys down here are shootin' real bullets. There's so much metal bouncing around under this trailer you'd think it was raining iron." Izz reached into his backpack as he lay on his side. He grabbed the last two white phosphorus grenades that his hands found and yanked them out of the pack as another bullet spun off the metal surrounding him. He pulled both pins from the grenades and piled them into one hand. He rolled over on his opposite side and pulled his arm back. With a super effort he heaved the grenades, long armed style into a high, arching lob. The grenades fell to the ground about 25 meters south of his position. Both Sean and Izz could see the grenade's smoke deploy. Izz waited until the cloud of smoke from the two grenades fully developed. It was his only chance to cross the unobstructed ground and get to the position that offered the best vantage point where Sean was located. They mercury vapor lights of the rail yard created 10 shadows for every one man. It was difficult to see exact numbers. Izz thought that they would probably have night vision devices. The smoke would help cover his movement.

"Here, I come Sean. Keep the volume turned up buddy!" Izz ran in a dead, flat out run across the ground, crouching low and trying to make his 6 foot frame as small of a target as possible. Izz could hear the sporadic fire from the security force. It wasn't as intense as before. The guard force fired conservatively into the dense smoke so not to waste ammunition on a target that they couldn't see. Izz covered the ground and began to scale the small slope that led to the top of the hill where Sean was firing and keeping the heads of the security force down. In between burst from his 5.56mm automatic rifle, Izz could hear the thumps of the grenade launcher as it fired the small High Explosive charges toward the reinforcing units as they approached. Izz pressed the detonator that was attached to the left suspender of his webbed equipment belt. The charges exploded in a series of ka-whumfs walking toward the guard force now turned attackers.

Izz was a body length from the depression where Sean was positioned as the smoke began to fade away with the help of a light breeze. The firing became more intense and Izz could see the dirt kicked around their position in amazing detail. It was as if he were moving in slow motion. He dove head first, arms outstretched into the depression. It seemed to take forever for him to reach the safety that the small shallow depression offered. He landed on his arms and chest. Sean watched out of the corner of his eye while he continued to alternately fire the rifle and the grenade launcher.

"I'll bet the judges would've given you a ten on that dive mate, hardly made a splash!" Sean said trying to keep both his and Izz's spirits up. Both of them were experienced enough to know that this was a bad situation.

"Yeah, I've had a lot of practice today. I probably would do a little better if the landing area were a little softer." Izz said as he scrambled up the side of the depression to face towards the direction were Sean was laying down the suppressive fire. Izz picked up the grenade launcher and was aiming at the tankers full of fuel oil.

"Sean, on my mark set off the charges on the plutonium rail cars. If I can light off a few of those tanker cars up at the same time, we'll create enough of a barrier to keep the reinforcements from reaching us." Izz said sighting in the string of tankers.

"If one of these penetrates the skin on those tankers, I'll feel a lot better about this situation. Sean, as soon as one of the tanker cars explodes, head for the underpass where we left the truck. Don't stop for anything...the data will be in my zipped chest pocket. Make sure that it gets to Kuerhle. We'll have less than two hours to get there. Here goes buddy. Get ready to sprint." Izz said as he carefully aimed the grenade launcher toward the center car on the rail lines farthest from their position and closest to the pursuers.

"I hope that I can win a dinner from you on these shots, Seth." He said under his breath to Seth that was miles away from his and Sean's position as he aimed. He took into account everything, he even carefully accounted for the slight breeze that he watched carry the smoke away from the rail yard. Sean dutifully kept firing into the grouped security force. If the grenades hit the mark, they could easily run down the reverse side of the slope and evade the pursuers before they fought their way around the exploding tankers. Izz squeezed the trigger on the grenade launcher.

The 40mm round arched high into the early, pre-dawn sky. He strained to watch its trajectory but was unable to see anything in the shadows that played in the rail yard. The explosion seemed to catch him by surprise. He thought that the hang time for the grenade would have been longer and didn't expect the explosion as soon as he did. His aim couldn't have been any truer. It was perfected by years and years of practice and experience. Seth used to laugh at Izz's ability on the grenade launcher. Seth would intentionally place acoustical reverberators at the firing range and set off the noise to see just how close Izz could come without sight but by only aiming by the direction of the sound. Seth would buy dinner that night for the team if Izz could destroy all of the acoustical reverberators. Seth always ended up buying dinner. The grenade hit the top of the tanker at a point where the metal skin was the thinnest. The 40mm grenade packed with high explosive ripped its way into the tanker car and ignited all 25,000 liters of high octane petroleum. The heat and flame from the explosion, along with the concussion expanded like the ripples of water caused from a stone thrown into a still lake. The concussion reached Izz and Sean's position and hit them with an incredible force. It squeezed their chests and emptied the air from their lungs. They were thrown against the opposite side of the depression and hit with a thud loud enough to be heard at close range over the explosion.

They both shook their heads to regain their awareness. "Jesus Christ mate, what the hell did you hit?" Sean said spitting dirt and mud from his mouth.

"Good things come in small packages buddy, let's get out of here before someone makes us pay for the damages." Izz said scrambling over the top of the depression.

"Let's go!" Izz added as he kicked up the dirt pumping his legs against the slopes loose soil.

"Come now, don't you want to stay and have a butchers?" Sean said recanting his cockney roots. The second tanker exploded sending more heat and a concussion their way.

"On second thought, don't slow down mate or you'll have my foot prints up your back." Sean said grabbing the bag full of unused ammunition and slinging it around his neck. The two men ran as fast as their tired bodies would carry them. The distance from their position to the underpass was a little less than two kilometers. They had made several mistakes in their haste and didn't properly plan the egress route. They had missed the guard tower that overlooked the rail yard and didn't see the two guards placed above the smoke. The two were now watching for them after being alerted by the screened guard force. The more senior man had seen the two running as the light from the second tanker explosion turned the night's darkness into daylight. If they would have made it over the top of a small hill in front of them they would have been concealed from the men in the tower by the rolling terrain. Izz had crested the hill and was one step down the other side as Sean was just about to crest the hilltop. The guard in the tower raised his 7.62mm sniper rifle and sight in on the back of the neatly place target at the crest of the hill. The image filled the snipers night vision sight. He paced a small illuminated dot in the sight on the spot just above the center of the man's back. He followed the movement and only when he was confident that he had the right lead for the targets movement, he fired two rounds in rapid succession. The high velocity bullets from the 7.62mm rifle covered the 170 meters in less than the time it takes for a man to exhale. Sean felt the impact of the single round to his back before he felt the pain of penetration. The force of the bullet striking his body carried him over the hilltop as if he had been pushed from behind. The force had the effect of accelerating his run at three times his speed. Izz saw him partly stumble, partly run as if he had gained too much momentum. He appeared to be running out from under his feet on the down slope of the hill. Izz saw that his legs folded under the weight of his body as they seemed to match the pace of his movement but no longer able to support his weight. Sean felt the deep burning pain as the bullet passed from the entry in his back just to the left of the spinal column. The bullet carried though his chest and exited on the left side. The impact squeezed the air from his lungs out of his mouth and nose. It carried with it the blood and tissue that was flowing from the wounds created deep in his chest.

As he lay on the partially frozen ground, in the dark, he had never felt so alone. He gasped Izz's name. Izz could barely hear him but knew that something was wrong. Sean rolled part of the way down the slope carried by sheer momentum. His position was now shielded from further shots from the sniper because of the cover now offered by hill between their position and the guard tower. The momentum and force exhausted, Sean came to a stop and tried to grab away the white-hot burning, deep and intense pain that was auguring into his body.

Izz slide to a stop, like a baseball player sliding safely after stealing a base very aggressively, near his friend. He pulled Sean over onto his back toward him and could see the blood that had collected on his face from his mouth and nose as the bullet mauled its way through his body. Sean gasped for air and tried to talk. His eyes opened wide looking into the Izz's eyes and pleading for help. He laid there, his mouth opening forming words without sound. Izz knew that Sean had been hit but didn't know how bad until that moment. Izz removed the field dressing from Sean's equipment belt and broke open the small ampoule of coagulant and pain killing narcotic. He smeared the liquid onto the khaki colored thick gauze and searched for the wound with the other hand. He felt the large exit would on the left side of his chest and immediately applied the dressing. He reached in his belt and pulled the other field dressing from its place on his belt and repeated the process, smearing it with coagulant and pain killer. He found the small but jagged entrance hole made by the bullet and placed the dressing squarely on the hole. In the dim light he could see the unstaunched blood flowing freely from the hole in Sean's back. Izz cringed without letting Sean see his expression.

"You are going to be fine my friend, in no time you'll be scrummin' on the rugby field with the boys back in Gloucester. Hang in there man. It feels worse than it is." Izz lied.

Sean tried to talk through the thick foamy blood that oozed from his mouth when he opened it. "This…is…the…second…time…you've had…to…carry…me…" Sean said in a hoarse, gasping wheeze. His eyes offering an expression of the deep trust that he had in Izz.

"Just be glad that I'm not Mike, he would've left your Scottish arse here and drank your beers to boot." Izz said.

Izz saw Sean try to smile through the pain as he hauled him up over one shoulder. Izz dug down deep for the strength and forced his body past the exhaustion that he felt. The added weight on his feet broke through the top layer of partially frozen ground. He dug in slowly at first and then picked up the pace as his body gained a little momentum. Izz covered the ground in less than 8 minutes, but the pain shooting up from his legs made it seem like hours. Izz paused at the top of the overpass before proceeding down the slope to the tractor. The detonations and secondary explosions from the petroleum tanker cars ripped into the cold air, reverberating through the yard. The thick smoke was billowing now in all directions. He couldn't even see the lights from the rail yard only two kilometers away. He was sure that no one could have followed their movement but it wouldn't be long before they expanded an organized search looking for them.

"Hang in there Sean, just down the slope buddy and we'll get you patched up." Izz said as he looked around carefully.

Their only chance now was to get out of here without being followed. Sean was dead weight hanging on his shoulders. Izz's breathes came in heavy, deep heaves now after the run across the muddy ground crusted over by the cold night air. Sean let out a wheeze that comforted Izz a bit. At least he was still alive. He could stabilize him in the truck and hopefully get Mike to come back in and pick him up with the fast flying Citation X.

Izz was more than confident that the explosions that continued in the rail yard had delayed the pursuers. He headed down the slope toward the Saratov diesel hidden under the metal framework bridge. Izz opened the door and climbed aboard carefully with Sean still slung over his shoulder. Izz could feel Sean go in and out of consciousness. His body would alternate between completely tense and total relaxation. Izz placed Sean on the small bed that was located in the compartment just behind the tractors cockpit. He pulled the aid kit from the to-go bag and pulled the morphine and plasma from the bag. He administered the injection of morphine and inserted the intravenous needle to start pumping Sean with synthetic blood type plasma. He rolled Sean on his side carefully and examined the entrance hole. The bleeding was staunched from the entrance wound but still flowed around the blood soaked field dressing over the exit wound that Izz had placed back when they were on the hill. Izz removed the field dressing and looked for the bleeding artery. The pulmonary artery on Sean's left side was nearly severed. The only reason that he didn't bleed to death already was that the gauze from the field dressing acted as a plug and slowed the bleeding. Izz removed two hemostats from the aid bag and clamped each end of the severed artery leaving about a 12mm end exposing from each. He flushed the cavity created by the bullet's exit with a sterile solution. Izz removed one of the devices that looked like an open ended tube, halved along its length and clamped the ends of the cut artery into it. Izz closed the tube over on itself and effectively joined the damaged artery and allowed blood to flow past the damaged area. Izz reduced the blood flow to nearly half of what it was, but there were too many small damaged small arteries to repair. Sean was losing blood too terribly fast. He placed more of the coagulant on the dressing and finished bandaging the wounds. Sean had lost a lot of blood and was still bleeding internally.

"Hang on Sean, we'll get out of here and on our way to Bhutan. In about four hours we'll meet up again with Seth and we'll be on our way. Warmer weather and sunshine awaits us my friend. Hey what was the name of that little town where you live now?" Izz talked as he finished hopefully trying to spark a deeper fight for survival in Sean.

Sean glanced up at his friend as Izz finished the bandaging. "...A fine place Izz...you'd really love it Izz...Marlow...Marlow on the Thames." Sean said through wheezes barely audible. Izz noticed the smile on Sean's face and returned one to him.

"You're be there in no time Sean, you'll be there in no time." Izz pulled the blanket up around Sean and elevated his legs slightly. He fastened a seat belt loosely around him to keep him in place on the rough roads of northwestern China. Izz had seen badly injured men before. He had done all he could for Sean but he couldn't lie to himself as he did Sean. Sean would be lucky or jammy as Sean would phrase it himself to see the next day.

Izz climbed into the seat and started the Saratov's engine. He drove away from the rail yard for many kilometers before he turned on the headlights of the big tractor. They weren't out of the woods yet. Danger was all around them. Izz saw the helicopters swoop in low over the highway. The pilots of the helicopters made no moves toward them and appeared to be using the highway as a route into the north central part of the city. Izz tensed as he saw a military convoy pass him on the opposite side of the road. He breathed again once they had passed and made no threatening moves. He thought about Seth. Just as he did in the past, his decision to use the Saratov diesels saved their lives and contributed to the success of the mission so far. That was all that was traveling the highway this particular morning. The Saratov tractors were more common on the highways of China than Fords were on the highways America. He didn't see many Range Rovers though. It would have taken months for a large force to stop a search every Saratov tractor moving around the highways of China. Izz didn't know how Seth had known that it was time to trade the Rovers in, but he was very grateful that Seth had made that call. At least they blended in a little easier with the other vehicles on the road.

Izz drove along a little more before he reached in to his rucksack. He pulled out something to eat and watched the helicopters continue to pass overhead in the darkness. The moon was becoming visible through a veil of high cirrus clouds as they left the lights surrounding Urumqi.

The roughness of the road made the 400-kilometer trip seem even longer. Izz hadn't checked on Sean since they had left the outskirts of Turpan. Sean was unconscious, but alive. Izz had done the best he could for his teammate but still felt helpless. His emotion matched the moon's gray cast on the highway in front of him and it seemed to place more emphasis on the unknown that was ahead of them.

Izz glanced at his watch. He had less than one hour to cover the remaining 40 kilometers of rough road leading to the rendezvous point in Kuerhle. He checked the data in his chest pocket on the disk from the digital recorder. All he could think about was how expensive this information was to retrieve. It probably will cost a man's life. He prayed that it would be all worth it.

Izz thought to himself, "The world will never realize the sacrifice you made for humanity Sean, but you know it and that's all that matters."

25

The Road to Bhutan

Seth drove the big Saratov into a densely forested area just south of the city of Kuerhle. It was not unlike any other moderate sized city in northwestern China. Most of the industrial areas were in the center of the city and the agricultural areas surrounded the city center apartment complexes. There was a small forested area near the lowlands south of the city. The rugged mountains to the east and north provided a white snow covered backdrop to the rather quaint and beautiful city.

Seth pulled the Saratov off the secondary road and onto a small access road that led into the forest. He could see the road that they would use to head south toward Bhutan. It was the same road that the truck convoys used to take their cargos south. Seth pulled the digital satellite phone from the one of the containers that they had unloaded from the aircraft. He unfolded the phone's antenna out of its container and opened the door of the Saratov. He glanced upward. He needed to place the antenna in a clearing that had a good view of the southern sky.

The night air seemed colder than it was in Urumqi. The light breeze flowed from the mountains to the east. The air cooled against the snow-covered slopes, un-insulated by the layers of atmosphere that kept the bottomlands a little warmer and flowed down the mountain like a gentle tide.

Seth kept his radio on and listened via his earphone for Izz or Sean to call back. He glanced at his watch and the silvery light from the moon through high overcast illuminated the dial of his watch.

Twenty minutes remained until the preset rendezvous time. He heard several crackles of static in his earphone as he approached the truck. Other than that, the radio was silent. The cold night air was refreshing and Seth decided to take advantage of the down time. He walked at a relaxing pace back down the small sandy path toward the highway away from the Saratov. He couldn't help but think about how pleasant this little patch of forest was. Even in the darkness, it was illuminated with ambience and presence. It would be a wonderful place to rest for a while. Seth continued his walk to where the forest and road met. He looked down the road. It was empty in both directions. The convoys probably didn't leave Kuerhle until early in the morning. The highway would soon be alive with the large trucks pulling their loads toward the southern parts of western China.

The stillness of the night air was so peaceful, so remarkable that the contrast between what had happened in Urumqi less than 90 minutes ago seemed ages old. Seth turned to walk back toward his transport. He glanced again at his watch. It was five minutes past one. He'd wait until the designated time but no longer. He quickened his pace as he walked. Time was not something he had an excess of on this mission. Seth heard the low growl of a heavy truck's engine coming up the road. He turned on his heels and moved to the tree line for concealment out of habit. The truck downshifted and was running without lights. Seth felt confident that this would be Izz and Sean.

The truck slowed and turned off the roadway on to the forest road. Seth could see the white outline of the big Saratov as it made its way through the forest. It passed his position heading towards the area where they had agreed to rendezvous. Seth checked to make sure that they weren't followed and then ran to their position to meet them.

Seth saw Izz get out of the drivers station and jump down from the tractor's cab and his feet hit the sandy soil of the road. He moved with such urgency that his shoes kicked up small piles of sand as he walked. He caught him by surprise as he approached from behind.

"Izz." Seth said in a low voice. Izz stopped and turned around. "How did everything go?" Seth said reading the expression on Izz's face. Izz was in the process of pulling the disk that contained the data from his chest pocket. He was handing it over to Seth.

"Sean was hit bad Seth, I don't think he'll see the sunrise." Izz said as Seth took the disk. Seth looked up at Izz. He wanted more details.

"We were egressing and a sniper in a tower that we didn't see got him as we were heading back toward the truck. He's lost too much blood Seth. I tried to keep him stable once we made it to the truck."

Seth interrupted, "He's in the truck?" Izz nodded. Seth climbed in through the door of the diesel and stuck his head into the sleeping compartment.

"Sean, hey mate, you weren't supposed to come back with any more holes in you. That wasn't part of the deal." Seth said speaking to Sean in the darkness. Izz was right behind Seth turning up the lights. Seth was standing next to Sean holding his wrist.

"Sean…" Seth stopped not feeling a pulse in his wrist. Seth moved his hand quickly from his wrist to his carotid artery. There was nothing there. Sean's skin felt cold under Seth's touch. Izz turned up the lights up brighter. The bunk was blood soaked. Sean's skin had a pale gray cast to it. Seth gently opened Sean's eyelids. There was no movement in the lifeless pupils.

Sean was dead.

The damage caused by the sniper's 7.62mm bullet was too extensive. Izz's effort was valiant, but even a trauma center couldn't have been able to save Sean.

Seth turned to look at Izz. Izz's expression was showing the wear that the mission was placing on him physically and mentally. Seth stood and placed his hand on Izz's shoulder. Although the two were close in age, he looked him in the eye with the expression that only father could give a son.

"Izz you have never put yourself before anyone on your team. Sean was hit badly. You did everything that was possible. You know that. I need you to reach down inside and keep your head on straight. It's only you and I now for the rest of this mission. And the tough part happens in Bhutan. We have less than 53 hours to get to Bhutan, get the data and call in the troops. Don't quit on me now. I am asking a lot from you, but I wouldn't if I knew that you didn't have it to give." Seth said to Izz.

Izz's eyes moved to Sean's body. "I don't want you to think that I failed by allowing Sean to die. I know that I did everything that I could, but I still came up short."

"We are human Izz. Sometimes we fail in the individual battles to give ourselves strength to win the war. Hesbulah must lose. If he doesn't this time, there will be many other battles were good men like Sean will continue to die. Sean died for something greater than humanity. His life and death was a perfect example of selfless service. He did this for the right reasons. He wanted life on earth to be filled with wonder and contentment. He wanted to leave our world better than he found it. He wanted peace. He did it for the same reasons that you're doing this Izz.

You didn't fail, you have never failed anything in your life Izz." Seth understood what Izz was thinking. He didn't want Izz's self –confidence shaken, not here, not now. They both needed to compartmentalize now and drive on with the mission.

"Izz, we'll have Sean taken care of. Some of the CIA operatives in the area will help us get Sean out of here. You and I have to head for Bhutan." Seth said as he climbed down the ladder from the truck's cab. Izz closed and locked the door. Seth saw Izz place the key on the topside of the fuel tank, under the ladder platform. From the outside nothing appeared abnormal. It simply appeared that a weary driver had pulled off the highway for some rest. They were walking back to the other Saratov.

"Izz, send the data back to NSA and I'll transfer the fuel from the other truck to this one. Every little bit will help." Seth said pulling opened the access door that contained a fuel transfer pump and hose.

"Roger Seth, I'll send it back. Any other messages?" Izz asked looking over his shoulder as he climbed into the cab.

"Yeah, tell them about Sean and tell Joshua that we'll expect full honors for Sean's arrival. It's the least they can do for a hero that was killed trying to save everyone else." Seth said with complete conviction.

Izz nodded an affirmative with a tight-lipped expression on his face.

It only took fifteen minutes for Izz and Seth to complete their tasks. While Seth was waiting and watching the fuel transfer he placed a call to Nick. He asked how McKensy was resting and laughed at Nick's reply. He knew that the narcotic that he had given her would make her fall into a full night's sleep. She wouldn't wake up for another five or six hours. He then asked him for one other favor. Nick sensed the solemnity in Seth's voice as he told Nick about Sean. Nick would take care of it for Seth, that Seth did not doubt. Seth terminated the call and secured the satellite phone. He finished stowing the fuel transfer gear. Even though the Saratov's carried plenty of fuel, they'd have to borrow some fuel from some other unsuspecting driver's truck on their way to Bhutan. He went back over to the other Saratov and removed all of the gear that was theirs. He took Sean's identification and personnel items with him. When he was confident that the truck that contained Sean's body was sterile and would not relay any clues to a hostile, he closed and locked the door. He paused for a little prayer and let the memory of the when he had met Sean replay in his mind. He glanced up toward the heavens and felt the familiar comfort of many looking down upon him. He knew that Sean was now one of them.

The moon's light was now stark as it moved from behind the high overcast. It offered full reflectivity of the sun's intensity to the ground below it. Seth could see with nearly the same detail as daylight. Seth made one last check of the area as Izz was securing the satellite antenna used to uplink the data. They both climbed the ladder on the driver's side into the cab of the Saratov.

"Everything's secure inside Seth, the information has been sent and acknowledged by the watch officer at NSA. I noticed that you don't have your partner with you." Izz said.

Thanks Izz, good work, at least part of the data that Karl needs is in his hands. McKensy fell asleep with a little help from me. She's in good hands and some friends picked her up after we briefed outside of Urumqi. She'll be heading back to Australia by morning. She did her part by getting us in here. There was no need to get her further involved." Seth said trying to quell Izz's curiosity.

"We'll keep the satellite phone up and on secure to monitor any last minute changes. After we clear Kuerhle, and head into the Tarim Basin, we'll discreetly mount the satellite antenna on the truck so that we can receive the Intelligence Summaries for Bhutan on the road. We should have a clear satellite link in the lowlands." Seth said as he started up the diesel that powered the Saratov. He backed the truck out of the hide position and headed toward the main road.

They both looked at Sean's temporary tomb as they passed it out of respect. Seth had the truck up to 150 kilometers per hour and was accelerating as they proceeded south toward Bhutan. The experienced drivers that made this route planned 48 hours to cover the 2300 kilometers. Seth planned to cover it in less than 30 hours. That would leave them 24 hours to finish the mission and gather the information on the launch sites in Bhutan.

"I'll take the first shift Izz. Why don't you get some rest buddy? I don't plan on stopping, except for fuel and that won't be anytime soon. I filled the tanks by transferring the fuel from the other truck. We should be able to nearly make it all the way with this machine. Just make sure that the weapons are ready before you nod off. I don't expect company, but if someone drops in unexpectedly, I want to have a proper welcome ready for them." Seth said as Izz was climbing out of the seat and into the living quarters in the rear of the cab.

"Not a problem. Make sure you wake me if company drops in. I don't want to be rude you know." Izz said. Seth smiled. Izz was regaining his sense of humor.

"Nothing more to do now but cover the miles and follow the plutonium that was on the trucks from the complex in Urumqi." Seth said as the barren highway passed beneath the truck's tires.

"Hey Izz, I wonder if we'll see a McDonald's on the way. A vanilla shake sounds great to me. How about you?" Seth said and waited for Izz's reply. He looked in the rear mirror that looked into the living quarters of the Saratov. Izz didn't hear Seth. He was sprawled out on the bunk sound asleep. He'd sleep straight through until they switched. Seth figured it would be a long eight-hour shift. He was long passed exhausted. He couldn't even remember what a comfortable bed felt like. He let his mind run away with thoughts as he drove through the night.

The kilometers clicked off as he steered the Saratov a crossed the vast ocean of barren desert. The stars met the night sky horizon abruptly. The tapestry just ended. There wasn't a gradual transition from earth to sky. It just ended. The Takla Makan region of China was a huge void, so vast that it would appear to anyone that the end of the world was just ahead.

Seth hoped that his analogy wasn't a premonition.

26
Tashi Gang Dzong

Bhutan, March 2, 0620 hours

"Mike, what does it feel like being back in headquarters? Are you getting enough to eat, showers hot, getting your mail?" Seth said as he chided Mike about being in a support role.

"Boss you really know how to hurt a guy. Just for that I'm skipping dessert tonight. Speaking of mail boss, General Woodsen is here. He handed me a letter from Elizabeth. He wants me to make sure that you get it." Mike finished in between bites from a piece of celery. Seth could here him deliberately crunching it as he talked.

"Just kidding buddy, if you weren't there coordinating the attack phase, one of those bomb happy zoomies would probably drop one here in my lap." Seth said referring to the air force targeting officers that staffed the Army command posts.

"Mike, we are at the RP near Tashi Gang Dzong, about an hour of a flight for you to the north. Latitude 27 degrees, 19 minutes north, Longitude 91 degrees, 38 minutes east. Frank, see if that checks with your fix on our transmissions." Seth said over the secure satellite phone talking to Mike who was positioned in Calcutta and Frank in Burma.

"Yeah, Frank and his bums are on track just to the south. You are within range of the RC-680s. They'll pick up your low power transmissions from now on and get it back to me. We shouldn't need the secure satellite communication any longer. Frank sent me a map plot of your position just as you came up a few minutes ago. Which tree are you standing next to? " Mike returned on the other end.

"Good work Mike. Great job Frank. Keep things together on the validation." Seth said as Frank was listening to the conversation from nearly 800 nautical miles away.

Frank had the high-resolution video array zeroing in on the intercept plot but couldn't actually see Seth because of too much atmospheric haze. A smile broke upon Frank's face, the first one in days, since he had been notified that the validation exercise was being moved to Allanmyo, Burma. Frank had set up the Processing Facility up near a small aerodrome on the south side of the Irrawaddy River. Frank had been notified, packed up, moved and was operational in less than seventy-two hours. He was given orders to participate in the newly created annual exercises with Vietnam. It was as good of front as any he thought.

"Mike, there's a small highway to the north of our position, with about a 2 kilometer stretch that looks better than where we landed in Alma-Ata. Do you think you can do it?" Seth quipped.

"I see it. You just be nearby boss. I'll land it and we'll be outta there." Mike said as he saw the highway that Seth was talking about on Frank's imagery transmission.

"Mike, if you don't hear from us, land there in 24 hours. If we are still alive, we'll be there. Also coordinate the timing with General Woodsen and Josh McAdams to have the strike force prepared and ready to come in as soon a we are on board or you come in and find an empty nest." Seth said arranging the downed crew pickup point and confirming the plans for the air attack. "And Mike, make sure that you do your homework buddy. We are probably gonna come out of here hot, with the bad guys on our trail." Seth added.

"Hey boss, like Izz always said, if you see one hot landing zone, you've seen 'em all. I'll be there, with the cavalry circling overhead, but I'll be there. You just stay alive and watch your six. General Woodsen would kill me if I don't deliver this letter to you. Just make it to the LZ boss." Mike said to reassure Seth. Seth did not need reassuring; he knew Mike was as good as his word.

"Roger Mike, stay on top of things in that cushy office there in Calcutta. Stephens out." Seth terminated the connection with the secure phone. The termination sequence took several seconds longer. The routing would be switched in hundreds of combinations to prevent an adversary from backtracking the call. If someone was trying to capture and triangulate the small footprint signal, the connection may show a termination in as many as four hundred different locations.

Mike was ahead of the situation. He had already been in contact with Joshua McAdams and Gen Woodsen.

Karl Linder's discoveries were accepted unanimously by the United Nations. All that was needed was the information that Seth and Izz were about to collect.

A British and US Naval task force with two carriers each was already positioned in the Indian Ocean, just as they had always been for the spring exercises. The Air Forces from 6 countries would also support the campaign. The US Air Force would launch its B-2 Stealth bombers from Whitman AFB Missouri in six hours to be in position off of the coast of India ready to come in on order. The United States Army's newest attack aircraft deployed from Korea to Northwest Thailand for the annual exercise with Vietnam. Frank Nellis had already moved the Army's RC-680A Multi-Disciplined aerial reconnaissance aircraft into position to support the mission by feigning support for the combined US-Vietnamese exercise. The forces were already positioned for a response to Bhutan and was now being prepped as Seth and Izz observed the compound. The forces would coordinate their attacks and it would be executed with unmatched military precision. Anything that Maxwell Woodsen touched was flawless in the past and there was nothing that suggested this operation would be any different.

Joint operations were old hat now and after both Iraqi wars, Afghanistan and Iran, combined operations between the world's military forces were very well practiced. Gen Maxwell Woodsen would be leaving in twelve hours for the campaign area. Joshua McAdams would make sure that the briefing to the U.N. Security council went off as planned. As soon as Seth sent the targeting data back and the U.N. voted on the resolution, the campaign would begin. In less than twelve hours, Hesbulah's capability would be reduced to a smoking pile of ruble by the most powerful armada ever coordinated.

"Izz are you ready?" Seth asked.

"Always ready." Izz answered.

The two carried everything that they had as to-go gear, ammunition, explosives, remote mortars, electronic equipment, everything. They nearly doubled their body weight as they prepared to move and gather the information that would convince the world that Hesbulah and his agenda had to be stopped. Karl Linder would be addressing the United Nations Security Council in less than 30 hours. The final part of this briefing would gain the world's support to expose Hesbulah and his powerful political alliances everywhere in the world.

Joshua McAdams would asked for an immediate resolution to allow aircraft and naval forces from 28 countries to destroy the capability in Bhutan and southern China where the bomb making was in progress. Forces had been alerted by the Chairman of the Joint Chief of Staff,

General Maxwell Woodsen and were preparing for the assault. They only needed the council's resolution to deliver their weapons.

Seth had parked the Saratov in a remote truck park, next to an old transport that he followed the last 130 kilometers across China and into Bhutan. The driver had seen Seth in the rearview mirror and smiled and waved several times. Seth and Izz laughed when he pulled an American flag out of his shirt pocket and tied it to the rear mirror of his old transport and waved as they passed the old tired truck that he drove. Seth placed a note written in his best Chinese, along with the trucks ownership papers, bestowing the new Saratov to the old Chinaman. Seth smiled as he drew a picture of the Chinese and American flags waving side by side on the bottom of the note. Compliments of Uncle Sam he wrote as he concluded the note.

The sun was coming up over the eastern horizon. Seth and Izz wanted to be in position to observe the compound during the day and collect their data under the advantage that they had hoped darkness would give them. Izz carried a palm computer that contained the satellite photos and intelligence summaries that he had downloaded from NSA during the drive from Kuerhle.

The two men spent the next 45 minutes moving into a perfect hide position overlooking the possible entrances to the Hesbulah compound. Izz studied the satellite photos. He and Seth decided that the mountains to the southwest of the compound and the city of Tashi Gang Dzong, along the Dangme Chu River would offer the most options for an approach into the compound.

The compound straddled the Dangme Chu River. The river was one of the larger tributaries of the Brahmaputra River. The Dangme Chu flowed like an ocean with the runoff from the Himalayas into the Bramhaputra, then to the Bay of Bengal and Indian Ocean. It was wide and deep enough to support navigation by the large boats that could transport goods from these isolated areas.

A large bridge that spanned the river connected the compound. From their vantage point, they could see that the bridge supported foot and vehicular traffic. The compound was very modern. It was constructed of concrete and steel. Several smaller buildings all connected by covered walkways surrounded the main building. The mountains surrounding the area were a source of geothermal energy and the plant took advantage of the cheap energy source provided by the tectonics that the Himalayas continually experienced. A large duct that connected the geothermal fields with the factory ran up adjacent to their position. It looked like any of the newer factories that lined the Dangme Chu. There were no clues given from its exterior that it contained more processed plutonium than any other location in the world.

"Izz, what's your guess on those large doors? The ones there that open to the river." Seth said as he looked through the high powered stabilized binoculars that also captured the data digitally.

"There's one of the satellite photos here that show the doors opened. You can see a few meters inside and it appears to be a water-side loading dock." Izz said pointing to the satellite photos and the hand held computer that stored the imagery.

"Does the river network prove to be navigable throughout Bhutan? How do they get the packaged plutonium to the launch sites? Road network or do they use river boats?" Seth asked furrowing his brow as he continued to observe the compound.

"I don't know boss. The last 4 days of satellite photos show the plutonium coming in. It's the same stuff that we traced from Urumqi, but nothing leaves. Maybe they haven't started to move the material yet. Maybe it is part of the launch plan to keep the material safe until just before launch. We have a lot of questions to answer boss." Izz said as he kept his eyes focused on the compound through the binoculars.

Something clicked for Seth. "Izz, we'll observe from this position for another hour. If we don't see any of the plutonium moving on the surface, we'll contact Mike and tell him to check all of the recent satellite photos along the river system in Bhutan. Hesbulah may be moving it around under water. Now that would make it difficult to track wouldn't it?" Seth said aware of the tight schedule that they were on.

The two continued to watch the compound. Nothing left. If Hesbulah were on the time schedule that Karl had talked about, they would have to move the plutonium packages by now. Satellite imagery would show any surface movement and they could track the plutonium easily once it left the compound. How was Hesbulah getting the plutonium to the launch sites? Seth wondered.

"Izz, time to move buddy. I think that the geothermal duct offers our best approach." Seth said as he gathered up his gear and hauled on his rucksack. The two had wished that they could move under darkness but the timeline didn't allow any addition waiting time. If they were to find the launch sites, they'd have to move now. It wouldn't be as easy as tracing the plutonium's movement by observation. They were going to have to make this a hands-on exercise if they were to give Karl Linder the undisputable evidence that he needed.

Seth and Izz used the craggy terrain and the overcast skies to their advantage. They moved in between the ridged outcrops of rocks that would conceal their movement. It would have normally worked if Hesbulah had not expected them. Hesbulah had set his security forces up so that nothing could have approached the compound unobserved. Seth and Izz moved into position near the geothermal duct.

"Izz, I'll make sure we have a way into the opening. Send this imagery back to NSA along with a SITREP. Make sure that they know that we haven't seen any shipments leave the compound and that we have to get inside for a look." Seth said as he dropped his rucksack and handed over the data disk to Izz.

"Roger." Izz replied as he positioned himself to cover Seth's moves and send the data via the satellite phone.

Seth moved in the shadows and kept his moves smooth, not abrupt. Hesbulah and El Hadin watched Seth's progress on the high-resolution video monitors that watched every area surrounding the compound.

"What do you think he will accomplish by destroying the geothermal duct? We have several energy sources that we can switch to in any event." El Hadin said as he watched from a step behind Hesbulah.

"Ah, this is the infamous Colonel Stephens. He moves like a panther. I do not believe that he is trying to destroy the duct. He is finding a way in. He is much smarter than you allow him. The thin housing that acts as an insulator for the geothermal conduits will allow him access directly into the compound. If we weren't expecting him, he could very easily gain entry and surprise." Hesbulah paused. "We will allow him to enter. I believe that he will be our best source of information. We will use him to find out what the Americans are planning since our staff in Washington is nearly incapacitated by their own stupidity. El Hadin, I want you to make sure that Colonel Stephens is treated appropriately until I say otherwise. We will see exactly how devoted he is. He may decide that his conviction only assures that he is underpaid. I am interested in this challenge. Make sure that we have his every move covered without him knowing. Perhaps I can convince him to join our side." Hesbulah finished and retired to his quarters within the complex to plan exactly how he would deal with Seth Stephens.

El Hadin took the lead to make sure that Seth and Izz were very welcomed.

"Seth, the data has been sent and receipt acknowledged. Did you find the key to the back door?" Izz said trying to interject levity.

"Yeah, better than that. The back door is opened. All we have to do is proceed down the void along the geothermal duct and we're in. We may have missed the trail somewhere and relied too much on NSA's information. If this were the main distribution point for all of the plutonium, you'd think that they'd have the security up a little more than it is. I don't know what to expect Izz, just be ready for anything." Seth said as he led the way to the duct.

In no time they had opened an inspection panel and had entered the duct. Seth was first in. The sidewalls of the duct were smooth aluminum sheeting welded at the joints of the plates. The incline down to the compound was slight initially, but would become steeper as they got closer to the compounds base cut into the mountain along the river. Seth put his rucksack in front of him. He planned to slide in to the compound as if they were on a larger version of a child's sliding board. The rucksack would absorb any impacts if they encountered a blockage. He rolled over into a prone position, night vision device in place, and 9mm at the ready position, resting on the top of the rucksack.

"Izz, reverse your position to cover behind us." Seth commanded. Izz threw his rucksack in and got into a feet first prone position to cover the rear.

"How does that saying go…you pay for your ticket, take the ride, and accept the chances. Stay close Izz and let gravity do the work."

Seth let go of the top bracket that supported the steam duct. He started his watch. His calculations said that they would slide down the shaft for nearly 17 minutes, give or take a few. They were off slowly at first and then gradually picking up speed. The ducts incline made its first change in the slope; Seth had a mental image of where they were along the duct. He glanced at his watch. So far his calculations were precise. The speed increased. They were sliding down the duct at speeds of nearly 40 kilometer per hour.

Twisting and turning in the darkness reminded him of a thrill ride, only longer. This would be a big hit in an amusement park he thought. Only they weren't in an amusement park. They had no idea what would be on the other end. The ride was fast and turbulent. And the end would offer the most suspense. He had to be ready for anything. Seth could see the proverbial light at the end of the tunnel through his NVGs. He switched them off and pushed them up out of the way from his eyes. The end was about 50 meters in front of him. He felt Izz boots pushing up against his so he knew that Izz was close by. Seth pushed hard on the toes of his rubber boots in an attempt to slow their momentum. The duct gradually reduced its incline to be level at the point where it emptied out inside the plant. Seth could now see the jumble of pipes that ran across the ducts opening. At least they would have some cover and not empty out into a large open area. The rubber on his boot's soles did the trick on the smooth surface and slowed their speed by half. They both came to a stop with four meters remaining in the duct.

Izz turned around to cover Seth as he inched toward the opening of the duct. Seth peered out of the end of the duct. The pipes were transverse of his position and offered about 3 meters of space from the ducts opening. He glanced left. A large heat exchanger coil assembly was 4 meters away from them. To the right was a walkway that proceeded for at least 15 meters before it turned to the left. He looked overhead and beneath. Nothing. He swiftly exited the duct and scrambled into a firing position beside the heat exchanger. He spent a few more seconds observing the area. Only when he was assured that there was no danger did he move forward and signal Izz to take his last firing position. They could not use the way in as an egress route so there was no need prepping the area.

The best egress route was across the compound near the river. They would reconnoiter the entire compound on the rivers west side trying to find out exactly where the plutonium being shipped in was being used and what was the ultimate destination for it.

The plan was to have Seth and Izz communicate live with each other to the command post via the secure radios and cameras that they wore. The RC-680s were orbiting within range and transmitted the information back to Mike in the Tactical Operations Center located in the American embassy compound in Calcutta.

Seth and Izz made it to the bend of the walkway and were looking down a small steel frame stairway that would bring them to ground level. Seth approached the stairs with Izz providing cover. As he descended he heard footsteps. He motioned to Izz to freeze. He could hear the footsteps fading away from his position. Whoever was there wasn't in any big hurry. Seth used his fiber optic camera to peer around the blind corner. He called Izz forward.

"Take a look. I think we walked right into the heart of the operation. I don't know if it was dumb luck or divine guidance." Seth said as he pulled away from the monitor.

"Looks like we found the assembly line Seth." Izz said as he studied the monitor.

"Izz, we'll keep the shoulder cameras turned on and continuous stream transfer up to the RC-680 aircraft. This way Mike can capture the data live and see exactly what we are seeing. Place the cameras transmitters on 40-millisecond compression burst. If anyone is watching for errant radio transmissions it'll look like static." Seth said as he adjusted the numbers on his transmitter.

The transmitter was a relatively low power transmitter that would send the digital imagery and voice data via compressed radio bursts. The system didn't have enough power to send the imagery up to a satellite, through the stratosphere. The Army's RC-680 surveillance aircraft were designed to act as relay antennae in addition to intelligence collectors. The information from Seth and Izz would be relayed to the aircraft orbiting airspace in India's Nagaland airspace, near Imphal. The transmitters could easily range the 400-kilometer distance to the RC-680s. There was nothing left to chance on this mission, everything was in place. As soon as Seth and Izz discovered the launch sites and plan, the information would be transmitted to the bases from where the aircraft would launch and uploaded into the targeting computers.

"Seth, it looks as if they are uploading the plutonium packages into multiple re-entry vehicles. The devices are too small to be the warhead or nose assembly of an ICBM." Izz said as Seth looked at the monitor over his shoulder.

Seth nodded. "We need a closer look." Seth looked for the best path over to the assemble area. There weren't many technicians in the area. Most of the assembly was automated. Izz maintained the over watch as Seth moved close to the location of the plutonium packages.

Seth studied the vehicles. They appeared as very sleek fuselages with asymmetrical fin assemblies. The larger fins were on the underside as he viewed the vehicles with two smaller canard or forward wings near the nose. Seth could see an air scoop or intake underneath and the same sized exit point at the rear of the vehicle. The vehicle's design seemed very odd for an aerospace vehicle. The lifting surfaces seemed to be misplaced and not large enough to support the vehicle in flight. It looked more like a sea-worthy vessel rather than an aerospace vehicle.

Seth moved closer. He peered up and down the assembly line before he moved next to a vehicle that was next to the conduits that he was using as cover. The vehicle was over 10 meters in length and about 2 meters wide at its widest point. Its circumference was flattened and almost resembled the profile of a shark. Seth looked at the open access panels of the vehicle. The widest panel was shaped to accept the plutonium packages and the area just aft of the intake accepted some type of engine. A guidance system or computer was mounted in the tapered area just aft of the power source area. The panels were heavy and not made of standard aircraft alloys or composites. Seth moved the entire length of the vehicle. His shoulder-mounted mini-camera captured all of the imagery. Seth made one final check of the area and then moved back to Izz's location.

"Izz, I think we made a mistake. I don't believe that these vehicles are going to be air launched. I'd place a bet that those vehicles are more seaworthy than airworthy. Mike, I hope that you're getting this buddy. Hang out the second lantern; they are coming in by sea. Make sure that you get this imagery sent back to NSA and have the vehicular engineers from both aero and hydro to look at them. My hunch is that the navy will be more interested in this now. Send a message for me to General Woodsen. Make sure that he hears about this at the same time that Joshua McAdams does." Seth said into his radio more so that Mike could hear him. The signals traveled through the RC-680A aircraft at the speed of light.

"I'm seeing it boss, but not believing it. Underground caverns, secret submarines, this guy must have been a big Jules Verne fan." Mike said as he was re-transmitting the data back to NSA and sending off messages to McAdams and Woodsen. He hit the send button and talked directly with Seth in a low voice.

"Seth we have the data and it has been transmitted back to NSA at Fort Meade. I have also passed the info to McAdams and Woodsen." Mike said acknowledging Seth's instructions to the letter. Mike spoke so that Frank Nellis would hear. Frank, make it clear to your mission managers that we'll need on station relief. I don't want any of Colonel Stephens' messages missed. Tell them to brief the aircrews. They sure as hell don't need to find out when the low fuel lights are blinking." Mike said thinking about how he and Seth found out about this mission that day back in Germany. Frank's mission manager was scrambling to take the notes accurately. Mike was shouting orders to the staff that was nearby. The last thing Mike wanted was to be part of a support team that wasn't supporting the mission. The people on the planning staff may be eating better, but they sure wouldn't be sleeping unless they could prove to him that everything would be perfect. He didn't want his boss, who was four hundred miles away wanting or needing anything. Izz and Seth had enough on their plates to try and digest.

"Izz, let's find out where the vehicles go after assembly." Seth said as he scrambled back underneath the conduits that ran parallel to the assembly line. They moved along the assembly line. Seth counted each as he passed them. There were at least fifty of the vehicles in the completion process on the assembly line. They reached the end of the conduits as the line moved into and opened into a larger hangar area. Seth and Izz could both see the large doors that opened to the river. The overhead gantry cranes and launch ramps suggested that many vehicles could be launched simultaneously.

"Izz, we may be just in time to stop a launch. It's no wonder why we couldn't track activity outside. They weren't sending warheads anywhere. This is the central launch point. They plan to put these vehicles in the water. We were looking for birds and he is using fish." Seth looked at the mass of miniature-unmanned submarines that were ready for launch. The small nuclear powered underwater vehicles could move about nearly undetected by conventional overhead satellite surveillance. Yet they would deliver a warhead large enough to incinerate New York City by pulling up into Flushing Bay. One of these submarines could nearly destroy each major city in the world.

"If he launches these Izz, we will never be able to destroy them all. My guess is more than 70-80% would get through. I'm sure he has already figured that out. We have got to destroy them before they are launched. Mike, more bad news buddy, by my count, there are more than 700 submarines ready to launch. If we don't destroy them here, we'll lose our one and only opportunity to get them in one place assuming that there isn't another launch point that we missed." Seth said into his radio.

Seth and Izz were fixated on the launch arena and didn't see or hear the security force that moved in from behind until it was too late.

"Mike, make sure that you contact McAdams and Woodsen. Tell them that we need to launch the strike force before these fish are in the water. Target our pos…" Seth didn't get to finish. The butt of the Chinese made AK-47 struck him at the base of the skull.

27

America, A Blessing from God

Manhattan, New York City, March 2, 1130 hours

The flight from Hanover to New York took a little over seven hours. The winds were light across the north Atlantic Karl occupied every minute of his flight asking questions from everyone on board. Everyone, from the flight crew of the Presidential 747 to the stewards that were sent along with Joshua McAdams into Hanover, had the chance to talk with Karl.

Their landing in the United States was at Teterboro, New Jersey. Karl stepped into the sunshine and cool temperatures of New Jersey for a few minutes before he was loaded on a military VH-60 helicopter and transported to a small Army base right in the center of Manhattan, but not before a little sight seeing up the Hudson River. They flew over America's beautiful lady, the Statue of Liberty, past the memorial to the World Trade Center and the Empire State Building. Karl hardly spoke a word but he took in everything with his eyes. Joshua wished that he had a dollar every time that Karl whispered the word magnificent. The helicopter turned south, down the Hudson before turning onto an approach path for the military base.

"Karl, we have a very full schedule lined up for you while you are here in New York. You and your family will have the guest residence of the Fort at our disposal." Joshua said as they looked out the side window at the landing area. "The small base is used to provide Military Police security contingents to the United Nations."

"Karl, see over there?" Joshua said as they passed the UN building again. "We will use the East River diplomatic entrance to the rear of the building. The entrance is more secure and allows us a little more discretion." Joshua McAdams said as they passed over a convoy of armored Chevrolet Suburbans passing the front of the UN Building on First Avenue.

He watched as Karl and his nephew looked at every site New York City had to offer. "There is Secretary Newman's office, the United States UN representative. She doesn't have far to go, just across the street." Joshua said as they passed the rows of office buildings to the west.

Karl and Peter noticed the bronze globe of the World in front of the UN building that was presented to the United Nations as a gift from the Government of Italy.

"Your country is a gift from God. There is no other society like it on the earth. I can't believe the diversification of the cultural groups. Everyone lives so well with everyone." Karl said as he had just experienced the most wonderful thing life had to offer, peace and harmony. He, Peter and Joshua watched as businessmen walked to their offices. Joggers, roller-bladers, and exercise groups in the river plaza... the city was teeming with life and excitement. This didn't present an atmosphere of hatred or doom. People did not only know, they knew how to apply life's lessons. They seemed to strike the perfect balance of teamwork and individuality. The two were separated by a very wide margin of respect for life and freedom. Those two ingredients were absolutely necessary for humanity to thrive as magnificently as it was doing here in this marvelous city.

The helicopter landed in the center of the landing area that was surrounded by the vehicles that would take the party to the United Nations.

"Karl, we will go directly to the United Nations and take care of some administrative requirements before tomorrow's briefing." Joshua said as he led the way into the vehicles.

The convoy of Suburbans pulled into the same discreet entrance that they saw as they approached in the helicopter. The escort and guards took their positions to offer maximum protection to the NSA Director and Karl Linder. Soon Karl Linder would reveal Hesbulah and his destructive plan to the world.

The elevator ride to the subterranean levels of the UN Building took only seconds. The lower levels of the building were dug during the construction of FDR Drive after the initial construction of the original building before it was determined to house the UN. The surface structure was the tourist part. Far underground was where the very important meetings took place.

They were below a floor that was shielded by hundred of tons of natural granite, steel and concrete. Karl was escorted to a room that was occupied by several technicians that had taken his data, both pictures and words and worked it into a multimedia presentation that would be accepted by the United Nations councils. The UN briefings were told more by pictures rather than words. Long gone were the days when Khrushchev would stand and give long orations while attempting to pound in emotion with his shoe. Today's briefings were pictures and very few words for fear that their meaning and intent would be lost at times in translations. Karl would review the briefing for the next several hours to make sure that it matched his original briefing exactly and carried with it the intent that he wanted to relay to the world's leaders. He knew that he would have one and only one chance.

He glanced at his clock and wondered about Seth and his team. Without the details to update his briefing, it would be difficult to convince the council members that these events were taking place in their countries, right under their noses.

Joshua McAdams walked into the room. "Karl, I have just received a message from Seth Stephens. He has traced the plutonium to Tashi Gang Dzong, a town in Bhutan. He is inside what appears to be the factory and has found the vehicles that are being uploaded with the plutonium from Russia. He is sending a constant stream of data back to Calcutta, where one of his colleagues is stationed. We have received the latest of his imagery and we are prepared to include it in your briefing."

"I would like to see the imagery now if I could Joshua." Karl said.

"Yes, of course. Can you show us the unedited imagery from the Tashi factory? Joshua requested from a technician after realizing the impact that this information would have on the outcome.

Karl sat back in his chair as he was instantly there with Izz and Seth, placed on Izz DeConcerio's left shoulder through the lens of the camera and carried around the factory. The image was unstabilized at first and then became steadier as the camera anticipated the movements of the camera's platform. They could see the inside of the factory and they watched as Seth in the lead, would stop, observe, move. The camera view switched from Izz's shoulder camera back to Seth's. Karl straightened in his chair as Seth's camera showed a close-up of the delivery vehicles.

Karl spoke in a low solemn tone, quoting a biblical verse, "a third of mankind was killed by the three plagues of fire, smoke and sulfur that came out of their mouths." Karl continued to watch the imagery.

"Can you go back to that image of the entire vehicle?" Karl asked Joshua.

"Yes of course. Go back and freeze when we get to the frame that shows the entire vehicle." Joshua said.

The technicians did as instructed.

"He will try once again to send them by the sea!" Karl said as he viewed the vehicles. Before the technical analysis had been completed Karl was certain that Hesbulah would use the sea as his medium to transport his nuclear weapons.

McAdams narrated. "The Japanese tried that in World War II. The Japanese had launched two fast attack kamikaze cruisers intent on making their way to Los Angeles and detonating nuclear bombs. The cruisers were sunk only hours before the Enola Gay dropped her atomic bombs. The Enola Gay sighted the cruisers as she approached Japan and radioed escorts to intercept and destroy the cruisers before they could relay information about the Enola Gay. Unfortunately, the cruiser's commander was under radio silence orders and was more afraid that they Enola Gay would attack them. We found out about the cruisers and their nuclear bombs and sent recovery crews to locate them. We found them in relatively shallow waters near the Bikini Atolls. Have you ever seen pictures of the supposed first Hydrogen bomb ever detonated near the Atoll? We weren't testing any bombs there. We were just detonating the two bombs that Japan had made to target America. It was a very close race. Fortunately, we were there first or things would have turned out a little different. A nuclear bomb detonated on the American west coast would have crippled our war making capabilities. Our historians say that Japan and her allies would have defeated us if their bombs had made it. Our first strike was more of a prevention than President Truman let out for fear that Americans would have forgotten how to gracefully win." McAdams said.

"Yes of course, we were abreast of the situation. Hesbulah was pressing Hitler to use his U-boats for the attacks on the eastern coast and the Japanese to use smaller submarines launched from Hawaii to assault the west. The importance of Pearl Harbor was apparent to Hesbulah and Hirohito. If they could have taken the islands, they would have had a better launch point for the weapons. There was genius in his plan, but it assumed to many variables. What we are seeing here has a much better chance of success. Technology has grown to where Hesbulah can use the nuclear weapons to achieve the same results as he set out to almost 70 years ago." Karl said with certainty.

"Get me data on how many of these small submersibles with a moderate yield bomb, given the dimensions that we see in the submersibles would be needed to kill over 2 billion people." McAdams said to one of his assistants.

"It is imperative that we incorporate this information into this presentation Joshua." Karl said.

"Gentlemen, excuse me. I have Major Mike Thomas calling. I'm sorry for the interruption gentlemen, but he said that it was of utmost importance." A female technician said apologetically to McAdams and Linder. McAdams grabbed for the phone in a manner that would have made a hungry wolf devouring a piece of steak look polite.

"Mike, hello. It is good to hear from you. Have you maintained contact with Seth?" McAdams said eagerly.

"You bet Sir, he has been breathing in my ear. We have just received the latest information from he and Izz and communications stopped. You should have the imagery now. I just want to confirm that you have it. I think that things are heating up in Bhutan and we may have to send in the Rangers to help Seth and Izz get out." Mike said into the secure phone from Calcutta.

"Standby Mike, let me check on the data." McAdams placed the phone on mute and asked the technicians if they had received the latest imagery transmission from Seth.

"Mike we have it and they are running it as we speak..." McAdams was now glued to the monitor as he saw the hundreds of submarines lined up waiting to go out the doors. Karl Linder saw it too and was staring in awe at the incredible force that was harnessed in the dockside hangar.

"Mike we have it. We'll complete the analysis and present the information to the United Nations. Extract Izz and Seth now. We are still on track for a strike force within twenty-four hours. There will be more iron falling on that place than you'd care to discuss. I believe that we'll have United Nations authorization as soon as they hear Karl's presentation. I'll brief President Abrahams and General Woodsen immediately. Get the team out of there as soon as you can Mike." McAdams said.

"Roger Sir, Thomas out." Mike signed off.

Karl was already prompting the technicians to continue reviewing the briefing. McAdams excused himself to call President

Abrahams and update him on the situation. Then he called General Maxwell Woodsen who was already in route to Calcutta were the Indian government had authorized the United States unrestricted use of all government facilities for the efforts.

"Maxwell, Joshua McAdams here. I'm sending you an update of imagery sent in by Seth. Karl and I have made a quick analysis of the information and given the situation we believe that the majority of the weapons are still located in the facility in Bhutan. Max, we're hanging out two lanterns. We believe that they are coming in by sea. The vehicles that Seth has seen in Bhutan are most assuredly submarines. The launch sites that we were seeing in China were a ruse. There's hasn't been any activity in them that shows us that they are being prepped to launch from those sites. There's good and bad here Max. If all of the submarines are still in Bhutan, we'll only have one target. If they are allowed to leave the facility, then we are going to have a nightmare on our hands trying to track the submarines that have left. I just finished briefing the President and he has given full approval to the plan. As soon as the United Nations has voted, we need iron falling on the factory in Tashi in order to prevent the vehicles from leaving." McAdams finished.

"Joshua, keep me posted. We have enough hardware to complete the mission. As long as the plutonium packages haven't been coded for triggering, we'll only have a disposal problem on our hands in Bhutan. The Himalayas will contain most of the radiation if any leaks develop, but we may have a problem with material leaking down the rivers. I suggest that we block the rivers flow into the Bramhaputra before we destroy the facility." Woodsen suggested.

"I concur Max. Keep me posted." McAdams finished.

"Let's get this information back to the Pentagon immediately. I want the planners to review this and put the details in place to make this happen with near zero collateral damage." Woodsen barked to his staff assistants.

"We'll need God's help if those devices have been coded. Half of Asia will be uninhabitable for centuries if they have been coded for triggering." Woodsen said more to himself than to his assistant.

Karl had reviewed the briefing and was looking at his notes when Joshua McAdams approached him. "Karl, you have spent your life exposing this man. Where did you get the focus and drive to continue? Joshua asked.

"Hesbulah is the epitome of evil here in our world. I watched him systematically command the annihilation of 6 million people in Europe alone. Three of which were my mother, father and younger sister. They were taken from their home in Schaffenburg one evening. I had led him straight to them unknowingly. My parents were helping Jews escape into Slovenia, Croatia and Italy. As a young man I believed strongly in the propaganda and lies that were told by Hitler and his Nazi party. But his lies became apparent when he started murdering the people that he had placed in the camps. These were some of the German people that stood against him and his empty promises. My older brother and I vowed to do everything that we could to expose Hitler as a fraud. Robert and I vowed to never give up the fight. When Robert was killed after the war in America, I continued the fight with the men and woman that he and I organized. My brother Robert Linder as you also know him was a great man. His nephew Seth is so much like him. We have been involved in this fight against evil for centuries. We are very close now to Hesbulah's final defeat. We are very close to ending his chaotic influence to the people of our world." Karl said looking off into the light. Joshua could see a tear forming in the corner of his eyes.

"Karl, Robert Linder was Seth Stephen's uncle? How do you know that Seth is Robert's nephew?" Joshua seemed more confused that ever. The question was written all over his face.

"I know this, Joshua because Seth is my son." Karl said with the proud voice and tears that could only come from a father.

28

Caught Fishing in a Private Pond

Bhutan, March 3, 0647 hours

Seth felt as if he had spent a week out on the town. His head was pounding and the bright lights of the room penetrated his brain like laser beams directed at his optic disk. He tried to move his hands but couldn't. He felt the metal bindings tightly encircling his wrists. He looked around the room as his eyes slowly adjusted to the blinding light. It was almost too painful to open his eyes beyond the smallest slits that he could possibly allow. He rested his eyes on the dark spot to his right. He could barely make out Izz's face. Izz hadn't faired as well, Seth thought. His head was hanging over his left shoulder. He was either still unconscious or worst yet, dead.

Seth waited a few minutes and let his eyes adjust gradually before trying to determine where they were. He remembered being in the balcony overlooking the holding area for the submarines. Then he was in this room with the incredibly bright lights. He took a quick survey of his bodily functions, trying to determine what was working and what wasn't. He tried to feel his body to see if they had inserted any needles before they may have completed an interrogation. He felt nothing that would give him the indication that he had been administered any drugs. He continued his survey of the surroundings. The room wasn't arranged the way a professional interrogator would have had it set up. He considered he and Izz fortunate that they hadn't been turned over to Hesbulah's Intelligence goons. For now at least he was confident that they hadn't used any modern drugs to conduct an interrogation. Other than the dull pounding in the back of his head he felt all right.

Then he surveyed the room again with more attention. The room was empty except for the two chairs that he and Izz occupied. The walls, ceiling and floor were white and the glaring light reflected off of the surfaces so brightly that it was almost nauseating. Seth knew that they were being observed. It was a tactic commonly used by people trained in older methods of intelligence. They may not have been experts but they could still administer pain. They had sequestered him and Izz in a room where it was obvious that they were being held captive. They were hoping that he and Izz would discuss some information amongst themselves. It was surprising how much you could learn from this simple technique. Usually, a lot of information could be garnered by this tactic, if the subjects themselves hadn't used the same technique. When Izz came to, Seth thought, they'd give them a conversation full of worthless information. When you were a captive, you bought time by metering out your information. Let them make it uncomfortable, knock you around a little, tell them some information. Sooner, rather than later your body releases more endorphins to mask the pain and you can hold out a little longer each time. By that time they'll either kill you and move on to someone else, or stick you in a holding cell until they decide they haven't got enough information. In any case, you don't tell them everything you know. After they empty your brain and get the information that they want, they'll kill you. Knowledge reserved equals time alive. It is a direct equation.

The room's lights were becoming more bearable. Seth's eyes adjusted to the bright lights and he continued to survey the room. The 8 meter square room wasn't designed as an interrogation room, which was a good thing. It meant that they probably weren't dealing with interrogation professionals. Seth figured that they cold stall the bastards until the strike force came in a blasted a new depression into the landscape of Bhutan. Either way, the chances of them leaving Bhutan alive were grim and getting less optimistic each moment. Seth could see Izz stirring out of the corner of his eye.

"Izz, good morning. This is great, getting paid to sleep on the job. The good news is that you are still alive. The bad news is that I'm not sure for how much longer." Seth said.

"So this wasn't a nightmare that I was having. I was hoping that I would wake up in bed thinking that I was having a bad really dream." Izz said.

"No luck Izz. I am afraid it's their move again. We'll just wait them out and see when an opportunity presents itself. Let's just sit here and stare at the camera over there. That'll really piss these guys off." Seth said.

As he expected the door opened and in entered the entourage of goons.

Seth summed it up instantly. These guys had no idea what they were doing. They were amateurs. With any luck they'd bat he and Izz around a little more rather than resort to drugs and skilled interrogation. If they started the rough stuff that secured his belief that they were amateurs. If they didn't, they'd find out everything that they wanted to know within minutes.

He had seen professional interrogators take Sadam Hussein from his palace in Baghdad one evening in August of 1990, just after the Iraqis moved into Kuwait. The rangers went in, bagged him while he slept, took him to the Ishtar Sheraton, gave him 20cc of Methyl-Q and ask him about anything. By the time he had finished, we knew the codebooks, his plans, his childhood problems, his weaknesses, and to top it all off, we gave him some new instructions. The interrogator laughed when they found out that he and his Ambassador to the United States had torrid homosexual adventures in his palace at Basrah.

When the interrogations were finished, they put him back in his bed and he didn't know the difference. He woke up with the best night's sleep that he had ever had and didn't even know that we had him. Everyone was wondering why we didn't try to blow him up. Everything had gone according to plan until Al Quaeda operatives began diverting the oil for food money into the terrorist hands. Hell, he would have still be there if that didn't happen. Since we had liberated Iraq, we lost one of best sources of information. Even now, he's following the instructions that we had given him and telling the interrogators all about his terrorist connections. People wonder why after his capture just before Christmas of 2003, little else about him has been told. Even highly placed informants are well taken care of. If the terrorists only knew that he was being played by the United States, he would have been ousted long ago.

Even Osama Bin Laden was one of the CIA's most reliable informants. He was more valuable in the field than hundreds of intelligence agents.

In any case, Seth was almost sure that these clowns didn't use these techniques. They liked the technique that he and his fellow officers used to laugh about, HOSEINT. HOSEINT was a finely developed technique where interrogators used a rubber hose to beat the subject into submission and collect intelligence. Seth watched as the room filled with goons just aching to take a few jabs at he and Izz.

I think we are about to be compromised Izz." Seth said to Izz with disappointment lacing his voice. Izz looked at Seth and shrugged his shoulders. "What did you say about taking your chances boss? Izz replied.

Seth smiled at him and began talking like he was turned the corner on a street in his hometown and ran into an old friend. "Remember Izz, it's all about perceptions. If you are about to get run out of town and the crowd is hot on your heels, smile and make it look like you're leading the parade." Seth casually said as smiled in front of the welcome committee.

In a brash display of confidence, Seth looked each one of the goons over from his chair as if he were conducting a pass and review. El Hadin was more shocked at their display of attitude than Seth was to find himself in this predicament. El Hadin had rehearsed the small greeting that he would give. In his greeting, he planned to console the two Americans and make them stop begging for their lives. Use the old good guy, bad guy routine, but Seth wasn't acting according to El Hadin's plan. He wouldn't get to use his speech. Seth acted as if he were already well known and well thought of invited guest. El Hadin was speechless.

Hesbulah watched over the monitor and realized that his challenge of converting Seth to his team would be as, if not more, difficult as converting the entire world. Stephens' confidence was astounding.

"You appear to be the leader of this group." Seth said to El Hadin. "What's your next move? I'm sure that you have some kind of plan. You obviously weren't sent here to just stand there." Seth finished.

"You should be grateful that you are still alive Colonel Stephens. You should be on your knees begging to live." El Hadin shot out, overcoming the initial shock of Seth's confident display.

"Well, you have disappointed me twice already. I come here looking for a good fight and you just stand here. Now you show me that you haven't done any more homework on me other than knowing my name. I hope your boss is more understanding than I would be. I'd have you busted back to cleaning out cattle pens." Seth said in a loud whisper squared off staring at El Hadin. Seth's eyes burned the words into El Hadin's mind.

Only one other man had spoken to El Hadin in that manner. Hesbulah. This man Stephens had the leadership qualities to inspire men that few others possessed. El Hadin only acted now because he knew that Hesbulah was watching. If El Hadin could choose on his own, he would not place himself in the middle of this torrent that was about to take place.

Hesbulah almost immediately deduced that Stephens would be a worthy adversary. His mannerisms, confidence and stout character told him that he would dominate El Hadin. El Hadin was a strong leader and if thrown into a crowd of millions, would come out on top. But he was no match for this American. Hesbulah left the small room where the monitor was and went directly into the room where the action was being played out.

"I believe, Colonel Stephens, that you would rather address me. I am the Hesbulah." Hesbulah said in a deep powerful voice that would have intimidated most men but not Seth.

Seth heard the voice and knew, before he turned around that it was Hesbulah speaking. Without looking at Hesbulah, but gradually turning to speak at any object as a show of disrespect, Seth spoke. "I see that you received my message Hesbulah. I tried to leave you a trail so obvious that any one could have stumbled upon it and found me." Only when he was finished talking did he turn and look at Hesbulah.

"Release Colonel Stephens." Hesbulah commanded and two of the goons moved to release Seth.

Seth stood and turned to appraise Hesbulah. Seth knew that this was the first part of combat, the appraisal of the adversary. This was the time before combat began and each combatant would survey his opponent for a weakness. Seth would look for any sign that he could use against this man. He was ready for this. This was the final battle of his life.

Izz could see what was taking place. Seth appeared sharper and more determined now than Izz had ever seen him. It was incredible what he was witnessing. Izz felt as if he were watching the final battle of good and evil take place. It was the battle of the Titans. He couldn't move. Every breath hung on the actions and response that the two opponents made. Izz pulled himself away from the action to watch the original eight men that were positioned earlier to meet them. The stood unready, weapons slung over their shoulders, unprepared. They were glued as he was to the drama that was unfolding before them.

Seth was almost disappointed when he saw Hesbulah. He was expecting fire breathing, mountain of flesh that had a grimace so evil that it would turn men to stone where they stood. He was not what he had expected. Seth saw right through the image that Hesbulah displayed. He saw that there was no substance of a man, only an empty shell. It was easy for Seth to gain moral ascendancy over Hesbulah. There was nothing beneath the facade. Hesbulah was a life empty of conviction and selflessness. There were no beliefs, no faiths, and no values. There was nothing there. Seth could see the empty promise that his eyes held. The soul of this man did not exist. His eyes were empty and lifeless. It was as if he were looking at a store window manikin in an expensive Manhattan men's clothier shop.

Hesbulah stared at Seth working the intimidation that he had used so many times before. He wanted to strike terror in this man's heart and gain a superior position. The more that Hesbulah looked into Seth's eyes, the more he saw things he did not want to. Seth Stephens was not a weak-minded idiot, the kind that also thrived on the chaos that Hesbulah promoted. This man was strong and held deep core beliefs. Even he would surely buckle under Hesbulah's intimidations and tactics, everyone did eventually. Hesbulah had to keep reminding himself that Seth was only a man, it would be no different. He would eventually fall to his knees and serve Hesbulah. No one had ever successfully resisted.

Seth turned now and fully faced Hesbulah. Hesbulah paused to release a nervous laugh to himself. He was furious inside because he felt threatened by the weak American. He could not believe that Seth had already shown disrespect by not talking to him directly and then not averting his eyes when Hesbulah had stared at him. Hesbulah began to move forward casually and reposition himself in front of Seth. Seth moved forward to him and thwarted Hesbulah's symbolic move of aggression. As he moved toward Hesbulah he placed his hand on his heart and traced the cross over it like he had done before every battle. Hesbulah noticed the gesture even though Seth had done it discreetly. Hesbulah felt the corners of his mouth unconsciously turn down in disdain.

'There's his first weakness,' Seth thought to himself as he stopped, facing Hesbulah, just out of arms reach.

"Perhaps you should show a little more respect to your host, Colonel Stephens. We could very easily have killed you and your colleague." Hesbulah said with slitted-eyes still pressing a bad attempt at intimidation and closing the gap between them.

Seth watched him, ready for anything. Hesbulah stopped. He only moved closer to play the intimidation out a little longer. That was the mistake that Seth had hoped for.

"Perhaps." But then you wouldn't have the opportunity to find out what I know and if you could tempt me to forfeit my mission." Seth returned, not shaken in the slightest.

Hesbulah burst out into laughter. "I can see that you are a very industrious man Colonel Stephens. Won't you please allow me to show you my hospitality before you cast an unfitting judgment? There is much that we can learn from each other. You are trying me and although I am patient. I do have my limits." Hesbulah said immediately shifting his strategy.

Seth knew that Hesbulah would either come at him full steam ahead or back up and regroup. Hesbulah was evil, not stupid. He knew from Karl that there was no one more adept at creating chaotic turns of events than Hesbulah. Seth realized that he was playing a dangerous game, but one that he had to. If he didn't he'd be dead in any event.

Seth only maintained his position and said nothing in return to Hesbulah.

"El Hadin, escort Colonel Stephens to my chambers. I am sure that he is hungry and would enjoy some dinner." Hesbulah half looked at Izz and looked out of the corner of his eye to watch Seth's expression. "El Hadin," Hesbulah continued, "You may kill Major DeConcerio. We have no further use for him."

Seth waited no longer. He knew that Hesbulah had intended to kill them. Seth could delay his death by parsing out bits of data a little at a time. But he couldn't play the waiting game at the expense of Izz's life.

In one quick move Seth reached for Hesbulah's weapon and pulled Hesbulah against him in an arm-neck lock. Seth was effectively cutting off Hesbulah's air supply and preventing him from speaking. Every ounce of energy that he could draw was focused on this effort. Before Hesbulah knew what had happened. Seth had the pistol forced into the side of Hesbulah's neck. Hesbulah was momentarily shocked. He had never been threatened in this manner, let alone grabbed and held at gunpoint.

"Release him now." Seth commanded. El Hadin looked at Hesbulah for instructions. "Don't look at him, he is no longer in charge. I am! Do it now!" Seth commanded in a voice so forceful that the dead would have risen to obey the command.

El Hadin moved to release Izz from his chair. "Have the rest drop their weapons or I will kill Hesbulah immediately." Seth would have loved to pull the trigger, but it Hesbulah was his only bargaining chip.

"You continue to make mistakes Colonel Stephens. What do you hope gain by taking me hostage? You will never leave here. If you don't kill me, I'll kill you. If you do kill me, my men will kill you. Anyway you will die." Hesbulah said with no resistance.

Seth couldn't disagree with him. He knew as well as Hesbulah that he wouldn't play this out. "My life in trade for yours? Hardly seems worth it. But you do have a point. This is the part were we negotiate a little. I'll tell you what. If you give Major DeConcerio a chance to leave, you won't die right now. Maybe time will improve your chances. Other than that, I'd say that I'm in the position to name the price. After Major Deconcerio leaves, you'll still be alive and have me to interrogate. Sounds like a very sound deal to me Hesbulah." Seth said as he pushed the barrel of his gun further into Hesbulah's temple.

"For the moment, you have me at the disadvantage." Hesbulah said as he and Seth looked over at the eight men all armed with automatic weapons trained at Seth's head. Seth could ascertain the obvious. He would die if he killed Hesbulah right now. Would that end the reign of terror or was there something else in place that would merely continue where he left off? Seth couldn't risk it. Hesbulah would have to live until he found some answers.

Izz knew what Seth was doing, buying him time. He quickly got up and gathered up an AK-47 to cover the goons that stood awestruck at the turn of events. The situation had turned in their favor, but Izz wasn't sure for how long. Seth was backing for the door as he placed Hesbulah between he and the goons. Hesbulah was regaining his situational awareness. The three had made it out the door and had locked it after their exit.

"That should keep them quiet for a few minutes." Izz said as he secured the door with the padlock and tossed the key out and down the hallway.

Seth saw their equipment thrown in the corner of the observation room. "Izz gather up our equipment. We need to head for the Landing Zone. This place is going to have more aircraft overhead than LAX in less than one hour. Give Mike a call and tell him that we'll have one more passenger with us."

Hesbulah began to laugh, and then he flung his head back and rammed Seth with a powerful head butt. Seth's grip unconsciously loosened and Hesbulah reached and grabbed for Seth's gun hand. Seth couldn't remember ever being grabbed with such force. It was as if his hand was caught in a vise. He fought off the pain and struggled to maintain control over the gun.

"You simple fool, do you believe that I would let you just walk in and destroy my final opportunity. The submarines have begun to leave. There is no way to call them back. You have lost Seth Stephens. Soon the submarines will reach their destinations and the nuclear weapons will begin to detonate. The world will be in chaos, it will be looking for any one to fill a leadership void. I will succeed in uniting the world under one leader. I will have the only infrastructure remaining in place to distribute food and water. How does it feel to be impotent? You tried as hard as you could to disperse my plans but failed. The might of the greatest power on earth will soon be beaten. There is nothing that you can do, nothing!" Hesbulah said wincing and glaring at Seth.

Seth fought to return the pistol to the position against Hesbulah's head. The best that he could do was a stalemate. Hesbulah matched each increment of force that Seth could muster. Izz stood by watching the conflict his gun aimed at Hesbulah, waiting for Seth's command.

"Izz, shoot for Christ's sake! Shoot us both Izz! Take the shot Izz!" Seth commanded. Hesbulah had seen it coming and rolled with Seth as he heard the command. Izz couldn't get a clear shot.

"Izz, for Christ's sake, shoot us both, don't let this bastard leave here alive." Seth commanded as he struggled with an inhuman power.

Izz couldn't just shoot. The thought of Sean dying and now killing Seth would not let him fire the shot. Sweat was pouring from his brow into his eyes as he fought to get a clear shot.

He yelled, "Seth, pull him over toward me on my count, One!" Izz fired. Hesbulah resisted the roll and instead broke free and fell under the railing of the catwalk to the deck below. The shot impacted the deck inches away from Seth's ear, narrowly missing him.

Seth shot a look at Izz with teeth gritted tightly together. "You just lost the war for us Major." Izz saw the determination in Seth's eyes as he jumped over the side of the railing after Hesbulah. Izz followed and snapped the radio in his ear as he ran.

"Seth, here!" Izz said as he threw Seth's CAR-15 and bag of explosives down to him. Seth looked up and grabbed the equipment as it reached his level.

"Izz contact Mike and meet him at the Landing Zone. Work with General Woodsen; stop as many of those submarines heading out as you can. Do it now!" Seth was not willing to discuss his command. He was off running after Hesbulah. Perhaps he could find a way to prevent the detonation.

"Thomas, this is Izz, over…Thomas this is Izz, over…" Mike heard the radio transmission, as he was about to taxi the aircraft toward the active runway in Calcutta. Mike switched the radio selector knob over to the satellite communications.

"Izz, this is Mike, I'm just about to take off. I'll be at the Landing Zone in 54 minutes over." Mike responded.

"Mike, switch us over so the command post can monitor our conversation." Izz commanded as he was on the full run after Seth. Izz would try and prep their escape route to the Landing Zone. Mike heard the security claxon ring through the satellite communications. Izz heard it and stopped in an alcove to his right to see what the response would be. "Seth has followed Hesbulah, he doesn't have his radio. They have moved the launch up earlier. The submarines have begun leaving the facility. Whatever happens, you are to bomb this target heavily. Do you understand? Do not change the plan. With a little luck we'll be at the LZ in time to meet you. If we aren't there, don't wait around for us Mike. Just make sure that no more submarines leave this installation." Izz said into the satellite phone.

"Izz, this is General Woodsen. We copy your instructions son. The strike force is on its way. Time on target is 42 minutes. I say again 42 minutes." Woodsen said as he checked the status of the aircraft inbound. The B-2's would be in first followed by the F-117s, and then a mix of Army Hawks to clean things up. The first wave of B-2 would use shaped charged bomblets to try and close the Dangme Chu River where it passed a narrow valley on its way to the Bramhaputra in order to prevent any material from leaking down away from Bhutan. The plan would also close off the river so that none of the submarines would pass that point, only if they closed it off in time. Wooden paced back and forth in the command center and kept the communications opened for calls from the Intelligence Team, Joshua McAdams, or the President.

Mike was airborne. He glanced at the Flight Management System. The system showed 34 minutes to the coordinates where the landing area was located.

Seth winced from bullets fired at him by the goons responding to Hesbulah's alarm. The facility was not designed as a kill zone and offered too many places for a man to find cover. Pipes, stanchions, platforms and conveyors blocked the bullets before they reached the target at which they were aimed. Seth could see the small room to where Hesbulah had retreated. He was determined to find Hesbulah. He rounded the turn to where Hesbulah had tried to make the elevator and retreat to his bunker. If he made it there, Seth would not be able to get to him. He had to get him now. Seth ran against the hailstorm of lead that was streaking toward him. He felt the hot lead pass within centimeters of his face as he ran uncaring toward Hesbulah. He was closing the distance but not fast enough. He reached over the railing and threw himself over it, landing on the ground level of the facility. He could see the elevator shaft just ahead. He pulled a package of explosive out of his bag and rigged it as a grenade while he ran and ducked the bullets aimed for him. On the run, he reached back and threw the rigged explosive at the elevator shaft. The small charge of High Explosive landed at the base of the exposed elevator and its shaft.

Seth ducked under a heavy worktable as the explosive detonated. The explosion shook the facility on its foundation and pushed the elevator cab from it rails and jammed it in place. Seth was thrown against the wall. His pistol was forced from his hands. A group of goons that had the mission to make sure that Hesbulah was secure was thrown clear of the area and landed in the conveyors and machinery that surrounded them. Hesbulah was thrown into a wire meshed caged that held bottles of oxygen. Hesbulah grabbed for the fire axe that was attached to the wire mesh cage and ripped it from its mounts. He held it like high over his head and walked at a quickened pace toward Seth, who still lay on the ground bruised by the explosion.

Seth quickly regained his faculties and saw Hesbulah coming at him with the axe raised overhead.

"You should have escaped me while you had the opportunity, now I'll hack your body to pieces, Seth Stephens." Hesbulah said with a rage laced voice as he pulled the axe down toward Seth's torso.

Seth forced the haze from his head and rolled in time to avert the powerful swing of the axe. The axe sent a shower of sparks and flying concrete into the air as it contacted the hard floor with enormous power. Seth rolled to his feet and charged Hesbulah head down like a linebacker plowing through his opponent's line as Hesbulah raised the axe for another blow. Seth's head and right shoulder drove into Hesbulah mid-section, compressing his kidney as if it were a pillow driven over by a heavy roller. The incredible force would have ruptured internal organs in any other man, but Hesbulah wasn't any other man. Hesbulah shook off the charge with hardly a wince at the pain. The axe fell to the ground harmlessly as Hesbulah was forced off balance. Seth lunged back for the axe and threw it overhead into the center of the factory.

Hesbulah leapt toward Seth. His hands and arms were out forward towards Seth trying to encircle his neck. Hesbulah was fully enraged; an animal with no rational thought, his only thought was to go for the kill. Seth calculated the landing point while Hesbulah was in mid flight and pulled a sharp triangular piece of metal that was ripped from its mount in the blast into Hesbulah's path. Hesbulah landed on the jagged debris with his full weight. The jagged metal penetrated his shoulder and neck. Slightly dazed, he stood pulling the metal from his neck and shoulder.

Seth shook his head in amazement as he watched Hesbulah stand after he landed on the jagged metal. He charged Hesbulah again, taking advantage of his dazed state. Seth aimed his forearm and elbow at the wound that was oozing blood from near Hesbulah's neck. Seth's forearm caught Hesbulah with his all of the power that he could bring to bear. Hesbulah folded into a heap as Seth landed on top of him. Seth pummeled Hesbulah's face and neck with his balled fists. They hit like hammers driving a spike into a piece of soft wood. Seth felt the flesh and muscle give under his assault. No one could have survived this beating, except Hesbulah.

Hesbulah grabbed Seth's hand as it was coming down for another blow and stopped it solidly as if there was no force or momentum behind it. Seth rolled free from Hesbulah grip and fell back near the whirring pulleys of the conveyor belt. Hesbulah stood and charged at Seth. He grabbed Seth with one hand and pinned him to the wall. With the other he smashed into Seth's ribs cracking several with one blow. Seth's sharp instinctive reflexes brought his right knee up and into Hesbulah's groin. The impact forced Hesbulah's release and he doubled over but almost instantly regained his strength.

Seth dropped and swung his legs under Hesbulah to cut him down. Hesbulah lost his balance and crashed into the framework that supported the conveyor belt in the facility. Seth saw an opportunity and lunged at Hesbulah's raised arm as it rested on the framework.

"If I can't beat you whole, I'll do it piece by piece." Seth said as he grabbed Hesbulah's arm and rammed it between the conveyor belt and the pulley. The machined steel pulleys ground and tore into Hesbulah's flesh. Skin tissue, muscle and bone were ground off of Hesbulah's arm as the pulley sawed away. Hesbulah pulled on it as if he were pulling on a fallen tree branch. It was as if the pain didn't register. He only grunted and pulled harder.

Seth watched in disbelief and took advantage of Hesbulah's painful preoccupation. Seth drove his knee into the side of Hesbulah face as Hesbulah struggled to free his mangled arm. Hesbulah head spun as Seth's knee forced it to one side. Hesbulah continued to struggle with his arm.

Somewhere above and behind him, Seth did not know exactly where it came from, but he heard the staccato of machine gun fire. He threw himself to the ground out of instinct. The rounds from a gun aimed at only him impacted the floor and ricocheted off of the machinery all around him. He rolled under the framework of the conveyor for cover. He looked up and saw the gunners moving to get a clearer shot.

Seth saw Hesbulah roll free from the entanglement. His left arm was shredded. The fabric of his clothing, the skin, muscle and bone were all twisted together in bloody strands. 'At least the bastard bleeds.' Seth thought.

Hesbulah rolled and stayed clear of his gunner's line of sight. "What are you waiting for...shoot him!" Hesbulah commanded in a deep growling, almost inhuman voice.

311

Seth squeezed himself into the recesses of the framework as he heard the report of at least two machine guns fire. He had no solid cover, only the lattice of framework hiding him. He expected the rounds to tear into his body as he winced at the sound of the gunfire. Nothing came his way. He looked up and over the lattice to see Hesbulah pull himself up with one arm and scramble down the hallway as the gunfire sprayed his, not Seth's, footsteps.

"What the…" Seth mouthed as he tried to see where the additional firepower was coming from.

"Hang in there Seth. Help is just around the corner." Izz said, but not loud enough for anyone to hear. Izz had more than enough firepower to manage the poorly trained goons that stood with Hesbulah not because of conviction but because of pay.

"Your six is clear boss." Izz said as he held two M-8s in each hand.

"Izz, get on the radio, broadcast what is going on here. The reconnaissance aircraft will pick up your transmission. Tell them that I have gone after the submarines that have been released and tell them to block the river passage. You make sure that the strike force levels this place. Make sure that you and Mike stay close to assess the damage after each wave." Seth said glancing at his watch. "You've got less than twenty minutes to get to the Landing Zone and clear out of here." Seth commanded as he moved in after Hesbulah.

"What about you Seth? I just can't leave." Izz asked with deep concern for his friend's life.

"Major you have twenty minutes to get to the LZ and make sure that this mission is completed. If those planes don't hit this target and annihilate it completely, it'll go on your record as just another failure for you Major. I'm tired of covering up your screw-ups. When are you going to figure it out, Huh? It'll be your failure, Major. Your orders are to get to the LZ and captain the strike force. Do you got it or are you really that stupid?" Seth knew that he'd have to say something to anger Izz and make him leave. Even though it wasn't how he felt. He needed to alienate and give him the responsibility to make sure that the strike force destroyed the submarines in order for him to leave.

Izz knew what his commander was doing and he also knew that someone had to assess the damage that the strike force caused. Satellite imagery may not be able to provide the immediate detail. Nothing here could remain intact, Izz would make sure of that. Tashi would be a smoking hole in the Himalayas. Izz turned and watched as he his friend ran off down the corridor after Hesbulah, wondering if he'd live. He keyed his radio's microphone and spoke solemnly. The chances of Seth surviving this mission were next to nil.

"White Horse Watch this is White Horse Two, Transmitting in the blind. Be advised that..." Izz relayed all of the information that Seth wanted him to, without knowing if anyone would hear the transmission.

"Also, relay to White Horse Rider that I am proceeding to the landing area for pickup, White Horse Two out." Izz finished the transmission and moved out of the facility to the loading dock and jumped into the first vehicle that he found. With a glance back he detonated the remote explosives in the facility as planned. The explosions rocked the building and blocked the route of Izz's pursuers.

"God be with you Seth." Izz said stealing one last look around for his good friend and commander. Izz sped off toward the landing zone to make sure that the strike force would deliver the payload on target.

29

Uniting the World

The Address to the United Nations, March 2, 1530 hours

"Distinguished Ladies and Gentlemen, it is my distinct honor to introduce Mr. Joshua McAdams, Director of the United States National Security Agency. Mr. McAdams has served in the Armed Forces of the United States for 28 years retiring as a flag officer. He has served as the Security Advisor to two Presidents and has been an ally to the United Nations throughout his very focused career. I have requested this assembly because the United States, along with the United Kingdom, has discovered a series of events that threaten the sovereignty if every nation on earth. As the Secretary General, I felt that is was necessary to act as a unilateral body on this matter with only one objective in mind. We must work to ensure stability in our world, to solidify the progress that we have made toward peace and the eradication of hostile leaders and their intent to spread terror and chaos at every turn."

The Secretary continued. "Over 65 years ago, Robert Linder Stephens, was recruited into the Waffen SS by the Nazi party. Then Field Marshall Erwin Rommel, the commander of Hitler's Afrikorps, recruited Linder to serve on his intelligence staff. Rommel knew of Karl's family from Schaffenfeld, Austria. Karl had key qualities that Rommel desired. He knew Karl was educated in the United States. Rommel hoped that this education would allow Karl to gain an insight on American tactics and strategies. It did and it propelled Rommel into the history books as the amazing tactician now known as the Desert Fox. Rommel's astuteness on the battlefield allowed him to get inside the Allies decision cycle and seemingly know their every move. Rommel by his own hand in his book lends credit to his Chief of Intelligence. We know that it was because of Robert Linder Stephens. It didn't take long for Hitler to recognize Stephens as a leading intelligence analyst and request that he be promoted to Field Marshall in order to lead the intelligence efforts for all of the Nazi war efforts.

Robert delicately balanced his position and realized that he was in position to influence many Nazi leaders. He did just that and formed and underground of inside leaders that were secretly battling Hitler and his forces at every turn. Many attempts to overthrow Hitler were thwarted but still Robert, his brother Karl, and his colleagues continued to play this dangerous counter Nazi role.

Linder's efforts included, delivering the enigma encryption device to the allies, identifying V-2 construction sites and target lists, and leaking the key strategic plans of Hitler himself to the American and British intelligence forces. Because of his tremendous efforts, Robert was asked to attend a post-war meeting with Prime Minister Churchill and President Truman. In this meeting, Linder discussed how Hitler and Hirohito, meet with a man only known as Hesbulah.

Hitler referred to Hesbulah as the Furher. Ironically, Hitler even subtly acknowledged that the Furher was Hesbulah. Author Ronald Stuart Kain discussed in his book <u>Europe: Versailles to Warsaw</u>, published in 1939, Hitler's foreign policy and his exceedence of all expectations by bringing all groups and forces under his absolute control. Hitler recanted Hesbulah's statement on a radio address one evening, "…every man, woman and child must be gathered up in a mighty sacrifice to one resolute will when great things are to be accomplished." Robert and Karl were present and heard Hesbulah make this statement as a command to Hitler and Hirohito at a secret meeting on the Island of Socotra in July 12, 1939. Only three days before the Anglo-Japanese negotiations on China opened in Tokyo where Japan demanded assent to the New Asian Order. The Great Will was the directive of the man known as Hesbulah. President Truman and Prime Minister Churchill agreed to open the investigation titled PROJECT VICTORY to uncover this unknown man named Hesbulah. The United States recently opened the file once again after a series of discoveries. To describe this further I would like to present Mr. Joshua McAdams, the Director of the National Security Agency for the United States of America."

"Thank you Mr. Secretary." Joshua McAdams began his introduction. "The Army Security Agency worked with the British Intelligence agencies and hoped to track and eventually uncover the man that Linder discussed in his meetings with Churchill and Truman. A tragedy occurred after we had Field Marshall Stephens come to the United States to begin the formal investigation to determine if a character named Hesbulah actually existed. He had just finished his first day of questioning and was leaving the Pentagon to head for Camp Meade. A train destroyed the car in which he was traveling. No one was sure how it happened. There were no witnesses. We only suspect that is was a train accident because the vehicle was found in pieces, nearly consumed by fire, at a railroad crossing near Greenbelt, Maryland. The destruction was so complete that it took us days to verify that it was the vehicle in which Linder was a passenger. We now believe that the accident was arranged to prevent progress with the investigation. The United States attempted to continue the investigation, but without Robert Linder Stephens, there was simply nowhere to go. The report was shelved until this past February. Then a most amazing thing happened. It is something that surprised us all frankly. It was something that we would have never expected. In a moment, I will introduce to you an amazing man. This man has dedicated his life's work to intelligence collection directed at exposing this man Hesbulah. His fusion and analysis capability was many years ahead of its time and still remains as an amazing contribution to the world's stability and peace. Ladies and gentlemen of the United Nations, what this man is about to tell you is true. It has been substantiated by several major intelligence organizations throughout the world. No matter how incredible it may sound to you, please know that every single statement is backed by indisputable evidence. This imagery that you are about to see was taken just recently today. Men of the United States Intelligence services are now, as we speak, fighting for their very lives. They were sent to bring back this evidence so that we could unite and take action against a very hostile and evil force."

Joshua McAdams stopped in surprise as the back doors opened in the chamber. The two secret service agents preceded the President of the United States as he took his place in the visitor's gallery. McAdams straightened himself and smiled. He knew that President Abraham was there as a show of support. The leader of the most respected government in the world thought that this was important enough to attend. Many of the Ambassadors who weren't paying attention, just as always, had now turned their undivided attention to Joshua McAdams. He now had every ear bent and hanging on his every word.

"Mr. President, it is an honor to have you present Sir." Joshua McAdams said with sincere respect.

"Ladies and Gentlemen, it is vital that we act as soon as possible. A threat to the existence of every government on earth has been uncovered. It is a situation so grave that I have coordinated with each country's leaders of every member country of the United Nations. They are hearing and seeing exactly what you are experiencing now by videoconference. Please, my fellow leaders, as you hear the evidence that is about to be brought forth, do not delay. We are prepared to act immediately on your decisions. This is an historic occasion. Never before have all of the leaders of the governments of the world been united in such a manner. Never before has the sovereignty of every nation on earth been threatened. It is imperative that we all hear and unite to support this as our common goal. We must stand together, at least this one time and hold our differences in abeyance as we make our decision. It is a decision that breaks through every boundary that we believe and hold important. As we listen to this evidence I ask you, along with each and every leader that you see before you cast a decision made by knowing what you truly know is right and not by an alliance to any flag. The people of the world are today, looking for wisdom in our actions, wisdom that will save them from a life of despair and agony without freedom."

The President paused as the final monitor came alive with the image of every leader of the worlds governments represented.

"Fellow leaders, Thank you for your attention and Mr. McAdams…thank you for pardoning my intrusion." The President quickly took his seat amidst the whispers and hushes. He sat as a humble servant of the people of the United States supporting his subordinate's actions. Joshua McAdams smiled inside at the show of support. The atmosphere of unity in the chamber was almost so real that he could hold onto it.

Joshua McAdams spoke in a low humble voice, out of respect for not only his President, but for all of the world's leaders that were now in attendance.

"I would like to introduce to you a man that has given his life in pursuit of world peace and stability. He began this pursuit many years ago when as a soldier, with his brother, Field Marshal Robert Linder Stephens. Together, they worked to undermined Hitler's Nazi government and helped to defeat Hitler. Throughout the years since then they have secretly worked to maintain peace and stability and defeat tyranny at every turn. Today, Mr. Karl Linder Stephens has come to us as a friend and an ally to present to us his life's work at great personal risk. He has earned our respect and attention this historical day. The work that he and his colleagues have prepared will fill volumes and each of you is now receiving data on your monitors in your native language." Joshua concluded as Karl Linder walked out form behind the door to McAdams left.

The chamber was as quiet now, even completely filled during the working hours, as it is normally is at midnight in its solitude. All eyes watched as Karl Linder, head held high, dignified, walked toward the podium from where he would address this honored assembly. He turned as he reached the podium and took the time to measure the sincerity of each member in attendance by making eye contact. The assembly remained completely silent as Karl lowered his head and paused. In a few fleeting moments and without a sound he won the respect and admiration of the assembly. It was as if they were each touched individually by his hand as his gentle green-brown eyes met with theirs. He seemed to ask, without words, for their openness and serious attention. He received it from each leader and each ambassador present either in person or by the marvel of technology. They were his audience. He held their undivided attention. Many were startled by his gentle voice breaking through the silence. It was one of the most sincere and genuinely personal experiences that they had remembered.

"As I stand here in this chamber, filled with the greatest leaders that humanity has known, I have two thoughts passing through my mind. The first is of my son and my wife, whom I love dearly. The second is of your families and the children of our world."

Karl paused to collect his thoughts. "What is the one thing that we would give our lives for? It of course is our families. Our wives, our children and their happiness is what we would give our lives for. No man of this earth would jeopardize his children or his family for the sake of his own personal gain. Yet there is one man among us that would sacrifice his children and his wife for his own gratification. There is someone that preys upon our human frailties and weakness. His name is Hesbulah and he is among us today. He is but the final descendant of a family has had only one objective for over two thousand years. That is to dominate the earth and see that a reign of chaos and terror is brought to humanity..."

Karl continued to describe to everyone those events that led up to the present day. He described in complete detail the study of ancient writings that told of Hesbulah's reign. All eyes and ears were wide opened and attentive as he described World War I, World War II and every major recent conflict up to the 911 event, Iraq, Iran and Africa. He used facts, maps, radio transmissions, and images to set the facts solidly with each member. Everyone in attendance was shaking his or her heads in disbelief.

Karl concluded with the imagery and details of Hesbulah's plan to launch the submarines. The assembly was awestruck as they watched Izz DeConcerio and Seth Stephens move through the facility with images taken only hours before. Karl's case was iron clad. Doubt was not possible. He had boiled the facts uncovered in a lifetime down to a three-hour briefing. The briefing in itself was a display of sheer genius. He had made the case against Hesbulah and built it form the ground up. In every ones wildest imagination, they couldn't have assembled a story as unbelievable as this, but yet Hesbulah had done it. He carefully and painstakingly used every strategy possible to turn brother against brother and father against son. He had succeeded more times that Karl cared to recount. What is Hesbulah's only desire? Plunge the world into chaos for his entertainment while subjecting every human to his whims and eliminating freewill.

"Ladies and Gentlemen, I leave you hopefully with the thoughts of your families and their welfare as I leave with the same two thoughts of my family and the prayers that my work will help you to defeat this evil. Thank you for you attention and patience. May God be with you as you cast your decision." Karl concluded his recounting of his life's work. As he left the podium, one by one, the members of the assembly stood with him in prayer. It was a deeply moving and emotional experience to watch this very gentle man, a man that had spent his life in the service of humanity, bow his head and pray.

"Distinguished members of the United Nations, I propose that resolution 1487 be unanimously approved. This motion will authorize the Armed Forces of the participants of this resolution and grant complete authority to discharge whatever force necessary to destroy the facilities located in the country of Bhutan and defeat the plans of Hesbulah. It further authorizes the arrest and arraignment for trial of the designer of this plan, Hesbulah. This action will be carried out as soon as feasibly possible to prevent the launch of submarines containing nuclear weapons. Please indicate your decision before ten minutes has passed. As you confer with your country's leadership please bear in mind that we can and will act to prevent the domination or destruction of our world. We cannot sit by and let the desires of one tyrannical dictator wipe from the earth the thousands of years of progress toward human freedoms. We will continue to pursue freewill and not allow the world's peoples to fall to the desires of one tyrant. The brave men that are fighting and preparing to fight for all of our freedoms must have the full support of their countries. It is with them that our future now belongs. Please make your decisions know." The Secretary General of the United Nations finished by casting his affirmative vote on the computer touch screen at his desk.

The entire unanimous vote took less than four minutes. There were no doubts among them. Hesbulah and his plan were real and that they had proceeded orderly to a vote and stood beside each other like never before in the history of man. All because of the courage and conviction of one family and one man.

30

Hesbulah's Escape

Dangme Chu River, March 3, 1630 hours

Seth had hurt Hesbulah, but he was far from finished. He knew now that the Americans would relay the information about the facility back to intelligence organizations or an aerial armada determined to destroy his facility and final plan. He heard Seth's shouts back to the other American and knew that he had no time to spare. Seth had prevented him from retreating to the central control room so now he had to get to one of the submarines that was already heading down the Dangme Chu. He refused to allow his plan to be derailed by the American. Instead of using the control center to change the submarines programming, he'd use the lead submarine to transmit the detonation commands to the others once they reached their targets.

Seth had to make sure that Izz followed his instructions. He didn't feel good about it but it was necessary for the success of the mission. Izz was a fine soldier and he would never denigrate one of his men. Izz's loyalty certainly didn't need to be questioned but Seth knew that he had to put some distance between he and Izz or Izz would have stayed. Now he had to find out what Hesbulah was doing. If he let him slip past them now, they would never end his reign of terror. He would just reorganize and continue to find another means to bring humanity to it knees under his self-serving control.

Hesbulah moved like he was uninjured. Seth on the other hand was starting to feel the combined strains of the mission. He pushed those thoughts from his mind and tried to keep Hesbulah in sight. Winding around the facility, through the conveyor and over the tops of the machinery designed to build each one of Hesbulah's submarines. Seth was closing the distance since Izz had cleared the trail behind.

Seth could see Hesbulah jump into one of the sleek watercraft with a tandem cockpit only designed for two people. As Seth turned the last corner, Hesbulah opened up with 12.7mm automatic machinegun fire and sprayed the area where Seth was standing. Seth dove behind two of the dry-docked submarines for cover. The machine guns armor piercing bullets dug into the sub's titanium alloy hull.

Hesbulah continued to fire in Seth's direction and then started the powerful hydro drive motors on the boats. Seth picked himself up and ran for the cover that the next submarine offered. The armor piecing bullets tore through the thin masonry construction of the factory. As Seth reached the cover of the last submarine, a loud explosion shook the facility.

Seth ducked under the heavy framed scaffolding that was erected around the dry-docked submarine. Debris from the explosion and shards of concrete fell around his position. He looked in the direction of the explosion and then checked his watch. Thankfully it was too early for the strike force's arrival. He saw that the explosion came from where He and Izz had planted the charges used to slow any pursuing force as they retreated to the Landing Zone.

He felt confident that it was Izz following the egress plan. With any luck, Izz and Mike would be soon leading the strike force into the target area and providing instantaneous bomb damage assessment.

Hesbulah crouched behind the gunner's shield on the machinegun that he was firing. He too could see that the explosion was not destroying critical areas and felt that it was either a diversion or an attempt to destroy his facility. Hesbulah fired one last burst in Seth's general area. The shots were poorly aimed but the 12.7mm rounds would cause substantial damage even if they had come close.

Confident that he had either killed or wounded Seth, he turned the guns on the pursuit boats that remained parked in slips next to the boat that he manned. The bullets ripped into the fiberglass and aluminum hulls like a very hot poker would through soft butter. Secondary explosions began to erupt immediately as the bullets found fuel tanks and ammunition storage areas. Hesbulah made one last glance but he could see no adversary on the dock because of the smoke that had obscured his view.

Hesbulah jammed the throttle of the pursuit boats full forward. The hydro drive motors bit into the water and the boat lurched forward, its bow climbing into to sky as if to take flight.

Seth moved toward the boats still docked under the cover of the smoke and fire. Seth could see Hesbulah's back as the boat shot out of the slip. Hesbulah cranked the steering wheel hard to the right and aimed the boat down the Dangme Chu. He could see the shallow wake of the submarines that streamed from the launch facility.

Hesbulah's pursuit boat had a 20-knot advantage over the speed of the submarines. Hesbulah would easily outrun them before the submarines made it to the Bramhaputra River and submerged before he could reprogram them. He did a quick calculation and figured that over 425 submarines would be launched and every minute that the facility remained intact meant another launch. He laughed at the feeble attempt made to foil his plan but cursed the weak American for shredding his arm. No matter he thought it is a cheap price to pay for control of the world. Soon he would be relaxing in Socotra listening to humanities cries for help from the few that survived his final holocaust anyway. The thought made his confidence and strength grow. He laughed out loud at the genius of his plan.

Seth found two boats farthest away from Hesbulah machine gun fire that miraculously remained somewhat seaworthy. Seth jumped into the first boat, the look of determination chiseled on his face. His eyes were narrowed by the taut pull of his furrowed brow. His lips were tight as he unconsciously worked his jaw muscles side to side creating what Mike had termed long ago as the ultimate war mask. Mike had described it as the combination look of an eagle locking on to his prey just before the final dive were it would drive its sharp heel talons into its prey and a cobra, muscles cocked and fully flattened in the final phases of its strike.

The engine of the boat choked itself to life more from Seth's will than out of mechanical design. Seth almost tore the throttle assembly from the console as he drove it forward, almost burying it into the instrument panel, trying to get every gram of energy from it. The stern dug in deep and the bow flung itself around in the direction of Seth's command as he spun the wheel. Seth noticed that the boat had very little fuel remaining in it. Hesbulah's machine gun's bullets tore into the fuel tank only inches above the tanks bottom and the fuel drained from the tank into the waters surrounding the dock. The boat now lightened by several hundred kilograms due to the near empty tanks was extremely over powered. Out of instinct, Seth pushed the already fully engaged throttle to its stops. The powerful hydro drive engines would make one final trip under Seth's command. Seth's boat erupted from the smoke filled docking building like an explosion propelled it. The hull had been weakened by the machine guns onslaught and strained against the resistance offered by the water and the engine's powerful propulsion. Seth could feel the boat protesting as it vibrated and shuddered like an unbalanced gyro trying to maintain its relative orientation as its revolutions dropped off. Still, he kept the throttle lever at maximum power. The only portion undamaged was the engine and it responded to Seth's commands oblivious to the hull's strains and vibrations.

Seth could see the wake of Hesbulah's boat in the distance as it arced high into the air, but he could not see the boat itself. Seth checked the instrument array and found that the once fully instrumented cockpit was reduced to a shambles. Only the wheel and throttle remained recognizable as controls. The machine gun had been torn from its mount by a direct hit from one of Hesbulah's bullets, the barrel bent and flattened at an odd angle. The Plexiglas windscreen had not been directly hit but could not withstand then shrapnel that was driven through it as a result of the bullets impacting near it. Seth now realized that he was riding a literal death trap, but he had no choice. The alternative was to let Hesbulah escape and Seth would not let that happen now that he was this close.

Seth strained his eyes against the rush of wind and spray as he plowed through the waters of the Dangme Chu River. The farthest he could see was the break in the jutting mountains ahead that allowed the Dangme to flow beyond Bhutan into India. He knew that the strike force would heavily bomb the rivers passage between the two mountains. They might have a chance at stopping the submarines before they could pass that point by forcing them aground. Seth estimates the distance to the pass at just over 18 kilometers. He strained to judge the rate that he would overtake Hesbulah. He pushed the boat harder and strained to maintain visual contact with Hesbulah's boat. In the distance overhead, he could make out a sleek silhouette streaking through the mountain pass in a knife-edge turn from the east. The water vapor was being squeezed out of the air into vapor contrail behind the streaking jet's wings in its hard turn. The monstrous sized engines in proportion to the razor sharp wings and narrow fuselage were characteristic of only one aircraft. Mike was driving the aircraft with the same determination that Seth was pushing the boat. Seth could see the aircraft roll wings level in a high-speed approach, its engines thunderously reverberating off the mountains sidewalls.

Mike could see hundreds of smaller wakes from the submarines navigating the Dangme Chu River. Their conning towers and the top part of the hulls only visible as they remained surfaced in the shallow waters of the Dangme Chu above India. Mike switched on the forward-looking radar and digital imagery recorder. The data was instantly transmitted to the command post back in Calcutta and NSA at Fort Meade, Maryland.

"White Horse two, this is Rider. I am four minutes out inbound to the LZ, break, be advised I have numerous targets proceeding along the axis of advance. Imagery is on its way." Mike spoke into his radio.

The signal's were picked up by the RC-680s and sent around the world back to NSA. Izz also received the message and was sitting in a binjo ditch along the road up to his waist, in sewage, waiting for pickup.

"Roger Rider, your LZ is cleared, as long as you get here in the next few minutes, after that it is anybody's guess." Izz said over the radio.

Mike followed the Flight Management Computers vertical profile and course to the LZ. He glanced up for one last look at the river full of submarines before he transitioned to full instrument guidance.

"What the hell?" Mike said as the X descended to just over 500 feet of the rivers surface. Mike could see two larger wakes, the trail one within several hundred meters of the lead boat. The trail boat had more pieces missing than it had together.

"Those poor bastards should have paddled their way clear of that facility. It must have been bad there for them to want to leave on a boat in that condition. Command, are you seeing this? Standby, I'll get you an up close and personal view of this boat. You wouldn't believe it if I told you this." Mike said in a proud voice. Just as Mike finished, the digital imagery from the X's sensor filled the screen. "Gentlemen, you are not going to believe this, that piece of sea trash is being piloted by no one other than Colonel Seth Stephens. Way to go boss!" Mike shouted into the transmitter. "Whatever or whoever he is following must be very important. I suggest that you have the strike force target that lead boat as a backup for Colonel Stephens." Mike finished as the X shuddered as if shook by a large unseen hand grabbing at it.

Hesbulah could see the aircraft come through the mountains just up ahead. He wasn't sure of its purpose, but he knew it was a result of the Americans intervention. He switched the 12.7mm machine gun to radar guidance and locked on the rapidly approaching target. The gun jerked into a tracking mode as it tried to follow the rapidly approaching jet. As soon as the computer was satisfied with its data it commanded the machine gun to fire in the high cyclic rate mode. 1,500 rounds per minute were filling the sky just in front of the X commanded by the radar-guided gun. Hesbulah could see the bright orange glow of the tracer rounds stream out of the gun like the flow of water from a garden hose. The tracers appeared to be on an intercept with the aircraft. Hesbulah laughed again out loud as he had thoughts of the aircraft bursting into flames and crashing into the mountains that surrounded it. Hesbulah saw the tracers meet the aircraft as it banked to the left to follow the rivers course. The gun stopped firing as it reached the mounts stops pointed nearly vertical. Hesbulah was disappointed when the aircraft didn't explode instantaneously, but was somewhat satisfied as he saw a white vapor streaming from its right wing.

Mike knew that he had been hit when he felt the aircraft shudder. The same way that he had felt it one night in South America as he and Seth just finished a photo run over a suspected cocaine processing plant in Columbia. His aircraft was hit with a 12.7mm in the tail and it felt like he ran into a bowling ball at 250 knots. After they landed, his crew chief dug the round out of his plane's tail and presented it to him. Mike kept it as one of his not good luck, but odd luck charms.

Mike quickly scanned the instruments. Nothing was falling apart or failing. That was a good sign. He breathed again and re-checked his instruments. The round could have just passed cleanly through a void area in the aircraft and not damaged anything but the metal skin. His optimism rapidly melted as he saw the red flashing fuel quantity reading on ht right wing. Mike focused on his fuel status. He switched the screen on the Multi-Function Display to give him a detailed look at his fuel status. 'It wasn't real bad news he thought, as long as the streaming trail of fuel vapor didn't ignite.' He was losing fuel rapidly. The right wing fuel tank would be empty before he reached the LZ. Mike acted quickly and transferred as much fuel as possible to the center tank before it all leaked into the atmosphere. At least he could save a little of it. He calculated his remaining fuel and distance that he could fly with it. They wouldn't make it back to Calcutta. Mike figured that they could either ditch in the Indian Ocean or fly as far as they could toward Thailand and make an emergency landing somewhere short of that destination. In either case, he broadcasted his options and intentions so that the RC-680 could relay it to a rescue squadron before they actually went down.

Seth watched with relief as he saw the Mike's aircraft escape the onslaught of machine gun fire from Hesbulah's boat. His was momentarily concerned with the vapor venting off the right wing, but knew that Mike would be able to deal with the problem. He quickly turned his attention back toward the pursuit. Seth now was within a stone's throw of Hesbulah's boat as the engine on his began to hesitate from fuel starvation. What little fuel that remained in the tanks was sloshing around because of the rough water on the Dangme Chu River as it approached the restriction of the mountain pass. It was Bernoulli's theory applied. The water had to increase its velocity to compensate for the decrease in area. Seth could feel the engine RPM drop off and then pick up again momentarily. Seth was within an arms reach as he removed an equipment belt and cinched the wheel to the seat adjustment lever on a course with Hesbulah's boat. Satisfied that he had steered to an intercept with Hesbulah's boat, he made one final check on the throttle. Seth climbed over the shattered windscreen like he was hoping a waist high fence. He climbed onto the bow of the boat as it sped toward its collision with Hesbulah.

Seth felt the RPMs dropping off. He looked at the distance between his boat and Hesbulah's and he was still closing in. Hesbulah had pulled the throttle back on his boat. Seth could see the wake from Hesbulah's boat trail off. Hesbulah was stopping. Seth saw that his boat was overtaking Hesbulah's much too rapidly. He would have to judge the timing perfectly. Too short and he would slam him into the stern of Hesbulah's boat. Wait too long and he would overshoot the cockpit and land on the bow in front of the 12.7mm guns in perfect position to be shredded by an un-aimed burst. All that Hesbulah had to do was press the trigger on the console.

Seth could feel the spray as he prepared to launch himself at the target area. Now! Seth jumped from his boat. An instant later the RPMs fell off to nothing and the boat decelerated to a stop as Seth landed on the boat behind Hesbulah's seat. The timing was near perfect. If the engine continued to run, the boat would have passed Hesbulah's and would have practically announced Seth's arrival. As he stretched the jump, his leg caught the rear deck of the boat as he was in mid air and spun him around wildly as he crashed to the deck.

Hesbulah hadn't seen or heard the impact of Seth with the cockpit deck and was intently studying the water in front of the boat. Seth thought for sure that his landing would have attracted Hesbulah's attention. Seth wanted to take advantage of the surprise and smash Hesbulah's skull with the spare machine gun barrel lying on the deck of the boat. He held back the rage that was boiling inside him, what was this maniac up too? Seth looked forward taking his eyes off Hesbulah only momentarily. The small conning tower of the unmanned submarine was breaking through the water in front of Hesbulah's boat. Hesbulah passed the submarine and continued to race forward, dodging the exposed conning towers of the submarines ahead. Seth looked ahead. The river was filled with hundreds of the small submarines. Seth wasn't aware of the magnitude of the capability but as he saw the wake created by the hundred of submarines it sunk in. Hesbulah's capabilities weren't only threatening words they were realities. If each of the submarines held the 20-kiloton warheads, he could easily pull of his plan of world domination.

Seth crouched low behind the seat's divider console. What was Hesbulah planning? Hesbulah sped ahead of the pack of submarines and aimed for the wake of the lead submarine. Hesbulah pulled his boat along side the lead submarine and matched its speed and direction. Seth watched as Hesbulah took two lines from his boat and tie off to the submarine. Hesbulah climbed over the side and stood next to the exposed conning tower of the submarine. He carefully removed an access panel on the side of the tower. After a few seconds the submarine began to slow. Hesbulah climbed back aboard the submarine in almost machine like movements and pulled the throttle lever back to idle. The boat and the submarine slowed to a stop. Hesbulah had manually commanded the submarine to a stop. Seth couldn't see what Hesbulah was doing. The controls were on the opposite side of his view. As Hesbulah turned to get back on the submarine, Seth quietly pulled himself up and over the side into the cold melted ice waters from the Himalayas that flowed into the Dangme Chu. The cold water took his breath away. Seth swam in a stealthy breaststroke to the side of the boat. From his position near the stern, he could see Hesbulah working intently at the control panel that he had exposed. Seth looked back at the river trying to see the movement of the other submarines before he swam out to get a better look at what Hesbulah was doing. Seth couldn't see any movement form the other submarines. They had all stopped because of the command from this one submarine.

The conning towers sat exposed in the cold waters of the river as if it were frozen in place. Hesbulah was using the lead submarine as the command ship now that he couldn't access his control room thanks to Seth's well-placed explosion! Seth patience had paid off. He moved into position to see the command console exposed. Hesbulah was working furiously typing in commands. Seth could buy time for the strike force here and he swam toward Hesbulah. Seth positioned himself to strike.

In an explosive effort, Seth pulled and launched himself up at Hesbulah's back. He grabbed him around the neck in a double arm hold. Hesbulah swung wildly around in an effort to throw Seth off.

"You fool, you should have escaped while you had the chance." Hesbulah said in a deep demonic sounding voice. "It makes no matter, whether you die now or die in a few days." Hesbulah screamed as they struggled on the narrow ledge of the submerged submarine.

Hesbulah reached up and grabbed Seth's head with his good arm and pulled Seth over the top of him with amazing power. Seth landed on the hard partially submerged deck. Hesbulah swung with a low kick aimed at Seth's kidneys. The tip of his boot caught Seth where he had aimed. Seth rolled off the side of the submarine to move with the kick's force. Seth felt the air explode from his lungs as he sunk into the cold frothing water. The kick knocked the air out off him and he struggled to right himself and stop his descent.

He reached and grabbed the horizontal stabilizer at the back of the submarine. At that instant, Seth felt the submarine lurch forward and begin to accelerate. He could feel the waters swirling past him as it was drawn into the fast powerful spinning propeller. Seth's legs trailed behind within inches of the saw-like spinning blades. Another inch closer and the propellers would have cut through his flesh like a razor edged saw and continued to draw him in and carve away his flesh and bones.

Seth fought the urge to kick and used his powerful upper body to pull himself away from the razor sharp propellers.

Seth could see from under a shallow layer of water Hesbulah replace the access panel as he pushed toward the surfaced. The submarine began to gradually submerge as it reached a point in the river where the waters deepened. Seth lurched upward out of the water and grabbed at Hesbulah pinning his one arm to his side.

Hesbulah began to laugh. "Once again, you are too late and impotent Colonel Stephens. The submarines can run on external programming. Do you think that I wouldn't have thought through a contingency? You cannot defeat me. I am the focus of all the power that you hold against me inside you." Hesbulah said as he forced them both from the boat. Hesbulah twisted and swung his pinned arm free. He grabbed Seth and forced him into a strangling arm hold as they fell into the waters. Seth punched at Hesbulah groin and kidneys with no affect. The chokehold remained vise-like and strangling.

Seth felt the side rail of the submarine brush past as they descended into the cold waters. He reached out and grabbed the rail. Hesbulah maintained his grip around Seth while holding the bar of the craft. Their legs trailed horizontally as the accelerating submarine dragged them forward. Seth looked at Hesbulah as he tried to loosen Hesbulah's hold. Seth saw into the empty eyes that looked back at him. He seemed to feel the hate and evil flow from them like the waters flowed out of the Himalayas. Seth's eyes narrowed with sheer determination as he inched his way along the rail back toward the churning propellers while still held fast in Hesbulah's death grip. Seth fought the blackness associated with the impending loss of consciousness. He pulled and rolled Hesbulah over him toward the submarine. Seth felt Hesbulah's grip tighten as the veins bulged in his strained neck. Seth felt the blood stagnate in his head and the pounding of his heart as his brain commanded an increase in pressure to compensate for the restriction. The oxygen-starved cells of his optic nerve began to send erratic impulses to his brain that resulted in Seth seeing a perception of millions of twinkling lights in a black background. Seth was straddling the fine line of unconsciousness. He was half in and out at times. He forced his body to follow the last command of consciousness. He used every last ounce of strength that he could squeeze to maneuver Hesbulah into the inside position. Seth realized that he wouldn't survive this encounter, but he wanted to make sure that Hesbulah didn't either. Hesbulah seemed nearly unaffected by the lack of oxygen. He kept tight his grip. Hesbulah was sure that he would win the war of attrition and last longer without oxygen than the American.

Seth felt the horizontal stabilizer strike his knee and knew from his previous experience that he was close to the spinning blades. He forced himself one last time to kick and strike at Hesbulah's legs. Seth's timing was perfect. The spinning, high-torque, blade caught the heel of Hesbulah's boot as it pulled it inch by inch further into the revolving razor sharp blades. Hesbulah felt the pull of blade on his leg and his eyes widened. Each revolution sawed off more and more of his boot's leather heel. Hesbulah felt the following blades slice into the flesh of his foot. The pain that shot from the sliced open flesh caused Hesbulah to loosen his grip enough for Seth to force himself to the surface and suck in a deep breathe of air. Hesbulah pulled harder at Seth and forced him under again. Any other man would have released his grip completely, but not Hesbulah. Hesbulah felt the pain now as a dull ache, but not the sharp slicing pain that anyone else would. He pushed against the submarines hull with his free foot against Seth's force. It was a useless attempt. Seth had grabbed the rail of the submarine with both of his powerful arms and held Hesbulah into the position as if he were a piece of lumber being sawed into thin sections. The razor edges of the propeller sliced an inch at a time into Hesbulah's leg. The power of the spinning scimitar like blades drawing water into the vacuum and each successive blade pulled and positioned Hesbulah's leg for another slice. Hesbulah fought to free himself from the pull of the propellers slicing disk with no success. He kicked against the side of the hull as he tried in vain to release his leg from the suction and the pull of the nuclear powered, spinning, titanium propeller.

Seth realized the suction created by the spinning propeller would draw him in too. He wedged his leg in under Hesbulah and between the submarines rail and hull. He could feel his body stop as the suction continued to draw Hesbulah inward slicing off a centimeter at a time. The water surging near the propeller was cloudy with the blood that poured from the severed veins and arteries; it was nearly impossible to actually see the blades slicing into Hesbulah's limb. Hesbulah continued to fight without result. The powerful spinning turbines pulled at Hesbulah. He would have needed twice the amount of all of the power that he could muster to break free from the propellers suction and the pull.

The blades had completely sliced off his foot one centimeter at a time up to his ankle. The propeller ground and sliced through the bones, ligaments and tendons like a deli meat slicer gone awry. The sound frequency was modulated perfectly to travel through the water. Seth could almost hear the bones sliced away in protest. Hesbulah was beginning to realize that escape was nearly impossible as the propeller continues to draw him in and slice away at him. He was now more determined to maintain his hold on to Seth and pull him in with him.

Hesbulah had relaxed his hold on Seth just enough to allow the air through to his lungs, but tight enough to have him locked into his grip. Seth could feel the tension on the leg that he had wedged between the rail of the submarine and its hull. He knew that he wouldn't be able to keep it in place as the suction pulled Hesbulah into the whirring propeller. Seth held his breath and released one of the arms that were wrapped around Hesbulah. Seth tried to grab for his boot knife. Hesbulah's head was trashing about like the head of a dragon Seth had read about in his childhood. His teeth were gnashing and grinding trying to take chunks out of Seth. Seth dodged each movement. He continued to hold fast with one hand and leg. He tried desperately to reach the boot knife as his body was twisted, pulled, and slammed against the hull. Seth made one last desperate attempt at the knife as Hesbulah's teeth bit into his chest just below his shoulder. Seth threw his arm against Hesbulah trying to break the clenching teeth tearing into his flesh. Seth pounded at Hesbulah's head in a futile struggle. He tried again to reach for the boot knife. Hesbulah's leg was sliced away already, nearly to the hip yet Hesbulah maintained his hold. Seth's leg was beginning to loosen from the railing. He had to force Hesbulah's hold free of him. The water was turned red by the blood flowing from Hesbulah's arteries. The surface watercolor was in stark contrast. The cold, almost blue, icy water held its line of definition against the red and pink froth bubbling up from under the surface created by the wake of the spinning propellers. Seth made one final grab for the knife as his body began to protest the commands sent by his brain. The cold water and lack of oxygen was about to win out. He had wracked his body before and forced it to endure much more physical adversity than any other man could stand, but he was still human. He felt his numbed fingers grab the heel of the knife and he consciously forced the command to wrap his hand around the knife's handle. He no longer had any tactile sensations. His capillaries had restricted trying to conserve whatever oxygen and body heat remained to keep his trunk and head normal. It was a losing battle. The cold waters sucked the heat from his body faster than his cells could generate it. Seth looked down in an attempt to see if he actually held the knife. The bright lights triggered by fatigued optic nerve endings were beginning to reappear. The combined effects of hypoxia and cold were far past any human limits. Seth was driving himself again on sheer will. He couldn't tell if he had the knife but made one last command to his muscles. He could still vaguely feel Hesbulah's teeth dug into his chest. He forced his arm to stab at the spot where he could feel the pain.

Seth didn't know that his thrust had met with Hesbulah's head. The knife's eight-inch blade found its mark by piercing and pushing through into Hesbulah's left eye. The interruption in brain activity involuntarily commanded his muscles to release. Seth felt the grip around his neck loosen. He didn't feel Hesbulah's teeth release from his numb chest. All he felt was the pressure sensations or the absence of them. With his leg still locked in the rail, he reached for the surface.

His head broke through the water and he sucked in a deep cold breath. He could feel the air burning in his lungs. He regained his situational awareness as his brain was supplied with fresh oxygenated air. He forced his leg free from the railing and grabbed the top of the submarines conning tower to prevent being pulled into the spinning propellers. Within seconds he was fully aware of what he had begun and realized that he had to go after Hesbulah. He had to make sure that the submarines went no further. With another deep breath he pushed himself below the cold surface.

With one look at the gruesome sight, he knew that his struggle with Hesbulah was over. Karl knew all along that Seth would defeat Hesbulah. Seth felt like he had fought the final battle as he saw Hesbulah being sawed apart centimeter by centimeter.

Hesbulah head continued to thrash about under the sea wildly. His brain hadn't had any oxygen for nearly eight minutes but yet he was still conscious and alive. Blood was pouring from his torso as the blades sliced through his midsection. His limp arm, the one damaged by the conveyor was pulled into the blades and was being hacked at while the blades sawed more and more of him away. Seth could see Hesbulah's other arm reaching at him as his head swung wildly about. One eye was fixed at him, glaring complete hatred and evil, the other was sightless with Seth's knife protruding from its socket. Seth didn't want to watch the carnage any more but felt that he had to make sure that Hesbulah didn't escape. He was still alive and until Seth watched his body completely disappear he wouldn't move. He continued to watch.

The blade sliced cleanly through Hesbulah's ribs and sternum. Seth could see the muscle that was Hesbulah's blackened heart explode as the blades tore into the outer chambers. The intense release of blood was apparent as the heart burst open with one last beat and released it bright red contents to the icy water. The tissue and ligaments that held the internal organs in place acted like guide strings and wrapped around the spinning shaft that drove the propeller. In quick jerks, Seth watched as what remained of Hesbulah was jerked into the spinning propeller. The two parts that remained were now separated. His arm and head were drawn individually into the slicing blades. Seth watched as Hesbulah's eyes turned toward him in one last glare of hate. His lips formed a sinister laugh but it was quickly sawed away by the blades. Centimeter by centimeter, Seth watched the blades grind away any trace of Hesbulah. In one final flash, the top of his skull and head were pulled through the propeller. It was over. Hesbulah's body and evil was sliced up and spread down two kilometers of the Dangme Chu River. He would never be put back together again.

Seth shot up from the depths. His ordeal wasn't over yet. He had to make sure that the submarines didn't make it through the pass less than 250 meters away. The submarine was still tied off to the boat that was trailing now behind at an odd angle. The submerging submarine's program did not compensate for the buoyancy force of the boat that Hesbulah had tied off. It ran at an odd angle lifted in the front with the front part of the conning tower just below the waters surface.

Seth scrambled for the control panel that was now under water. Hesbulah had secured the access panel. The panel would not come off without first removing the screws. Seth instinctively reached for his boot knife. In an almost dream he remembered that he had last seen it stuck in Hesbulah's eye. Seth climbed over the deck of the boat that was being dragged through the water by the submarine. He clawed through a compartment trying to find something to use to access the panel. Reaching in he picked up a knife used to splice ropes and turned back toward the submarine. In one step he cleared the boats gunwales and jumped onto the submerged conning tower. Seth worked at a blinding pace, feeling for the screws under the water, trying to gain access. As he loosened the fasteners, he glanced at the distance remaining to the pass between the two mountains. Less than 100 meters remained. The last screw was loosened and Seth pulled the access panel off. He could see the blurred glow of the digits and illuminated switches that were under the panel. Seth took a breath of air and dove under the surface of the water to examine the control panel. He started pressing the unmarked switches hoping to find something that would look familiar. The submarine changed course gradually. He attempted the same sequence. The submarines hesitate for a few moments and then change course in the same direction again. Seth repeated the process until the submarines where heading back in the direction of the facility.

Seth could barely make out the sounds at first. It sounded like rolling thunder in the distance. As the sound grew louder, he could make out the thunderous roar of the B-2s and F-117s. He could see the black specks grow larger in the sky as they approached the target of the mountain passes. The other submarines were now turning away from their original course and were following the lead submarine. Seth had successfully diverted the submarines from the river's passage point. With any luck the F-117s would succeed at forming an obstruction to keep the waters of the Dangme Chu from reaching the ocean. Things were finally looking up.

The lead F-117 rolled in on the pass and dropped its bomb load. The aircraft were in a tight and low formation designed to have the entire ordinance dropped and falling as the aircraft pulled away from the target. The bomb load streamed down on the nearly vertical slopes of the mountains on the east side of the river. The 2,000-pound convention bombs detonated on the bull's-eye. Seth felt as if he had been hit in the face as the concussion form the blast hit him and pushed him under the water. In succession the bombs exploded sending tons of rock and dirt sliding down the hills into the Dangme Chu River. As he surfaced he could see that the submarines were changing and turning back to their original course. He didn't have the code to program a permanent course change. The submarines were heading back to the Bramhaputra River. Seth surfaced to survey the damage. The dust and dirt cleared and Seth worst scenario was about to play out.

"Command, This is Rider. Bomb Report follows, Target 12, Objective not achieved, 50 percent of river remains navigable, over" Mike said as he orbited the pass and kept the sensors trained on the target areas.

Seth could see the F-117s heading for the facility. It would take at least five minutes for the targets to be assessed and reprogrammed. Seth had to make sure that he kept the submarines north of the passage. Their SONAR would allow them to navigate the river and avoid the obstructions that the Stealth fighters had created. Seth tried the input that made the submarines turn. It had no affect. Without the encrypted code, he couldn't make another change. Seth pressed more keys on the control panel and nothing happened.

The pass was again only about 75 meters ahead and the submarines were heading in the direction. If they passed the restriction created by the mountains, there would be no stopping them. They would make it out to sea and find their targets. Once in position they would detonate and even though Hesbulah had been chopped into small slivers, his plan would be achieved.

Seth keyed in any random number combination he could think of. He wanted to find anything that would delay the submarines progress through the passage. He tried the codes that made the submarines turn in reverse order. He tried the random numbers. He keyed in numbers in any order. He fought hard to thing of as many different combinations. Numbers came to his mind and he put them in. Nothing. Seth looked up at the pass, it less than 50 meters the submarines would be in the gap created by the mountains. Nothing would stop them after that.

Seth looked toward the heavens and paused. As if in slow motion and in complete calm everything was blanked out. He was focused solely on one thing. It was as if he was watching himself. He looked back at the panel and brought his hands up slowly to it and deliberately, as if knowing, punched the keys on the panel. His final push was on the enter button. As soon as Seth pressed the button, the button submarines engines stopped. Seth looked back at the other submarines the wakes trailed off into nothing. He had succeeded in stopping the engines. Seth looked back at the panel almost afraid to move. The panel went blank. Seth almost began to breath again and look away as the panel came back to life.

Seth's eyes fixed on the panel. The numbers 2:30 registered and began to count backwards in reverse order. 2:29...2:28...2:27...Seth was frozen as he watched the numbers. He knew what was happening. He pressed the stopwatch function on his watch. It was a countdown sequence. Seth had keyed in the detonation sequence for the submarine. In two minutes and 26 seconds a 20-kiloton nuclear weapon would detonate. He broke out in a cold sweat as he watched the countdown proceed. He had to warn off the strike force. They would be the only casualties if the bomb detonated. The high mountains would contain the blast and the nuclear fallout would be blown clear of major populations centers. If there was a place over land ideal for this, he was there. Seth scrambled back aboard the boat, but not before cutting the lines that tied it to the bomb submarine. Seth looked at the control panel and located a radio. He switched the frequency to 255.4, the military guard radio frequency.

"Mayday, Mayday, Mayday. All units, this is White Horse One on guard. Yorktown, Yorktown, Yorktown (the codeword for a nuclear detonation) in two minutes and fifteen seconds. All aircraft immediately turn away from the target area. I authenticate Yankee Bravo Hotel." Seth repeated the radio call as he started the engine on the intercept boat and jammed the throttle against its stops. The boat's stern dug deep into the water as the powerful engines accelerated to maximum revolutions.

"Shit Izz that was Seth. Get on the radio and make sure that Gen Woodsen knows that that transmission came from Colonel Stephens. Izz make sure that there is no doubt that a nuclear weapon is about to be detonated. " Mike said as Izz was switching the radio frequency to the command post frequency.

"White Horse One, this is Rider on guard. What is your location now? Over." Mike said with urgency into the radio.

"White Horse Rider this is One. Clear the area. I have the perfect location to wait out the storm. I'll be on the other side of the country with this boat. You all don't think that I set off this thing without putting some distance between it and me do you. After the detonation, contact me on guard and we will coordinate a pickup location. Mike, I'll make sure that I personally see to your Court Marshall if you damage that jet. I repeat clear the area immediately Mike. You have less than one minute and 28 seconds to detonation. White Horse One Out!" Seth said as he watched the X streak low over the river between the mountain pass.

"Mike, you aren't going to obey that order are you? How in the hell can you just fly off knowing that he's still alive in the face of a nuclear detonation?" Izz said thrusting his chin out in defiance.

"Look Izz, I'm a soldier and I follow orders. Your boss and mine gave us an order. He didn't ask for our opinion. He told us what we were to do. If we don't get out of here, and we get caught in that blast, there won't be a rescue attempt." Mike said with a battle going on inside him. If Izz only knew how Mike wanted to land the jet and pick up Seth, he wouldn't have pushed the issue. "Izz there's one other thing...don't ever question my loyalty toward the men in my team." Mike concluded. Izz realized that he was out of line by questioning Mike's judgment. He sat there and kept the digital imagery sensor focused on Seth as the X streaked toward the south. Both men hoped that they be alive to laugh about this ordeal when they got older.

Seth would have rather been on the aircraft speeding along at 300 knots rather than 50 knots on this river. The Citation X would be more than sixteen kilometers away when the bomb detonated. Seth would be lucky to be two kilometers. He knew that his chances of survival were thin, but that was nothing new for him. At least he met his objective and watched Hesbulah die painfully. Seth rounded the corner and was on the other side of the mountain pass. He had put as much of the mountains mass between himself and the blast as possible. Seth checked his watch as the swift current carried his boat almost 2 kilometers downstream. The submarines drifted almost into the center of the pass. With any luck the explosion would trap the other submarines in the river. The submarines that weren't damaged or destroyed by the blast would be trapped.

Seth checked his watch, 22 seconds left until the bomb detonated. Seth wanted to be much farther away than he was. He pulled the throttle back to its stop as the seconds ticked away and dove into river.

The trail elements of the strike force had heard Seth's radio call, as did the RC-680s. The information was relayed to the command post and the order was given for the strike force to clear the area. The aircraft streaked fast away and climbed to try and buffer the effects of the 20-kiloton blast.

Izz and Mike had the X throttles fully forward with the engines over sped to try and get as much distance between the blast and them. Mike looked at the fuel gauge and it was near empty.

"Izz, look for a spot where you'd like to wait out the storm. Pick a good one. We may be there for a little while." Mike said into his intercom as he pulled up the terrain analysis map.

"Mike, hard right turn heading 220, there's a small peninsula jutting into the river." Izz almost shouted into his intercom.

Mike had seen what Izz was seeing on the map view. He turned the airplane toward the small stripe of land and lined up the aircraft for a landing. He had neither the time or fuel to make a low pass to recon the landing area. The Citation X half landed, half crashed onto the gravel peninsula. The aircraft engines had just enough fuel in them for Mike to pull the throttles to idle and initiate the shutdown as the last drops of fuel ran through the fuel lines into the engine.

The white-hot explosion appeared immediately without a sound. The air surrounding the detonation was instantly heated to a temperature of more than the heat energy produced by the surface of the sun. The air molecules expanded so quickly and so rapidly that they created a complete vacuum in the atmosphere around the submarine. Everything including water, air and earth was pushed from the wide riverbed. The total nothing that remained was impossible for the mind to perceive. On the inside of the white-hot expanding explosion shell it was black. It created an expanding void, as black and empty as the farthest reaches of deep space or the empty void of hell. The blackness pushed further and further outward, consuming whatever it could before it reached the limits of its chaotic unrestrained power. Millions of liters of river water were vaporized and twenty times that amount boiled into steam. The titanium hull of the submarine became part of the chain reaction of the explosion as it was torn into molecular sized pieces. The hard granite and basalt rocks that formed the mountain were crushed and several million tons fell into the narrow river valley, creating a dam for the water and energy of the explosion. Water that wasn't vaporized or boiled was pushed by the blast with tremendous force and moved as a wall nearly 70 meters tall that cascaded through the upper valley. Everything that was caught in its path was pulverized. The other submarines closest to the blast melted into unrecognizable shapes of metal. The others farther away were crushed into solid form of metal. No space remained in their hulls. The explosive packages of titanium contained in these were deformed to greatly to create a sympathetic detonation.

Seth's last conscious experience would be feeling the crushing force that squeezed his body as if it were pressed from every side and angle by heavy iron plates. His body was compressed from all sides momentarily as the hydraulic forces created by the nuclear blast pressed in on him. The air that was trapped in the recesses of his body was squeezed out. His cheeks and hollows of his abdomen pressed inward

336

until it meet with equal forces from the other sides. He had never felt pain so intense or continuous in all of his life. Death would be a welcomed relief from this agony.

His wracked body was lifted high on the monstrous inland tidal wave and carried with it as it sped at nearly 300 kilometers per hour down the valleys. He would never feel the rocks slam into his body or feel the wild gyrations of being rocketed across the flat lands as the tidal wave flooded over them. His mind froze in the thought that he had been successful at life. Through the excruciating pain and lonely blackness, he smiled inward. If he had to die, it was just as well that he should die as he lived giving his all in the selfless service of others. The thought that he had lived a life of no regrets would be with him through eternity as he passed from consciousness and faded out. His mind flashed from the beginning of his life to this the end in what seemed like an instant.

He'd see his mother and father for the first time as he was looked at them as a child. They were the faces of contentment smiling down at him and gently reassuring him through his life. They were proud of him. He had made a difference. He relived is first day outside as a child, the air filled with a new bouquet of fragrances. He felt the breeze brush against his face as he watched the clouds float effortlessly through the sky. His mind would replay over and over again every pleasant memory that it had ever experienced as it worked against the physical pains. That would be his eternity. His life lived with peace and inner harmony. He had found his heaven as his mind replayed these last thoughts of his eternity. Seth would receive something now that he never asked for in his life. He was content knowing inside that he gave his all for peace. As his body was pushed down the lonely isolated cold depths of the river waters fed by the mountains that touched the heavens, his father was proud of him and was telling of his battle to many and they listened intently. The sun would eventually shine on his body and wrap it in its warmth as it floated out to the sea.

Colonel Seth Stephens would be remembered and celebrated as a great hero by untold millions whom he had never known but would know of him.

31

In Memoriam

RAF Northolt, March 4, 1140 hours

"Situated just north, on the outskirts of London, is Royal Air Force Base Northolt. It is only a short drive from Windsor Castle, home of the Royal Family and Queen Mother of England. It is normally a place reserved for the arrival or departure of the Royal family and other highly placed public officials of the United Kingdom.

Today, RAF Northolt will become a meeting place for the world's leaders to honor a fallen hero. The Royal Airman assigned to Northolt will receive the body of Major Sean McLowery. Major McLowery died in the line of duty several days ago in a part of the world many of us have never heard of. Urumqi, China a city located in the northwestern portion of China. Major McLowery and his joint operations team were assigned to gather intelligence on a plutonium smuggling operation.

The plutonium operation originated in Russia and followed a convoluted trail south from Novosibirsk through Urumqi and on into Bhutan. Yesterday's nuclear detonation on the Dangme Chu River, just south of the city of Tashi Gang Dzong, Bhutan was triggered by the international team to halt the deployment of hundreds of nuclear weapons programmed to sail to destinations throughout the world.

As reported yesterday by our BBC correspondent at the United Nations, the deployment of nearly 1,000 remotely programmed, unmanned submarines, each carrying twenty-kiloton nuclear devices had the capability to kill nearly 3 billion people throughout the world.

In an unprecedented vote, every member country of the United Nations unanimously supported the joint offensive action against the bomb making facility as proposed by the President of the United States. The spearhead of this force consisted of four intelligence officers assigned to this team. Three are accounted for and one American is still listed as missing. Major McLowery's body, the team member killed in action in Urumqi will arrive from Germany's Ramstein Air Base, accompanied by an international honor guard.

The guest list of the memorial ceremony for Major McLowery includes every leader of the world, including those of China and Russia. The feeling here is one of sadness mixed with jubilance. A very real threat to the world was exposed and in a relatively short time reduced to inconsequential by the world's unity and resolve. These men worked discreetly to gather information that united the world as never before.

Our thoughts and prayers are with the families of Major Sean McLowery and the American soldier still listed as missing. From RAF Northolt, the United Kingdom, this is Jonathan Donegal of the BBC reporting."

Jonathan Donegal was weary as he continued the BBC's coverage of the events that led up to Sean's Memorial Ceremony. His thick British accent crackled several times as he choked down the rising emotion realizing just how close the world had come to ending.

Joshua McAdams looked over at Karl and Elke Linder Stephens as they drove from Mildenhall, England on the M11 highway. They were just south of Cambridge, on their way to RAF Northolt. The 747 that they arrived on, departed from New York's JFK, had landed only 30 minutes before. The 5,500-foot runway at Northolt couldn't comfortably accommodate the heavy 747, so they decided on RAF Mildenhall's 9,227-foot runway as an arrival location.

The report on the radio summed it all up. The four men were modern day heroes. They saved the world's peoples from a catastrophic end. No one could offer a solid argument otherwise.

Major's DeConcerio and Thomas were recuperating in a hospital by now. Major Sean McLowery would be eulogized this afternoon and buried tomorrow in the Cemetery of the Parish Church of All Saints, on the north side of the Thames across Tierney Suspension Bridge in Marlow.

Colonel Seth Stephens was officially listed as missing. He would remain on the missing in action roles like many other heroes from wars past have done for many, many years. Unless his body or remains were found, he would be remembered as a monument made of stone, cold gray stone. It was a monument that was so much unlike Seth, who beamed with life and warmth.

Joshua knew what was going through Karl's mind. He had sent Seth off as a child and only saw pictures of him throughout his life as he grew into manhood. Now he was part of a decision that sent him off as a man, never to see him again. Karl had dedicated his life to defeating Hesbulah, a life that he could never reclaim. Joshua tried to answer the question in an unbiased manner, but couldn't. Could he have remained so dedicated to one cause, forsaking his family? The turmoil in his soul, which Karl kept disguised so well, must have been overwhelming at times. Joshua could see it as Karl looked off, staring at nothing. His eyes fixed on a thought that his mind perceived as a reality.

The Bentley in which the three rode smoothly negotiated the exit off the M11. They turned onto the M25 near the exchange at Epping and headed west towards Northolt. A brown sign that indicated the exit for the Waltham Abbey passed on the left of the roadway. Karl seemed to snap momentarily out of his deep thought and focus on the sign. The driver moved about 30 miles per hour faster than the traffic and Joshua figured that they would arrive at least 30, if not 45 minutes before the ceremony began.

More news stories would break in the next few days. The United Nations decided, and rightly so, on full disclosure of the events leading up to the historic vote authorizing yesterday's actions. The United States had offered to Karl, with the concurrence of the German Bundes Chancellory, a 12 person staff to help Karl with the demands placed on him by the world's news organizations. It was important to give the news agencies the details and have them report the facts to the world. Otherwise they would fill in the blanks of the facts that they gathered with conjecture and propagate an already active rumor mill. There were no secrets to be held back. The United Nations served the free people of the world and they had a right to know everything that there was to know. The news wire was full of the briefing that Karl had given in his address to the United Nations. The only rebuttal came from two-bit dictators whose days were numbered now anyway.

The world easily saw through the fabrications that they offered and some massive overthrows were already happening. The long time members of the family leading Cuba had been placed under house arrest as a revolution against them had begun. His countrymen charged them as conspirators of Hesbulah. The United States and Cuba began to discuss plans to lift trade sanctions. The momentum for righteousness would continue. Any move to promote chaos was met with force. The unity of the world against immorality grew to unheard of levels. It was politically correct to be politically moral and tell someone that they were wrong if their actions went against harmony and peace.

Karl Linder Stephens had sent the world a wake up call by showing the difference between those who embraced chaos and those whom embraced peace. It was easy now to determine where you stood. You were either right or you were wrong. Karl would be sought after to speak at groups and offer his philosophies to many that sought his point of view. The week was full of ceremony, interviews and meetings with country leaders wanting to meet with Karl Linder Stephens. The German government had agreed to honor his continued service in the Vehrmacht for the past 63 years and settle his pay account. The amount would easily cover his living expenses for the rest of his years. His speaking honorariums and book rights alone would make him a very well off man by anyone's standards.

His organization's members, based in locations throughout the world had the opportunity to receive their back pay and resign or remain on duty if they wished. They would be absorbed by the Central Intelligence Agency, World Events Branch. The branch was newly established to support the United Nations. After the case that Karl had made in New York, no one could effectively argue the need for a highly networked and efficient intelligence organization. One that kept a look out for global threats, not threats to a specific country.

The Bentley turned off the M25 at exit 16 and headed east toward Northolt. Joshua could see the aircraft arriving from the west landing on runway 07. The car turned into the Air Base and headed toward the large ceremonial hangars, located on the base's north side. The U.S. Air Force sent additional Military Police from Lakenheath and Mildenhall to help with the security of the ceremony at Northolt. The ramps and roads were crowded with more security personnel than guests.

"Prime Minister Banbury will deliver the eulogy for Major McLowery along with President Abrahams. All I can say is that it is the least that I expected. Your son and his men saved us all. Your life's work made everyone a believer in the good that man has to offer. The world doesn't realize it yet but they will eventually. There would have been nothing. We would have had a world with no hope. Everyone of us would have wished that we didn't survive the nuclear blast after a few days of the new world order." Joshua said as the Bentley pulled up next to a contingent of officers.

The car door was opened by a stract young Royal Airman. "Admiral McAdams, General and Mrs. Stephens, please allow me to escort you to your seats." The young airman said.

The three left the car and proceeded to their seats in the hangar where Major McLowery's body would be placed. The hangar was painted freshly with white floors, white walls and even the ironwork forming the ceiling trusses glistened. A small pedestal was placed in the center of the rows of seats. A backdrop of flags from every United Nations member country lined the back wall. Flower sprays sent by every country filled the back wall of the huge hangar.

The mood was somber with very light conversation taking place outside the hangar before the distinguished guests took their assigned seats. Karl looked hard at the level of detail. It was magnificent that they should honor a soldier in this fashion. It said a lot about a country, they way that they treated their military men. If they weren't willing to give the finest for these men, the true heroes that gave everything that they had for everyone, then for what cause would they feel it was worth?

An usher came through and quietly whispered in proper etiquette that the ceremony would begin in 3 minutes. The guests moved to rows of wood and leather chairs dotted with brass tacks to keep the thick upholstery in place.

The huge gray-camouflaged C-17, U.S. Air Force, transport airplane taxied up to the awaiting ground guide. It seemed to bring a cargo of tears that welled up in everyone's eyes. The ground guide that directed the arriving C-17 commanded the crew to stop and the huge machine smoothly rolled to a stop. The engines were immediately shut down and the ramp of the C-17 lowered in silence as the unseen band played a somber selection from Beethoven's sonatas.

At first only the sharply creased pants and highly shined shoes from the casket bearers were visible as they moved from inside the aircraft down the lowered ramp. Their steps were the slow, somber and hesitant gait as they carried Sean's body down the exit ramp of the cargo jet. Karl glanced over at Sean's parents, Mr. And Mrs. McLowery out of respect. The both were trying desperately to hold back a flood of emotion. They had given their only son to the Queen's service and were proud that he lived his life the way that he wanted but felt cheated today because they couldn't enjoy his passion for life any longer.

The casket bearers, with Sean's casket draped with the flag of the United Kingdom firmly held in their grasp, executed a perfect ninety degree turn to the right when all had reached the bottom of the ramp. They proceeded into the hangar and passed the rows of dignitaries seated on both sides of the aisle. As they placed the casket on the lonely pedestal, Prime Minister Banbury moved from his seat to the podium and faced the crowd. The news cameras were asked to remain in one corner of the hangar and the lenses of each zoomed as far forward as possible onto the Prime Minister as he moved to the podium. The casket bearers stood at attention guarding their fallen comrades remains. The silence was almost deafening as all eyes turned toward the Prime Minister.

"Josephine and Milton McLowery, we have come here today for only one purpose; that which is one that would honor the spirit of our beloved fellow countryman, our brother and your wonderful and loving son, Sean. Sean gave us everything he could as he lived his life. He was a fine man. He carried the ideals and values inside him, that we as a nation hold so dear. Values that define us as a people intolerant of tyranny and true lovers of the freedoms that God has bestowed upon us. Sean's life stood for God's gift of freedom. As a man he stood for us all embattled against the tyranny that would repress our spirit's want of freedom.

As a young child you watched him as he played in the fields of Marlow on the Thames. He ran laughing and shouting, full of life and filled with compassion. Everyday was an adventure for Sean. Everyday was filled with love, happiness and freedom. We look back on those days, days that seemingly weren't that long ago with envy. You remember the time that he took his first few steps. They were happy achievements for Sean, but sad for us because you knew that was the beginning of his journey that would take him farther away from your love and care. Then he started to run and push ever farther from you as he expanded his horizons searching for his purpose in life. The one that would make him feel that he was making a better world for you after you had for so long provided it for him.

The example of selflessness that he lived had begun at that tender and early age. If only we could have them back. If only we could have changed something back then, something that could have made the world a better place for our children. If only then we could have changed something, perhaps Sean would still be with us, laughing and enjoying life to the fullest. Showing us how to love and be loved. He would have been a leader in that respect too.

Today, as we honor Sean and his life and his love for us and of every people on this earth, we pray that he will look down upon us and have kind words for us as he takes his place next to God. Just as we pray today, a new mother and a new father is looking down on their newborn son. They are overwhelmed by his perfection and want to make sure that the future will be bright for him, just as you, Josephine and Milton, did when Sean blessed your family. This newly born lad too will grow, walk, run and play, just as Sean did in the fields of Marlow. But the similarity will end there. You see Sean made the difference in that little boy's life. His parents, we pray, won't have to sit here one day as we are now and remember him as we do Sean, under these conditions. His life will be free from tyranny and the threat of trampled freedoms. Sean made the difference by making sure that the world will be safer for not only him, but also for every little boy or girl born today, in any country and in any culture now and in the future. Sean is celebrated as a hero today. To Sean, his brave teammates, and our military forces that serve to protect our freedom, we owe so much. For what is the price of freedom I ask each of you? What is it that makes freedom worth the lives of our sons? Sean answered that for us a few days ago as he fought for us in a country far from the fields where he played in his childhood. A place where he never imagined his first steps away from you, Josephine and Milton, would take him. He answered it with a voice so loud and so strong that is resounds about the earth and heavens. Freedom was worth everything that he could possibly give! He gave his life for us and the freedom that we enjoy. He gave his life to keep the freedoms that we have fought for with others and amongst ourselves for so long. He gave his life and through his own God given free will made that decision, one that we owe our complete gratitude.

Sean, as you look down upon us today. Know that we will miss you and know that your mum and dad would give their lives, just as I would, to have one more minute to hold the child that smiled on us not long ago as they held you in their arms. We can only pray that we can prove ourselves worthy to you one day when we meet in heaven.

Sean, this is not a final good-bye. Rather, until we see you again, bless us with your courage, forth righteousness, and faith. I speak as the voice of the citizens of our great countries when I say that we are deeply grateful and proud to serve in your example of selflessness in the name of freedom. Pleasant journeys dear Sean."

Many in the audience quietly wept as Prime Minister Banbury completed his eulogy and moved silently back to his seat.

The soldiers that served as Sean's casket bearers lifted the casket in one precise movement. The casket was lifted not by six individuals but lifted as if the hand of God had simply lifted it off of the pedestal and smoothly moved it to the waiting caisson. Sean was on his final journey, one of peace and contentment, back to the village of Marlow.

The weight and impact of the Prime Minister's eulogy was apparent not only to Josephine and Milton McLowery, but also to Karl and Elke Linder Stephens. The realization that their son had died and he didn't even know of or that his mother and father loved him all of these years would be the most difficult regret for them to live with. In all of Karl's wisdom, why didn't he take the opportunity to tell Seth everything that he wanted to the last time that they had met? Karl and Elke looked over to Josephine and Milton and fully understood the pain that they felt.

Not much was said as the guests made their way to the waiting cars that lined the roadway in front of the ceremonial hangars. Most of their emotions delicately balanced on the edge of control. Some managed gentle smiles in passing as they walked. Others needed the full concentration to maintain the balance. Any external distraction would push the teetering rock over the edge and allow the avalanche of emotions to crash upon them. The somberness of the late afternoon made many realize that chaos and destruction was the result of war and the illogic of it was to be avoided at any and all costs.

The high and low tides of the emotion that many of the dignitaries would experience wasn't over yet. Tomorrow was the burial service for Sean McLowery in Marlow. And perhaps the next day, a day that Karl and Elke Linder Stephens hoped that they would never see, they would meet again to honor their son Seth. Karl prayed for a miracle as they drove from Northolt to Marlow. It was a silent drive through the back roads of England. The setting sun provided a spectacular backdrop on the late winter almost spring evening as they passed the serene fields of farms, where the freshly plowed earth filled the car with the earthly smell of the coming of spring and new life. It gave hope and restored the faith of those that experienced it as they honored the dead. The irony of the moment was nearly overwhelming.

Elke pulled closer to Karl as every living thing reminded her of what she had given up to defeat Hesbulah. She prayed like she had never prayed before for Hesbulah to burn in hell for all of eternity and feel the agony that she would feel for taking away the son that never knew his mother.

32
A Day of Remembrance

General Maxwell Woodsen's Command Post, Calcutta, March 4, 0540 hours

Colonel Todd Murphy had gathered his briefing and was presenting it to General Maxwell Woodsen.

"Here is the most recent satellite imagery taken of the area Sir. The RC-680s have just finished the final sweep with all sensors active. 148 milli-roentgens of residual radiation remain in the 6 km radius around the facility. The outer radius residual radiation drops rapidly to about 18 milli-roentgens. About as much as our aircrews experience during high altitude flight. The destruction of the facility and the damming of the Dangme Chu River tributary appear complete. The Corps of Engineers is developing the full survey and we should have preliminary results within the next 72 hours or so. We have detected multiple concentrations of plutonium near the facility and in the river upstream of the debris dam. The submarines have been well contained by the valley after the river was dammed up. We will have the 3ʳᵈ Marine Squadron go in 12 hours to conduct the ground reconnaissance of the area. From every indication, all of the objectives have been achieved. Sir, we believe that Colonel Stephens may have been the only friendly casualty. The RC-680 high-resolution imagery showed that Colonel Stephens was inside the blast area on a boat seconds before the blast. Post detonation imagery confirmed that the area was decimated by the blast moments later. There are no indications that anyone would have survived in that area. Even the riverbed itself sustained substantial damage. All that remains is the sand and some newly formed elements of

Trinitite." Colonel Murphy paused gathering his composure before he continued.

"The world will never know just how close it came to a catastrophe. Colonel Stephens and his men saved a lot of lives today Sir." Colonel Todd Murphy finished saying as he presented the information to General Maxwell Woodsen.

Woodsen was thinking of the mission and the success. Colonel Murphy words hung on him like they were pinned on. He knew all along that Seth wouldn't fail. He also knew that this mission was the toughest that he had ever imagined and that the chances of survival were next to nothing. But he was a soldier and he had made decisions that sent many men in to harms way. This one would remind him forever of his frailty. He had sent men off to die. He saw each of their faces in the late night hours just after he would fall asleep. He would see them sometimes as he closed his eyes for a brief rest. He would see them in the faces of their children and widows. It was something that he couldn't forget only something that he had learned to live with. But to each one, he could answer that their lives were not given in vain. They were sent to battle and to die for an honorable and worthy cause. Their lives were sacrificed to secure the world from oppression and tyranny. They all knew and understood why. They would have given no less for their wives, children, mothers, fathers, brothers, sisters, friends and fellow soldiers.

They were the heroes and they deserved to be honored. They deserved it much more than the so-called athletes that were only motivated by their paycheck. Sports figures weren't heroes at all compared to what his men had to do. They were just modern day court jesters and buffoons that provided a fools entertainment in our hours of boredom.

His heroes, each and every one of them, were bigger than life. He hoped that when he met them in eternity that they would allow him to sit with them, even though he didn't deserve their company. He'd like to talk with them just once more and wrap his arms around them and tell them, each and everyone just how damn proud he would be to sit with them, in their company.

He would now add one more face to his long list of heroes. He turned away from his staff as the tears flooded his eyes. The memories of the last time he and Seth talked seemed like only moments ago.

Colonel Seth Stephens had done the impossible. He saved the world from a fate that most would never know.

General Woodsen reviewed the imagery taken only moments before by the Army's RC-680 reconnaissance aircraft. The high mountains of the Dangme Chu Valley contained nearly 100 percent of the force of the blast. Anything or anyone inside the blast area was certainly obliterated. The force of the blast visibly altered the ground itself. From the high altitude imagery, General Woodsen could see the ground ripples that remained emanating from the center of the blast area. The ripples that formed in the ground from the blast heaved and rolled in the same way that water would form concentric circles when a stone was tossed into it. Only the ripples would stay visible for a very long time on the ground. He looked at the pictures straining to see any detail that would suggest someone would have survived. He wouldn't know it then, but someone did survive.

33

Survival

As He lie on the ground and felt every bone and muscle in his
body ache. He looked into the bright late afternoon sky. He was almost
blinded by the bright sun that shone as he opened his eyes after being
knocked unconscious and swept away by the wall of water that careened
through the river valley. His vision was still blurred and he could just
make out the light and dark areas of the earth and sky contrast. He was
afraid to try and move for fear that something may not respond.
Gradually his memory was coming back. He had just made it into the
water before the blast swept over him.

He could remember being picked up by the overpressure and
thrown repeatedly in and out of the churning river. He remembered
hitting the water and then he was struck unconscious by the debris that
hammered his body. He could hear the pulsating assault of the
overpressure in the water but this was different. The thumping was
growing louder and louder. At least he could still hear and see. The
thumping grew louder still.

He finally recognized the beating of rotor blades as they
approached his position. He turned his head in the direction of the
pulsing sound. Another good sign, he could turn his head. He moved his
arm and hand to clear the sand and mucous that had dried around his
eyes. His cleared eyes could see the Army tilt-rotor aircraft approaching
his position. He forced himself up on his elbows and allowed himself the
time to regain his orientation. He felt like a heavyweight boxer that had

just taken a solid punch to the head. He was still in a fog and his inner ear was struggling to gain its balance.

The tilt-rotor landed about 30 meters from his position and kicked up the swirling sand on the beach where he was laying. Two flight helmeted medics ran from the rear ramp of the tilt-rotor. Their helmet visors were still down protecting the eyes from the swirling sand as they examined him.

He could hear them call to one another in the fog of his mind. "Over here, bring the litter, double-time." One of the flight medics called out.

"Major Thomas, sir, can you hear me, sir." The first medic to reach Mike pushed his helmet visor up to see more clearly. Mike looked up and smiled a weak smile.

"I'm not dead yet. Do you think that a nuclear blast would do me in? You don't know the Thomas' family very well. We come from a tough bunch." Mike said, his vocal cords struggling to produce the raspy words. He hurt so completely that even the vibrations from his vocal cords pained his entire body. Mike's senses gradually returned and he sat straight up, fighting through the pain.

"Thank god you guys are here, we've got to go and rescue two others." Mike said as he immediately thought about Seth and Izz.

"We've got one other on board already sir. There are three additional MEDEVACs combing the area for anyone else. We'll find them sir. You job now is to get well." The medic said as they worked rapidly to make sure that Mike was stable enough to transfer to the tilt-rotor.

The medics continued to talk to Mike as the conducted their assessment of his injuries. He looked much worst than he actually was. His flight suit was nearly shredded by the rocks and debris that was sent hurtling through the air and water by the blast. Cuts and bruises that were still bleeding covered his body, but miraculously, no arteries had been severed. The medics made sure that there were no broken bones or spinal cord injuries and were satisfied that they could move him back to the aircraft. They picked him up in a firemen's carry, ignoring the litter and double-timed back to the tilt-rotor. Mike could feel the sensations in his lower extremities and sighed in relief. Everything was working.

The inside of the tilt-rotor was configured as a medical evacuation aircraft. Mike could see the other medics bandaging and splinting another casualty on the litter on the opposite side where he was placed. A female medic turned from the other litter and began examining Mike's injuries.

"Make sure that you take care of that guy first Doc, he looks like he is in pretty bad shape." Mike said trying to see the extent of his injuries before the medic.

"He'll be just fine. He is a tough one. He was stuck in a tree when we found him. He was screaming and hollering about some SOB that had landed him on an island in a middle of a tidal wave. After we removed the tree branch that was stuck in his thigh, he calmed down a little." The medic said as she cut away what remained of Mike's flight suit. Mike turned his head to look over at the other patient. He saw Izz looking back at him smiling.

"The next time partner, I'm driving. The last two flights with you, I've had to land at some place other than a runway. It's a wonder they allow maniacs like you to keep a pilot's license." Izz said as he grimaced against the pain caused by all of poking and prodding.

"License? I don't have a license. You don't need one in the military. Anyway, what are you complaining about? You're still alive aren't you? I can't land at airports Izz. I don't have a license. They'd throw me in jail." Mike said. He could feel the tilt-rotor lifting off the beach along the river as the tilt-rotor's engines developed more power.

"Where are we going to Doc? Have you guys picked up Colonel Stephens yet?" Mike continued now regaining his old form.

"Oh you'll love it, a little helicopter carrier in the Indian Ocean. I've already talked with the pilots and they have heard from the other aircraft. I'm sure that Colonel Stephens is already they're waiting for you." The medic had no idea if they had found Seth or not but wanted to keep her bedside manner positive.

"Are you sure Doc? If they haven't picked up Colonel Stephens yet, you may as well turn this bird back around and pick him up." Mike said, his veins bulging in his forehead.

"The first rule is to trust the person with the sharp knife trying to fix you up Major Thomas. The command post has launched every MEDEVAC in the area to find you guys. I am sure that Colonel Stephens is just fine. We'll get you all fixed up in no time and ready for your next crash." The Medic trying her best to keep Mike calm and injecting some humor along with.

Mike was relieved at what the medic told him. He wasn't about to head back to a ship away from the area without Seth.

"See that Izz, we'll get to take a cruise surrounded by beautiful women too! Hanging around with me is good for your social development." Mike said trying to raise his friend's spirits.

"The only consolations here is that you're not flying. Mike." Izz turned to the medic. "Whatever you do don't let that guy at the controls.

"Oh that really hurt Izz, that really hurt buddy." Mike said confident that his friend would be all right. They both turned away and looked out the side windows of the tilt-rotor as it flew south toward the Indian Ocean. As it gained altitude they could only hope that Seth was on another aircraft heading to the helicopter carrier as well.

The daylight was rapidly fading.

Frank Nellis had the RC-680, or Seth Stephens' RC-680s, actively searching for any other signs of Colonel Seth Stephens. The high-resolution digital imagery was combing the search grid and sending back imagery that could find a dinner plate lost in the sand. Any and every active sensor was being used. Imagery and Signal collection were being used by not only the RC-680s. Satellites were sending back imagery in streams of information and ground reconnaissance teams were searching under debris and wreckage. No stone was left unturned. If Seth was out there, they would find him. General Woodsen would turn the Dangme Chu valley inside out if needed to find Seth's body. This man deserved to be buried in a place of honor, not some unknown river valley in a place never heard of. He would make sure that Seth's body would be taken back to Arlington Cemetery and given a military burial with full honors.

"Joshua, this is Maxwell. We have recovered Majors DeConcerio and Thomas. They are on their way to the helicopter carrier Pittsburgh as we speak. They are a little beat up but should recover without complications. Although, I am afraid that I have some bad news, we have turned the river valley and the surrounding area inside out. We haven't found Seth or his body. Joshua our imagery had him in the primary destruction radius before the blast. Imagery taken moments later shows the same sight as completely obliterated. I fear the worst at this point." Maxwell Woodsen said relaying the information back to McAdams.

"Maxwell, I want you to keep the search crews in the area as long as possible. You have the President's authorization to use whatever resources necessary to find Seth or his remains. I am heading back to Europe with Karl Linder." Joshua paused thinking how to break the news to Karl. "Karl will take the news very hard." Joshua said to Maxwell thinking about what Karl had told him earlier in the day.

"No disrespect Joshua, but no one feels worst than I right now. Seth and I have been through a lot together. That man is like a son to me as well." Maxwell wanted to continue but McAdams interrupted.

"Maxwell, He was a son to Karl Linder." Joshua said to Woodsen. Maxwell Woodsen was silent on the other end of the connection.

"What do you mean Joshua?" Was all that Maxwell Woodsen could stammer out.

"Karl Linder told me early this morning. His name is Karl Linder Stephens. Seth is his son. He was sent to the United States to live with relatives soon after he was born rather than be raised in the Goslar complex. I'll tell you more when I see you. We should be arriving in Farnborough tomorrow afternoon for the memorial ceremony for Sean McLowery. President Abrahams and Prime Minister Banbury will attend. I'll see you then. Maxwell, keep me posted if there is any more news.

Maxwell Woodsen would have walked through hell for his men but there was little that he could do for Seth. He would keep the crews searching a few more days out of loyalty. Reality was slowly sinking in. Seth Stephens was dead. Out of loyalty and a strong sense of devotion for Seth, Woodsen would keep the crews searching for his body for the next forty-eight hours. He was thankful that Mike and Izz were safe and being cared for on the helicopter carrier Pittsburgh. The President and Congress had already received his request to award three Medals of Honor. One of which would be posthumously awarded.

"Captain Jennings, contact the C.O. of the Pittsburgh. Get a SITREP on our two heroes." Woodsen said to one of his staff members closest to him. "Yes sir." The young officer replied.

Woodsen reviewed analyst's reports that were flowing in from at least a dozen different Intelligence agencies. The entire operation was over in less than 24 hours execution time. The well-developed intelligence picture clearly defined the objective. As a case study there was no better example of deterrent force. The force was applied to eradicate a problem. Collateral damage was minor comparatively, as well as well of resources committed. One very corrupt man's ideas were stopped before they could materialize. It was a painful lesson that we had learned painfully, time and time again.

"Sir, I have the Pittsburgh for you." Captain Jennings said handing the remote satellite handset to Woodsen.

"Thank you Captain." General Woodsen said in a low voice to Jennings.

"To whom am I speaking?" General Woodsen asked.

"Sir, this is Major DeConcerio." Izz said from the infirmary on the third deck of the Pittsburgh. General Woodsen could hear the muffled beating of helicopter rotor blades from several decks above the Infirmary.

353

"Izz, it is good to hear from you son. I saw the imagery from some of your mission. That was hell son; you did everything that you could. How are you doing?" General Woodsen said sounding genuinely concerned.

"No worst for the wear Sir. Sir have you heard anything about Colonel Stephens?" Izz said without concern for himself.

"We have the search teams hot on his trail Izz. We won't give up. Tell me, how are you and Mike feeling." Woodsen offered.

"We're fine sir. Mike and I are really enjoying the hospitality of the crew of this floating palace. I think shuffleboard is on the schedule this afternoon." Izz said with his voice filled with sarcasm. Woodsen detected the hidden meaning. These men were thoroughbreds. The only way they'd be happy in that ship is if the were near dead and in a coma. Other than that, he wouldn't be surprised if they jumped overboard and swam to where the action was.

"Izz, you and Mike need to be where the action is. As soon as you two are ready, get over here and get back to work. Sean, Major McLowery's memorial service will be held in Farnborough tomorrow afternoon. Catch a flight off of that ship and get to Calcutta. You and Mike can ride with me to England. Izz, you and your teammates saved us all. You are the heroes. Tell Mike that I said that. Well done Izz, Well done! See you tomorrow, Woodsen out." Maxwell forced the end of the conversation as he thought about the two men that lost their lives on this mission.

Mike Thomas was just walking back in from the ship's gymnasium. He had taken the flight suit that they had given him and cut off the pant legs and sleeves. He looked like he belonged at a surfing meet rather than on a tightly run naval vessel. Mike was carrying some of the food that he had picked up in the dining room. He had managed to bring back enough in his arms to feed the infirmary's staff. Izz was still seated at a small gray steel desk that served as a watch officer's post and communications console. Mike threw one leg over the side casually and was spreading out the bounty that he had absconded from the galley.

"Izz, can you believe the way these Navy guys live. You should see the gym. It is better equipped than the one at Huachuca and we thought that it was great. Here you go, have some dinner. Eat hardy buddy. We are leaving as soon as the deckhands service one of the tilt-rotors. The bastards are about ready to postpone the search for Seth after nightfall. I don't think that I can allow that so we'll resume the search Army style. Postpone is not in my vocabulary. We either achieve mission objectives or die trying. Here try this cream puff. I've already had two. This'll put some fat on your skinny ass. You can replenish all of those

354

calories that you've been losing this month with just one of these babies. No wonder the smallest size on this ship is a size 38 waist." Mike was primed and ready. Without a hint of his plan to anyone on the crew, he had already developed the groundwork to borrow one of the V-22 Osprey tilt-rotor aircraft.

"Mike, General Woodsen called. The three of us need to get to England by tomorrow for Sean's memorial service." Izz said with solid defiant determination.

"Three of us, who's the third?" Mike said quizzically. "You and I and Colonel Stephens. We either go as a team or not at all. We've already lost one too many members of this mission already." Izz said with his mind already made up.

"Now you and I are on the same page of the operation's order. Did General Woodsen say that we could borrow one our sister service's aircraft?" Mike said not really caring about the answer.

"The key here is that he didn't say that we couldn't Mike." Izz said with a devil may care attitude. Mike's influence, good or bad, was beginning to show on Izz and he for one thought that was a good thing.

"I've got a few things to research before we head out." Izz said.

"Not a problem, I'll get a few items for the road. Maybe I can convince the supply officer to get us some flight gear. I'd hate to fly around in this one. I do love the slippers though. They are really comfortable." Mike said as he glanced down at the brand-new Navy issued infirmary slippers he was wearing. They were sort of a brown leather covered soft-soled sneaker that would have stolen the fashion scene if sold at Neiman-Marcus.

Izz could only laugh at the thought of he and Mike searching the Dangme Chu River Valley for Seth dressed as a couple of vacationing Americans. He would have liked to laugh a lot harder but the thought of Seth still out there dead snapped him back to reality.

The flight deck was quiet as the crews turned in for the evening meal and a briefing on the success of the mission by the commanding officer of the Pittsburgh. Only the Duty Officer stood watch along with the ships bridge crew over the flight deck. They were mostly concerned with navigation and trying to catch the C.O.'s briefing over the closed circuit video monitors. No one noticed the two characters clad in standard issue navy flight gear and equipment taking the tie downs and chocks away from the tilt-rotor parked on near the stern of the ship.

"Mike, when was the last time you flew a tilt-rotor?" Izz asked as they strapped into the front office seats. "Moffett Field, California, NASA test pilot assignment. Probably the best training an aviator can get. That is what put me over the line of being a great pilot to the world's best pilot, without a license." Mike said as he switched on the battery and ran through the pre-flight tests of the avionics and warning systems.

Izz pulled a map and a data cartridge from the pocket on the flight suits leg and brought up the Multi-Function Display. He keyed in the data cartridge and pulled the information off of it and placed it on the navigation overlay. The big 25 by 30 centimeter display had all of the information needed to keep the flight crew aware of the situation. Izz keyed in the information with a few more buttons.

Mike had started both engines and was preparing to engage the rotors after they were unfolded from the shipboard stowed position. He looked over at Izz and shot him a smile from under his flight helmet. Izz looked down at Mike's feet on the combination rudder and anti-torque pedals of the tilt-rotor. He shook his head as he noticed that Mike had taken off the heavy soled flight boot and switched into his ship's slippers.

"What, they are great for flying." Mike said as if responding to Izz's negative comments.

Mike flipped the switch and the rotors of the large tilt-rotor aircraft spun to life. In less than 10 seconds they reached flight RPM. Mike scanned the cockpit for one final check before he pulled the collective upward. The tilt-rotor clawed its way into the sky effortlessly and hovered as the ship moved out from under it. As the ship cleared, Mike lowered the collective control and let the ship mask their departure. Mike used a completely non-standard ships departure for an aircraft that could hover but that was the least of his worries. The crewmen in the ship's bridge were glued to the monitor and didn't even notice the tilt-rotor depart.

Mike pushed the cyclic control stick of the tilt-rotor forward and pulled on the collective control that both increased the blades bite into the air and the engines power to drive the rotors at the same constant RPM. Izz brought up the navigation display and transferred the flight director screen to Mike's side of the cockpit.

"Mike, I put together some data from the ship. Here are the overlays of the area. This one shows Seth's position before the blast. Here is the data of the rivers course and velocity a split second after the detonation. Here are the winds and currents in time segmented recordings. I took the information and had the computer come up with an estimated position of an object Seth's mass and assumed that he would be unconscious so his extremities would probably flail about in the currents. Here is the computers estimated position accounting for as many variables that I could think of. The computer has given us this Error ellipse estimation. The larger outer ring shows standard deviations from calculated position. It meant that Seth should be somewhere in this 5 nautical mile ring. With a little more manipulation of his model, Izz reduced the center ring to a 200-meter radius and hoped that the 93% confidence interval would be substantiated. The computer's prediction for his location is right here. The grid coordinates are up on your screen. It is saying that we have only a 86% chance of finding him there when it considers all of the variables." Izz didn't have a chance to finish, Mike cut him off.

"Izz, I haven't really understood or heard anything that you have said. You and I get along better if you use sign language. Just point me in the right direction and we will start there. You tell me where you want me to go and I'll get us there. I trust your judgment implicitly Izz. There's no doubt that with you pointing and me flying that we'll find Seth. If he's out there he's coming back with us." Mike said admitting that he had no idea what Izz was trying to show him.

The flight management display showed 128 nautical miles to the point where the computer estimated that Seth should have washed out of the river. That was if he didn't first get boiled by the extreme temperatures of the river or slammed into the sharp rocks that were normally above the rivers waterline. The tilt-rotor had transitioned fully to horizontal flight. The large rotor disks were near full vertical as they powerfully pulled the V-22 through the air back toward India and the portion of the Bramhaputra River where Izz calculated Seth to be.

"I hate to see Seth's face Mike when you tell him that you wrecked the Citation X." Izz said trying to stay optimistic.

"You're not kidding Izz, I'd rather face another nuclear explosion." Mike said reflecting equal optimism.

The V-22 approached the eastern most portion of India where the Bramhaputra River broke into fragments as it emptied itself into the Bay of Bengal. The land here was very flat and the spring melt waters of the Himalayas had not yet reached the lower portions of the river. The sudden surge of water pushed down the river had already crested and fallen. In fact, so much water as forced down stream by the explosion that the river was now at a record low. Portions of the delta were exposed that hadn't been in hundreds of years. The silt and mud that had collected here over the years of flooding and spring melts formed a soft and pliable surface that absorbed the crashing wave that broke over the banks.

Daylight was only a memory for this day. The sun had moved too far beyond the western horizon to provide anything more than a thin shimmering light glowing on the earth's curve far west of India. The red and orange sky reminded Izz of an old sailors phrase that would come to mind every time he took notice of a red sky at night. 'Red sky at night, sailors delight, red sky in the morning, sailors take warning.' At least there was one good omen that the twilight held more optimism and promise.

"Mike we are about 12 nautical miles from the target area. I'll be glued to the FLIR so my attention is inside the cockpit." Izz said as he started adjusting the intensity on brightness on the FLIR.

"Roger Izz, You just tell me where to point this machine and I'll get it there for you." Mike said over the intercom as he continued to shift his scan from the flight instruments to the outside.

The damage from the wave caused by the blast was about the same as the spring floods down the Bramhaputra. The United States had already coordinated the aid packages for the damages in Bhutan and India. The Indian Air Minister had restricted the air over the areas affected and kept it under military control. ATC was conducted by the AWACS which provided the same services that any other air traffic control organization would. By morning, fleets of huge C-17 transports and V-22 Osprey tilt-rotors would be shuttling food, medical supplies and drinking water to the thousands of people that were affected by the blast. Mike could see the Army's hovercraft assembling near several transport ships that would move the heavier building materials more difficult to move by air. The hovercraft would be moving up the narrow waterways that formed the delta of the Bramhaputra. The United States had been so practiced in providing relief aid to devastated countries that this was simply a standard drill. Everything would work like a well-oiled machine.

"Mike that small outcropping of land over there is the target area predicted by the statistical analysis. Let's set down over there and nose around." Izz said as he scoured the area looking for any signs of Seth or worst his remains.

Mike deftly landed the big tilt-rotor machine gently on the hard, beach-like surface that they could see was clear of any debris or more specifically any bodies. Izz was already unstrapping from his seat as Mike secured the engines and shut down the electrical power. He quickly prepared the engines for a quick start just in case they needed to leave in a hurry.

Izz was slowly walking the area looking for any signs that Seth may have washed out of the wave at this location. The area was on a slight bend in a small outer finger of the delta that normally was well above the waters flow except during the annual spring thaw. The sandy soil was freshly washed and would make easy the task of tracking a recent movement. Izz looked at the ground searching for any clues. The hand held GPS receiver was programmed with the calculations and showed that he was within the predicted area, plus or minus 10 meters. Mike joined him as they moved in circles covering the ground. The two tenacious men would either find Seth or his remains before they would give up. As they expanded their circles, they moved from the sandy beach into an area where sparse river grass clumps were growing in the rocky soil. The chest high river grass was matted and tangled in spots where the fast water pulled and twisted it as it flowed past. Izz and Mike spent more time searching these areas as they worked their way outward from the center of the prediction target. The sun was well below the horizon and the moonless early evening provided no illumination. They searched with their halogen flashlights for any trace of a man or his body.

They looked for scraps of clothing, boots, fabric, metal clips, buttons or anything that looked like it was man-made and deposited by the wave of water. Mike's lights contrasted off of something on the edge of a tangled mess of river grass. The way that the light played on the ridge of sand covering the fabric looked as if it were part of an arm bent at an odd angle and buried beneath the water swept sand. He stopped in his tracks and fell forward on one knee, too anxious to move, his breathing halted. He moved closer to the piece of cloth. The fabric was partially buried in the sand. He bent down to examine it closer. It almost looked like a sleeve cuff off of a flight suit. The Velcro tab was impregnated with sand and the muddy waters stained the material that trailed from it. Mike began to feel the disappointment sink in as he reached to pull on the tattered piece of fabric that Seth might have been wearing or even worst, still attached to.

Mike felt himself hold his breath as he pulled on the fabric. With a gentle tug it gave way and came loose from its sandy burial. Mike felt relieved momentarily as the 12 by 22 centimeter shred dangled free of the sand in his hand, unattached to an arm or body. Mike examined the fabric closer, it appeared not be a flight suit but a...

"Mike, Mike, over here, over here!" Shouted Izz. Mike dropped the tattered fabric and ran towards the sound of Izz's voice. Mike felt the anxiety rise once again, not knowing what to expect when he pulled up next to Izz. He could see Izz's light play on the ground a few meters ahead as if it were searching a specific area. Mike stopped close enough that his shoulder overlapped and pushed against Izz's. Mike could see the ground where Izz was shining his light. It looked as if something was dragged across the ground. Two distinct footprints followed by striated imprints in the sand led away from the site. Something was deposited here in the sand by the rapidly receding water. It could have been anything. Mike and Izz searched the area for more answers. There was nothing there. The only thing that remained was an indentation in the sandy soil that looked like an object had slowed the flowing water as it erased the distinguishing marks that could have helped them identify what was there.

"What do you make of it Izz?" Mike asked through partially clenched teeth as he moved his light back and forth, rapidly searching for more clues.

"I am hoping that it isn't what I think it was Mike. The only way to find out is to follow the tracks." Izz started off following the tracks as he pressed a button on the GPS to mark the location of the indentation.

The tracks headed off to the southwest slightly away from the rivers edge and up a gentle slope. The tracks and indents were easy to follow in the freshly washed sand. No other footprints or markings were visible. It was like the first tracks left on a beach after a high tide. Izz and Mike rounded a small hill and could see several lanterns and fires burning in stoves in an area that looked like a nomad's campground. Cloth collected and sewn together formed tents and coverings for structures made out of anything available. Cardboard, scraps of lumber and dead tree limbs washed white by the river were piled up to form walls and roofs. The crude shelters were typical of the poor that inhabited the valleys of eastern India. They lived very meager and impoverished lives. With the millions of people living in India, the more fortunate ones found respite in the least desired lands.

Starvation and disease was as common here as the sands that lined the Bramhaputra river valley. Death wasn't feared it was celebrated. It was a release from the pain of living and watching others escape the tortures that the poverty offered. The dead were revered almost as gods. They were the representatives in the life that followed death. The celebration of the death of a person was viewed as an opportunity to gain a guarantee for a place in heaven next to the departed. The more elaborate the death celebration the more favor one was given by the dead. If the people of this camp had found Seth's body, they would celebrate his death as they would someone that they knew. He would be guarded and not left alone until the burial ritual that would accompany the celebration.

Izz's heart pounded as he approached closer to the camp. He could hear it in his ears. It drowned out the swishing sound that he made plowing through the thicker dense river grass that was growing out of the flood plain. He couldn't hear Mike's heavy breathing, but they were so close, he could feel his breath. The moved at a rapid pace, afraid of what they would find here, but unable to stifle the desire to find the answer. The answer may not put them any closer to finding Seth or his body. Izz tried to think of other things that it could have been, but his intuition, supported by the analysis of the information led him to the same conclusion. He could only hope that they would find his friend, somehow, still alive.

Izz was within sight of the small camp. He made no attempt to be discreet. He had no reason to believe that these peaceful people would have cause to do him or Mike any harm. Izz broke out of the river grass and bramble that formed a ring around the cleared area for the camp. The people of the camp had seen the approaching lights and began cautiously moving toward the direction from where it came.

The camps leaders whispered back and forth to each other as they tried to determine who would be approaching with the artificial lights. Izz stopped as he and Mike broke into the clearing. They were met with silence as they looked into the curious stares, ghostly illuminated by the reflection of the lights that they carried. Izz fastened the light to his thigh pocket. He made a non-aggressive gesture by placing his hands at his side, palms up. He spoke in a gentle voice, deeply ingrained with sincerity.

"I am looking for my friend." Izz said as he looked for clues that his message was understood. The front row of the men in the group that met him looked at one another. Izz could see that they had interpreted his gesture as peaceful. They looked at each other to try to determine what he had said. Mike and Izz watched as someone from the back of the group moved toward them. The front row of the group parted and allowed a young man through.

"What is the name of your friend?" The small young man that came from the rear of the group questioned in perfect Queen's English.

"His name is Seth, Seth Stephens. He is my friend and my commander." Izz responded. "He may have been washed up on the river's edge near your camp by a very large wave of water. Please, he may be injured badly, have you seen him?"

"We have seen no one, but if we do how would we recognize him? Can you describe him?" The young man asked. An air of suspicious overtones floated in the sound of his voice.

Izz very carefully reached into his flight suit pocket as the group opposite him followed his hand's every move. By now the crowd had become much larger. The young man translated Izz's replies to the men standing with him as Izz pulled a small waterproof wallet from his breast pocket. Izz unzipped the wallet and thumbed though it, gently pulling a photograph from its center. Izz approached the group as Mike stood with his hands, palms up. They both hoped that these people could help him and Izz find Seth somehow alive.

Izz gave a photograph to the young man that showed three men standing in front of the flag of the United States, dressed in the Army dress blue uniforms, smiling at the camera. "This is my friend." Izz said pointing to Seth's image on the photograph.

The young man stared at Izz as he spoke, before he looked at the picture. He gently moved the picture to the light shining from Izz's flashlight. He studied the man on the left and looked up at Izz. He looked at the man on the right and looked over to Mike. The two men in the picture matched the two that claimed to be the man in the middle's friend. The young man sensed that the two were soldiers and that they were genuinely sincere in their intent to find their lost friend.

"My name is Rasheed. My father, Jaimirr, is the governor of the camp here. Through your actions, I know that the man in this picture is your friend." Rasheed turned to who Izz assumed to be the camp's Governor, Jaimirr and spoke in Indian to him. After several minutes of conversation, Rasheed turned back to Izz.

"Please follow me. I am sorry for what you will find here." Rasheed said as he turned to walk up toward the camp's center, following his father. The group parted as the two made their way into the camp toward a large hut erected in the center. Izz turned to Mike almost afraid to move. Mike moved first and followed Rasheed. Izz turned and followed Mike. The two approached the hut almost shaking with fear of what they would find inside. These were men that were afraid of nothing. They could fight their way out of any situation and survive when others gave up long before them in the most adverse conditions. Yet now, they each felt like a small lonely child, being led away, into the darkest room in the middle of the night, wide-eyed and too afraid to scream. The fear of the unknown of what was inside the hut nearly paralyzed them.

34

Marlow on the Thames

Marlow, England, March 6, 0800 hours

The spring like weather that enveloped England was holding fast under a high-pressure system that stagnated over the country longer than ever recorded. It was nearly a miracle that the weather was this fantastic. A perfect day presented itself to the many hundreds that would visit the small town where Sean McLowery grew up to pay their last respects. Many of the guests stayed in the quaint Inns that surrounded Marlow. Some stayed in London and made the drive earlier that morning.

The RAF had set up a helicopter landing area west of the town on the north side of the Thames for the helicopters that would bring or had brought, the Queen of England, the Prime Minister of the U.K., the President of the United States and the President of Germany just to name a few.

Limousines shined and ready, parked in the grass fields next to the small portable control tower that had been brought in only yesterday. The newly arrived equipment sharply contrasted with the wooden fence and old the church situated across the Thames. The cows that were accustomed to grazing in that field were moved to an adjacent field early yesterday morning. They stood against the fence staring at the cool, dew covered grass now occupied by different sorts of animals that had metal rotors sprouting from their heads.

Just a mile down the Thames, located on the southern bank, just east of the suspension bridge sat a magnificent hotel. It provided lodging for the twenty or so distinguished guests from the United States. The

President and his entourage, Joshua McAdams, Karl Stephens and his wife Elke, were staying there. The guests arrived last evening and some woke early to relax in the quiet morning before the ceremony that day. It was a wonderful place. It would have been the source of fond memories for this group if it were under other circumstances. Even in this perfect surrounding, the day held an ominous foreboding feeling to all that attended. It was a time for elation, yet a time for sadness.

"It is nearly time to walk over the bridge to the church. Mrs. Abrahams and I have never walked across the Thames. We are looking quite forward to the stroll." The President said as he excused himself from the company of Joshua McAdams, Max Woodsen and Karl Linder.

The four met for an early breakfast before the funeral service. The three others rose to their feet out of respect as the President left the table.

The three sat back down as if to prolong the inevitable as long as they could.

McAdams steered the brief discussion. "Max, where in the hell did Thomas and DeConcerio go?" McAdams said as he reached for the coffee and poured the dark liquid into his cup.

"We have the AWACS radar data being analyzed right now. It seems that the two borrowed a V-22 from the Pittsburgh and made their way back into India. The commander of the Pittsburgh is embarrassed and felt that he had relief orders on the way. After I talked to him and told him about those two, he felt a little better. Put those two together and hell the gold a Fort Knox would be an easy target for them." Woodsen said as he broke another piece off his fresh blueberry scone.

"Maxwell, where do you think that they went?" Karl implied in a calm clear voice.

"There is no doubt in my mind. They went back to look for Seth, Karl. Once they found out that the search was being halted until morning, they couldn't just sit around and wait. They resumed the search on their own. I believe that I would have done the same thing. Your son had a way of leading men to where they would follow him to hell and back and be grateful to him for letting them have the chance. I have been a soldier for more years than I care to recount Karl and I have never seen a man as capable of Seth when it came to inspiring his men. His men were extremely loyal to him. He'll be a fine Gen…" Woodsen caught himself almost forgetting that Seth was missing and presumed dead.

"I am glad to see that you share in my optimism." Karl said with a weak smile as he grabbed Woodsen's forearm.

Joshua McAdams sat observing the two. There was nothing more than he had wished for than to have Seth back here with them. But he was a realist. He had to be. He had reviewed the imagery himself. One second Seth was there and the next he wasn't. The post detonation imagery showed the extensive damage surrounding the area where Seth was last seen. No matter how optimistic he would have like to have been, he couldn't dismiss the facts.

"Gentlemen, I believe that I will make my way to the church. The Lord knows that I could sure use a little more of his guidance. Perhaps a few minutes there will help." Joshua said as he pushed away from the table.

Eventually, everyone walked across the bridge and made their way to the church where the service would be held. The church was filled to capacity as the guests sat in solace. Some prayed, others fixed their eyes on Sean's flag draped casket that was guarded by the six military uniformed casket bearers.

The church was decorated magnificently. The white alabaster hand carved altar shimmered as the flames of the white candles danced in the reflections. The sunshine streamed through the leaded stained glass windows that lined the sidewalls of the church. The sun's light, wavering through the trees blowing in the light breeze and mixture of the colors used in the artist's works of stained glass made them seem nearly alive. The marble floors were highly polished and the smell of oiled oak, the paraffin of burning candles and the incense used in prior services filled the air. Occasionally, one would pick up a hint of a blooming flower's fragrance as it wafted on the slowly moving currents of air inside the church.

The organist played several unrecognized somber selections quietly. The courtyard outside the church began to also fill. The crowd of people gathered in and around the church increased the population of the town ten fold that day.

The pastor that would now conduct the ceremony made a discreet gesture to the organist from the rear of the church and she faded the somber selection of music into silence. The silence was broken as the pastor began to recite his chants of prayer as he moved forward down the aisle accompanied by two assistants and several young altar servants. They were all dressed in simple white long robes, adorned with black cords knotted around their waists. The pastor conducting the service wore a wide and long black stole, made of finely woven linen adorned with hints of gold silk thread, around his neck.

Karl could smell the incense as the priest waved the inscensor in a practiced movement in front of his body as he moved along the aisle.

As the pastor approached the casket, the guards parted allowing him access to it and just above the place where Sean's head would be inside. The pastor stood at the head of the casket and blessed it with the incense, water, and familiar cross-making gesture of his hand before moving, acting as the priest and cantor, to the altar. The organist subtly, almost faintly heard, resumed playing as the pastor moved to the lectern.

The priest paused. He turned his head as if to listen more closely. The congregation also heard it.

A helicopter or aircraft with large spinning rotors passed close to the village. Everyone could hear the large aircraft pass near the location of the church. The muffled beating of rotors ceased as the helicopter landed in the temporary landing zone west of the church and the pilot disengaged the transmission and secured the engine. The Pastor waited for the sounds to dissipate into silence before he resumed the ceremony.

The congregation of dignitaries stood as the pastor reached the altar and held the gold etched book high over his head. The Pastor proceeded to read passages from the bible that offered consolation to the heavy hearts that sat before him.

Several sobs were heard as the Pastor told of how he remembered the day when Josephine and Milton brought Sean into his church wrapped in blankets. They sought a baptism into Christ's church. The pastor spoke to them of how Sean would simply pass from the doors of this church through the doors of heaven.

Within what seemed like only several minutes, he paused again as the rear doors of the Church were opened. The congregation had no idea what was happening. They sat awestruck as if they would themselves witness a miracle. The atmosphere contained within the confines of the hallowed walls of the old church was vibrating with solacing presence. If rationality weren't the supposed rule many in attendance would have expected it to be Sean or another of the churches many divine souls walking among them.

The beautiful bright sunlight flooded the entranceway as the doors gradually opened. The pastor saw the lone figure of a man standing in the arched doorway. His form was backlight by the sun's intense and majestic light that made it difficult for his eyes to initially see his detail. As he slowly moved forward with the sun's rays dancing off of the particles of dust suspended in the air, his details came into view as if projected to the congregation in a sort of holograph.

His face held back the agony of both physical and mental pain as he walked down the aisle toward the guarded casket. He desperately appeared to be trying to catch his breath. His head oddly turned to survey those in attendance on both the left and the right of the aisle through the other eye that wasn't blood caked. He forced a smile from his dry cracking and dried blood stained lips. The guests restrained themselves by not staring, but still they tried to look out of the corners of their eyes. It was as if they were too afraid to look.

The pastor's eyes locked with the man's one opened eye and saw in it complete comfort and peace. He could not have held any ill feelings against this man who slowly and painfully moved down the aisle. His, was a vision of peace emitted from the inside out.

The man painfully moved closer to the flag draped casket. The two guards closest to his approach stood firm their position as they saw the man in their peripheral vision. They stared and positioned for defense.

His clothing was tattered and ripped, in places it was cut into strips that hung at his sides. His hair, once the color of golden oak was matted and partially torn away. His face was cut in hundreds of places and his hands hung at his sides as if to painful to be moved. He more dragged himself, than walked up the aisle.

The only thing that was in a nearly new condition were his shoes. They looked more like house slippers than shoes. The new brown soft-soled shoes looked sorely out of place on this poor tattered man.

He paused as his approach came to within a man's length of the casket to partially kneel and cross himself before continuing on. The people in the congregation were now mesmerized at the sight of this man and forgot their etiquette. They now stared at him, some with mouths agape. They were drawn to his presence. He painfully tried to right himself after kneeling. An airman, dressed in his finest dress uniform, seated on the end of one of the oak pews close to the stranger, noticed that the clothing he wore was barely recognizable as a type of uniform. He stood to offer his help to the man. The man paused to look into the airman's eyes as a sincere show of thank you, but no thank you. He was going to bring himself to this place by himself. It was the least he could do.

His colleagues that now stood in the back of the church had also offered him help, but he refused it. He wanted to say goodbye to Sean McLowery with his own strength. Seemingly as a way to tell Sean that he would give everything to be with him. It was a way of bringing closure to this nightmare of a mission.

The airman backed slowly away. He had never looked into such intense piercing brown eyes and looked into the soul of another man as he did with this stranger. They were eyes that conveyed a message of warmth and hope. Even the pain couldn't mask this man's his inner spirit. The tattered stranger finally stood erect again and continued down the aisle and was within an arms length of the casket.

A guard turned his head to confront the stranger, his last order was to guard the casket and he intended to do that. Without a word the stranger looked into the guards eyes. The guard also saw the same intense sincerity flowing from the stranger's eyes. He took one step back away from the casket to allow the stranger complete access.

As the congregation watched, seemingly in slow motion, they saw the stranger extend his hand slowly, with his palm upward, reach toward the casket. He placed his cut and badly bruised hand, open palm down on the place just above Sean's left shoulder and touched it as he had done in life but now in death.

"Goodbye my friend," he said painfully in an emotionally pained strain of a whisper. The tears welled in his eyes. It was all he said as he fell to his knees, head lowered in respect and pain, still touching the casket above Sean's shoulder.

He wavered and fell away, totally limp. Two men dressed in flight uniforms rushed from the rear of the church and moved down the aisle to help their friend.

Karl Linder Stephens was the last of the congregation to resist the urge to look. He felt a certain presence in the church as soon as the doors had opened, allowing the sun's warmth and light in. But he was too afraid to look. To afraid of being disappointed. He tried with all his might to rationalize away why he had felt this way.

Elke Linder Stephens too, felt the same presence, but she could not resist. She felt the attachment of mother and son as if he were still inside her. The separation of 40 years couldn't erase that bond. Karl could feel her shake and tremble as she grabbed for his arm. He could feel her gentle sobs and body heave as she wept.

Finally he could no longer resist. He heard the stranger whisper and knew before he looked who the stranger that had entered the church was. Without looking at him, he closed his eyes, pushed himself up into a stand and slowly walked to the side of the pew still looking forward. Elke remained frozen in emotion.

The congregation stared along with the pastor in awe at the incredible scene being played out before them. Karl moved in behind the stranger lying on the cold marble, behind the casket of his dead friend and kneeled on one knee.

In a most gentle and sincere manner, he placed his hand on his son's forehead trying to take away the pain. He looked in almost disbelief at his son and slowly moved to place his arms around him in a gentle embrace. Seth gradually opened his eyes for a brief moment and smiled a pained smile at his father. The tears streamed from his rock solid face without a sound. He looked into Karl's eyes and saw the eyes that in a distant memory he remembered from long ago. Karl held him as his eyes closed and his body fell into unconsciousness.

The congregation felt the full impact of the emotions there that day as Seth came to say goodbye to his friend.

Seth woke within what seemed like a few seconds to his bruised mind. He looked into a bright light, which was almost too intense to see as he regained consciousness. His eyes wouldn't focus. Time and space were a blur.

There was a woman seated next to him. He could see the outline of long hair but not the details of the face. He recognized the fragrance and lay there trying to allow his brain recall a memory but couldn't. The woman stood up and walked over to the window, continuing to keep her back toward him. The walk was familiar too. She watched outside, looking toward the voices outside the window that he too had heard.

He could hear children singing in play outside the window. His eyes began to focus slowly. He tried to pull in some meaning from the sensations that he was experiencing. Perhaps he could force the identity of this woman standing in front of him from his numb, half-awake senses. His eyes gradually focused on her face. She was unaware that he was waking but a moment later she could feel someone looking at her and she gradually turned her face toward him to look.

Seth saw her as she turned from the window, her face backlit by the diffused sunlight as it passed through the heathery curtains on the window. It was his angel, the one that he'd always seen ready to help him. Was he dead? He thought. Maybe he was experiencing something that he never had before. That would explain his disconnect between thought and feeling. It couldn't be, where he was headed wasn't this beautiful. In any event he couldn't complain. He just stared for what seemed like forever.

Her eyes connected with his. She hesitated and then rushed to his side.

"Seth, thank God! You're awake. Can you hear me? Do you recognize me?" Elizabeth said as she gently took his hand.

"I though that I was dead, but realized that where I'm going wouldn't be as pleasant and there are certainly no angels as beautiful as you there." Seth said as he pushed himself up into a sitting position.

"Seth, please don't move. You've been unconscious for nearly 10 days, since the ceremony. Let me get the doctor. Let me help you up.

Let me fix you pillow. Let me… Seth, just lay still until I get the doctor." Elizabeth said as a flurry of confused emotion washed over her. She fussed over him as he reached out for her other hand.

"Elizabeth, I probably look a lot worst, but I feel okay." Seth said smiling as he looked at Elizabeth.

She stopped and their eyes met. "Right now this is all that I'd like to do." Seth said as he studied her face. She looked even more beautiful in person than he remembered.

"Seth we'll have plenty of time. Let me get the doctor." Elizabeth said as she moved toward the door. He could hear her calling for the doctor as she rushed down the hallway.

Seth pulled the blankets away from his feet and took inventory of what was working. So far, everything was normal. The deep cuts and tears in his skin were healing. The damage to his body was miraculously repairing itself. He was surprised how good he felt. He tried to remember the last few days. The memories were slow to return to him. He swung his legs off the side of the bed and pushed himself up. Other than feeling stiff and like the blood was pooled in his backside, he felt fine.

He walked stiffly to the window to see the children playing across the way in the schoolyard. He smiled at the children and remembered the events that led up to today. One by one, the thoughts poured from his memory. 'My god, how could anyone want to destroy these precious little lives?' He thought. He could see a little boy running with his friends and latch on to a climbing gym.

The little boy stopped and turned to the window. He must have felt someone watching him and slowly turned his head to look up at the window where Seth parted the curtains to one side. Seth smiled and waved to the boy. The boy dressed in his navy blue pants and white shirt, complete with a tie looked back and gave him a toothless smile along with a wave and thumbs up before returning to play.

Seth smiled as he watched the young lad and his friends play out their adventures as he did once when he was young. 'How could anyone want to take away their dream?' He thought as he watched.

"Colonel Stephens lets not rush our progress." The doctor said making his way in a rush towards Seth side. "How do you feel? You've been asleep for a long while. Come here, let's have a butchers at you." Said Doctor Elliot Vance, an older gentlemen that lived near Farnborough as he walked into the room. He moved to the side of the bed in front of the window and examined Seth.

"Colonel Stephens, this is going to make my job a little easier. I now have a patient that can give me feedback. Here you go let's look at some of those wounds." He looked at the one that concerned him the most.

It was a large deep jagged gash at the base of the skulls occipital bone. Vance was concerned about damage to the cervical vertebrate and the spinal cord. The X-rays and MRI that he had done while Seth was unconscious revealed nothing remarkable. Dr. Vance thought that the wound was at least three weeks old because of the progression of healing. Vance could tell that a considerable amount of flesh had been torn away as if it had been caught on something.

"Seth, you are nothing short of a miracle son. I have never seen someone heal as fast as you have. The new tissue is growing in at an astonishing rate. You can consider yourself extremely blessed Seth." Said Vance, as he gently probed the tissue surrounding the wound that had now completely closed. Only the presence of the pink, tender new skin served as the evidence that an injury had occurred.

"Doc, I'll feel alright!" Seth said as he looked around. He stiffly turned at the commotion he heard behind him out in the hall just as Mike and Izz came plowing into the room. Both tried to squeeze through the door at the same time.

"Boss, how are you feeling?" They both said as they saw Seth up and walking.

"I feel good Mike, Izz. I feel good!" Seth said smiling as he turned back to look at the children playing in the school's yard, laughing and running about.

He watched and was fascinated at how perfect everything seemed. He felt that the world was right again, if only briefly.

The doctor released Seth from the infirmary at Marlow and allowed him to join his family and good friends at the hotel. He would examine him once more before he left to return to the United States a few days later.

35

Seth

The Village Park, Marlow, March 16, 1334 hours

I walked from my hotel, The Compleat Angler adjacent to the Marlow Suspension Bridge. Just a little over a month had passed since we received the mission, yet it felt like my entire life. I couldn't take but a few steps before I stopped to notice everything and the perfection that it inherently contained.

I read the signs, watched the cars go by, I looked at the people. I didn't just merely see them. It seemed that everything that I was experiencing was from a more positive point of view. Life held a deeper meaning now.

I stopped and read in detail that marker riveted to the girder of the bridge that had been built by Sir Tierney in 1832 as I walked across the Thames.

The day was just about as perfect as one in the month of March could be in England. The sun was shining, though not intensely, but diffused by scattered, cotton-like clouds that floated high above me as I crossed the Thames River.

The rivers gentle serenade as it fell gently over the falls was easy to isolate amongst the other sounds that it layered with. The sweet subtle smell of newly blooming Honeysuckle was wafting in the light, almost imperceptible breeze. It was the kind of breeze that you feel with only the small tender hairs on your neck and face.

It was as perfect summer-like day. Men wore shirtsleeves and cotton trousers and the ladies light cotton dresses, complete with a bonnet. It seemed the world had changed, perhaps not. No, it hadn't changed. It was the same. I changed. I looked at the positive influences more now.

I look for the good in everything. That was the difference. Nothing had changed except my perspective. I had to change my outlook after looking at the emptiness of Hesbulah's eyes. They were the empty eyes that revealed the void where a soul should have been. That was the essence inside each of us where God's grace stays for eternity.

The children still played as they had for centuries on the manicured green lawn among the cottonwood trees and elms in the Marlow Park along the Thames River. The sidewalks still were bustling with local folk out and about shopping. Straw-woven shopping bags filled their hands as the hurried in and out of shops.

I passed by the Parish Church of all Saints where we buried Sean the a few days ago. It was just on the other side of the bridge. The church is surrounded by a cemetery that is filled with aged and new burial headstones. Some have the shape of a traditional stone; others are very ornate or shaped like crosses. Sean's was the most recent. The scar of the freshly turned earth would heal, just as most have that date back to the 18th century. Most like Sean's carried the name of the beloved complete with age, date of birth and death date.

They too, just as Sean did a few short years ago, walked the streets of Marlow. Just as I, on this day was doing. I paused and said a prayer for my new found family, friends and for everyone before I continued on my way into the village center hoping to find the shop where Elizabeth, my mother and father were shopping. We were going to meet for dinner at an Italian restaurant on the way to the train station.

My mother had a lot of shopping to catch up on. After nearly 68 years, it was finally time for them to do something just for themselves.

Elizabeth, well she would never change. She wanted to buy something for everyone that she had ever known. I discovered something else that we now had in common, where we didn't before. She only accepted the positive influences in her life. She would turn ugliness into beauty and despair into hope. It had taken me nearly forty years to see positives rather than negatives.

As I passed the City Park where the children were playing, I noticed the memorial to the men who had lost their lives in the First World War. It was an obelisk similar to one memorializing George Washington in the Capital City of the United States. This one stood only about 15 feet tall. It would have been dwarfed by its larger likeness in America.

Two hundred and seventeen, was the number inscribed on the side of the monument, the number of men from Marlow killed in that war. On the top just above that inscription was the memorial's dedication to the men that gave their lives during World War II. The village revered the grounds surrounding the memorial; signs were placarded about asking for no one to sit about on the monument grounds or drink under its shadows. I appreciated that reverence and respect. I felt a bond with each of them. I wanted to be considered worthy to stand in their shadows.

I, like the villagers of Marlow, felt that it was hallowed ground. It honored the men, like Major Sean McLowery, that lived and grew up here. They didn't return to walk among its quaint shops and perfect spring skies as many others and I had the opportunity to do. They gave everything a man could give. They gave us their lives. Was it all worth it though? What if they didn't go? What if Sean decided to pursue another path in life? What if he wanted to be selfish and not serve his fellow man? What would be the consequences that this little village would suffer? Would it be the same if the tyrants that tried to conquer the world had succeeded? Would I be walking around enjoying this perfect day, in the shadows of this monument to those, the men, the heroic men that gave their lives? Would I be able to walking under a brilliant sun filled sky speckled with pure white clouds, surrounded by a blanket of freedom that is valued more than all else by the human spirit?

If the tyrants had triumphed, freedom would be only a dream. It would be something people would continue to strive towards under oppression and hatred. Each of these honored heroes; they did what was right. Their sacrifices made the world a better place for good people to live. They vanquished evil and stood as reminders that nothing would take away God given free will. They knew it and so do we all.

If we would take just a minute to think about the events that have taken place in our world, we would soon arrive at the same conclusion that those great men, the leaders of freedom, did as they marched from the tiny Village of Marlow in 1917 waving to their wives, children, mothers and fathers. As they did again in 1940, and as Sean did only a few weeks ago, not to return. They knew that they might never return. Each of them realized that they had to do this. They were the protectors of freedom and life. Each of them would be damned by their own conscious if they didn't fight to keep us all free.

As they left on that last day in their homes, they looked hard at every detail of their lives, the community that they had built, their wives, their children, their brothers, sisters, friends and acquaintances. They wanted those images to burn into their memories so as not to forget, in any event, what they held so dear.

The ones that are honored here, the ones that didn't return, they relived those fond memories as they fell in battle. As they lay there mortally wounded, their consciousness fading, these were their eternal memories. The memories became a reality as they saw, once again, their wives lovingly smiling at them, their children waving as they played in the garden, their mother's happiness and their fathers bursting with pride. These would be the thoughts of their eternity and a true measure of heaven.

They made a sacrifice that most of us cannot imagine. They had built a character that we should all strive to be like. They knew the secret of living and they did the right thing for us all. Their sacrifices haven't been forgotten by the countless others that walk in freedom throughout the village of Marlow or throughout the world. The spirit of freedom and God-given free will is indomitable and will not rest if contained.

The satans of our world and their harbingers of chaos must take notice. These Heroes of our times, our champions, they have proved that we will not give up the good fight. God and his gift of freedom will always triumph. We will suffer any pain, any hardships, and any loss to guarantee that we will live freely or not live at all. The good and decent people of the world have found a common bond that is within each of us. We will continue to band together to destroy the dictators that would stifle freedom's spirit. We will stand with each other in freedom or stand with each other, as we die defeating tyranny. When one falls, two will take up the fight, when those two falls four more will stand in their place. The spirit is indomitable. And the intention of God's perfect design for us will always be realized.

The men memorialized here are the true Heroes of our time and they have realized their contentment. They have, even as their bodies died, realized that the contentment that they felt and feel in eternity, was one brought from their hearts, knowing that this was the most significant offering they could bring to us from their lives. They made the world a better place for the children, theirs, and ours, that play in the park on a spring day. A day filled with the sweet fragrance of honeysuckle under a deep blue sky as an imperceptible breeze plays the air. Under this blanket of freedom, life in its wonderful contentment of God given and inspired freedom will always triumph.

"I'm glad to see you up and about sir. What happened to you? Does it still hurt?" It took a few seconds for the face to connect. Oh yes, it was the little boy from the schoolyard that I had seen the other day; he was asking me how I felt. His hair the color of golden oak and his eyes a deep and endless brown. His smile was dauntless and slightly tilted. Spaces where teeth will eventually be gave it even more character. He was now dressed in his play clothes. I thought him to be very considerate for such a young boy.

"Well, thank you for remembering me. I am very impressed." I said as I reached out to put my hands on the young man's shoulder.

"You were Major Sean's friend. Everyone knows you. My Dad showed us your picture in the paper. He told my Mum that you and Major Sean are heroes. He tells us the story about you and Major Sean at bedtime. It's fun to be the hero. My friends and me play it all the time. Sometimes I get to be you. Sometimes I have to be the bad guy. I hate being the bad guy cause I never win." The little boy continued to look at me, studying my wounds and the lines in my face. "Guess you have to go now, your wife's here." The young boy said as Elizabeth came up from behind and grabbed me around my waist.

Elizabeth and I exchanged smiles.

"What is your name?" Elizabeth asked.

"My name is Seth, just like yours. I hope that you'll feel better." The young boy said as he ran off waving, eager to join another adventure with his friends.

"What was that all about?" Elizabeth asked as she and I walked back toward the bridge.

"Seth...I saw him the other day from the window of the hospital. He was just sharing his adventures with me." I said as I looked at Elizabeth and then across to the children playing. "Probably off to fight another bad guy." I continued.

"I certainly hope that he wins." Elizabeth concluded.

"He will, He always will." I paused a long while and looked over at my new friend as he continued his play in the distance. I thought of Sean. The young boy stopped turned around with an expression that revealed a puzzling thought. He and I shared a moment as we smiled at each other.

The day was perfect. The sun was shining, perfectly diffused by scattered, cotton-like clouds that floated high above. The sweet subtle smells of God's gifts were wafting in the light, almost imperceptible breeze. It was a perfect day. Men wore smiles and greeted one another cheerfully and the ladies laughed with their children. The children's laughter reflected the new era of celebrating life and the countless adventures that we can share in a world not torn by negative influence. The young boy, my new friend returned his wave and skipped off into a run toward the Thames and another adventure shouting and laughing with his friends.

"We'll have to come back here someday." I said to Elizabeth as she squeezed my hand and smiled. From behind, I felt a familiar and comfortable touch on my shoulder. It was good to feel my father's hand again.

The day was perfect. It was most certainly, perfect!